# ROBERT WILSON

Robert Wilson was born in 1957. A graduate of Oxford University, he has worked in shipping, advertising and trading in Africa. He has travelled in Asia and Africa and has lived in Greece and West Africa. He is married and writes from an isolated farmhouse in Portugal.

He was awarded the CWA Gold Dagger Award for Fiction for his fifth novel, *A Small Death in Lisbon*.

Praise for Robert Wilson

## A DARKENING STAIN

'Unmissable . . . Unflinchin
hint of competition. First i

## BLOOD IS DIRT

'For once a novelist influenced by Raymond Chandler is not shown up by the comparison, matching his mentor's descriptive flourishes and screwball dialogue . . . A class act'
*Sunday Times*

## THE BIG KILLING

'Something special in the line of original crime fiction . . . If I come across as original and blackly funny a thriller again this year, I'll feel myself doubly blest' *Irish Times*

## INSTRUMENTS OF DARKNESS

'An atmospheric and absorbing debut, *Instruments of Darkness* vividly paints a credible picture of a world I know almost nothing about. Now I feel I've been there. Robert Wilson writes like a man who's been doing this half his life'
VAL MCDERMID

*By the same author*

THE COMPANY OF STRANGERS
A SMALL DEATH IN LISBON

A DARKENING STAIN
BLOOD IS DIRT
THE BIG KILLING

# ROBERT WILSON

# *Instruments of Darkness*

**HarperCollins***Publishers*

This novel is entirely a work of fiction. The names, characters and incidents portrayed in it are the work of the author's imagination. Any resemblance to actual persons, living or dead, events or localities is entirely coincidental.

HarperCollins*Publishers*
77–85 Fulham Palace Road,
Hammersmith, London W6 8JB

The HarperCollins website address is:
www.**fire**and**water**.com

This paperback edition 2002

1 3 5 7 9 8 6 4 2

First published in Great Britain
in 1995 by HarperCollins*Publishers*

Copyright © Robert Wilson 1995

Robert Wilson asserts the moral right to
be identified as the author of this work

A catalogue record for this book
is available from the British Libray

ISBN 0 00 647985 5

Set in Meridien
Typeset by Rowland Phototypesetting Ltd
Bury St Edmunds, Suffolk

Printed and bound in Great Britain by
Clays Ltd, St Ives plc

All rights reserved. No part of this publication may be reproduced, stored in a retrieval system, or transmitted, in any form or by any means, electronic, mechanical, photocopying, recording or otherwise, without the prior permission of the publishers.

*For Jane*
*and*
*in memory of my father*
*1922–1980*

## AUTHOR'S NOTE

The French West African currency, the CFA, was devalued in January 1994 from 50 CFA to 100 CFA to the French franc. All financial transactions in this novel are based on the old rate.

Although this novel is set very specifically in West Africa, and its backdrop is the Liberian Civil War, all the characters and events in it are entirely fictitious and no resemblance is intended to any event or to any real person, either living or dead.

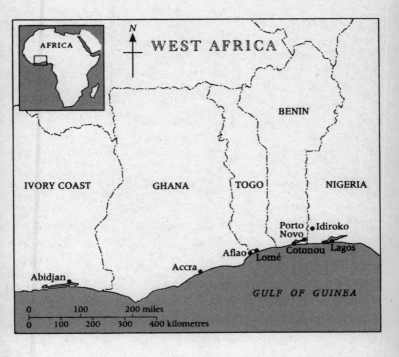

# *Prologue*

My name is Bruce Medway. I live in Cotonou, Benin, West Africa, along that stretch of coast they used to call the White Man's Grave because it was hot, humid, and full of malaria. It still is, but we don't die so easily now. Air conditioning and quinine have made us smell better and more difficult to wipe out.

I travelled across the Sahara a couple of years ago and stayed. I knew I wasn't going back before I came. I used to live in London where I made good money in a shipping company. The boredom crushed me, the traffic nearly killed me and the recession threw me out of a job.

Now I live in this warm, damp hole in the armpit of Africa and it suits me. The house is rented. I share it with Moses, my driver, who occupies the ground floor and Helen, my cook and maid, who lives with her sister nearby and comes in every day.

I don't make much money. I'd make more without Moses and Helen, but then, cooking and driving in 100 degrees isn't much fun, they need the money, and I like them.

I've got some work. I collect money for people, some of which is late, more of which is very late and most of which is so late it's stolen. I organize things for people – offices, transport, labour and contacts. I negotiate. I manage. Occasionally I find people who've lost themselves, some of them accidentally, others on purpose. I'll work for anybody unless I know they're criminal or if they ask me to follow their wives or husbands. My clients are mostly expatriates. A lot of them I wouldn't invite back to my mother's, and that's probably why they're here and not there.

They come here to trade as they have done for the last 500 years. They're a different crowd now – Lebanese and Armenians, Chinese and Koreans, Syrians and Egyptians, Americans and Asians. The Europeans are still here as well, toughing it out with the soggy climate. A lot of them drink too much, some because there's nothing else to do and others because they want to forget why they're here.

They trade with the Africans and the Africans trade with each other and they all move up and down the coast with the same aim – a fast, hard buck. In Ghana and Nigeria, the old British colonies, the bucks aren't hard and fast. Their currencies, the cedi and the niara, flop about with the price of cocoa and oil. In Togo, Benin and Ivory Coast the French keep a foot in the door of their ex-colonies by supporting the CFA franc (Communauté Financière Africaine) at fifty to the French franc so that's the hard, fast buck that everybody's after. When they get it, they want more. It's no different to anywhere else in the world.

# Chapter 1

There were a few worse places to be in the world than outside warehouse 2 in Cotonou Port, but I couldn't think of them. Moses and I were on our haunches in 105 degrees and – it felt like – 200 per cent humidity. I was losing weight and patience.

Berthed on number 2 quay, in air crinkled by the heat from the baked concrete, was the *Naoki Maru*. It was a 14,000-tonner dry cargo ship with a rust problem and an Oriental crew who leaned on their elbows at the ship's rail, waiting. Waiting to discharge my client's 7000 tons of parboiled rice from Thailand which was going to be sold to Madame Severnou, who I was waiting for to come and give me the money. Above us, on the roof, a couple of vultures were waiting for someone to make a mistake crossing the road. A driverless fork lift stood outside warehouse 3 with a pallet of cashew nut sacks a metre off the ground waiting to put them down. I could see the driver, waiting and doing some sleeping on some sheanut sacks in the warehouse. We were all waiting. This is Africa where everybody has mastered the art of waiting. Waiting and sweating.

The sweat was tickling my scalp as it dripped down

3

the back of my head. I could feel it coursing down my neck, weaving through my chest hair, dribbling down my thickening stomach and soaking into the waistband of my khaki trousers so I knew I'd have a rash there for a week. I wasn't even moving. The dark patches under my arms were moving more than I was. I looked down at my hands. The sweat hung in beads off my forearms and dripped down my knuckles and in between my fingers. Christ, even my nails were sweating. I looked at Moses. He wasn't sweating at all. His black skin shone like a pair of good shoes.

'Why you no sweat, Moses?'

'I no with a woman, Mister Bruce.'

'You do sweat then?'

'Oh yes please, sir.'

I had a newspaper in my hand called the *Benin Soir* which always came out the morning after the 'soir' looking unshaved, hungover and ready for nothing. I opened it and scanned the pages. There was nothing but smudged newsprint and black and white photographs of African people on black backgrounds. I tried to get some breeze from turning the pages.

I turned the last page and folded the paper in half. I was going to start fanning my face, which is what most people use the *Benin Soir* for, when I saw an almost readable item in the bottom left-hand corner with the heading: *Tourist Dead*. Cotonou had never had tourists and now the first one had died.

The article told me that a girl called Françoise Perec, a French textile designer, had been found dead in an apartment in Cotonou. There was a paragraph that finished with the word *sexuel* which I couldn't read at

4

all and I didn't need to. A police spokesman said that it looked like a sex session that had gone too far. I wondered how a policeman could tell that from a dead body. Is there such a thing as an ecstatic rictus? A drop of my sweat hit the page. I folded the newspaper and used the *Benin Soir* how it was meant to be used.

I was beginning to gag on the smell of hot sacks, stored grain and crushed sheanut when a pye-dog strayed out of the warehouse shade. It wasn't the healthiest pye-dog I'd ever seen. It definitely wasn't anybody's pet dog. It had the shakes. I could count its toast rack ribs and it needed a rug job. Its nose hoovered the ground. Out of the corner of my eye I saw one of the crewmen leave the ship's rail. The pye-dog moved in tangents. It stopped, clocked round a spot as if its nose was glued to it and then moved on. The crewman bounced down the gangway. There was a flash of light from his hand. He was carrying a cleaver.

Moses had pushed up his sunglasses and was frowning at the way things were developing. Inevitability was in the air. The pye-dog, its diseased hindquarters shaking, the crewman, his stainless steel cleaver glinting, closed on each other. The sun was high. There were no shadows. The instant before they met, the dog looked up, aware of something. The survival instinct wasn't operating too well inside that pye-dog. He looked right. The crewman came from the left and took the dog's head clean off with a single blow.

There was no sound. The dog's fallen body twitched with brainless nerves. The crewman picked up the dog's head and held it trophy high. The men at the rail burst into cheering and clapping. Moses threw off his Mr Kool act and was up on his feet, eyes rolling in horror, and pointing.

'Must have been a Chinese,' I said, before Moses could get anything out.

'Why he kill the dog?' asked Moses.

'To eat.'

'He eat him?' Moses was shocked.

'You eat rat. He eat dog,' I said, trying to balance the horror of foreign cuisine.

'Dog eat dog,' said Moses, laughing at his own joke, '. . . and I no eat rat. I eat bush rat and he no rat rat.'

'I see,' I said, nodding.

The crewman put the dog's head down and picked up the body which he tucked under his arm. The legs still twitched in memory of birds chased and rubbish investigated. He bent down again and picked up the head by an ear. He walked back to the ship. The dog's tongue lolled out of the side of its mouth. Its wall eyes bulged out. A dark patch remained on the concrete of number 2 quay.

'He go eat him!' Moses confirmed to himself as if it were a fair thing to do.

'Hot dog,' I said without smiling, knowing that Moses would roar with laughter, which he did. My best lines fall on deaf ears, my worst are a triumph. I think I satisfy his anticipation.

'Here we go,' I said, standing up.

Moses turned and saw the group of hadjis heading our way. Al hadji is the title given to a Muslim who has been to Mecca. Before air travel it must have been a big deal to have been a West African hadji. Now they charter planes and a grand will do the job. These boys have got money and Allah on their side and a long line in horseshit.

They looked quite something, for a bunch of businessmen, dressed in their floor-length robes, their black skins against the light blue, green, burgundy and yellow cloth, their heads bobbing underneath multi-coloured cylindrical hats. In another world they could have been showing a summer collection. Here they meant business. They were going to hassle me for the rice which wasn't mine to be hassled for. I reached for my cigarettes. They weren't there. I gave up last year. That's why I put on the weight. It all came back.

I heard an expensive engine. A grey Mercedes with tinted windows stopped with a squeak in between me and the hadjis. An electric motor lowered the window. The hadjis huddled together so that the car's occupant must have seen seven sweaty faces pressed into the frame of the window. One of them took out a hanky and wiped his brow.

Some African words came from the back seat of the car. The words sounded like they could move some sheep around. They had the hadjis rearing back. The group moved as one, turning and walking back to the port entrance. The window buzzed back up. One of the hadjis fell back to get a stone out of his Gucci loafers.

The Mercedes swung round to where Moses and I were standing. The driver, anthracite black, was out of the car almost before it had stopped. He opened the rear door and looked as if he might drop to one knee.

I got a short blast of air-conditioned cool and with

it came Madame Severnou. All five foot of her and another nine inches of sculpted deep green satin which sat on her head but could just as easily have made it to a plinth in the Uffizi. At six foot four I could put a crick in her neck, but as Madame Severnou knew, size wasn't anything.

'Bruce Medway,' she said, as if tungsten would melt in her mouth. She held out a small coffee-coloured hand encrusted with gold rings and jewels.

'Madame Severnou,' I said, taking her hand and thinking, this is one of the few occasions you put twenty grand into someone's hand and get it back. 'How's business?'

'Very good. I've been in Abidjan . . . Ali!' she shouted, withdrawing her hand and checking it to make sure she hadn't slipped a grand or two.

The driver, who had been standing to attention by the boot, opened it on cue. He took out the double bedsheet which had been drawn into a sack like laundry. Moses opened the boot of my smacked-up Peugeot estate and Ali dumped it on top of the tool box and spare tyre.

'What did you say to the hadjis?' I asked Madame Severnou.

'I remind them I am the seller. They know it but they forget sometime.'

Madame Severnou was petite from the waist upwards but downwards was the market mamma bottom, a bargaining tool not to be messed with. This meant that she didn't walk, she waddled, and the bottom did what the hell it liked. She waddled over to the Peugeot. Moses backed off. She turned to me and said: 'Six hundred and thirty-six million CFA. I hope you have some friends to help you count it. Not much of it is in ten thousand notes.'

She held out her hand and I put an envelope in it which she tore open. Her eyes flickered for a fraction of a second.

'This is a non-negotiable copy,' she said with an edge to her voice that I could feel against my carotid.

'It is,' I said.

'It's no Monopoly money in here!' she said, pointing at the boot. 'Ali!' she roared, whipping the air with her finger. Ali lunged at the laundry.

'Moses,' I said in a voice made to steady the thin red line. The boot came down and Ali was lucky to get away with his fingers still on.

'I'll count it and give you the original tomorrow,' I said to Madame Severnou. The ground frosted over between us but we both started at the two vultures which dropped down beside the dark patch where the pye-dog had been killed and broke Madame Severnou's concentration. She turned back to me.

'I give you six hundred and thirty-six million CFA and you give me a piece of paper.' Her voice came fully loaded. I said nothing. The look she gave me thudded between my eyes and I realized this was not the usual West African drama.

The two vultures, their wings folded behind their backs, paced around the patch on the quay like two detectives inspecting the outline of a murder victim.

'What about demurrage?' asked Madame Severnou.

'Time doesn't start counting until tomorrow noon.'

'What about my trucks?'

'I'll see you tomorrow. I've only got twenty-four hours to count all this.'

Something clicked in Madame Severnou's face. The points had changed. The boiling anger flattened to a simmer, her little mouth pouted and broke into a smile.

'OK. You come to lunch. I cook for you. Agouti. Your favourite.' Her smile was like a faceful of acid.

I got the panoramic view of her bottom as she climbed into her car. Ali closed the door. The window buzzed down. She had all the techniques and the technology to go with them.

'I do the snails for you as well. Just like last time.'

The window slid back up and the Mercedes moved out into the fierce sunlight between the warehouses. Agouti? That's bush rat which she cooked with okra and manioc leaves. 'Rat in Green Slime'. The snails, my God, the snails – they looked and tasted like deformed squash balls and the chilli sauce was so hot the last time, I woke up the next day still in a silent scream.

Moses hadn't missed the cruelty in those eyes as the electric window zipped up her face. He was fumbling for the door handle. I was nervous myself.

'Less go now, Mister Bruce.'

'Wait small.'

'Is lunchtime.'

'I know. I think is better we wait small. Let the traffic calm down. Then we go. We look at this ship now.'

We drove to the ship circling the vultures on the way. They were shaking their heads, then looking at each other, then staring at the ground. They knew there had been a death, a recent one, and a pye-dog too, but where the hell was it?

This was a first for Moses and I to be driving around with more than a million pounds in the back seat and Moses's clutchless gear changes were shredding metal and my inner calm. Madame Severnou hadn't made things any easier for us. At least she didn't know where I lived and I was anxious that she didn't find out. I had a feeling from the sweetness of her lunch invitation that well before we sat down to eat I was going to get a lesson in business etiquette that wasn't included in the Harvard course.

One of the crewmen took me up to meet the ship's Korean captain in his cabin. The generator rumbled like an old man in a bathroom but still coughed out some air conditioning which made my back colder than a dungeon wall. The captain poured me a cold beer. The first inch put medals on my chest. There was a photograph on the cabin wall of the captain with what looked like his local kindergarten.

'Which ones are yours?' I asked.

'All of them,' he said.

'All of them?'

'And another coming. I love childrens.' He said it like most people talk about pizza.

We chatted about rice, his home in Korea, storms in the Pacific and favourite ports. He wasn't an African fan. On the way here he had discharged containers in Abidjan and Tema, picked up some containers of old cashew nut in Lomé, and was now going to Lagos to discharge hi-fi and load cotton, then on to Douala or

Libreville, he didn't know which, and it didn't matter because he hated both. He liked Ghana. They had a good Korean restaurant in Accra. I knew it. They served me a gin and tonic there which came with a stretcher.

He walked me around the ship. I felt like royalty except I couldn't think of anything nice to say. It was one of those ships that takes a bunch of Koreans two weeks to build. Five holds, one aft, four forward with the bridge in between. The lifting gear on number 5 hold at the rear of the ship was broken; the captain put his hand on my shoulder and told me not to worry, that the rice was in the four forward holds. The fifth hold had the hi-fi in it for discharge at Lagos, and that was where they would fix the lifting gear.

We looked at the rice, which wasn't very interesting. How long can you look at a pile of sacks? The captain said something to a man holding a four-foot spanner who would never be clean again. I thought about showing some interest, but instead leaned on the slatted metal cover of number 2 hold and earned a first degree burn for my trouble. Moses stood by the gangway, not learning any Korean at all. It was time to blow. The smell of hot painted metal was taxing my nose's interest in life.

I held my hand out to the captain who said: 'You must have lunch,' and we both turned at the same time because Moses was showing us how to get down a gangway starting on his feet and ending on his nose.

'Moses!' I shouted.

He was holding the car door open for me which he had done on the first day he worked for me and never since.

'Yes please, Mister Bruce, sir.'

'Lunch?'

'You forget something, Mister Bruce.'

'No.'

'You have meeting.'

'I have?'

'The meeting with the man with the *dog*.'

'The man with the dog?'

'Yes please, sir.'

I turned to the captain and shook his hand. 'Sorry, I have a meeting with a man with a dog. Next time, I hope.'

As I got in the car, I saw Moses was sweating.

'I don't see no woman, Moses,' I said down my shirt front.

We drove off, me grinning and Moses shouting: 'You go make me eat dog! Mister Bruce. I no eat um. I no eat um never.'

# Chapter 2

The port was at a standstill; only the sun was out working on the scattered machinery and the corrugated iron roofs which creaked and pinged in the terrible heat. The shade of the buildings guarded sprawled stevedores who, rather than slow broil on the hot ground, lay across wooden pallets sleeping. The Peugeot's tyres peeled themselves off the hot tarmac.

There was no traffic outside the port. We looked left down the Boulevard de la Marina and fifty metres down the road a parked car's engine started. We turned right and headed east into Cotonou town centre. Moses's eyes flickered from the windscreen to the rearview.

The sun leeched all the colour out of the sky, the buildings, the people, the palms, the shrubs, everything. Through the open window a breeze like dog breath lingered over my face as I manipulated the wing mirror. A madman with dusty matted hair stood in dirty brown shorts inspecting his navel. He slumped to his haunches as we drove past and started parting the dirt on the road as if something had fallen out. We passed the agents' offices. The air conditioners shuddered and dripped distilled sweat into the thick afternoon air.

'He following us, Mister Bruce.'

'Slow down,' I said. 'Turn left.'

Moses dropped down to a fast walking pace and the

car, an old Peugeot 305, settled behind us. Vasili, a Russian friend of mine, had told me not to worry about learning about Africa, that the Africans would teach you all you needed to know. They weren't going to teach me anything about tailing cars.

'Left again,' I murmured. 'And again.'

We were back to Boulevard de la Marina, still with our tail. Three cars slicked past in front of us heading into town.

'Take them,' I said, and Moses's foot hit the floor.

We were past one car when a truck pulled out from the left, past two by the time its driver saw us. Moses didn't bother with the third car, which would have put us through the radiator grille of the truck, but with his mouth wide open preparing to scream, he swung between the second and third cars and went up on to the pavement where he took out two frazzled saplings, snappety-snap, and overtook the third car on the inside, crashing back on to the road just in time for the round-about which he took more briskly than he intended.

Behind us, the truck had slewed and stopped across the road, the second car was now facing the other way and the tail was up on the pavement with the car's cheekbone crumpled into a low concrete wall. Cyclists sizzled past giving the scene the eyes right.

'We lose him?' asked Moses.

'You lost him,' I said, straightening my eyebrows.

We came into the centre of town, which, far from being free of lunchtime traffic, was jammed with cars moving at the pace of setting lava with half a million bicycles swooping in and out of them like housemartins. In the mid-seventies the President had announced a

Marxist-Leninist revolution and forged links with the People's Republic of China who built a football stadium and then took the opportunity to sell the Beninois a lot of bicycles. All that remained of the old regime were some battered hoardings with Marxist slogans like *La lutte continue*, which had now become the white man's battlecry as he tried to make money in a difficult world.

We crawled past the PTT waiting to get on to Avenue Clozel and I noticed a tickering sound from the car when it was moving which must have come from Moses's off-piste run. A man with brown, decaying teeth put his head in the window and tried to sell me a stick which he said would keep me hard all night. I asked him if I had to eat it or put in my pants and he said all I had to do was hold it and I told him it would cramp my style. Moses said I should have bought it and I asked him how he knew I needed it.

We were trying to get to my house, not a place that I'd had to fight hard to rent but comfortable enough for me. The rooms were big. The open plan living and dining room had breeze coming in from two sides. The bedrooms each had a wall of window. The bathroom worked and the kitchen was big enough for me to create a lot of washing up when I did the cooking. There was a large covered balcony on one side of the living room where I ate breakfast, and dinner if I felt like having my blood thinned by adventurous mosquitoes. The furniture was a mixture, some of it cane which I didn't like but was cheap, the rest of it was carved wood which I did like, but couldn't sit on. There were a lot of carpets, mainly from Algeria and Morocco, and cushions covered in the same designs. I spent most of the time on the floor. You couldn't fall further than that.

There was a garage at the side of the house, and in the courtyard a huge and ancient palm tree with orange and purple palm oil nuts hanging off it in swagged clusters. The walls of the garden were covered in purple bougainvillaea. A green leafy creeper grew up the banister of the stairs at the front of the house which led up from the garage to my apartment.

The place I rented was on the west side of the lagoon. Most expats lived on the east side in Akpakpa or around the Hotel Aledjo. I preferred living with the Africans. They enjoyed themselves. The expats hated Cotonou. It was depressing to live with them and their wives who looked at you as if you could liven up their afternoons.

Moses kept up a monologue on Benin medicine, dog cuisine and great movie car chases he had seen. He let up occasionally to roar at cyclists so that they veered off and crashed into market stalls rather than hit the car.

'Africans fear dogs,' I said.

'Thassway we no eat um.'

'You fear them because they bite you.'

'Thass it, Mister Bruce, they bite us.'

'But if you eat um then you get the power of the dog and you no fear no more.'

Moses stopped the car, throwing me against the dashboard. A cyclist had come off in front of us. Two children put their hands through my window and were pulled away by a couple of Nigerians who shoved cheap ghetto blasters in my face. A girl offered Moses some water from a plastic jug on her head and another barbecued meat which congealed under greasy grey paper in a blue plastic bowl.

'You clever, Mister Bruce. You be right. But not the dog the Chinaman kill. He sick dog. You eat dog, you find big, strong dog, then you eat him.'

'You can't get near a big, strong dog.'

'Thassway we always fear the dogs.'

After half an hour in the traffic, with Moses yelling at cyclists to stop cadging lifts off the car, we turned off Clozel and started up Sekou Touré with nothing more to look at than crumbling, ill-painted buildings. The tickering noise from the car was still there as we turned left into the grid of mud streets where I lived. We bought some kebabs from a girl who was cooking them just outside the house. I opened the gate and, in the shade of the garage, saw Heike Brooke waiting for me, sitting on a step with her skirt up over her thighs keeping herself cool. She leaned forward and rubbed her shins and stood up letting the skirt fall to her knees. She leaned against her 2CV which she was considering taking off life support.

I'd met Heike two years ago when she was twenty-eight and I was thirty-six. It was in the Algerian Sahara about a hundred miles north of Tamanrasset. I was lying in a small square of shade under a tarpaulin fixed to the side of my dead car. The battery and the alternator were finished and I was on the way out. I had been there for three days without seeing anyone and was beyond the hallucinatory stage of thinking that every rock was a truck coming towards me. I was reading *Dombey and*

*Son* which was taking the edge off the 120-degree heat and just about letting me forget that I only had three and a half litres of water left.

When I heard the rumbling noise of a truck, I thought it was from the truck route that I couldn't see thirty miles to the east, but knew was there. Then I saw the Hanomag radiator grille from over the top of my book and I came out from under that tarpaulin as if I'd just had a kiss from a scorpion. As the truck came nearer I saw the driver and passenger were two guys, both with thirty foot of cloth wound around their heads and faces, so that all I could see was a sinister slit where the eyes should have been.

I was either going to be rescued or robbed. The truck stopped and the driver jumped out. The driver had breasts and hips and was wearing a calf-length tea gown; the passenger had breasts too and was wearing a denim shirt and a pair of baggy trousers that I'd seen the Mozabites wearing in Ghardaia. They unwound the cloth around their heads and revealed themselves to be two women in full make-up. In my confused state I thought that these hermaphrodites were the desert sprites that an Algerian soldier had told me about, or that perhaps I was having some contact with a strange simultaneous world where the genders had united. They introduced themselves as Heidi and Heike, two Berliners going to West Africa. They towed me to Tamanrasset which was a real enough experience and saved me from a thirsty death.

Heidi had driven back across the desert six months later, but Heike had stayed and was running an aid project in the north of Benin. Every few months she came to Cotonou to drink us into a very dark world beyond oblivion and find out if I was worth loving. I tried to tell her these two activities were not compatible but she insisted that for her alcohol was the only approach road to love. By coming to Africa she had thrown in her job as a TV commercials producer and left her director and first 'serious' boyfriend. She had discovered he was over-generous with nothing except one part of his anatomy and not exclusively to her. She was looking for a purer life, less complicated, but like a lot of us couldn't always make up her mind. The drink parted her from her memories, gave her just enough courage to try again and, like me, she liked it.

Heike was a beautiful woman despite this punishment. She was the daughter of a British army officer and a Berlin café owner which meant she was bilingual and disinclined to listen to anyone's bullshit. She was tall, just under six foot, with a long whippy body that wasn't skinny but carried no extra flesh. She had thick brown hair which she always wore put up in a way that looked as if she'd just slammed a clip in any old place, but it was always just right. The style accentuated her long neck and fragile bones. Her eyes were intimidating. They were very clear light blue and green, like aquamarines.

I knew from the beginning that although she looked breakable she was tough. She had access to a temper that on a few occasions had caused her rather large hands to form fists and lash out on the ends of her long arms and hurt people. People like me.

Sometimes I deserved to be hit, but never because I couldn't keep my trousers done up. That wasn't my

20

style at all. I found out early on in life that playing around messed up my head, dealt me the clap and gave me a better understanding of the blues than I really wanted. No, she would hit me, because she couldn't get in there. She would tell me she was breaking down walls. I wasn't always sure why the walls were up in the first place or what they were guarding, but whatever it was, she wanted to get to it. I wasn't disinterested myself.

Heike was standing in the garage, her hands on her slim hips. She was wearing a white broderie anglaise top which showed about a foot of lean torso between it and her skirt, which was red with a light brown and white pattern. The lips of her small mouth were pursed, she was gnawing at the inside of her cheek. She looked at me with disdain as I walked up to her and kissed her. She threw her long arms around my shoulders and kissed me back.

'I've been waiting for hours,' she said in a voice that had been waiting with her.

Moses slid past me into the garage, nudging me with the wing mirror. The tickering noise had stopped. He got out, opened the boot and pulled the bedsheet out, grinning at Heike who said hello to him in the form of a suppressed smile. He walked up the stairs and Heike and I followed.

'You've got a lot of laundry, Bruce.'

'The biannual wash,' I said.

Some money fell out from the top where the corners of the sheet were drawn together. She picked it up.

'You should empty the pockets first,' she said like a

21

good little *hausfrau*, which is one thing she isn't. The door to my part of the house opened straight into the living room. Moses threw the sheet on the floor. The knot gave and two corners of the sheet burst open and the money spewed out on to the floor. Heike was not impressed.

'Can you count?' I asked her.

'I think I've just forgotten how.'

'It'll all come flooding back once you get started.'

'Can I have a drink or do I just get straight down into it?'

Heike took a shower. I made a salad to go with the kebabs and broke open some beers and we sat on the floor and ate the food. Heike rubbed her wet hair with both hands and looked at the money as if it was sending her mad. We started counting. A light breeze blew through the mosquito netting over the slatted windows. Heike pulled up an ashtray. It was early afternoon. We had a long way to go.

# Chapter 3

Heike was smoking cigarettes through a two-inch holder which took out most of the tar. After the hundredth time I'd seen her cleaning it, I gave up smoking and took up watching. She held the holder between her teeth at the side of her mouth and snorted smoke while she counted bundles of small denomination notes.

In the late afternoon, we stopped for a while and drank some sugary mint tea. Heike lay on her back with her legs bent and crossed at the knee. She told us that she had persuaded the women in her aid project to plant aubergines which would grow in the poor soil up north. It had taken some time because the men were suspicious of a new vegetable. The clincher had been to get the men and women together and deliver a seminar on the aphrodisiacal properties of aubergines. She had selected a number of priapic specimens as examples and had nearly been trampled to death in the stampede.

We continued and the sun gave us a warm yellow light to work by, which quickly turned pink and then orange. Then the sun dropped like a penny in a slot and we turned the lights on. The atmosphere changed to smoky poker room and we cracked some cold beers.

At eight o'clock I stood up. Moses, sitting cross-legged on the floor, fell backwards. I picked up the warm beer, went into the kitchen and threw it down the sink. Moses said he was going to get some chicken. Heike came into the kitchen and drank mineral water from the bottle in the fridge.

'I hate money,' I said, looking at Heike who was reflected in the darkness of the window, looking at me out of the corner of her eye with the neck of the mineral water bottle in her mouth.

'Money's all right, but not all the time,' she said, pouring some of the chilled water into her hand and patting her breast bone. She walked over to the sink and I felt her body leaning against me.

'What are you looking at?' she asked.

I turned and our faces were very close together. We were breathing a little faster and my hand slipped to her bare waist. Her eyes were darting around and her mouth opened. I moved my lips to hers so that they were almost touching. Our eyes held each other's. My hand slipped around to the small of her back and I put two fingers on either side of her spine and pushed up very slowly. We both swallowed. Our lips touched. My fingers were nearly between her shoulder blades. A long arm snaked across my back and her fingers ran up my neck and spread out through my hair. She crushed my lips to hers and her tongue flickered in my mouth. I didn't mind the taste of tobacco and lipstick. I felt her breasts pressed to my chest and her legs trembling against mine. The inside of my body lifted as if I'd just hit a hump in the road. We both heard Moses coming back into the house and drew away from each other.

'It's been a long time,' I said, holding her wrist and letting my hand slip down into hers. She breathed

24

heavily, licking her lips and said nothing. Moses came in the kitchen. Heike looked across at him, her shoulder against mine. Moses grinned. His sex radar was infallible.

We ate the chicken with some hot Piment du Pays that I'd brought over from Togo. I opened up a bottle of cold Beaujolais that had had Heike's name on it for the last couple of months. Moses stuck to beer. Afterwards, we dragged ourselves back into the living room and carried on counting the money.

It was 10.30, we were taking it in turns sighing, me like a horse on a cold morning, Moses like a dog left in a car, and Heike like someone who's into her third day in Immigration. She stood up, stretched and went to her bag and came back with a pack of cards in her hand.

'Poker?' she asked.

Moses, who had fallen back with his head resting on some blocks of cash, sat up.

'You deal, Miss Heike.'

'Miss Heike beat us no small,' I said to Moses.

'There's nothing like playing with other people's money,' she said and riffled the pack of cards. The noise from the cards shot through me and I sat rigid. The tickering from the car, but not the car, the noise of a playing card flicking over the wheel spokes of a bicycle. There was always fifty bicycles behind you in Cotonou. That was the tail. The noise had stopped as soon as we'd got to the house. Vasili was right – Madame Severnou's first lesson. How to outwit the Oyinbo* without raising a sweat.

* Oyinbo – Yoruba for white man.

25

'Something the matter?' asked Heike.

There was a click at the gate. Moses turned on to his knees and was up at the window looking down like a cat.

'It's Helen,' he said.

'What're we nervous about?' asked Heike.

I found myself staring down at over a million pounds in cash and feeling things going wrong. With Heike here I'd lost concentration, hadn't thought things through. I'd had that feeling in the port this afternoon that Madame Severnou was going to be trouble. I'd done nothing about it and now lesson number two was coming. How to burn the Oyinbo for the lot.

Moses knew what I was thinking and was already packing the tied-up blocks of money into carrier bags.

'Let Heike do that,' I said, tying up the bedsheet. 'Tell Helen to go back to her sister and get the car ready.'

Heike was on the floor packing the money. I picked up four carrier bags and the sheet and ran downstairs. Moses was reversing the car into the garage. Helen slipped out through the gate. I flung the money into the boot and ran back up the stairs. Moses was out and opening the gates. I hit Heike coming through the doors telling me she had it all.

I left the lights on, checked the floor and dropped down the steps two at a time. Moses drove the car out and I closed the gates. The car pitched and yawed over the mud road. Heike leaned forward from the back seat. We parked up under some bougainvillaea that fell down the walled garden of the house on the opposite corner to mine. We could just see the gates. It was very dark and the light cast from the living room window was

26

blocked by the head of the palm tree in the garden. We sat with our breath quivering like sick men waiting to die.

After fifteen minutes the paranoia wore off. Moses played a drum solo on the steering wheel. Heike sat back, looked out the window and hummed something from *Carmen*. I sat with my back against the window and my arm hung over the top of the seat and played with her fingers.

'So,' asked Heike, with a little German creeping into her accent to show me she was annoyed. 'What's going on?'

'It's a lot of money,' I said, only half concentrating, 'and the person who gave it to me wasn't very happy about what she got in return. I think we might be getting a visit. We were followed out of the port this afternoon but I thought we'd lost them.'

'It's a lot of money for rice.'

'It's for parboiled rice,' I said. 'Seven thousand tons of it. The Nigerians won't touch anything else. There's an import ban, too, which gives it a premium.'

'You're going to smuggle seven thousand tons of rice into Nigeria?'

'Not smuggle, exactly. The Nigerian government have said that each man can bring in a bag of rice legally. We've got five hundred guys who are going to take two hundred and eighty sacks each, one at a time, through the border at Igolo, north of Porto Novo.'

'You can do that?'

'It needs a bit of help which is why my client, Jack Obuasi, cut this woman, Madame Sevenou, into the deal. She can oil the Customs.'

'Have I met Jack?'

'If you had it would have probably been in his bed, and I think you would have remembered that.'

'So who is he?'

'He's an English/Ghanaian who lives in Lomé. This isn't the first job I've done for him, but it's only the second time with this Severnou woman. She's not easy. For a start, I can tell there isn't enough money. I reckon we're short about fifty to a hundred mil. She's a greedy woman . . . with an appetite.'

'It was only Helen, remember.'

'So far.'

'And you've still got the documents?'

'Yes, but that doesn't mean very much. A non-negotiable bill of lading with a bit of tippex, some faxing and a couple of million CFA could get to be negotiable.' I gripped her finger and she bit back the next question.

Headlights lit up the mud road and were killed. A quiet engine cut out and a car rocked over on its expensive suspension and stopped in front of the gates to the house. The doors opened. Four men got out. They didn't close the doors. They weren't carrying violin cases but they did have long arms. They went through the gates. Moses started up the Peugeot which made a noise like a tractor and baler and we rode up on to the tarmac and went into town.

We bought some pizza at La Caravelle café to take away. We had a beer while we waited. Some white people came in. We must have looked tense. They walked straight back out. Heike had thrown away the cigarette holder and was smoking for Germany.

We crossed the lagoon and turned off down towards

the coast and the Hotel Aledjo where we took a bungalow and finished counting the money at three in the morning. The total was fifty million CFA short, a hundred thousand pound commission for Madame Severnou. By this time, I had a half bucket of sand up my eyelids and Heike was asleep sitting on the floor with her head on the bed. Moses and I packed the money inside the car so that it looked empty from the outside. Moses lay down on a mat on the porch of the bungalow with the bedsheet from the money.

I put Heike on the bed and threw a sheet over her; as it landed, she opened her eyes. There was nobody behind them. Her voice said, 'I'm going.' Her eyes closed. She was asleep. Normally, when she came down from up country, the first night we made love of the desperate, savage kind that two months' celibacy encourages. It was something we liked to do besides drinking, something that kept us going together. This time I left her a note. I gave Moses some money and told him to look after Heike in the morning and then drove the 100 miles west along the coast to Lomé, the capital of Togo.

# Chapter 4

They didn't bother to search the car at the Benin/Togo border and it was still dark when I left the Togo side of the frontier. I couldn't make out the sandbar at the mouth of the lagoon at Aneho but by the time I came to the roundabout for Lomé port, it was light. The morning was fresh, unlike my shirt.

After commercial Cotonou, Lomé was a holiday resort. There were European luxury hotels and restaurants which fronted on to the beach and air-conditioned supermarkets with more than tomato purée in them. Most of the buildings had seen paint during the decade and a lot of the roads were metalled and swept clean. There was greenery in the town which backed on to a lagoon traversed by causeways which took you out to the suburbs. Lomé is a free-port where booze and cigarettes are cheaper than anywhere else in the world. Life was a permanent happy hour.

The coast road passed the Hotel de La Paix, which still looked like the architect's children doctored the plans. It seemed empty. Closer to Lomé on the left was the five-star Hotel Sarakawa with a snake of taxis outside and a fight for rooms on the inside. The sea appeared motionless but didn't fool anybody. Nobody swam. The currents were well-known killers along this coast.

People were beginning to make their way to market. The polio cripples hauled their torsos up to the traffic lights and arranged their collapsible legs beside them ready for another day in the sun scraping together the money for a meal.

I drove past the 24 Janvier building and Hotel Le Benin, turned right and arrived at the wrought iron gates of the white-pillared pile that Jack Obuasi rented for a million CFA a month. The *gardien* opened the gates for me and I cruised the botanical gardens up to the house. The drive cut through a manicured jungle of shrubs and bamboo before breaking through a line of palm trees where the lawns started. The two bowling green-sized expanses of grass were rolled and snipped, snipped and rolled, by a gang of gardeners who could have had a football tournament between them.

The house was whiter than a Christmas cake and had a central portico with four fluted pillars. It was the kind of portico that should have had a motto carved in it. Jack favoured *La lutte continue*. There was an east and a west wing on either side of the portico. Each wing had five bedrooms upstairs, all with bathrooms and all air-conditioned, with white shutters, which, if you had the energy to throw them open, would give you a view of the old wooden pier that strode out into the Gulf of Guinea. Underneath these bedrooms was enough space for living rooms, dining rooms, games rooms, jacuzzi rooms and cricket nets if you felt out of practice. There was also Jack's office, and in his office, a desk that a family of four could have lived in without him noticing.

The walls of the office were bare, but, in the other rooms, were covered with African masks, animal skins and ancient weaponry. Man-sized carvings hung around the place like servants of long standing who couldn't be sacked. Some rooms were taken over by collections of African paintings which crammed the walls from floor to ceiling. The floors were entirely of white marble only broken by large rugs whose tassels were kept in line by Patience, Agnes and Grace, the three maids.

In the rooms he never used he had much better cane furniture than I did, which wasn't difficult. In the rooms he did use were tables and chairs of every hard wood the jungle had to offer, as well as armchairs and sofas from France and England that formed exclusive circles about the place like people at a cocktail party who wouldn't mix. The one failure was a table and six chairs carved from a single tree, but the table was too low and a man's bottom couldn't fit in between the snarling carved heads on the arms of the chairs even if it had wanted to.

There was a large verandah above the garage and maids' quarters at the end of the east wing and another at the back of the house overlooking the swimming pool. They were both surrounded by a nursery of potted plants. I parked the car behind Jack's Mercedes in the garage.

It was breakfast time. Patience, the most senior of Jack's maids, with the eyes of a murderess and the shoulders of a mud wrestler, came out of her quarters and pointed to the verandah above the garage. I locked the car. Patience adjusted her wrap and slouched off to the kitchen. Mohammed, a tall, rangy, immensely strong servant of Jack's who could polish a Mercedes down to the base metal came from the back of the house hunched over, holding a monkey by the hand. Jack had bought the monkey and found that Mohammed came with it. The monkey saw me and hid behind Mohammed's legs like a shy little girl.

'How are you, Mohammed?' I asked.

'Yessssir,' he said with the intensity of a truck's air brakes.

A parrot in a cage started running through its repertoire of clicks and whistles, calling for Patience and doing imitations of her cleaning the verandah: little sweeping sounds with the odd chair scraping thrown in. I walked up the spiral staircase to the verandah and heard the murmur of the video-taped soaps that were recorded for Jack and sent from England. He played them in the big gaps of his light-scheduled day. Christ, he played them all the time.

'Mister Jack will see you now,' the parrot said to the back of my head.

Jack wasn't seeing anything. He was lying on a lounger with a cup of coffee the colour of his skin on his stomach, the video zapper on his chest. His eyes were closed. One big finger was crooked through the coffee cup handle. He wore a pair of shorts and nothing else.

He was a large man, probably as tall as six foot four, with heavy shoulders and a broad chest which must have housed solid slabs of pectoral when he was younger, but was now on the turn to flabby dugs. He

33

had a big hard, round belly which shone like polished wood. He flicked his feet to keep the flies off and his sandals made a loud flopping sound on the soles of his feet.

Jack was a good-looking man, but it was the mixture of African and European in him that made him peculiar and fascinating. His hair was black but not as tightly curled as a full African's. His skin was the colour of a walnut shell. He had blue eyes from his English mother and a straight sharp nose with a mouth fuller than most, but not African. He had long flat cheeks that fell from his sharp cheekbones and he kept these and the rest of his face clean-shaven. He had small, perfectly formed African ears.

Jack's overall impression, which he'd had to work on, was one of lazy power. He was a lion that turned up for his prepared meals, ate, lounged about, never had to move too quickly but had a look in his eye when he turned his big head that told you who was the patriarch. He had great charm, a boyish smile and he loved to laugh. When he walked into a room of people all you could hear were women's hearts fluttering like a colony of fantails. He left a wake of despair. He was ruthless in his pursuit of sex. A man who couldn't sleep alone but couldn't bear the same woman twice. Women knew this. His bed was never empty.

He'd had another hard night. He slept more on that lounger than he did in his bed. The parrot tutted as if he knew. Jack's eyes opened.

'Bruce,' he said in a thick sleepy voice. He glanced at the coffee cup in his hand, leaned his head forward with an effort and drained it. 'My God,' he said, sinking back. It was difficult to find any sympathy for him. I took the zapper off his chest and shut down the TV which sat in its little roofed shelter in the corner of the verandah.

'Madame Severnou's left you fifty mil short.' I paused for a moment while his supine brain took this in. 'And last night she sent some muscle round to my house to pick up the rest.' Jack's eyes opened and flickered as he registered. 'And I'm pretty sure that right now she's unloading the rice without the original bill of lading.'

Jack didn't move for a moment until his tongue came out and licked the nascent bristle below his bottom lip. He stared down through his feet at the blank TV with half-closed eyes.

'Can you turn that on again?'

'Can you listen for a minute?'

'If there's any good news,' he sighed, staring off over the wall into the palm trees of the next-door garden with ostentatious lack of interest.

'I've got five hundred and eighty-odd million in the Peugeot.'

He let the hand with the coffee cup in it fall by his side. A dribble of coffee leaked out on to the tiles. He put the cup down and with a sudden jerk shot himself up off the lounger and walked like a man with diving boots on to the rail of the verandah. He leaned on it as if he was catching his breath. On his back were four deep, six-inch long gouges on each scapula.

'And this after you've been in bed with a polecat all night,' I said.

'A lioness, Bruce, a bloody lioness,' he said as if he was talking to someone in the neighbouring garden.

'What the hell's going on with her?' he asked his stomach, which percolated some coffee through his intestines. He turned and walked back to the table by the lounger, squatted with a loud crack from both knees and poured himself some more coffee and filled a cup for me. He took a croissant from a plate and bit into it. His brain wasn't getting the spark to turn itself over. He heaved himself on to the lounger.

'I got the beef out of Tema, it's on its way up to Bolgatanga,' he said without thinking and blowing out flakes of croissant on to his hairless chest. I checked the coffee for insects. He was telling me things I didn't need to know. Jack's mobile phone rang. On automatic, he pulled up the aerial, clicked the switch to 'Talk', and then said nothing, but listened for some time, his eyebrows going over the jumps. I took a slug of the coffee which kicked into my nervous system. It was robusta and strong and bad for you if you're the shaky type.

'Can I think about it?' Jack asked the phone, and then waited while he was told why he couldn't. 'I can help, but you have to let me talk . . .' He held out a hand to me with eyes that said you can't tell anyone anything these days. 'I can't. I haven't got the time,' which was a lie. 'I have . . . No you don't . . .' He turned his back to me and I missed a snatch; he came back with some more croissant in his mouth. 'I have to talk to him first.' Pause. 'Let me talk to him.' Jack looked into the earpiece, pushed the aerial down and switched the phone to 'Standby'.

'Look,' I said, 'I'll take this lot down to your man Jawa and then I'll get back to Cotonou.'

'What for?' he asked.

'If not the rice, Jack, the fifty million might be useful.'

'I have to think about this.'

'Did Moses call?' I asked.

'No,' he said thinking elsewhere. 'Moses didn't call.'

I listened to the sound of Lomé getting itself together. Some women walked past the wall at the back of the house with piles of washing on their heads and babies on their backs who were sleeping on the rhythmical movement of their mothers' hips. It seemed like a good place to be, rather than up here feeling seedy and bittermouthed from the coffee.

'You've done business with her before,' I said. 'She's always been straight with you, she's always paid, it's not as if you're a one-off. So what's going on?' Jack nodded at each element with his chin on his praying hands. I looked at the top of his head. 'Is it me?'

'I don't know,' he said, looking up.

I stared into his blue eyes and all I saw was a big problem. The phone went in the house and Patience's flip flops slapped across the tiles.

'It's Moses for Mister Bruce.'

'Can she put it up here?'

'Different line,' said Jack, and I went down into the house.

Moses said the rice was being off-loaded and that nothing had been touched in the house. Heike tore the phone out of his hand. She was angry and spoke to me in barbed wire German which left my ear ragged and bleeding. She was in no mood to be apologized to. I didn't try. The plastic split as her phone hit the cradle. I hauled myself back up to the verandah.

'Africa. Africa. Africa,' said Jack after Moses's news. 'I'll drop the money at Jawa's and go back.'

'No,' said Jack, holding up his hand. 'She's got the rice now. You won't even get in the port. I'll talk to her about the fifty million. I want you to do something else for me. My uncle in Accra needs some help in Cotonou.'

'I didn't know you had an uncle in Accra.'

'I don't. He's a family friend, a Syrian multi-millionaire. He did a lot of business with my father over the last forty years.'

'Was that him before?' I asked. Jack nodded. 'What does he want?'

'He needs someone he can trust in Cotonou and I'm volunteering you.'

'I'll give him a call.'

'He wants to see you.'

'What the hell for?'

'He likes to see people he employs.'

'I don't want to go to Accra.'

'It's good money.'

'To hell with the money. Heike's in town and she's bloody furious.'

'You didn't make her count the money?'

'What the hell else was she going to do?'

Jack shook with high giggling laughter and drummed his fingers on his taut belly.

'If you go now you'll be back in Cotonou this evening.'

'Ready for action,' I said.

Jack ducked his head and turned his mouth down.

'It's a new client for you. He'll pay you a lot better than anyone else around here.'

'You mean his currency is money rather than promises.'

'He does have money.'

'Giving-type money or keeping-type money?'

'Money-type money.'

'I don't care. I don't want to go.' I was searching for something. 'I've got lunch with Madame Severnou.'

'Lunch!'

'Yeah, first course is a ground glass soufflé.'

'You're not going to lunch.'

'No, and I'm not going to Accra either.'

'I'll get someone else. Fine. No problem.' Jack was giving me the lion look now.

'I owe Heike. We were counting until three in the morning.'

'No problem. Forget it.' Jack looked off into his neighbour's garden again.

'Jack,' I said. 'I'll go as long as you promise never to say "no problem" to me.'

'No problem,' he said smiling. I didn't laugh.

It was a game that had to be played. Jack knew I needed the money. I knew I needed the money. Jack knew that I owed him. But appearances have to be kept up. I also wanted to find out what was going on with Madame Severnou and I thought I might be able to catch Jack right now with the stabbing technique.

'What's going on, Jack?'

'With what?' he said.

'Madame Severnou.'

Our eyes fixed; Jack's were steady.

'Croissant?' he said, holding up the plate and shrugging.

'I've got to get rid of this first,' I said, pinching the fat on my stomach. Jack smiled and breathed out.

'You have nothing to fear, Bruce,' he said, standing up and slapping his wooden gut. We shook hands and clicked fingers Ghanaian style.

'My uncle's name is unpronounceable. Everybody calls him B.B. He lives on the airport side not far from the Shangri La Hotel. Ask for the Holy Church of Christ. His house is next door, on the left as you look at the church.'

I started down the spiral staircase, back into the garage.

'By the way,' added Jack, picking up the zapper, 'he's a little unusual for a millionaire.'

'He gives people money for nothing?' I said.

Jack laughed and the TV came on so I left him. I kept a few things in a room in Jack's house. I had a shower and changed.

Patience accepted my dirty clothes which she dropped on the floor and walked off to go and be surly somewhere else. Jack was leaning over the balcony waiting for me.

'What were the heavies like?' he asked.

'Big and heavy,' I said, not feeling like telling him anything.

'Did they have guns?'

'Either that or very long arms.' That impressed him.

'You keep me informed,' he said.

'What about?'

'About B.B. and things. You might need some help. He's not so easy to deal with.'

'Is anybody?'

'Come and see me when you get back.'

I got in the car and drove down to Jawa's compound near the DHL office in town.

Jawa's boy let me into the garage underneath the office and disappeared. I filled up some cardboard boxes with the currency and went upstairs to Jawa's office through several rooms of dead-eyed men counting huge quantities of money.

Jawa was a small, balding Indian with muddy quarter-circles under his eyes. He was thinner than an African dog. He didn't eat food, but nourished himself by chewing the ball of his palm. He sat at his desk surrounded by ashtrays, each with a burning cigarette, and took drags from them all in turn, as if he were a beagle in a scientific experiment. The idea was that he should be smoking in the same order at the end of the day as he was at the beginning. It was something to do in the gaps between making money. He poured some tea and started to play with a lump of gold, weighing it in his palm and looking it over.

'There's going to be more trouble here, Bruce.' He spoke very quickly, as if the words were going to outstrip him.

'With what?'

'This multi-party democracy.'

'Jack called me last week from the Hotel Golfe. He said he was trapped, they were throwing stones at each other in the street.'

'And shooting . . . There was shooting, too. It's going to get hot, Bruce, very hot.'

'How do you know?'

'I'm listening. The people are getting angry. They told me at the flour mill they asked for a hundred per cent pay rise. They're going to close the port and the taxi drivers are going on strike. It's going to get very, very hot.' He put the lump of gold down and leaned forward. 'Does he want this in London or Zurich?'

'Zurich.'

'They'll blame it on the Ghanaians, close the border, the usual things. But it won't work this time. They'll be fighting, looting . . .' He sipped his tea and kept some cigarettes going. He booted up the computer, took the slip of paper I'd given him and entered the money in Jack's account.

'How's Cotonou?' he asked.

'Still good,' I said.

'They had big trouble there, too. Nothing's easy in Africa. Nothing stays good for long . . . We're going to see blood.'

'You'll be all right, Jawa.'

'If they don't shoot me. You don't know these people. I know them. Tea?'

'I've got to get going.'

I left him worrying his lump of gold, scrolling through his accounts, smoking his cigarettes, chewing his palm, thinking about blood. He was a busy man.

# Chapter 5

I drove back down to the coast road and headed west to the Ghanaian border. The sun on the sea and the breeze through the coconut palms washed off Jawa's depressing office and morose talk. For a while, I kept pace with a young white woman on horseback. The dappled grey seemed to be smiling through gritted teeth as his hooves kicked up the sand. The girl was out of the saddle, her bottom in the air, her head and shoulders leaning over the horse's ears, her mouth wide open.

I looked at her and wondered what I was doing grubbing around in this half-lit world of trade and commerce, making a bit here, getting shafted there, listening to people talking very, very seriously and watching the insincerity flicking from face to face until all you could be sure of was that nothing was going to happen as agreed.

I crawled into the crowds around the border. The horse eased. The girl sat back a little. The horse's head came up with its front legs. She turned him and was gone.

The Togo/Ghana border was always full of people. The Ghanaians poured across with their goods to pick up the hard CFA. I parked up in the border compound and a group of money changers gathered around me intoning the names of the currencies like priests at Communion. I bought some cedi for petrol and Moses expected me to buy Ghanaian bread for him. I paid a boy to go and get my name entered in the exit ledger and have my passport stamped. A soldier with a rifle over his shoulder was enjoying himself frisking all the women traders. Jawa was right. They were expecting trouble.

I drove across the baked mud to the Ghana side. Ten minutes later, I coasted through the border town of Aflao and bought a half dozen of the usual tough, green-skinned oranges from an alarmed young girl who scored them for me and cut a hole in the top so I could squeeze out the juice.

It was a fast, flat, boring drive to Accra and I arrived at the airport roundabout in a couple of hours. It was hot. I drove past the Shangri La Hotel and thought about going in there for a Club beer or six and a long lie down. I found the 'uncle's' house four streets back from the main road. I followed the music. They were singing in the open plan church next door.

The garden boy opened the gates and I went up the short drive past a frangipani tree and parked in front of a double garage. There was a huge woman sitting in the darkness. All I could see was the size of her white bra, which must have been a 90 double Z. She threw a wrap over herself. I asked for B.B. and she pointed to a door at the back of the garage which led to the battleship-grey front door of the main house. The house looked like a municipal building. It was L-shaped and tall with white walls and grey woodwork. There was nothing pretty about it. There were no plants or flowers. It was functional.

I knocked. There was an echoing rumbling noise of someone clearing their throat in an empty room. The noise rose to a crescendo and ended in a cough and a sneeze which bounced around the walls inside the house. There was an exhausted sigh. A different noise started, a man with a stammer.

'Ra-ra-ra-ra-ra-Mary!' he finished surprisingly.

There was the neat sound of someone who picked up their feet when they walked and the door opened. Mary had a round bush of hair and a smile a foot wide to go with it. I walked up a few steps and found myself in the main living room. There was a table and a few chairs which dated back to the British colonial days, then a large space before a four-piece suite which I could tell was going to be hot from where I was standing. A fifties ceiling light of a cluster of brass tubes held in a wooden circle had six lamps but only three bulbs. The walls on either side had two massive grey frames holding eight columns of slatted windows which were netted against mosquitoes. Between the frames, the walls were bare and white. The wall at the far end of the room was occupied entirely by a scene of snow-capped mountains, pine trees and a lake which should have been in the Swiss Tourist Board's offices, circa 1965. I blinked hard at the hoarding because treetops rather than bottoms appeared to be coming out of the lake. I could see that a whole section in the middle was missing. Sitting in the left-hand corner of this scene was B.B.

'You like?' he said in a thick, throaty voice.

'I . . . there's something . . .' I fished.

'It get wet in de airport,' B.B. explained. 'You get de idea anyhoare.'

We shook hands.

'Bruise?' he asked, as if I did easily.

He stood up for some reason. He was holding his shorts up with one hand. He had such a tremendous stomach that they had no chance of being done up. He wore a string vest which stretched over his belly and creaked under the strain like a ship's rigging. The vest was badly stained with coffee and a few other things, one of which was egg. He had short, recently cropped grey hair and snaggled grey eyebrows which fought each other over the bridge of his fleshy nose. His mouth was small and sweet and looked as if it might whistle. His neck was like a gecko's. It hung from below his jowls and fanned out to his clavicles.

He crashed back into the armchair, swung his feet up on to the table and crossed them at the ankles. His big yellowing toenails arced out from the flesh by a couple of inches and he had hard pads of skin on his soles. They were high-mileage feet in need of some remoulds.

'Sit, Bruise,' he waved at a chair. 'Ka-ka-ka-ka-ka-ka-Mary!' he roared.

Mary was standing right behind his chair and said, 'Yessah!' which made him jump a bit. He turned as if he was in a seat belt and gave up.

'I see,' he said. 'You want drink, Bruise?'

I asked for a beer. He tried to turn to Mary again and it brought on a wince of pain so he relaxed. 'You bring beer for Mister Bruise and the ginger drink for me.' Mary hadn't even moved when B.B. said: 'No, no, no, no, no. Yes.' She went to the kitchen.

B.B. rapped the arm of his chair, alternating between his knuckles and the palm of his hand for a minute or two. Suddenly his eyes popped out of his face and he leaned forward as if he was going to say his last words, but instead let out a sneeze like a belly flop, showering me and the furniture. He pulled a yellow handkerchief out of his pocket and wiped his nose and took the sweat off his brow and then held it tumbling out of the back of his hand.

'My God,' he said. 'I tink I have a cold.'

I was 'tinking' I was going to get a cold when Mary came in with the drinks. He sipped his daintily with his little finger cocked. He dabbed his mouth with the handkerchief and put the drink down. His face creased with agony. He lifted himself off one buttock and then settled back down again. His face calmed.

'Yesterday I tink I eat someting funny. The ginger is good for the stomach,' he said. 'Lomé? Is hot?'

'There's going to be more trouble.'

'Africa,' breathed B.B. 'Always problem. It getting hot in Ivory Coast now. De people, dey want to be free. Dan when dey free dey don't know what to do. Dey make big trobble. Dey teef tings and kill. Dey ruin deir contry. Is very hot in Abidjan now. Very hot.'

I sipped my beer and felt very hot through the Dralon seat covers. B.B. went through a few more crises. I felt as if I'd been there a couple of hours. I didn't feel awkward; he seemed to have things to occupy him.

'Jack said you wanted to see me,' I volunteered.

47

'Yairs,' he said and sipped his drink and looked out into the garden.

Mary flipped in and flopped out again. It reminded him of something.

'Ba-ba-ba-ba-ba-Mary!' he hollered, and she reappeared.

'We eat someting?'

'Corn beef, sah!'

He looked at me, wanting some encouragement, so I nodded. Mary went back into the kitchen.

'Jack –' he said and stopped. The singing in the church stopped too and was replaced by a preacher who roared at his sinners, torturing them with feedbacks from his microphone. B.B. lost his track. His eyes looked up into his forehead as if he might find it up there. Something clicked, it sounded like a synapse from where I was sitting.

'Jack,' he repeated, and I flinched because his eyes had popped again, but the sneeze didn't come, 'is a nice man. His father too. His father dead now. He was a nice man, a good man. We do lot of business together. He know how to wok. We wok very hard togedder, all over Ghana, the north, the west side, east ... Kete, Krachi, Yendi, Bawku, Bolgatanga, Gambaga, Wa ... We wok in all dese places.'

He sipped his drink and I wondered where all this was going to. He breathed through his nose and mouth at the same time, the air rushing down the channels. His feet seemed to conduct an orchestra of their own. He talked for twenty minutes with a few coughing breaks in which he turned puce and became so still that I thought an impromptu tracheotomy was looming and

I took a biro out for the purpose. What he talked about is difficult to remember, but it took a long time and part of it was about how hard he had 'wokked' with Jack's father, which brought him back to Jack again.

'Jack,' he said, 'has never wokked. Everting has been given. Is a problem, a big problem. If money is easy, you always want more, but more easy evertime.'

He winced again and leaned over, raising his left buttock as if he were about to break wind ostentatiously in the direction of something he disagreed with. The pain made him lose his track but his random access memory came up with something else. 'Cushion,' he said, and I looked around. 'Cushion!' he said again, wagging his finger with irritation. 'When you want to cross the road you always look, if you walk and no look you get run over. Cushion. Always look. Take your time. Don't be in hurry. Cushion is a very importarn ting. Jack is not careful. He no understand the word cushion.'

B.B. sipped his drink. 'Respeck,' he said, holding up a different finger. 'Respeck is very importarn ting. If you no have respeck you no listen, if you no listen you make mistake. If you make mistake in Africa you get lot of trobble. Jack he no listen. He know everyting. He no respeck. You know Africa, Bruise?' he said suddenly, so that I wasn't sure if it was a question.

'Not as well as you,' I said, throwing a handful of flattery.

'Now listen.' He looked at me intently. 'You see, I am still small boy. In Africa you learn all de time. If you tink you know everting you stop learning, dan you get big trobble. It come up on you like a dog in de night.

49

You hear noting until you feel de teeth.' He grabbed a buttock with a clawed hand so that I got the picture.

'Smock?' he asked, and I looked puzzled, so he lit an imaginary cigarette.

'I gave up.'

'Me too,' he said, annoyed.

He saw someone over my shoulder in the garden.

'Ra-ra-ra-ra-ra-ra garden boy!' he yelled.

Outside, the gardener was looking around as if he'd heard The Call. He ran towards the gate.

'Bloddy fool!' said B.B., standing up, grabbing his shorts and walking with an old footballer's gait to the window.

'Ra-ra-ra-ra-ra-garden boy!' he bellowed and banged on the window frame.

The gardener worked it out, ran to the door and knocked.

'Come,' said B.B., searching his pockets.

The gardener, glistening with sweat, stood with his machete down by his side, naked apart from some raggedy shorts and a willingness to please. B.B. had performed the Augean task of cleaning his pockets out of old handkerchiefs and found nothing.

'You have some monny, Bruise?' he asked.

I gave him some money with Jack's words sticking in my craw. He told the gardener to get him some Embassy.

He was about to walk back to the armchair when Mary came in with the food. It was chilli hot corned beef stew with rice and pitta bread. B.B. sat down and ripped the pile of pitta bread in half like a phone book. He reached over and scraped exactly a half of the chilli and a half of the rice on to his plate with his fork. He fell on it using the pitta bread as a shovel. Most of the food went in his mouth. I used a knife and fork and wore my napkin on the arm nearest to him.

The gardener came back in with the cigarettes and B.B. grunted at him. He finished his food and tore into the packet of cigarettes and chain-smoked three of them without speaking. He picked rice out of his chest hair and ate it in between drags. I picked the Cellophane wrapping of the packet out of my corned beef. He stood up and walked back to the chair, cigarettes in one hand and the shorts in the other. I finished my food and sat down in front of him again. We sat in the silence left over from B.B.'s breathing. I was getting a little frustrated now and had started thinking about Heike. B.B. was fretting over what was on his mind.

'You see, Bruise,' he said, 'I giff this man a job. He's a good man. He been here before. I know he haff no money. He haff big problem. So I giff him job and now he's gone. I no understand.'

I didn't understand either, but I realized we were talking about what he wanted me to do for him in Cotonou.

'Who is this man?'

B.B. muddled about with some papers on a side table. The phone went and he picked it up.

'Hello,' he said looking up into his forehead again. 'John. Yairs. OK. Cocoa? . . . Coffee? . . . Dollar? . . . Parn? . . . Fresh Fran? . . . Swiss Fran? . . . Arsenal? . . . Oh, my God! Tankyouvermush.'

He put the phone down and went back to the papers. He pulled one out and waved it at me. I took it from him. It was a photocopy of a British passport. It belonged to a man called Steven Kershaw.

'When you say he's gone, what do you mean? He's quit the job. He's flown back to the UK or what?' I asked.

'He disappear,' said B.B. 'He never dere when I call.'

'So what do you want me to do?'

'Find him,' he said. 'His wife keep calling me and I don't know what say to her.'

'Have you got a photo of him?'

He reached over to the papers again, winced as some ash fell into his chest hair and he slapped himself hard there, coughing the cigarette out which fell into his crotch and he came out of the chair roaring like a bull elephant. I got the cigarette out of the chair. He sat down again and took the cigarette off me as if I'd been trying to steal it and plugged it back into his mouth.

'My God,' he said. 'Is big problem.'

He found the photo. Steven Kershaw was early forties and dark. He had dark brown hair, dark skin, and dark eyes. The hair was thick and cut short with a side parting. He had a moustache which rolled over his top lip into his mouth. From his face he looked as if he carried a little extra weight but wasn't fat.

'Is he English?' I asked.

'Yairs,' said B.B. 'But his mother from Venezuela or someting like dat.'

'How tall is he?'

'Smaller dan you.'

'Most people are.'

'Yairs. Less dan six foot.'

'Is he big?'

'He not fat like me. He fat small.'

'Does he have any scars, or marks?'

'I don't know.'

'What about the moustache?'

'I tink he shave it.'

'What was he supposed to do?'

'I organize flat for him. I organize warehouse for him. I organize bank accoun' for him . . . everting.'

'To do what?'

'Sheanut. I buy sheanut from Djougou and Parakou in de north of Benin. It come down to Cotonou in trucks. He weigh de sheanut, pay de suppliers and store it. When we get contrack we ship it.'

'How long has be been missing?'

'Since last week. He supposed to call everday. He no call.'

'What about the money in the account?'

'No, no. He no teef man,' he said waving the cigarette at me. 'He no chop de monny. De monny still dere.'

'What sort of cash does he have?'

'Expense monny. Four hundred parn, two hundred thousand CFA, someting like dat.'

'Credit cards?'

'I don't tink so. He declared bankropp in UK. Thassway I giff him de job.'

'Car?'

'Nissan Sunny. ACR 4750.'

'How do you know him?'

'A Syrian friend. He introduze us.'

'What's his name?'

'Dey call him Dama.'

'His address?'

'You know de road out of Lomé to Kpalimé. You cross de lagoon, up de hill, he has de big house on de right at de traffic light.'

'You said Kershaw's been here before?'

'Das right. Not wokking for me. For his own accoun'.'

'Doing what?'

'I don't know . . . but I tell you somet'ing, Bruise, he a very capable man, he understan' de business very well. A very good head for trade and a good attitude, you know.'

Either that was true or B.B. found it necessary to cover himself for his poor judgement to a complete stranger.

'What do you think then?' I asked.

'I don't know. Maybe . . . You know Africa . . . dese African girls . . . maybe he lose his head. Dese girls dey change your head. Dey make you weak. Dey drife you mad.'

B.B. sounded like a man who knew. 'You know dey get beautiful girl mush more beautiful dan English girl, dey fall in lov and deir head come off.'

'Where's the flat?'

'In Cadjehoun. When you come into Cotonou from Togo on de right side.'

'That big block?'

He nodded and gave me the flat number. He wanted me to organize the sheanut business for him as well until I found Kershaw, so he told me where the warehouse and office were and gave me a set of keys. He also told me about a weekend house that Kershaw used in Lomé near the Grande Marché. It was a house that belonged to an Armenian friend of his who wasn't using

54

it. He asked if I wanted a fee. I said yes and he ignored me. He asked me if I wanted a game of backgammon. I asked him if he meant instead of my fee, which he didn't understand, but it meant that he heard the word 'fee' again.

He lit another cigarette in addition to the two still smoking in the ashtray. We walked out of the house to the garage.

'What's he like, Steven Kershaw?' I asked. 'What's he like doing?'

'He like to go to bars. He like girls. He like to play cards. Yairs,' he said, thinking, 'he's a lively fellow. He like to tok a lot. He like to tok to women. Thassway I say maybe de African girls give him trobble.'

'What about his wife?'

'Dere he haff problem. De monny. It break de marriage.'

'She still calls him?'

'Yairs,' said B.B. thinking about that. 'He like to draw. His wife say she going to send art material to him in Lomé. Yairs, he always sketching, you know – trees, birds, people. He show me a drawing of myself. I tell him thass no very good. He say, "Why?" and I say it make me look like baboon.'

'My fee is fifty thousand CFA a day plus expenses.'

'Whaaaaaat!' he roared. His face fell and his coal eyes bored into me.

'Fifty thousand CFA a day plus expenses.'

'My God, maybe I do de job myself.'

'Two hundred and fifty thousand CFA in advance.'

'Whaaaaat!' he bellowed, and stormed back into the house. The big woman in the garage smiled at me. I smiled back. B.B. returned and handed me a sheaf of notes.

'Is good business you're in,' he said, subdued now.

'I don't earn fifty thousand everyday.'

'Is true,' he said, smiled and shook my hand.

I left B.B. standing in the garage holding on to his shorts and smoking and talking to the big African woman. The preacher was still giving them hell on earth in the church next door. The palms looked bored stiff. I drove back past the Shangri La and kept going to the round-about and turned right on to the motorway to Tema with the bit between my teeth and Heike on my mind. At the toll booth a boy tried to sell me a Fan Milk yoghurt, then a set of screwdrivers and finally a duster. I blew him out on all three.

At the Tema roundabout, I saw the dark clouds hanging over Togo. The storm was heading this way. The women at the side of the road were already packing up their long oblong loaves of sweet Ghanaian bread. I stopped and bought some for Moses.

I thought about B.B. as I moved towards the storm. The old Africa hand who's 'still a small boy' but shrewd as a grifter. The millionaire who lives like a student on a tight grant. The guy who doesn't have to do anything but has to do something. The guy who's got a bit lonely over the years. He enjoyed having a crack at Jack. He was enjoying the Kershaw intrigue. He enjoyed men and their weaknesses. He was bored by strengths. You didn't make money out of people's strengths.

The first drop of rain burst against the windscreen. The tarmac turned to liquid. The windscreen wipers went berserk. I felt cool for the first time in a week. The thunder rumbled like a wooden cart on a cobbled road. Sometimes I felt the car floating, aquaplaning along. The road didn't feel solid and I wasn't sure whether I was in control.

# Chapter 6

The patches of tarmac – which were all that was left of the road – in Aflao were steaming after the rain and people wandered about in sodden clothes looking like refugees. The rain had made the town look ten times dirtier than it was, which was inconceivable. I stopped and bought some grilled plantain to chew on.

The border had become a lake on the Ghanaian side. The flow of traffic was going back to Ghana now and I was through in five minutes. The traders on the Togolese side stared out from under plastic sheeting, hollow-eyed and dismal behind their banks of cigarettes, tinned tomato purée and sardines. Mud worked its way up the buildings of this strange quarter of Lomé that butted right up against the wire of the frontier. The sea was grey and the sand looked hard and dark. Africa, after rain, was a place of the living dead.

I drove around town before going to Jack's house. Through the drizzle still whimpering over the city, I saw the red lights marking the height of the 2 Fevrier Hotel, its glass walls reflecting the greyness of the late afternoon. The smell of the rain made me think of London on a November evening. I had a sudden nostalgia for a dim pub with warm beer and a cheese roll with courtesy lettuce.

There was no light at Jack's house or in his area.

Parked behind Jack's Mercedes was a larger, longer Mercedes with Nigerian plates and windows tinted so that only a squat version of myself was visible on them. Looking in, I'd expected to see a bowling alley at least.

Jack was glowing strangely in the yellow light of a hurricane lamp where he sat by the french windows of the living room. His legs were stretched out and his hands were clasped behind his head. He was nodding as if he was listening to somebody, which was unusual because, as B.B. said, he never did. The guy he was with must have been important or Jack would have been flicking through *Hello* magazine and playing with his nose.

Mohammed came over and directed me towards the spiral staircase leading to the breakfast verandah. I got a back view of Jack's guest who was sitting in a cane two-seater sofa which wasn't reacting well to the circumstances. This man was wide and made wider by his suit whose cloth and tailoring values could still be discerned in the oily light. He moved for his drink and the sofa cracked like a splitting redwood.

His hand buried the glass. A heavy gold watch hung on a thick loose chain from his wrist as if he wanted to shake the worthless thing off. The light shone down the back of his shorn head and revealed three horizontal creases in the skin where there was supposed to be a distinction between where the head ends and the neck begins. It was a thick neck, a working ox's neck. I wouldn't have liked to be the man to strangle it.

Night fell faster after the rain and I stood at the rail of the verandah and looked down into the darkness of the garden. A drink had fitted itself into my hand with no complaints from me. I heard the booming laughter of a man who hadn't found anything funny but knew a cue when he heard one. There was more cracking from tortured furniture and the heavy footfall of a man who walks little.

The huge Nigerian appeared at the bottom of the portico steps. Beneath his pewter grey super lightweight suit his black shoes shone with a better shine than patent leather. A chauffeur appeared from nowhere. He must have been sleeping on top of the tyre under the front wheel arch. He opened the car door which swung out with magnificent weight. Mohammed stood holding a torch so the Nigerian could see where he was.

Jack was saying something I couldn't hear which was probably just as well. Mohammed moved the torch's light between Jack and the Nigerian, drawing attention to himself. Jack's voice told him to stop being a bloody fool. Mohammed held the torch steady. The Nigerian was jangling something in his pocket which must have been the keys to his Swiss bank's safe deposit box because he didn't look like a man who'd ever heard of loose change. He was chuckling a low, rich, deep chuckle that he must have bought in Harrods and displaying great white teeth and a thick, pink tongue. He walked in a stumbling way to the car following the pool of light from Mohammed's guiding torch. Jack appeared between the pillars of the unlit portico.

The big man bent over and got into the car while the chauffeur danced around him in case something stuck and needed to be levered in. He must have thrown himself back into the seat because the Mercedes's suspension coughed politely, just to show that it hadn't really been a problem. The chauffeur pushed the door to and it closed with a satisfying thunk.

The engine of this car was no louder than Heike breathing in her sleep. The car rolled backwards, arced on its power steering, negotiated a few bumps and floated off into the black shrubbery. Jack was waving, maybe the Nigerian waved back or maybe he gave him the finger. Jack will never know.

The spiral staircase shivered against the house as Jack climbed up to the verandah. He made it to the drinks tray and poured himself a beer. He drank and sighed the sigh of someone who has been so unfortunate as to have made such money.

'Who was Mr Big Shot?' I asked.

'That was Mr AA International Commodities Traders Limited,' said Jack with a smug look that would have earned him a dead leg anywhere in the world.

'He looked like Mr Kiss My Arse from over here.'

'Sometimes, Bruce, arses have to be kissed.'

'Tell him before you do it, or he won't notice.'

Jack drank some more beer and ignored me.

'How did you get on with B.B.?' he asked.

'He gave me the job and he paid me an advance.'

'I told you.'

'I bought him a packet of cigarettes first.'

'He likes generous people.'

'Millionaires do.'

'Did you get the lecture?'

'On wok, you mean.'

'He loves eating Chinese.'

'He spoke very highly of you.'

'He tink I neffer haff to wok for my monny.'

'Someting like dat,'I said, and we both laughed.

I put my empty glass down and poured us both some whisky into fresh glasses with ice.

'Do you know anything about Kershaw?' I asked.

'I know what he looks like.'

'You've never spoken to him.'

'B.B. likes to keep things separate.'

'You got anything to tell me?'

'He lost a bit of weight.'

'Thanks, Jack, don't strain your brain. Did you speak to Madame Severnou?'

'She's calm now.'

'I'm glad about that,' I said, mustering some acrid sarcasm to spread on my tone. 'I was worried for her. I'd hate to think of her out of pocket or inconvenienced. It must be tiresome to have to send the hit squad out every time someone questions your integrity.'

'Bruce,' said Jack, 'calm down. What I meant was that the misunderstanding that made her do that has been cleared up.'

'What misunderstanding was that, Jack? It must have been a pretty big one, and if they're that big I normally see the dust cloud coming over the horizon well before.'

'She thought that when you gave her the non-negotiable copy you were acting on my instructions. That ... and she didn't like the way you handled it.'

'Look, I know this woman is used to people throwing themselves on the ground in front of her so that she doesn't get dust on her toenails, but she has to understand that I'm there representing you in a deal where with very little effort she gets to make fifty thousand dollars.'

'Without her . . .'

'Spare me the horseshit, Jack. You could sell that rice to anyone. They're screaming for it. You're doing *her* the favour and, don't forget, she did short you by a hundred thousand pounds.'

'I'm going to tell you this, Bruce' said Jack in a voice that wasn't used to getting annoyed but when it did it was time to hit the deck, 'and then I want you to mind your own fucking business. The fifty million CFA is for some cotton fibre I've bought from AAICT and her fee. I didn't know that she was going to turn it round that way but it's done now and it works out the same. More important, she got me the contact with AAICT and this is her payback.'

'What about the four suits coming round to my place with half a brain between them?'

'Madame Severnou trades with other people's money. If she loses it, they get upset. She has to protect herself . . .'

'Against me?'

'She was annoyed with me and she was going to send the message back through you. She wanted to remind you of your position in the deal. She wanted to show you that she was a principal and that principals have to be respected.'

Jack wanted to think of another five reasons why Madame Severnou should have sent the gunmen round but couldn't, so be poured himself another drink and refilled my glass. He was calming down now. He forced one of his cheesy grins on me which I swatted away.

'Why didn't you just give her the original?' he asked in one of those voices of disarming simplicity that normally get the people who use them hurt.

'She's the sort of woman who you shake hands with and she checks her jewellery, you check your fingers and when you get home you find she's taken the shirt off your back and some of your skin's gone with it.'

'She's not that bad.'

'She resents the fact that you're breathing air that she could be breathing.'

'You'll warm to her eventually.'

'Like I will to a puff adder on coke. And anyway, why didn't you explain all this shit to me?'

'I didn't think you'd give her the copy.'

'You pay me to manage things for you in Cotonou. If you want a gofer . . .'

'All right, Bruce. I admit it. I should have been clearer.'

Jack defused rows by conceding but not giving an inch. We both sat down on a couple of wooden loungers with foam rubber mattresses. Jack balanced his drink on his belly and looked up at the stars which weren't there. He pulled a pack of cigarettes out of his shirt pocket and offered me one without thinking. He plugged one into his mouth, lit it, and drew on it as if he was trying to keep his cool in the trenches. He let the smoke trail out of his nose and from between his teeth and it disappeared off behind his ear.

He leaned forward and split his legs on either side of the lounger. He reached for an ashtray, put it in front of him and winced with his right cheek and eye.

'I have no sympathy for you, Jack. You get less than you deserve.'

'I bear the scars of love,' he said, as if it was a terrific bore.

'Love, Jack? I didn't think that was your scene.'

'Love, African style,' he cautioned me with his cigarette.

'How does that go?'

'She likes me. I want her. She lets me. I pay her.'

'I'd forgotten how romantic it was.'

'The women here aren't fools.'

'Who said they were?'

'They're not fooled into thinking romance exists. They *know* what exists.'

'Let me guess. Money and power?'

Jack somersaulted the cigarette in his hand and stabbed the air with it. 'Exactly. Haven't you noticed, I don't go with white women any more?'

'I haven't consulted my black book recently.'

'Well, I don't. They're too complicated.'

'You don't have to pay . . .'

'. . . money. That's what I mean. You sleep with them and before you know it you've got a relationship, they've moved in and they're supervising your life like it's a school project. Jesus. What I want is . . .' He trailed off.

'What *do* you want, Jack?'

'I don't want that.'

'Whatever you do want, you're not finding it.'

Jack wasn't listening any more. I had exhausted his attention span between thoughts about sex. He smoked an inch of his cigarette in one drag and let out more smoke than a bonfire on a wet November afternoon.

'There is one white woman I would like to have,' he said from behind his smokescreen. I didn't respond but sipped my whisky and did some passive smoking.

'Elizabeth Harvey.'

'Never heard of her. Is she a movie star?'

'You know her. She's married to that American banker.'

'Clifford Franklin Harvey the seventh.'

'The seventh?'

'Americans always have Christian names like surnames and numbers like royalty.'

'What do you think?'

'She doesn't look like one night stand material to me.'

He gave me an alarming grin followed by a diabolical laugh and some vestiges of smoke left in his lungs from the last toe-reaching drag came out of it.

He took the final drag from his cigarette, which was so hot he had to whip it out of his mouth before his lips blistered. He crushed it mercilessly into the ashtray.

'You're right.'

'I think she's Catholic, too.'

'You've seen her kicking with her left foot.'

'I've seen her coming out of a Catholic church.'

'Perfect,' said Jack. 'To attain the unattainable, Bruce. That's an excitement in life. What are you doing hanging around churches?'

'Hoping for a bit of salvation to rub off.'

Jack laughed, a high-pitched giggling laugh, and shook his head.

'Oh Bruce,' he said with mock pity, 'sometimes I think you're my brother, other times my son.'

'Naivety's one of my strongest suits.'

Jack looked up like a dog over its dinner. He lit another cigarette and rolled it across his bottom lip. The paper and tobacco crackled as he drew on it.

'I forgot to tell you. Heike called.'

'Thanks.'

'I told her you'd gone to Accra. She said something in German.'

'Did it hurt?'

'She said she was going to Porto Novo tonight and she'd be back at your place tomorrow afternoon.'

I chewed my thumbnail for a minute and Jack inspected the video zapper which told me the interview was over. I asked if I could stay the night, saying I'd go to Charlie's bar and see if anybody there knew anything about Steven Kershaw.

'Do you want to bet, Bruce?' Jack asked as I juddered down the spiral staircase.

'On what?' I said without looking up, just hearing his voice.

'That I can bed Elizabeth Harvey before you find Steven Kershaw.'

'You're a sick man, Jack. You're making too much money. It's creasing your moral fibre.'

He wasn't listening. The soap opera voices had started another crisis in another world.

# Chapter 7

I showered and changed and went out into the cool night and the smell of wet grass. The cicadas were practising. The inside of my car smelt of wet newspaper and damp carpeting. I shut the car door waiting for the satisfying thunk and heard a chord from a cheap guitar with a broken string.

The lights were back on in downtown Lomé and the place was full of music. A shop selling cassettes had set up some speakers on the street and for half a mile nobody was walking without a wriggle or a jerk. Three girls with snack food in large aluminium bowls on their heads stood together and bobbed up and down and turned around in time.

I came out on to the coast road and headed east out of Lomé. A wind was blowing through the low palms along the beach. The stiff leaves knocked against each other and made a harsh clapping noise like a few sarcastic people in an audience.

The Hotel Sarakawa looked like a recently landed space craft illuminating the dark and attracting humans for observation. The port was lit and it looked as if there might be work going on. Charlie's bar was on the beach a mile beyond the port. There was a rough track through some wasteland from the metalled road up to his compound which continued a further two hundred yards to another bar called Al Fresco's where the track looped back to the Lomé/Benin road.

At the entrance the *gardien* checked the car and opened the barrier. I parked outside a huge paillote which was the restaurant part of the bar. The paillote was a massive thatched cone supported by wooden beams. There was seating for a hundred people and a bar underneath. It was empty. It always was after rain. Next to the paillote was a concrete building which Charlie had built a couple of years ago with profits from all those fingers he had in all those pies. This was the real bar. A huge open plan room looking out to sea with a thirty-foot bar on the back wall, seating for fifty around a piano and a lot of room to stand and fall in.

I walked into the air conditioning and piano music. The hum of the distant generator that ran Charlie's compound disappeared. A light-skinned African girl with close cropped hair and a long neck was playing some Billie Holiday and looking out to sea through the arched windows. There was nothing out there except the dark.

At the bar, balancing on one leg of a four-legged stool, was a Lebanese guy in his early twenties. He had his palms flat down on the bar, his head hung at a level which gave him a perfect view of the whisky in his glass as he spun from one side to the other on the axis of the bar stool's leg. A Togolese girl was drying some glasses and looking at her single customer with concern and disdain. I stood at the bar and the Lebanese looked at me from under his armpit. His lips hung slackly.

'Charlie?' I asked the girl.

The Lebanese swung his head up to look at her too

quickly and too hard and it took several adjustments for him to focus. The girl shrugged at me with her eyeballs. The Lebanese gave me an exaggerated translation which was too much for his tenuous equilibrium. The stool spun violently on the axis of the single leg and sent the Lebanese crashing against his back into the bar. The stool slipped away from him and entangled itself in his legs, impairing his recovery so he had to throw himself on the mercy of two other bar stools who wanted nothing to do with him. He came down hard on the tiled floor with the chrome bar stools bouncing around him like a street gang. The pianist stopped, swivelled around on her bottom and gave us a clanging discord with her elbow on the middle section of the piano keys. It had been a very quiet evening.

The Lebanese needed plenty of help but looked as if the exercise might sober him up. I walked to a door at the end of the bar, opened it and caught a faceful of sea air. It was only four or five yards across some damp, hard ground to Charlie's house. There was a light on. I closed the door on the Lebanese who was finding new ways to say *putain merde*. Billie Holiday resumed.

Charlie's maid answered my knock as if she'd been waiting on the other side of the door all evening. I stood in the hall which had a single light in it, shining down directly over a plinth with a slim-necked pot on it which spouted a flower with a long green stem and a head like a bird with an excited comb.

I was trying to work out what this image was saying to me when Charlie's maid returned and led me down a dark corridor to the living room which, like the bar, looked out through arched windows on to the sea.

There was no sound of air conditioning but it was very cool in the room, and although there was no smoke, the smell of Gauloise was strong.

Charlie was sitting on the edge of a ten-foot white leather sofa, right in the middle with his legs apart, his forearms resting on his thighs and his large hairy hands dangling in between his knees. There were two women each sitting in a corner of an identical sofa opposite him. There was a tiger skin rug laid out diagonally between the sofas held down by a large glass-topped table with three glasses and an ashtray the size of a cymbal on it. One of the women had her bare foot in the tiger's mouth; a long canine slid in and out in between her big and second toes.

'Bruce! My God!' said Charlie in his expansive American businessman's way. 'How ya doing?' He came over and clapped me on the shoulder and shook my hand in his strong paw. Charlie looked shorter than he was only because of his width. He was six foot and a little slimmer than a brown bear but with no less body hair. It would be a big mistake to say he was fat and an understandable mistake to think it. He had a covering. Something for the winter, he would say as we sat outside on a December evening in ninety-five degrees, sweating like pigs, drinking dry martinis made with gin and an olive and held in the general direction of Italy for the vermouth.

He was bald and employed no techniques for disguising it, although I'm sure he could have trained some hair up from his shoulders and worn his collar up if he'd wanted to. His bare head was tanned dark brown and shone like polished teak. His remaining black hair was cut very short. He had strong black eyebrows which you would have thought would meet in the middle but didn't, and a thick bristly moustache. His eyes were dark green with long dark lashes, his cheekbones high, his jawline solid and square at the chin with a dimple on the point. The bottom lip of his mouth was full and tanned so that when he licked it, as he often did, it was the colour of fresh liver. Like most Americans, he had ten thousand-dollar teeth which were all his own but didn't look it.

Charlie had a big head, a big tanned head for a big hairy body. He was very strong but with no use for his strength other than drumming figures into a calculator. He was benign when sober, hard but not unpleasant when he was doing business, affable and charming when he was being social, but when he was drunk there were probably only a couple of things in the world more unpleasant – a fighting bull that's caught your eye in an open street is one of those things that springs to mind. He was wearing a pair of dark blue chinos, a yellow short-sleeved shirt and no watch. He kept that in his pocket on a long chain connected to his belt.

He introduced me to the two women who had both looked up with their eyes. Jasmin, who had her tanned foot in the tiger's mouth, had very long legs inside some equally long, baggy blue jeans. She wore a white T-shirt with what looked like her DNA on the front. She had short, straight blonde hair, very big blue eyes, a long and pointed nose and a mouth full of £25.50 teeth which were all her own and looked it. She had to be English, which she was.

Her arms were long and slender with small hands, one of which played with a lighter, the other held a cigarette. She smoked like a schoolgirl, the cigarette held at the very tips of her fingers and puffed at like a pecking hen. She was nervous despite the relaxed sprawl. There was a lithe sexuality to her boyish body and a surprised innocence to her eyes which I am sure triggered off base thoughts in the minds of a lot of men. I realized that she was the woman I'd seen on horseback that morning on the way to Ghana.

Yvette, who sat at the other end of the sofa from Jasmin, had more sophistication than the rest of us put together. She had very dark, shoulder length brown hair, styled with a nostalgia for the fifties movie star. You could see the same head of hair with one of the non-hats and some netting that they used to wear in those days. Her eyes were quite wide apart and, although large and rounded, narrowed at the edges with an Oriental sharpness that wasn't done with make-up. They were violet in colour and made her look more feline than any woman I'd ever seen. Her nose was small for her face, which had high wide cheekbones and a wide, full-lipped mouth with a pronounced cupid's bow. She wore a pale purple lipstick and her teeth were small and white with a gap between the front two which she had a habit of tickling with the tip of her tongue. Her skin was perfect white with not even the first hint of a line or a crease. I was looking too hard and too long.

'Did I miss something shaving?' she said to me in a deep, cracked voice with a French accent.

'No,' I said, taking the opportunity to look over her

face again. 'Very close, no cuts. Perfect . . . not the first time, right?'

She threw her head back and laughed through some gravel in her throat which trembled the white skin and light blue veins of her neck.

I sat down opposite her and took another look while Charlie did something about everybody's drinks and looked over his shoulder at Yvette – a lot. She wore a pink crêpe jacket, and a blood orange crêpe sarong which was split to mid thigh. The jacket wasn't fastened and I could see from her exposed waist that she was naked underneath it. A long orange and pink silk scarf dropped down from around her neck and covered her breasts. Like Jasmin, she sat low on the sofa, her legs crossed at the knee, and her bare feet nodding. She smoked an untipped Gauloise, thick and fat as a chalk stick, with the relish of a true professional. Charlie handed me a Scotch with ice and sat on the sofa next to me.

'Yvette tells me they don't believe in marriage in France,' Charlie said as he sat down. 'Says they have this thing *concubinage* instead.' He strained his whisky through his moustache. 'Sounds kind of interesting, you know, concubines and that. Sounds to me as if you could trade 'em.'

'Like pork bellies, you mean?' I asked Charlie, wondering how they got to be talking about this kind of stuff.

'I was thinking more onna lines with "1987 Concubine convertible. Low mileage, one previous owner, swap plus cash considered".'

'I think you're over-romanticizing it, Charlie,' I said.

74

'No, no, Bruce, you gotta understand, marriage – that ol' roman'ic institution – is old-fashioned. Strictly wartime only before you fly off to a certain death. That's what the lady says.'

'Don't you think so, Bruce?' Yvette dared me, having dug deep to pronounce my name.

'I've heard there's a very high success rate when the man dies immediately.'

'Whose side you on?' asked Charlie. I ignored him.

'The woman is left with a memory of perfect love and consummation . . .'

'Yeah,' said Charlie, with no encouragement.

'. . . and, if it's really a perfect marriage, a load of money.'

'Now here is a man who really understands,' said Yvette, uncrossing her legs and leaning forward.

'And the guy?' said Charlie. 'What the hell does the guy get out of this perfect marriage?'

'The guy gets to die at the pinnacle of his achievement. Wedding night followed by heroic death.'

'What more could a man want?' asked Jasmin.

'To do it again?' asked Charlie.

'It's never as good the second time,' said Jasmin, 'and anyway, men are always looking for the ultimate thrill.' She pecked at her cigarette. 'Sex and death. In Japan they don't always need the sex . . . I've seen them sit down to eat puffer fish knowing that if the chef's carved it up wrong any one of them could get the chop.'

'Raw fish,' said Charlie, 'is not my kind of thrill.'

'Yes,' said Jasmin smugging at her Gauloise. 'I think the spider gets it right. She shows her mate a good time, gets herself pregnant and has a problem free dinner.'

'I think I'm coming round to *concubinage*,' said Charlie. 'I don't wanna give you indigestion or anything.'

'Don't worry about us,' said Yvette. 'We have huge appetites. You must think of it as an act of kindness. We're saving you from yourselves.'

'Kindness was not the word I had in mind,' said Charlie.

'All this talk and now I'm hungry,' said Yvette. 'It's time to eat.'

'Will you be our guests?' offered Charlie.

Yvette had stood up and looked Charlie over.

'You look too tough for me. I like my meat very tender,' she said baring her teeth.

'The tender bits are inside,' I said for Charlie.

Yvette raised an eyebrow. 'Can I use a phone?'

Charlie pointed to the desk at the far end of the room behind our sofa. He saw Yvette hesitate. 'Sorry, it's the only one inna house. My rules. Somebody wants to use my phone, I wanna know what they're saying. It's business . . .' he smiled, 'something personal.'

She gave Charlie a look which left me charcoal broiled and I was only sitting next to him. She walked over to the phone and punched out some numbers.

'Camilia?' she asked and started speaking in Italian. Charlie nodded and drank some more and sneaked a look at Jasmin who had stood up and walked to the window to look at the dark.

Yvette put the phone down and walked back over. 'I'm sorry . . .' she said.

'I heard,' said Charlie.

'You speak Italian?' she asked.

'I am Italian,' he said. 'Carlo Reggiani.'

Yvette and Jasmin slipped into their shoes. 'We have to go. Tonight we are meeting someone for dinner who says they know somebody who probably knows lots of other somebodies who might be able to sell me something I want,' explained Yvette.

'That's the only kind of business they have here,' said Charlie.

'African art, Bruce, is a terrible business. The worst,' she said, smoothing her scarf inside the lapels of her jacket.

I put my drink on the table and we all walked out to the private parking area at the back of the house. There was a taxi with a powder blue furry dashboard waiting for them under a low palm tree. Charlie was kissed soundly on the cheek by Yvette, which might have disappointed him but he didn't show it. The two women got into the car. The taxi took a while to get going and circled us before disappearing behind the paillote.

# Chapter 8

Charlie shivered.

'She does something for me, that woman.'

'Confuse you?' I said.

'There's one thing I'm not confused about,' he said, turning and putting his hand on my shoulder to steer me into the house.

'They don't make them like that any more,' I said.

'Right.'

'Now that we're all being genetically engineered.'

'Something went wrong in my test tube,' said Charlie, looking down at his big hairy body.

'Not us, Charlie. You can still see the ape in us. In the future they'll iron out all those blips and glitches that make someone extraordinary like Yvette and we'll all look like leads from shampoo and shaving ads. We'll be the bathroom people from planet Earth.'

'You know, Bruce' – he stopped and looked at me from under his eyebrows with his hand resting on the back of my neck – 'you're kinda weird, but you're OK ... I think, anyways.'

We went back into the house and sat opposite each other on the sofas with big tumblers of Scotch in our hands and a bottle and a bucket of ice on the table. We drank and refilled without speaking. I took Kershaw's photograph out of my shirt pocket and flicked it across to Charlie.

'I'm looking for this guy. His boss wants me to find him, says he hasn't heard from him in a week. He describes him as missing.'

'Steve Kershaw,' said Charlie, rolling his glass across his forehead. 'English. Buys sheanut in Cotonou.' He spun the photo back at me across the table.

'When did you last see him?'

'He was in here about three days ago with a blonde girl, French I think, I didn't know her. Nice looking though. Great legs, nice ass.'

'Three days doesn't sound like he's very "missing" to me.'

'You asked me a question,' he shrugged.

'Was he intimate with this French girl?'

'Kind of,' he patted his bald head with his hairy hand. 'Sex rather than marriage type, I'd say.' Charlie twisted his leg under himself and winced. 'You know, this *concubinage* thing confuses me, Bruce. It sounds . . . financial.'

'It's like a common-law wife,' I said, my eyes widening with the whisky on an empty stomach which was loosening off the gab more than I wanted it to. 'I know you Americans are keen on marriage. Divorce, too. But in Europe now, marriage is out. People live together, they don't need to tie the knot in front of God any more. It keeps the divorce rate down. I've met quite a few Americans who've had three or four wives, which to Europeans sounds like upgrading, like we do with computers. The Africans? Well, they have all four wives at once, it shows they're making money. But then they say divorce is not a cheap option in the US. Is it a status symbol there yet, Charlie?' He didn't answer but stared at a bookcase with no books in it.

'You been married before, Charlie?'

Charlie, who was sitting sideways on the sofa with his arm thrown over the back of it, gave me a sideways look as if I was trying to cheat off him in an exam. He held up two fingers and took a large slug of whisky from his glass, including a lump of ice which he crunched.

'And you'd like to make Yvette number three?'

Charlie didn't react well to that dart into his private life. He'd shown me more than he'd wanted to earlier and, being a businessman always on the lookout for leverage, thought I could be the type to abuse it, which is the sort of thing he would do. The look he gave me told me so. It left me with frost bite down my front. His face lost expression, his eyelids closed a little, and he spoke in a soft voice. 'We were talking about Steve Kershaw.'

As he said this, Charlie's brain spun and clicked into a different mode. He was not a man to reveal what he was thinking. I had caught him off guard. Charlie knew that I knew that Yvette had got through, if not to the heart, then at least to the fillet steak. He leaned back with his elbow on the arm of the sofa, straightened his leg and sipped his whisky, licking the liverish lip to show that he was relaxed. He put his glass down on the carpet and rubbed his face with his hand.

'Steve Kershaw,' said Charlie in a voice that had a very straight edge to it. 'Can I call him Steve?' he asked, not expecting an answer but just to show me he was back in town. 'Steve Kershaw used to come in here with a lot of different women. He only came in at the weekends. I never once saw him with another guy. I saw him in here with black girls, white girls, Orientals, Indians, tall girls, short girls, beautiful girls and ugly girls but I never saw him with a guy.'

'He likes women,' I said, shrugging my eyebrows.

Charlie drew a straight horizontal line with his hand. 'I don't trust that kinda guy.'

'Did you know any of these women?' I asked.

'The only woman I knew to talk to was a woman called Nina Sorvino. She works in the trade department of the US Embassy. She liked him but thought he was kinda intense. I don't know what happened but something went wrong. She was here last night giving me the lowdown. I think he was into weird sex. She wasn't specific.'

'D'you mind if I talk to her?'

'Try her. She'll tell you more than I can. She might know some other people. I'll call her tomorrow, let her know you're gonna be in touch.'

'Did you ever talk to him?'

'Uh huh. Like I said. Not my type.'

Charlie poured himself a very stiff whisky and did the same for me. He took a gulp out of his as if it was nothing more than a cold beer. He grunted as the alcohol hit his system. The blinds were coming down in my head and I could see Charlie was beginning to paw the ground with his hoof.

'Whaddya think's gonna happen, Bruce?' asked Charlie, slapping the back of the sofa and lapsing into a more pronounced American drawl. It was the usual thing – Charlie on the hunt for information. He was a businessman, a trader, one of the good ones who realized that information was everything and he didn't give a damn about the source. He knew better than anybody else that not hearing the vital piece of news in Africa wouldn't just mean that you missed out on some action, it could cost you your whole business and, in bad times, your life.

He also knew that the boy who packed his groceries last month, or the young army sergeant at the road block could, with not very many twists of fate if he didn't draw the line at shooting people, become a high-ranking minister, or even the president himself.

'The President might survive this one, but it's going to be painful,' I said. 'He's losing the support of the people. France is edging away from him. There's going to be a question mark about future US aid. He's been around too long. It's happening everywhere else in Africa. The day of the dictator is over. They're all feeling the cold wind now. Africa's going to be a different continent by the end of the century.'

'What about here?' said Charlie.

'The army's the problem. You're never safe until you've got the army with you. The army's full of northerners from the President's tribe. They're not going to want to see their man go.'

Charlie finished half a tumbler of whisky in one tip, poured himself some more and added another half inch to mine.

'The southerners will get their election. The President probably won't get in, but whoever does will be under threat from the army from day one.'

'A coup.'

'The first thing any civil administration will want to do is weaken the army. Generals in the US don't like that and they don't like it here either.'

'Is anybody talking about this kind of thing on the street?'

'On the street they just want multi-party democracy. They don't know what it means beyond free elections with more than one party, but they want it. Some of them *think* they know what it means but they don't realize how much choice complicates things. They see France and Germany with democracy and they know how wealthy those countries are. So they think, if *they're* rich, *we'll* be rich. But there're some big gaps and a lot can happen in the gaps.'

'It's gonna be a fuck-up, in other words,' said Charlie, his voice thick with the drink.

'It's just the next stage. Africa's been dominated by the Europeans and now it's going to be dominated by their systems. It's the only road.'

'The only road they know is how to fuck things up.'

Charlie started pacing up and down the room. His forehead was glistening despite the air conditioning. Somebody had put a couple of bags of cement on my shoulders. I drank some more to see if it lightened the load.

Some hours later, which turned out to be minutes, Charlie stopped wearing a trail in the carpet and fixed me with a malevolent, drunken eye. Maybe I hadn't been answering his questions, or maybe it was just the time of night when it occurred to him to start disliking company. I decided not to look back in case it stirred up his machismo and I caught the full force of Hurricane Charlie in an enclosed room. Wherever I *did* look, things either came towards me or I went towards them. I realized from the silence burning behind his eyes that the subject was going to change, and for the worse. As always with Charlie, it was going to get personal and it was going to be about sex.

'How's that babe of yours, Bru?' he asked.

'Heike, Charlie. Her name's Heike.'

'Yeah, Heike. Kraut, right? Ossa Kraut like inna sack?'

'Maybe it's time for me to go.'

'Come on, Bru, ossa Kraut like inna sack? I went with a Thai chick once, she was tighter'n a duck's ass.'

'That's not something I'd know about.'

'On account of what, Bru?'

'On account of English ducks are suspicious of people who come at them with that kind of thing in mind.'

Charlie poured some more whisky into my glass and topped up his own.

'You think you're smart,' he said, shaking his head and panting a little from the alcohol crashing around his system. 'English people. They think they're smart. Nina. She likes English guys. Me? I think they're all faggots. But Nina . . . when you meet her she'll tell you she likes English guys. She says: ''They don't fuck you with their eyes.'' '

'Now that's true, Charlie, once we've been told what to do it with, we remember.'

'You don't know when to shut the fuck up.'

'I'm drunk. That's what happens. It just keeps pouring out of me.'

'I thought you could take it.'

'I can. I like it and I can take it. But I can't take it and keep my mouth shut.'

Charlie drank half his tumbler and nodded to me. I took a gulp which blazed its way down my oesophagus. He topped me up so that I had neat whisky to the brim and did the same for himself.

'Cheers,' he said, and took an inch off the top, to show me that the real men were on his sofa. 'The first English guy I met was at my brother's. My brother makes films in LA.'

'What kind of films?'

'Thrillers, comedies . . .'

'Right, I was just making sure he wasn't a Pasolini or anything.'

'He does skin movies too, if he has to. Pays the bills.' Charlie liked to talk tough.

'The English guy?'

'Yeah. My brother throws a party, like he has to, to get work now and again. It's one of those parties, lot of girls. Lot of working girls, you know what I mean. They going round with the blow, little white piles of it on silver platters with spoons. I'm talking with these two guys. One of them is English. He's a writer. Calls himself Al 'cos he's in the States. His real name is Algernon. What sort of a fucking name is that? Anyways, Al's got a plate with some canapés on it. The girl comes round with the blow and Al picks up the spoon, loads it with blow and sticks it onna side of his plate. Then

he says to the girl: "You got any celery to go with that?"
Now that is what I call one big asshole.'

'I laughed.'

'I heard you,' said Charlie. 'You wanna see one of
my brother's films?'

'No thanks, I got to go.'

'It's a short,' said Charlie, leaning over, picking up
the zapper and the TV came to life. There was a picture
of African straw-roofed mud huts and two girls pound-
ing yam.

'This is Africa.'

'This is Togolese TV, asshole.'

Charlie clicked on the video and a dark ill-lit picture
came on in which only the movement of things could
just be discerned.

'Is this wildlife or something?'

'Kinda.'

As the camera pulled back, Charlie turned the sound
up and the telltale tinny music and sobbing ecstasy
accompanied a shot of a woman laid out face down
on a bench, her wrists and ankles tied underneath. A
huge and hairy man who looked as if he drove trucks
during the day held her thin waist in large and sinisterly
gloved hands while he worked on her from behind.
Another man sat in dazed concentration at the other
end of the bench with the woman's head nodding in
his lap.

'Good night, Charlie,' I said, and lurched out of the
room.

'Good night, chickenshit,' he shouted after me, without taking his eyes off the screen.

\*     \*     \*

86

I needed some fresh air. Things appeared cut together like a film. There was no feeling of time passing. The dark corridor, the bird-like flower in the pot, the door, the warm wet darkness, the bar door. The bar door was locked. I walked down towards the sea.

I knew there was a steep bank of red earth down to the sandy beach but it was very dark and the bar was shut down so there was no light. I eased forward with one foot ahead of me until I felt stupid enough, then I stopped and looked out. My eyes got used to the dark. I was very close to the bank. It was closer to the bar than I remembered it. The sea was slowly eating its way into Charlie's compound. It wasn't going to be long before it all tipped into the Gulf of Guinea.

Standing in the dark was giving me sensory deprivation rather than sobering me up. I walked back to the bar; Charlie was still sitting in his living room, his brother's film flickering on the screen. I fell heavily on my shoulder and kicked out at whatever I had fallen over, which groaned. I crawled back, and in the dim light I could just make out the slack features of the drunken Lebanese. I called the *gardien* and we hauled him up to the paillote, which left me speechless with a huge quantity of blood crashing through my head. The boy was covered in ants and his face and hands were swollen with mosquito bites. The *gardien* said he would put him in one of the guest rooms. After ten minutes, my pulse went back down from my ears to my wrist and I got in the car and drove back to Lomé.

There were street gangs operating in the centre of town and on the coast road at night. They wanted money in the name of democracy. I decided to go around town and headed for one of the causeways across the lagoon that hardly anybody used at night. There was no street lighting. There was nobody out. The noise from the cicadas closed in. A tyre burned in the middle of the road, the thick black smoke making the night thicker and blacker.

A group on a piece of wasteland stood around a blazing oil drum whose flames slashed out at the night. As I approached the lagoon, two kids ran across the road and into the dark. Further on, a young woman trotted with her hands covering her cheeks. A young man stood at the side of the road as I rolled past with my elbow out of the window. He slapped my arm.

'Go back. Go back,' he said.

I cut the lights, got out of the car and looked down on to the causeway. A car was parked diagonally across the road, its headlights flaring out across the lagoon. In the light, three people stood looking out into the lagoon, their hands behind their backs as if inspecting something. They crumpled forwards off the road. The sound of three shots, delayed, cracked across the water. The black, still lagoon rippled out in silver lines before the lights died on the causeway.

'Go now. They're coming,' the young man said to the back of my head.

'Who's they?' I asked.

'Nobody knows,' said the young man.

We heard the car approaching. The young man ran, his shirt tail flapping. I drove down a side street and parked by a house out of sight of the road, got out and looked back down the street. A single car drove past at walking pace with no lights on.

Ten minutes later I drove across the lagoon. The mosquitoes screamed across the water.

# Chapter 9

*Thursday 26th September*

By morning, my face was welded to the bed, I had an arm like a plastic leg and a brain as dry as a monkey nut and no bigger. Something rattled in my inner ear as I sat up. I drank the best part of a litre bottle of water and felt intimidated by the brightness of the sunlight slanting through the slats of the shutters forming white bars on the marble-tiled floor. I stared into them for a while until they lost what little meaning they had.

I made it to the shower and rehydrated to full size underneath it. I shaved with limited success. I flossed for the first time in a month and ended up with a cat's cradle in my mouth. I dressed as if I'd done it before but could use some maternal supervision. I flipped off the air conditioner, opened the shutters and staggered back as the sun slapped a white rhomboid across the room. By the time I'd got to the bottom of the stairs I was ready for bed.

On the verandah, Jack was asleep in the lounger with the radio murmuring on his stomach, the TV quiet for once. I poured some coffee, ate some pineapple and retreated to a shady corner with a pair of sunglasses.

'Morning,' said Jack.

'Should be,' I said.

Jack opened one eye and found me with it.

'What happened to you?'

'Man to man with Charlie. The usual. Half pints of whisky, no water.'

'Did he get ugly?'

'He's never been pretty.'

I sipped the coffee. It was that robusta again. It rippled through my system as if I'd mainlined it.

'They found twenty-one dead bodies in the lagoon this morning,' said Jack.

The black and white images of last night played themselves through my head.

'There's a taxi strike. We're going to have trouble,' he said.

'Who did it?'

'Nobody knows.'

'That's what the guy said to me last night.'

'Which guy?'

I told Jack what I had seen.

'Did they say whether they came from the north or south?' I asked.

'Both.'

'A mixture?'

'No. Some people say all northerners, others all southerners.'

'Who's trying to scare who?'

'I'd say the army were scaring the southerners.'

'And the army says the southerners are trying to discredit the army and are killing their own people.'

'Dead people make everybody think about what's going on. Everybody's thinking twice about changing their nice, boring stable lives. Trotsky's bloody omelette;

just give me fried eggs sunny side up any time,' said Jack, with a full stomach and an empty head.

'Don't talk to me about fried eggs.'

'Restraint . . .'

'Don't talk to me about that either. You are no authority.'

'I myself had an evening of ecstasy and restraint.'

'Acid house comes to Lomé?'

'I spent an evening in the company of . . .'

Jack who was already supine managed to sink even further back into the lounger.

'Elizabeth Harvey. You don't waste your time.'

'It's my challenge.'

'What are you doing on your lounger then?'

'I didn't restrain myself *all* night.'

'I'd hate to think you were slacking.'

I finished my coffee and called the US Embassy and arranged to meet Nina Sorvino at the German Restaurant for lunch. She said she knew who I was from Charlie, so I didn't need a carnation and a copy of *The Times*. Her accent was from the wrong side of the tracks. I called Dama, the friend of B.B.'s who had introduced Kershaw. We arranged to meet after lunch in his house up the Kpalimé road.

I drove to the house where Kershaw was supposed to stay at the weekends. Lomé was very quiet, the taxi strike had taken hold. The house was a big place near the Grand Marché, not far from the US Embassy. It was smart, but not so smart that it didn't have a mud road outside full of puddles with kids playing in them. I pulled up outside the front door and a solid-looking iron gate that needed a new coat of paint.

The house was colonial French with long shuttered windows and wrought iron balconies. The front door had a tiled porch with creeper growing over it and the door a large knocker of two brass ducks hanging upside down with a bar in their beaks. Hanging from the bar was a tortoise. I identified with that tortoise. The gate was locked. To the left, in a small courtyard to the side of the house, was Kershaw's Nissan Sunny.

There was another house over a high wall on the other side of the car. It was crumbling badly, and the roof was several hundred tiles short of a full head. The windows were boarded up and the visible part of the front door had a plank nailed across it. To the right, a couple of hundred yards away, a smaller crowd than usual waited to file into the Grande Marché. On that side of the house there was only a wasteland which should have been filled with people selling what they'd grown, but was empty because of the strike.

In front of Kershaw's car were some large wooden gates. There was a boy lying face down on a bench like the abandoned child he probably was. I gave him a 'Bonjour' and he snapped to attention, holding his bench under his arm. I asked him if anyone was in, but he didn't seem to understand. The wooden gates to the courtyard of the house were locked, so I climbed the iron gate and used the knocker on the front door. It made an impressive noise in what sounded like a hollow house. There was an alleyway at the corner of the courtyard which led to the garden at the back, and down this was a side door to the house. An aviary stood at the far end of the garden. I crossed an overgrown lawn through a smell of bad drainage and found, hanging upside down from the ceiling, a single grey parrot. He looked at me and slowly showed me his grey tongue as if encouraging me to show him mine. He wouldn't have wanted to see it.

By the garden wall which butted on to the wasteland was a ten-metre long swimming pool which was covered with a scum of green algae and next to it, against the wall, a stone bench with a small patio and stone urns at each corner except one. There were some very tall palm trees around the garden.

The back of the house had the single twisted trunk of something dead crawling up the middle of it, like a subsidence crack. It was a secluded garden, quite dark even on a day like this and, like the house, melancholy.

By the wall that gave on to the abandoned house was the garage and maid's quarters. The maid's door led out on to the garden. There was nobody in the maid's room, but the door opened. In the room was a bed with a Bible on it. There was a dent in the pillow and the bedclothes were pulled back and hanging off the end of the floor.

A set of keys hung out of the lock of the side door to the main house and the door was open an inch, which made me wary. I walked down a corridor between the large kitchen and the staircase into a living room with a wooden floor like a squash court. To the left, was a set of french windows to the garden, two sofas, an armchair next to a table with a phone/fax on it and, in a gloomy corner, a wood carving. The living room occupied most of the ground floor, and the ceiling was made by the wooden beams of the roof of the house.

A floorboard creaked in the long and unrestrained way that puts five years on a burglar's life. Standing at the top of the stairs was a man in the office worker's uniform of a worsted short-sleeved suit, buttoned up to short, sharp lapels above the sternum with no shirt or tie. A handbag hung from a loop around his wrist so that he didn't have to carry anything in the four pockets of his suit and ruin the cut, which wasn't one that Chanel would have been proud of.

'Who are you?' I asked in French.

'Yao,' he said, as if he'd just barked his shins on a low table.

'What are you doing here, M. Yao?'

'And you are?'

'Bruce Medway.'

'Doing what, M. Medway?'

'I thought I just asked you that question.'

'That's true.'

'And?'

'I'm looking for M. Kershaw.'

'So am I.'

'He's not here,' he said, walking down the stairs and turning into the corridor.

'Any reason why you're looking for him, M. Medway?'

'His *patron* wants to speak to him.'

'So does mine. *Bonjour*,' he said, and was gone.

I ran up the stairs into the master bedroom which overlooked the street and watched from the window as Yao climbed over the gate, straightened his suit, opened his bag and took a pen and paper out; he then wrote down my registration number. This shouldn't have concerned me too much, except that on one of Yao's lapels I'd noticed a small badge of the Togolese flag, which meant that he was a civil servant and that his *patron* was likely to be a *grand fromage* – a whole *gruyère* to my little *crottin*.

I paced out of the bedroom with a thumbnail between my teeth and looked at the gallery which ran along the alley side of the house. The walls along the gallery were completely covered in a primitive jungle painting. The green rainforest flashed with exotic flowers was the background for leopard, monkey, antelope, a variety of punky tropical birds and a large life-size baboon. The walls were ten-foot high and ran for forty feet. It looked like something Henri Rousseau would have done.

There were figures in the forest, smaller than the animals. Some were standing amongst the trees, some moving with spears in their hands and over their shoulders, others drinking at a pool into which a waterfall cascaded down one of the door jambs of the bedrooms. I saw something in the corner about a foot above the floor which stirred. It was a lizard and it moved to reveal the signature painted in tiny letters. It said, simply, 'Kershaw'. B.B. had said he sketched, which made him sound like a street caricaturist, but the man was an artist.

In the bedrooms, the walls were dedicated to people, mainly women, some naked with fruit, others wearing wraps of African print. In one room, two women occupied a wall each and looked across a third wall where two young boys played catch on a beach with a lemon.

Most of the wall was an aching blue sky with only the yellow fruit sailing through it to the wild outstretched arms of the catcher. In the back room, overlooking the garden, was an unfinished painting of a fisherman hauling on a boat line.

I went back into the master bedroom whose walls, I'd noticed before, were bare. A double bed with a carved wooden headboard was positioned in the centre of the room. The ceiling had been painted like a break in the clouds. Grey at the edges turning to gunsmoke, then yellow becoming an intense white light at the centre of the room where the single, bare light bulb hanging from a thin flex became a joke.

On the stretched white counterpane of the bed was an overnight bag. There was a Ghana Airways tag with Kershaw's name on it. I opened the bag and took out two white shirts, a pair of khaki chinos and a washbag. Underneath, was a pair of black lycra cycling shorts. Under them, what felt like a bunch of shoelaces. They stuck to my hand and fell through my fingers. They were strips of black leather encrusted with dried blood. I tipped the bag out on the bed. There was a horse whip, stained with dried blood, two lengths of insulated wire with crocodile clips. One of the clips had a flake of something caught in its teeth. There was also a piece of wood with two holes in it; a two-foot length of cord had been passed through the two holes and knotted. It was the kind of device where if you slipped the loop over someone's head and then twisted the wood, it would allow you a controlled strangulation of your victim.

I looked up at the ceiling and down at the bed. I

walked out of the room, on to the gallery, and found the leopard staring at me from the painted forest with eyes that had already eaten. I was trying to square what I'd found in the bag with what was up on these walls and I couldn't. I went back to the case and the mess of equipment on the bed and repacked the contents as I had found them. I gave the house a cursory search. There was hardly any furniture in it apart from a wardrobe and a chest in the bedroom with a few clothes in the top drawers.

Yao had said Kershaw wasn't here, but I'd found that his bag was, and I had no idea why someone would want to leave a bag full of that kind of stuff out in the open. It hadn't passed me by that Yao was keen to get away. It could have been because he'd found what was in the bag, or because he'd left the bag there himself. Either reason was a good one for getting out of there.

I was feeling hot and sick by the time I got back in the car. I had tried talking to the young boy again, who was forthcoming but spoke nonsense. At one point, he had let out a noise like a far off cry (not uncommon from Africans of all ages) and I thought we might be getting somewhere, but he followed it by blubbering his lips. He saw that it was a response that puzzled me so he raised his eyebrows, opened out his palms and smiled. He was the lemon catcher in Kershaw's painting.

I went to see a friend of mine who was a sergeant in the Sûreté to see if any dead bodies had washed up on his desk. He told me there were lots of bodies found in the lagoon that morning, but no white bodies had been found anywhere in Lomé yet. He grinned at the word 'yet'. When I asked who was responsible for the bodies in the lagoon, he drew a finger over his lips and told me not to ask that question anywhere in Togo.

# Chapter 10

The day had worked its way around to one o'clock and I found myself sitting in the open part of the German Restaurant with a beer in front of me that was so cold it steamed like liquid nitrogen. There was a mixed crowd in the dozen or so cubicles. Some trans-Saharan travellers giving themselves a luxury, some German businessmen not talking to each other and plodding through large hunks of roast pork and sauerkraut with huge jugs of beer, a French couple having a sibilant row like two cats fighting, and an ascetic looking Scandinavian who sat at the table next to me reading Kierkegaard and eating his paper napkin.

I turned round from the French couple whose row had reached a crescendo of hissing and terminated with a loud slap that had silenced the restaurant. A young woman in her late twenties stood at the edge of the table. Apart from her height, the bewildering curvaceousness of her figure and the dangerous length of her fingernails, the thing that jolted me about Nina Sorvino was her hair. There was a hell of a lot of it, enough to stuff several bolsters and have spare for a couple of scatter cushions. It was also very black. It wasn't dyed, because I could see it shining midnight blue in the sunlight that fell through the raffia matting above us.

'Bruce Medway,' she said, arcing her hand down in a way that might have opened up an unwary person from the neck to the abdomen. We shook hands.

'Nina Sorvino?' I said.

'Dat's me,' she said, with a lot of Bronx in the accent. She sat down and her hair drew around her like a heavy shawl. The waiter appeared and I ordered an omelette and salad while Nina asked for a rare entrecôte steak and fries.

'You a vegetarian, Bruce?'

'I don't look that ill, do I?'

'You need protein, need some blood in your veins.'

I looked at the quantity of protein coming out of Nina's head and fingers and reckoned she was on a cow a week.

Nina wanted some wine so I ordered a cold Beaujolais which the waiter brought straightaway. He poured a taster for Nina who beckoned him with a fingernail saying: 'Don't be shoy.'

The waiter filled the glass and fled. She took some Camels out of her handbag and holding the cigarette between the pillar box-red razors of her nails, lit it with a match which she blew out with the first exhalation of smoke. She tinkled the wine glass with the other handful of nails and looked at me looking at them.

'Dey're all my own,' she said, and gave me a little kick with her foot under the table which I winced at.

'Don't worry,' she said. 'I cut my toenails, I can't afford the sheets.' She laughed with a snort and so did I, forgoing the snort. This was almost too much for a single hangover to bear on its own, so I downed the cold beer and struck out for the wine.

She had a tough look to her face. It wasn't a mean look, it was a look that could stand up for itself when the chairs started flying in the saloon. She had very straight black eyebrows over dark brown eyes. Her nose was blade sharp and her nostrils arched from the blade like the prow of a ship through water. She had the habit of breathing through her nose and her nose alone, which meant the nostrils flared occasionally giving an air of impatience. As her nostrils flared, her red and glossy lips pouted. She knew this. The smoking was a diversionary tactic. The effect was of getting the come on and the knee in the groin at the same time. She wore a dark blue raw silk blouse and a white cotton skirt. She was dressed for work but I felt there was a racier wardrobe elsewhere.

She was looking at me with her head to one side. She dropped her bottom lip and showed me the straight line of her white teeth.

'You know, don't ask me why, but I kinda like English guys.'

'Any particular reason?'

'I said, "Don't ask me why."'

'I thought you were being rhetorical.'

'You ever been to New York?'

'Yes.'

'What happened?'

'I came out of Penn Station and asked a cop the way to Fifth Avenue, he said: "Piss off, jerk."'

'Not very rhetorical, right?'

She pulled on her cigarette and licked her lips, taking them into her mouth, and then pouted out smoke at me.

'I tell you why I like English guys, because dey don't strip you down wid deir eyes, dey don't sniff arounjew like a dawag, dey don't speak wid deir dicks and dey keep deir hands nicely folded in deir laps.'

I put my hands on the table to show I was the dangerous type and thought about Nina's impact on the Togolese Minister for Trade. She started laughing.

'I'm puttin' you on, Bruce,' she said with her eyebrows raised.

'I see.'

'You think I'd get a job in the US Embassy if I torked like dat?'

'You tork like dat to Steve?'

'Yeah. That's why I did it. He liked it. De Bronx, Southern Bey-elle, North Carliiiina 'n' all.'

'Very good.'

'No, but it's true I do like English men,' she said, putting her hand on mine, making me flinch. 'I sanded down de edges. I might graze you but you won't need stitches.'

'I thought the English were too boring. Not enough wisecracks.'

'Hey, look, buddy, I've had men cracking wise at me all my life, nobody said anything to me I ain't heard already.'

'D'you scare people?'

'I didn't scare Steve.'

'No?'

'He was too sure of himself to be scared. He just loved the act. Not many men I know can take a woman being too funny for too long.'

We drank some more wine. The food arrived with

a large bowl of salad and some bread. She stubbed out the cigarette, pulled all her nails off and poured them into her handbag like loose change.

'What can you tell me about Steve?'

'How long's he been missing?'

'About a week according to his employer, and three days according to Charlie.'

'Not so long.'

'Long enough when you're supposed to be working for someone.'

She nodded and forked some salad into her mouth.

'Did you ever go to his place here in Lomé?' I asked.

'Yep.'

'What did you think?'

'The guy can paint.'

'Did he tell you anything about himself apart from his job?'

'He didn't talk about his job; I liked that.'

'Was there anything you didn't like?'

'You tried his apartment in Cotonou?' she said, riding over my question.

'Not yet.'

I finished the omelette, ate some more salad and started to clean the plate with a piece of bread.

'In a crowd he was a very nice guy to be with. He could make you feel like the most interesting person in the place. He wasn't the type who'd sit around and look at everybody else over your shoulder, winking and waving like a bookie at a racetrack. I've had plenty of those. He only looked at me. It was great to feel intimate with someone like that.'

'But?'

'But when it was just the two of us the intimacy kinda changed to intensity, and hey, I'm not the frothy type, but I mean, he was obsessed.'

I didn't say anything. She finished eating, lit another cigarette and sat sideways sipping her wine.

'I'm not used to talking about my private life. I mean, I spoke to Charlie and he says you're cool, but it doesn't make it any easier. I've talked about sex before to my girlfriends. Hell, everybody talks about sex in America. You gettin' it, you not, does he do this, does he do that, he got a big cock, he got a small one . . . he sucks your . . . to-o-o-o-oes? Gad . . . did you have time to shower?

'We have talk shows about sex. We have cable channels dedicated to sex. We have books about sex. We have stars who have sex and write books about it and show us photographs of how to do it. Which is good because sometimes I forget how and it's always nice to know there's someone there to help.

'I mean, if you're not getting it in the US of A then you gotta talk about it, you gotta complain, you gotta go to the authorities and shout 'n' holler: "Where's my sex? I am an American citizen!" I think we're weird. Don't you?'

'It's your culture.'

'Culture? Wow! You mean, like you've got Big Ben and the Queen and we've got sex. That's a bad deal for Britain.' I laughed, I could feel the Scandinavian not reading his Kierkegaard, listening.

'The money culture,' I said.

'Now look here, sonny, I ain't never paid for it . . . not never, ever! And I ain't never, ever, never goin' to neither. Yo hearin' me, bo!' She jabbed at me with her index finger.

'Do you have sex in England? Or you just got beef-eaters and those fuckers in the furry helmets?'

'We have sex but we don't talk about it . . . all the time.'

'What do you do when you're not talking about it?'

'We're suppressing it. Then we go to apartments in Mayfair and ask formidable women to tie us up and give us the lash.'

Nina didn't laugh. She stubbed out the cigarette she was smoking and lit another one and blew the match out thinking.

'That's what Steve was into,' she said.

'Domination?'

'No. The other way round. He wanted to tie me up and stuff. He started off talking about spanking and then it was: "Why don't I just tie you to the bed?" and, I mean, I'm not into that stuff. I didn't know the guy that well. I didn't want to put myself in that position. We got crazy fuckers back home who tie you up and the next thing you hear is the chainsaw starting up in the garage. That ain't no fun.'

'So you finished it?'

'Well, it went on for a while. But then he tried to ease me into it. You know, being a bit rough, pinching, biting too hard. He got a kick if I cried out. I just found it creepy. I quit.'

'When did you last see him?'

The weekend before last. He was in here. We didn't speak. He was with another girl. Like I say, he didn't look up.'

A strong smell of grilled beef, fried pork and chips was beginning to thicken up the air. People were leaving for siesta. Nina and I talked for a while, but not about Kershaw. She didn't hit her previous form. I called for the bill, paid and walked her down to her car.

'Yo give me a call sometime,' she said, getting into her car. 'I like English guys.'

She left and I waded through a half-dozen hawkers who tried to sell me Cartiers and Rolexes. A persistent and rakish young man insisted I bought a video whose cover had some anatomical detail that a trainee surgeon might have been interested in. I told him to move along and he rushed off to the Scandinavian who'd just come out of the restaurant and who took the video and his eyebrows nearly stood out of his face and left him. He threw it up in the air like a hot piece of toast and ran.

# Chapter 11

I came into Dama's house the back way. A large crowd lined the main Kpalimé road which ran by Dama's house up to a crossroads where a knot of people hung around waiting for someone to do something. The *gardien* opened the gate and I parked behind Dama's Peugeot. The owner of the funeral parlour next door picked up the board with his coffin prices on it and took it back into his shop. A few people on the road looked back. There was nothing aggressive about them. Dama's garden was full of people painting his cane furniture.

Dama sat in a large wicker chair on a verandah in front of his living room watching the painters. He was a small, muscly, pugnacious man with thinning short grey hair. His eyes darted about in his head as if he was playing bar football. He sat forward in his chair, a packet of cigarettes in the breast pocket of his white shirt and his grey trousers hitched up so that his hairless shins were visible almost to the knee. He rested his elbows on his thighs and bobbed like a lizard in the sun.

We drank Perrier water with ice and lemon. Dama swirled his ice around in his glass and looked down the vortex.

'There's an advantage to living next to a funeral parlour,' he said.

'A discount,' I said, 'but you can never be sure they'll give it to you.'

He held up his glass. 'Ice,' he said. 'They've always got ice.' Which made me check for floating hairs.

Dama had met Kershaw three times in the bar of the Hotel Sarakawa before he told him about B.B.'s job. Dama liked him. Kershaw had drive, he said, and he laughed at his jokes, which was always seductive.

'The ladies liked him and I knew B.B. would like him too,' he said, 'because there was something . . . different about him.'

'Different?'

'You know, he might need some control but things are going to happen around him. Life won't be dull.'

'B.B. likes "different" people?'

'He doesn't need any more money. People are all that's left.' He offered me a cigarette and then lit one for himself. 'Where have you looked for him?'

'His house here. I've spoken to Charlie and a woman from the US Embassy he knew.'

'Charlie? What did Charlie say?'

'He'd seen him three days ago.'

'How did Charlie look?'

'Like he always does.'

'I hear he's taken some bad hits.'

'Trading?'

'Gold. Was he drinking?'

'He's always drinking.'

'Of course, but was he sipping or gulping?'

'What's your interest?'

'We compete. I want to know if it's true. Charlie

never tells anybody anything; we have to find out for ourselves. I think the rumour is true.'

'He was gulping.'

The crowd in the road roared. Dama and I walked to the edge of the verandah, which was higher than the garden wall, and watched. There were more people now and a road block had been set up. It was a large rock. It meant that cars had to drive close to the pavement, where the crowd drummed on their roofs with the palms of their hands. Occasionally, someone stalled and the car was surrounded by the exuberant crowd who developed interesting rhythms on the bodywork until the panicked driver managed to get it together to move on.

Dama and I noticed two or three young men in coats. At 110 degrees, it wasn't coat-wearing weather. They introduced some more elements to the road block. The traffic stopped. Drivers began to get annoyed. There was a loud gong sound as a rock hit a car roof. The driver started trying to move the road block. A group closed around and there was a lot of pulling and shouting and the odd flash of a fist.

There was the sound of an army diesel truck pulling up at the crossroads, its engine still running. Dama and I went into the house and upstairs to a balcony outside his room where there was a view of the road, crossroads and some wasteground, which was one of the largest taxi ranks in Lomé. It should have been full of people coming from outside Lomé to work and sell, but today the wasteground was empty because of the strike.

Another army truck pulled up. The knot of people around the road block loosened. A rock arced out from the crowd and hit the radiator grille of the truck in front. The truck edged forward and the engine roared. The crowd squealed at the reaction. Three more rocks clanged in. We heard the rubber soles of army boots jumping off the trucks. They lined up with batons ready behind the trucks. A helicopter stuttered in the distance.

More rocks rained in on the trucks, some of the wilder ones skittered around our feet and rattled the shutters. The furniture painters ran for cover. A group of soldiers moved off behind Dama's house. Another group moved in the opposite direction heading for the wasteland. The second truck drew alongside the first and they both moved over the crossroads.

We lost the sound of the helicopter until it clattered over us, wheeling low around the rooftops. The crowd raised their fists and roared. The helicopter pivoted on an unseen axis over the wasteland, and bucking and roaring like a rodeo bullock, it kicked up a dust cloud about fifty yards wide which it manoeuvred towards the cheering crowd.

Troops appeared in the side road by the entrance to Dama's house. The crowd saw them late, panicked and ran towards the wasteland and into the dust cloud. The troops chased them, some lingering and fanning out to close off escape routes. On the wasteland, through the haze of the dust cloud, we could see from our height the other troops waiting for them, their batons ready, angled for the first cut.

The helicopter tipped to its starboard side and rolled off over the lagoon. The cloud stayed, the panic continued. People tried to climb over Dama's wall and were hauled off. Some were pushed around, others were given a beating and thrown into the back of a van, red running down their black skin and soaking into their shirt collars.

The dust began to settle. A young man, head down, was pushing his bicycle up the hill from the lagoon. There were no cars on the road now. He pushed the bicycle off the pavement and on to the rough grass leading up to the wasteland. He didn't know what was going on. A soldier with a baton confronted him and for the first time he looked up. The baton cracked him on the side of the head and he fell down flat in the grass as if his feet had been whipped out from under him. His mouth had opened in surprise but nothing had come out. He lay there, arms by his side, his cheek in the dust and the bicycle wheel spinning behind him.

The van with a dozen bloodied young men moved off. They looked frightened. They were headed for another beating. The soldiers moved back towards the trucks. We turned because of a ferocious shout by the gate. There was the booming sound of juddering sheet metal and one of Dama's houseboys vaulted the gate and landed on the roof of my Peugeot. The soldiers started to climb over and Dama shouted at them. They trotted off. The houseboy slid off the roof. A cut across his forehead bled down his face and white T-shirt, which had a faded black and white print of Jimi Hendrix on it.

Dama told me that there had been a bad scene at the port in the morning. The dockers had refused to open the gates. There was a fight with the soldiers. A minister had turned up and promised some pay rises.

The gates were opened but no ships were unloaded and no ships came in.

The people were smelling desperation. But nothing was clear. Who was who in the rioting? There had been provocateurs in the crowd. Men and women had been shot last night. Twenty-one bodies floated in the lagoon that morning.

Ambitious men were getting hungry and people were behaving like a herd of antelope that's smelt the big cats in the long grass.

Dama had nothing more to say to me. He hadn't seen Kershaw since he started working for B.B. I drove back down the hill into central Lomé. It was very quiet now on the streets. The helicopter still circled above to remind people that somebody was watching.

An impromptu police post had been set up in the road and I stopped and showed my passport. The junior officer called to his senior and asked me to park up by the pavement. The senior officer asked me to get out of the car. He checked my mug against the shot in the passport and called over two other policemen who were armed with rifles. They marched me around the corner and told me to get into the police car. When I tried to sit down in the back, they shouted at me to lie on the floor. The senior officer's eyes told me that this wasn't a time to get huffy, so I lay down in the footwell. The two policemen got in and rested their feet and rifle butts on my back. My arms were pulled behind me and tied with plastic cuffs. The senior officer said something in his own language and a blindfold was tied over my face. The car moved off.

It was difficult not to be scared by the scare tactics, but I've found on the few occasions this has happened to me that deep breathing helped and not getting angry. Getting angry often earned a rifle butt in the face and you still ended up blindfolded and in the footwell, except your throat was full of blood and your looks altered for good.

After fifteen minutes, the car stopped and I was pulled out into the smell of motor oil on concrete and helped along into a building, and then a room in which there was an overhead fan but without the usual smell of the municipality. They sat me down and left the room. My nose told me I was in the company of leather and books.

'There's nothing to be afraid of,' said a deep voice, in French.

'There isn't?' I asked, the sweat pouring down my face under the blindfold.

'Very English of you, M. Medway. Don't worry, this won't take long.'

'I'm feeling more cheerful already. You are M. Yao's *patron*?'

I heard his fingers slap on the edge of his desk.

'I am. He tells me you are looking for Steven Kershaw. So am I. Why do you want to find him?'

'I have a client.'

'Who is?'

'A businessman in Accra. Kershaw is supposed to be buying and shipping sheanut for him out of Cotonou . . .'

'Is he?'

'. . . and he hasn't called him for a week.'

'I see.'

'And you?'

He didn't answer. I heard him get up from a chair whose leather farted against his bottom. A desk whinged as it was knocked into by a large thigh. Then the big man spoke, but this time all the charm was stripped out of his voice which now clicked and snapped like bolt cutters through chain link.

'You will find Steven Kershaw, M. Medway, and when you find him, the first person you will tell will be me. You will not contact your client until I give you permission.'

'Any particular reason?'

'Have you ever spent time in an African jail?'

That kind of response meant that I didn't have to tinker too long balancing out the pros and cons. The curious dog in me which liked to sniff around other people's affairs suddenly came across one of its own kind, dead under the sofa, and cringed away, asking to be let out into the garden.

'Is there an easier way of making contact?'

'You ring this number and leave a message on the answering machine.' He tucked a piece of paper into my top pocket and walked to the door and knocked. The police bundled me back into the car and we drove into the centre of Lomé, where they released me a short walk from my car.

I went back to Jack's house and lay down to sleep in a darkened air-conditioned room, but sleep never came. My head was full of Kershaw's paintings, black leather strips, Nina Sorvino's hair, broken heads, the lagoon at night, floating bodies with a single black hole in the base of the skull, blood red fingernails and the voice of a man who could make life very painful for me.

# Chapter 12

By four o'clock in the afternoon, I felt no worse than an old horse that's come into a yard to find a man waiting for him with a black hood and a hammer. I decided to go to Cotonou and see if Kershaw's apartment threw any light on him.

I heard Jack playing snooker with the TV on in some far off corner of the house. He was alone in the games room, unless you call *Neighbours* company.

'You're winning as usual,' I said.

'Fancy a frame?' he asked.

'I'm going back to Cotonou.'

'Any news?'

'Nothing here,' I said, deciding to keep him out of it. 'You heard any dirt on Charlie?'

'He got burned playing with gold,' said Jack, his cue stroking the underside of his chin as he aimed. 'But is it true?'

'You know Dama?' Jack nodded. '*He* thinks it's true. Who did you hear it from?'

'Jawa. He said he went down for seven hundred thousand dollars, but Jawa loves to exaggerate.'

Jack hit the ball which cannoned off all the cushions, hitting nothing, which was an achievement with only two reds off the table.

'You been practising that one long?'

117

'Goodbye, Bruce, safe journey . . . and' – I stopped at the door – 'let me know how things go. You need anything – call me.'

In the centre of town, the afternoon heat was close and fierce. The World Service news had reported an 'uneasy calm'. There was nothing calm about these streets and there was a great deal that was uneasy. They were empty. Doors opened a crack as I rolled by. Split fruit, dizzy with flies, lay spattered in the middle of the road. A pair of empty blue flip flops sat neatly on the pavement. A wrap used for carrying a baby hung off a parked car's bumper. A soldier stood on a street corner, more stood on others.

On Rue du Commerce there were broken paving stones across the street. A hi-fi shop had been looted. The people weren't hungry, they just wanted to listen to music. The street was normally full of people buying and selling, full of hustlers offering you currency, and full of mammas cooking food. Balls of paper and torn plastic rolled in the dust, the stalls were empty – there was nobody. A torn poster attached itself to the windscreen advertising flights to Rio, 14 days for 150,000 CFA. I pulled it off and threw it in the back seat.

Rue du Commerce joined the coast road. The beach was empty. There was no sign of life at the Hotel Sarakawa. Maybe it looked a bit drawn with all those rich people inside, worrying. There were ships outside the port stuck in the silver water of the late afternoon. The port was dead. I took a diversion past the flour mill. It was closed. A huge number of small birds covered the trees in the compound. The noise they made tore at the afternoon air like cat's claws down glass.

There were a few more road blocks than usual on the way to the Togo/Benin border. The soldiers were tired and they weren't looking to give me trouble. At the border, I gave an immigration officer 2000 CFA to have a look at his ledger, but didn't find Kershaw's name in it. It cost me another 2000 CFA to look in the card holder's ledger for frequent travellers. I found Kershaw's name quicker than I expected because it was an entry detail for the day of 23rd September: an entry into Togo. His exit had been on 22nd September. He had left for Benin on Sunday and come back to Togo on Monday. I looked through up to the last detail. Kershaw hadn't left again through this border.

I thought about going back and checking the Ghana border, but it was probably closed following the afternoon's rioting. I thought about going to the airport and finding out if he had skipped the country, but B.B. said he didn't have enough money and no credit card. I thought about a lot of things and got myself out of them every time. I wanted to check out Kershaw's flat in Cotonou and I wanted to see Heike tonight.

It was no cooler in Benin. There were people though. They moved slowly, some not at all. There were food stalls but nobody had any appetite. I waited in the border compound for the Customs inspection. A goat was doing little by way of self-promotion. It bleated constantly at such a pitch that it made despair sound like a relatively comforting state to be in. The Customs man gave me a release paper without looking.

Outside the compound, through a break in the stalls, a goat was strung upside down between two posts and two men were flaying it while its mate looked on, tethered to death. That was the bleating. The two men worked with the attentiveness of caring barbers. One of the men finished flaying, took two strides to the goat and straddled it. With a quick jerk of the right shoulder came silence. It was like a burglar alarm being killed in a London street after a long weekend.

Twenty miles further on, a policeman asked to see my fire extinguisher. Three other policemen sat in a palm leaf thatched shed chewing cola nuts under hooded eyes. One spat some white pulp out into the dust and another chased some gunk around his mouth with his tongue. I've never owned a fire extinguisher – one in a long line of negative achievements. I gave the policeman 500 CFA and the others rubbed their thumbs and forefingers together. It took another 1000 CFA to lift the barrier.

The front tyre burst on the other side of Ouidah. In two minutes, I was joined by a group of children who taunted me with makeshift frames which had dead spatchcocked bush rats in them. They looked like road kills. When I didn't buy them they thought I was being fussy about the meat so they pushed forward a boy who held a fistful of dead partridges with bloodied beaks and slack necks.

In Cotonou, the sky ahead weighed a ton and could barely get itself over the rooftops. The bright, low sun behind me produced a sickly orange light against the massive black clouds shouldering their way over the town. The ugly block where Kershaw had his apartment appeared on my right, one large blank wall shone in the unhealthy light while the front, in the shade, looked dirtier than a pit head.

I parked in an empty car park outside the block. There was nobody around. A piece of cardboard on the pavement looked as if someone had been lying there next to whatever they'd been selling. The apartments looked unlived in, although there was some ragged clothing hanging out to dry on the top floor. Maybe Kershaw had just thrown in the towel when he saw this place.

The block looked like one in a housing estate in Belfast, except there weren't drifts of used syringes in the stairwell of the ground floor. It was an all-concrete affair and it bore the stains of the rainy season in long dribble marks below the windows. The paintwork that existed was a faded hospital green. I wouldn't have spent any time here, especially if I could paint.

I walked up to the third floor. The stairs were dark and mean and in another city would have been crowded with boys with no-sleeve T-shirts whetting their flick knives on the concrete. Some ambient noise would have helped. A radio, a child crying, a row developing, even a scream – even the sound of someone sharpening an axe followed by a scream would have been better than hard silence. The sixth sense, which people in horror films never have, was not encouraging.

On the third floor was Flat 3B. I listened at the door of 3A; there was the sound of dust building up on tiled floors. The door to 3B was not quite shut and it opened with a push on well-oiled hinges. The pre-storm pressure was building, which didn't help the atmosphere. The heat was thick and still. I wasn't embarrassed to find myself sweating. Only I knew it was cold.

The flat was dark. There was a short hallway into a living/dining room. The blinds were drawn and so were some unlined mustard-coloured curtains. To my right was the dining room table with no chairs. Off the dining area was the kitchen. To my left was a sofa and two armchairs. They were cheap, just wooden frames and foam rubber covered with the same mustard material as the curtains. In front of me were three doors.

The room on the right contained two broken chairs. The next room was a bathroom with quite a few tiles missing from the walls which were stacked in the corner. One recently fallen had shattered in the shower tray. The third room had a little more light in it and a bed and two chairs, but did not contain Kershaw hanging from the ceiling rose.

The mattress on the bed had a green flowery pattern. In the middle, there was a big stain of the sort found on old mattresses in student digs. Kneeling at the corner closest to me, I saw a stain that was the rust colour of dried blood. Then there was a noise behind me which I'd heard before, but never live. It sent something dancing up my spine and rushing over my scalp. It was the sound of an old-fashioned revolver being cocked.

An African voice, in perfect English, asked, 'Mr Kershaw?'

'No,' I said. 'Bruce Medway.'

'Can you put your hands slowly on to your head, please?' It was a very polite and relaxing voice, considering it had a gun.

122

The barrel of the gun was cold on the back of my neck. A black hand came over my shoulder and felt my chest. It lifted my fat, super-large British passport out of my shirt pocket.

'Please stand up and turn around, Mr Medway,' the voice said.

I turned and stood to face an African man who came up to my shoulder. He was dressed in a dark blue rain-coat, a white shirt and a pair of dark blue trousers. He had no gun, but his hand was held in the shape of one. He opened one side of his mouth and gave a perfect imitation of a revolver being uncocked. He pulled a thimble off the end of his finger and put it in his pocket.

'My name is Bagado,' he said. 'I am a police detective.' He produced an ID card from his pocket which he held in front of my face.

'You thought I was Kershaw?'

'No. I just don't like the expression "Freeze mother-fucker".'

'You're looking for him.'

'It would be interesting if he turned up.'

'It's getting to the point, Mr Bagado, where it might be easier to count the people who aren't looking for Steven Kershaw.'

'Is it?' he said. 'May I ask why *you* are looking for him?'

'Because he hasn't called his boss for a week, and I'm being paid to find him.'

'A comparatively bland reason, Mr Medway.'

'Bland?'

'A woman was found dead in this room on that bed.'

'Dead as in murdered?'

'Possibly.'

'How?'

'Strangled.'

'Self-strangulation is difficult.'

'You'd be surprised.'

I remembered the newspaper article I had read in the port. 'Françoise Perec?'

Bagado raised an eyebrow and frowned with the other.

'The tourist?'

Bagado raised the frowning eyebrow to join the other.

'A sex session that went too far?'

'That was the way the newspaper chose to report it. Our journalists learn their skills from Europe. She was found on the bed naked and strangled. Her wrists and ankles were very badly torn and indicated that she had been bound with leather which she had strained against. She had been beaten severely with a whip on the back of her legs, her buttocks, her back and shoulders. So severely that blood had been drawn. There was evidence of vaginal and anal penetration and of electricity having been applied to those areas and her nipples. She had been strangled with a rope made from hemp, and from the marks it has been deduced that she came close to death by strangulation several times. All evidence of this ... "session" ... has been removed.'

Bagado delivered the report on Françoise Perec with little emotion, his voice was as tired as his eyes. He stared unblinking at the bed. He was a good-looking man, difficult to know how old, his skin, like most

Africans', gave no clues. He had a light dusting of grey on his hair as if he'd dabbed it on a ceiling still wet with paint. His forehead was strong; it wasn't rounded but had defined surfaces and between the frontal lobes there was a vertical ridge which ran from his hairline and petered out just before two creases above the bridge of a strong, sharp nose. His face was lean and you could see the muscles working; this gave an impression of forcefulness which his tired brown eyes didn't. He had a severe mouth, it was wide and thin-lipped, it didn't look as if it did a lot of talking but when it did it got listened to. He had a cleft in his chin with a small scar in it and his jawline was clear and sharp right up to below his ear. His muscular neck indicated that his body would have the same whipcord tautness of his face. He looked like the sort of man who knew and saw things that a lot of other men didn't.

'I have worked in Paris and London, Mr Medway. I have been in hotel rooms which looked like abattoirs. I have seen worse than the suffering of Françoise Perec.'

'Isn't it easier to carry a gun rather than sound like one?' I asked.

'It is. However, I cannot afford one.'

'You must practise a lot.'

'I learnt it from a fellow in London who held me hostage for forty-eight hours. Every fifteen minutes he would cock his revolver, hold it to my head and say: "BOOM! The nigger dies", then he would uncock it. It is a noise that has stayed with me.'

'Your English is very . . . superior.'

'I have a Nigerian mother, and my father was Beninois. I speak both English and French.'

'Do you know anything about Françoise Perec, Mr Bagado?'

'I think it is your turn to tell me something, Mr Medway.'

'I know where your evidence is,' I said, showing him the photograph of Kershaw.

'That would be very useful,' he said, turning the photograph over. 'Are you, may I ask, a private dick, Mr Medway?' The word 'dick' sound like a dart hitting a board.

'I'm an odd job man. I do things for people. Sometimes I'm asked to find missing persons. I am being paid to find Kershaw and to run the business he was supposed to be running.'

'Which was?'

'Sheanut.'

Bagado gave back the photograph of Kershaw and chewed the fleshy part of his thumb.

'Where is this evidence?' he asked.

'Lomé.' I told Bagado what was in the bag in the house in Lomé. He nodded and frowned.

'Why are you here, when he is obviously there?' he asked.

There was a thump of wind around the block of flats. The door of the apartment slammed shut. We both started and walked into the dining room and Bagado pulled up the blinds. It was dark. A cardboard sheet was sliding down the street, propelled by the wind and chased by a young girl with sputnik hair. A line of coconut palms bent at an absurd angle and shook their heads like rock stars who can't sing. The dust swirled in mini tornadoes which crossed the street and thrashed through the high bushes of the houses opposite. There was the sound of a tennis ball hitting the window. It was the first drop and was followed by a moment of tension before the rain crashed down. The road turned to a river. The rain, buffeted by the wind, lashed the cars, trees and houses. It was suddenly cold.

There was a clap of thunder which sounded as if it had cleaved the apartment block in two and a flash of lightning rendered Bagado a negative of himself.

'That seemed quite close,' said Bagado.

'I wasn't counting.'

We gave up talking because the rain didn't like being interrupted. It came down in a solid sheet of water with the noise of a snare drum crescendo. We lost sight of the houses across the street and the car below. It continued like this for ten minutes, with Bagado resting his forehead against the glass and me with my arms folded, leaning against the window frame.

The rain eased. My car became visible. The thunder boomed in another quarter. The rain moved off after it but the darkness remained. Night had fallen during the storm. It was half past six.

'A lot of people think storms portentous,' Bagado said, still looking out of the window. 'In Africa it just means it's the rainy season. It's a lot more sinister when it doesn't rain.'

'I'm relieved.'

'Which is as it should be.'

'Do you drink whisky, Mr Bagado?'

'When someone has the decency to buy me one. Whisky, like guns, is beyond my means.'

\* \* \*

Bagado locked the flat. There was six inches of water at the bottom of the stairs and a rat doing side stroke in it. We drove through Cotonou with wet feet and tide marks up our trouser legs.

Bagado told me how he had waited in the apartment since the body was found on the afternoon of 23rd September. Kershaw's maid had found the body. She came in every afternoon to clean and cook an evening meal for him. The first time she'd seen Françoise Perec was face down on the bed, naked, beaten and dead. The woman had been in shock since and they hadn't been able to get any sense out of her.

Bagado had spoken to the owner of the apartment who had only ever met Kershaw once. The landlord had never heard a company name and Kershaw hadn't been talkative. He didn't even know the business Kershaw was in. Nobody in the expatriate community knew Kershaw, he seemed to have no connections in Cotonou at all. Bagado had spent three days and nights in the apartment waiting for his break.

'Why wait in his flat. Didn't you check the borders?' I asked.

'The efficiency of my staff, the fastidiousness of immigration and the total lack of pay received by all for the last two months conspired against us. We are still awaiting a reply. I chose to pass my time in the flat because it seemed likely that someone would have to drop by . . . eventually.'

'It doesn't sound like much of a police force you're working for, Mr Bagado.'

'It doesn't, does it?'

Bagado had no car, no gun, no umbrella and no pay.

He had a raincoat, a badge, two sets of clothes, a wife, three children and a house within walking distance of my own.

'More children than trousers,' he said. 'They are my wealth. I had a lot more pay in Paris but I still felt a poor man until my children were born.'

We arrived at the house, there was no light. There was a lot of water in the compound and Moses was standing in it. He had sandbagged the door to his apartment and was bailing out. I asked him about Heike and he shrugged. We stood under the dripping palm and I introduced Bagado in the yellow light of a hurricane lamp. Upstairs, we sat at the dining room table with a candle, a bottle of whisky, two glasses and a bowl of melting ice. Bagado leaned forward and droplets of water slid off his hair like globules of mercury.

'Are you going to tell me something interesting about Françoise Perec, Mr Bagado?'

Bagado put up his hand and picked up his glass of whisky which he held to the candlelight. I picked up my glass.

'To life,' he said. 'The dead can take care of themselves.'

Helen came in from her sister's with an aluminium pot of food. She crossed the living room and went into the kitchen without a word. I poured some more whisky. Bagado sipped his and blinked with pin-ball eyes.

'This,' he said, 'is outstanding booze.'

I was about to say something, but he rode through me without a pause and, instantly drunk, told me in a stream of near unconsciousness about other moments in his life in which outstanding booze had figured.

'Wait,' I said, after ten minutes of unpunctuated surrealism, and called Helen who came out with a bag of groundnut. Bagado tore them out of her hand and went into a frenzy of cracking shells and throwing nuts in his mouth so that in a matter of minutes there were red flakes in his hair, a slag heap of groundnut shells in front of him and an empty bag which he flattened with his hand.

Helen brought a mountain of rice to the table and swept the shells on to her tray. She came back with the aluminium pot of groundnut soup – chicken in a chilli hot peanut sauce. I gave Bagado a meat platter and three kilos of rice and half a chicken which I covered in the sauce. He polished it off before I'd finished serving myself. He served himself the same again. That was the only time I've seen a man put on a stone in front of me. Afterwards, I had to help him to the cushions on the floor where he slept like a python for an hour.

'You must forgive me,' he said when he woke up.

'You haven't eaten for three days?' I asked.

'And three nights. I was on my last reserves.'

'I saw you chewing your thumb earlier.'

'It kept me going.'

'Didn't anybody bring you food?'

'They didn't know I was there.'

'What about your family?'

'They are used to me disappearing for a few days at a time.'

'Couldn't you buy some food?'

'I have no money. No pay, remember?'

'Didn't Kershaw leave anything?'

'My colleagues cleaned out the cupboards. They left some coffee filters of little nutritional value.'

'That was it?'

'There was a lizard, too. It appeared on the morning of the second day, high up on the living room wall. I stalked it for ten minutes but I only managed to catch it by the tail, which came off in my hand.'

'Did you eat it?'

'That afternoon, I caught the rest of it. It was a long campaign which I won't bore you with.'

'How big?'

'Four inches.'

'More of an *amuse-gueule*.'

'Not even that. I've eaten monitor lizard, it's very good, like chicken, but it is three-foot long. The other problem was that my colleagues had taken the matches. I had nothing to light the gas with. I couldn't cook it.'

'You didn't eat a raw lizard?'

'I decided to keep it for breakfast the next day, and spent some time thinking that the Indians use preserved lizard as a love potion, but when I woke up I couldn't face raw lizard. I put it off until lunch. By lunch it smelt very bad, very bad indeed. No fridge, you see. The landlord cut the power. It stank like a toad's breath. I threw it away. Still, it served its purpose. It filled my day.'

'You've got to, haven't you?'

'Police work is a terrible work.'

'The way you do it, yes.'

'The stake-out is the worst work of all.'

'You got your break.'

'You have been the ultimate break, Mr Medway. You brought information, drink and food. No man could wish for a better break.' He rolled on to his knees. 'I have to be going now.'

'But, Mr Bagado, you haven't told me anything about Françoise Perec.'

'Tomorrow. Tonight was for the living. Tomorrow we'll sort out the dead.'

I stood at the top of the steps and watched Bagado leave. He walked like a heavier man. At the gate, he turned.

'Six o'clock, Mr Medway. We need an early start.'

I took a cold shower and changed into a cotton night-shirt that Heike had bought for me from Berlin. I arranged some cushions on the floor, put a new candle in the holder, poured a very weak whisky and waited for Heike to come home.

The candle was low and guttering when I woke up. In front of me was Heike, lying on the cane sofa. She was up on one elbow looking at me. She swivelled her legs into a sitting position and unhooked the white broderie anglaise top and let it slip off her shoulders. She unhooked her skirt and slid the zip down. She stood and the skirt fell to the floor. She stripped off her white panties, the palms of her hands brushing down the length of her thighs. She lay back down on the sofa.

I knelt, pulled the nightshirt over my head and flung it somewhere. I crawled towards her and kissed her feet, the insides of her ankles and ran my tongue the length of her calf. I kissed the insides of her thighs, ran my lips over her hot triangle of pubic hair and kissed my way up over her flat stomach to her hard nipples. I kissed her breast bone and throat and up and over her chin, trailing my hand between her thighs. Before our lips met she said: 'I've been waiting for hours.'

We rolled off the sofa on to the floor and made love, which left us pouring with sweat in the humid night. Afterwards, Heike found her cigarettes and holder and lay on my arm smoking.

'I'm going back to Germany,' she said, after three drags of silence.

'When?'

'A few weeks, when I've finished at the project.'

'When you've finished what?'

'My contract.'

'You're not renewing?'

'No. I'm going back to Berlin.'

'For good?'

'I think so.'

We lay on our backs, two people in an African night after rain, going nowhere.

# Chapter 13

*Friday 27th September*

At 5.30 I woke up with a clanging discord of comfort and anguish. Heike's breathing and warmth under the sheet we had thrown over ourselves told me that she was there in the morning darkness. I made coffee and split open a pawpaw which wasn't as ripe as I would have liked. I dressed and stood over Heike, sipping coffee, and combed through a tangled, knot-ridden ball of thoughts which got me as far as it gets anybody in that situation.

Her eyes opened and she rolled on to her back to look at me. I knelt over her and kissed her, the coffee still bitter on my tongue.

'Where are you going?'

'I have to go back to Lomé again.'

'Are you here tonight?'

'Yes, unless things get complicated.'

There was nothing to say after that. I had the same feeling as when I once looked over the shoulder of a telephone engineer into a street exchange box to see half a million tiny blue, yellow, green, black and white wires all with somewhere to go. She just ran her hands through my hair again and again until I felt like a dog being absent-mindedly stroked. It wasn't unpleasant.

I've always thought that dogs have a very good life. Heike was trying to formulate something with the same measure of success as I, so she continued to run her hand through my hair harder and harder until I saw the luminous dial of my watch saying 6.00, and I kissed her and left.

Bagado was waiting under the palm tree, talking to Moses in a low confessional voice. The morning was cool and earthy with a layer of woodsmoke running through it. We got in the car, Bagado and I in the back, and drove in silence until the sun got up, just as we were crossing a causeway where some fishermen from a village on stilts were paddling out into a lagoon.

'Françoise Perec was thirty-four years old,' said Bagado. 'French nationality. She had a degree in English from the Sorbonne. She did a course in textile design at St Martin's College of Art in London. She spent four years working for a design company called CHIRAC in Lyons. For the last three years she has been running her own design company in Paris. She was here for a month's working holiday.'

'That's not very interesting.'

'It sounds like a good life to me,' said Bagado.

'Doesn't sound like the type to get herself killed in those kind of circumstances.'

'People get murdered all the time. Everyday people are murdered every day. Attractive, successful, talented, middle-class French women are not immune.'

'I hope your theories are more interesting than your facts.'

Bagado sat in the corner of the back seat and pressed

his hands between his knees. He was looking a lot better than he had yesterday. He had filled out, losing that taut, drawn look that hunger had given him.

'First,' he started, 'Kershaw killed Miss Perec in a sadomasochistic sex session that "went too far". He is naturally terrified at having to explain the death and this kind of behaviour to the Benin police who, he quite rightly suspects, will find this sexual deviancy bizarre in the extreme. He flees the country.'

'Africans aren't into bondage?'

'We don't have to be. We've been in bondage for centuries.'

I could tell from the back of Moses's head that he was listening and not understanding, but that he was sure it was interesting.

'So Kershaw planted the evidence on himself,' I said. 'I like it, Bagado. And anyway, what Françoise Perec went through was a little more serious than a sex session.'

'You and I may think that, but I have seen a great deal worse. Cutting, burning, clubbing, and crushing are also things that these deviants enjoy.'

'But electric shocks . . . strangling.'

'Strangulation, I believe, intensifies the sexual sensation. For instance, I myself have had to cut down half a dozen people, some hetero, some homo and one hermaphro, who had accidentally hung themselves. They arrange a rope and chair, stand on the chair, put the rope around their necks and then step off, doing whatever it is that they do. Then they try to get back on the chair, but if they've left it too late they start to panic and kick the chair over, or in some cases, they are already blacking out before they even think of saving themselves. I've seen people strangled in bed with a nylon cord fed through a pulley system attached to their feet. I've found a man in his wife's clothing throttled by gardening twine passed through the handle of the kitchen drawer. I found a man hanging from a toilet chain with a peacock's feather up his arse, his feet only two inches from the ground. They were all very sad, Mr Medway, very sad and lonely deaths.'

'Unsafe safe sex. I don't buy it.'

'But it is possible.'

'Does she have any history of masochism? Was there any evidence on her body of previous "sessions"?'

'As far as I know, the First World hasn't got round to keeping readily available data on individuals' sexual proclivities or diseases. I suppose it may come.' Bagado rubbed his nose with his thumb and forefinger. 'She wasn't HIV positive. She didn't have any scars consistent with this kind of punishment. Her father is an industrialist manufacturing sportswear who has barely seen his daughter in the last ten years; her mother died when she was young (not that parents know anything about their children's sex lives); she was an only child. There aren't many people to ask and there's probably no one who would tell anyway.'

'Boyfriend?'

Bagado shrugged. 'If she did, nobody knew about him.'

'People in her business?'

'It's not the sort of thing people know about.'

'Was she a lonely person?'

'She kept herself to herself. She wasn't high profile

on the Paris fashion scene. People say she was reclusive – worked hard and slept. She was on a working holiday.' Bagado threw up his hand. 'Who comes here for a holiday?'

'No close friends?'

'She was born in Nice and spent her childhood there. Then her family moved to Lyons when Miss Perec was twelve. Five years later she went to the Sorbonne, then London, then back to Lyons and finally Paris. She was never in one place long enough to have the kind of friend who would know.'

'Where did you get this information?'

'The French Embassy.'

'What about the evidence?'

'Kershaw has removed the evidence. Not a stupid thing to have done. He goes back to his house in Lomé trying to think what he is going to do. He then makes a snap decision to run. He gets into a pair of jeans and a T-shirt, buys a cheap bag, gets on a bus and he could be in the southern Sahara by now.'

'Why not destroy the evidence, or take it with him?'

'That kind of stuff is difficult to burn and hard to throw away without being noticed. I wouldn't like to travel in Africa with those kind of things on me. People are always getting searched, especially now in Togo with the trouble.'

Bagado ran his hand down his face to clear the board.

'Second. Miss Perec inadvertently came across something in Lomé, probably criminal, maybe politically harmful, maybe personally harmful. She is friendly with Kershaw, she sticks with him and goes to Cotonou to get away from an ugly situation. Kershaw goes to work on the Monday morning. The person who Miss Perec has been fleeing from catches up with her. He tortures her to find out what she knows and kills her, leaving the body but taking the evidence to plant on Kershaw. Kershaw returns and for the same reasons as in the previous scenario disappears. Or he was killed as well and transported to that lagoon we have just passed and dumped and then the evidence planted.'

Bagado held on to the back of the front seat with both hands and bent his forehead to rest on the head support.

'Third. Kershaw is involved in a group indulging in criminal activity which Miss Perec finds out about, or is even involved in herself. Kershaw discovers that she knows without her knowing that he knows, but persuades her to come with him to Cotonou where he kills her in this bizarre fashion, taking the evidence with him to plant on someone else who is also involved, or not involved at all, only to find that he has been second-guessed and is killed himself by the third party who plants the evidence on the deceased Kershaw.

'Fourth –'

'Bagado! You're out of the real world now.'

'I don't think so. You see, we know so little and human beings are so devious . . . It could be any of the above or a combination of all three. We have to examine every possibility, however strange. We are also in Africa, where anything can happen and regularly does.

'Fourth. You'll like the fourth. Kershaw has come across something in Cotonou. He is killed. The killers go to search his flat and find Miss Perec designing textiles. A perverted member of the gang comes up with this brilliant solution to the situation. They kill Miss Perec in such a way as to make it look like a "session" gone too far. They dump Kershaw's body and plant the evidence in Lomé. Thus focusing our investigation on Kershaw and Miss Perec. It is for this reason we must keep an open mind.'

'Nobody would sit in Kershaw's flat in Cotonou designing textiles.'

'We know' – Bagado lifted his head off the back of the front seat and held up his hand – 'nothing. We know about these people, what we know about almost everybody, even those closest to us . . . nothing. That's why most murderers are "known" to their victims. That's why most burglaries are committed by "neighbours". That's why children get abused and women get raped. We trust people who are close to us, we trust people who conform to stereotypes, we think we know them, we have no objectivity about them. The fatherly man with his arm in plaster trying to do his trousers up is your killer.'

'There's no middle way with you, Bagado.'

'Like many before me, I choose absurdity to make a point.'

'There are exceptions. We're not all naive.'

'Who do you think they are, these exceptions?' Bagado asked.

'Those with a reliable instinct.'

'And how do they get that?'

'Disappointment.'

'Let us hope that the first person to disappoint you is without an axe.'

'Or that you're not a child.'

'I think we are being unnecessarily gloomy.'

'I think you are sick people,' said Moses.

At the border we went through the formalities. I hadn't seen Françoise Perec's name with Kershaw's when I came through the last time, but that was because she was in the regular ledger which Bagado checked. Kershaw entered Benin with Françoise Perec one day and left on his own the next. I pointed out that this put paid to the theory that Kershaw was killed in Benin, and Bagado asked me how much did I think it would cost to have a name entered into a ledger.

'Remember, these people have not been paid,' said Bagado, getting into the car. 'They would tell you anything for a few thousand CFA. If we relied on their brand of veracity we wouldn't find Kershaw for a year.'

We arrived at Kershaw's house after nine o'clock. The young boy was there lying face down on his bench. Bagado was intrigued. The boy snapped to attention as we got out of the car. Bagado took the bench out from under the boy's arm and sat on it. The boy looked from one end of his bench to the other and then up at Bagado. Bagado took him round the shoulders and spoke to him in Ewe, an African language spoken in Togo and Benin; then in Hausa, a language spoken in the northern regions of West Africa; and finally in Yoruba, a southern Nigerian language also spoken in Benin. The boy listened very carefully. When Bagado had finished, the boy drew himself out from under Bagado's arm and danced a small and inept dance. Bagado frowned at the boy who stopped and held his hands open as if he had accomplished what he'd been asked to do. Bagado got up and walked past me saying, 'The boy is an idiot.'

In the house, Bagado walked up the stairs slower and slower as he took in Kershaw's murals. He walked to the far end and paced its length looking at the work.

'Kershaw?' he asked, and I nodded. 'Very good,' he said, going into a bedroom. 'It's the boy, isn't it?' he said from inside.

Bagado came out and walked into the master bedroom. He looked up at the ceiling and opened the bag. He emptied the contents on the bed and his head dropped down on to his chest.

He opened the wardrobe, flicked through the clothes and rumbled about amongst the shoes in the bottom. He came out with a camera which he threw on the bed. He went through the chest of drawers. In the bottom drawer, which I hadn't bothered to search, he found something that made him snort – a stack of SM mags. Bagado knelt and looked at the front cover of a blonde woman looking over her shoulder, her hands and feet bound to the four corners of a metal frame. There were weals across the back of her legs and her back. A thick, evil-looking black whip lay across her buttocks. She wore a black leather choker which was fastened by leather laces at the back. Bagado shut the drawer without touching the magazines. Still on his knees, he turned and crawled over to the bed, looking underneath it. He stood, picked up the camera and checked to see if there was any film.

'There's twenty-two in here,' he said. 'Can we get them developed?'

I called Moses and Bagado left the room. Moses left with the film and I went into one of the other bedrooms and looked at Kershaw's work.

On one wall there was a naked, tall, muscular African woman of the Amazon warrior type. She had short hair in the shape of her skull, a long neck, and long arms held in a way that suggested flowing and falling like water. She held one leg up bent at the knee, the toe pointed downwards like a dancer's. Her skin was as shiny black as an olive, as if she had just come out of water. The background was the dark green of the rainforest and red parrots exploded upwards to an unseen sky.

Across the room on the opposite wall was a naked Indian girl lying on her side, supported by one elbow on a white sheet, again with a rainforest background. Her other arm lay along her slim girlish body, the hand resting flat below the hip. There was a bowl in front of her piled high with mangos and pawpaws. She looked across the room with the curious effect of looking straight through me. I backed away until I was up against the water dancer; the Indian girl's eyes now focused and I remembered Charlie talking about Kershaw and his women – 'black girls, white girls, Orientals, Indians'.

Bagado called from a back room which contained all Kershaw's painting gear. He was standing by the window looking down into the garden.

'Can you see what I see?' he said, moving me into his position.

There was the wall, the seat with the small patio and the green swimming pool. I turned, Bagado had gone.

He had left by the french windows and was striding across the garden to the aviary. There was a large tree there with a long pole leaning up against it. Bagado took this pole which had a net on the end of it and started to skim the algae off the surface of the water. In the middle, not far from the edge of the pool, he hit something.

He brushed the algae away from the object and as it dispersed we could see, in the green water, a body standing as if to attention. A sulphurous smell bubbled up as Bagado disturbed the body. It was the stuff of projectile vomiting. We coughed and ran for the aviary.

The smell was no better, but we acclimatized and returned to the poolside. By kneeling down and stretching out, Bagado managed to grab hold of the hair which came away in his hand with a patch of scalp. We pulled on the shirt collar and there was a scraping sound of stone on stone.

'The fourth urn's weighing it down,' said Bagado.

We got the body to the side and reached down into the water and took an armpit each. We stood up and pulled. It was as heavy and stiff as a statue. I could feel a couple of hernias about to pop, so we put it down and called Moses, who had just come back from town. The three of us pulled and this time, as the body's thighs came out of the water, I threw my arms around them and heaved up with my shoulders. Bagado shuddered backwards and to the side with Moses crashing against him. The body slewed. There was an ugly cracking noise and the body landed on its side, partly on the grass and partly on the edge of the pool but wholly across Moses's leg; he was kicking at the body with his free foot and bellowing.

'Was that your leg, Moses?' I asked.

'Is my leg, Mister Bruce, is my leg!' yelled Moses.

I lifted out the urn and raised the body's legs and Moses, hollering worse than a sacrificial victim, was pulled out by Bagado. Moses got up on one leg and put his weight on to the other. It held, and in a matter of seconds he was walking around like a child trying on a new pair of shoes.

'My leg. Is not my leg,' he said.

'Of course it's your leg!' roared Bagado.

'No. Is his leg.'

I undid the ropes at the ankles and rolled up the trouser leg.

'You won't hurt him,' said Bagado, standing over me, still laughing at Moses.

Just above the sock was a sharp piece of bone which had torn through the skin.

The parrot gave Moses an appreciative whistle.

The body was covered in green slime, which reminded me never to eat Madame Severnou's bush rat dish again. I wiped away the strands of green weed from the head. What was left of the face was white, one eye was missing, the lips were swollen and partially eaten away, as were a cheek and part of a nostril. The tongue protruded and was thick and purple and the tip was missing.

'Kershaw?' asked Bagado.

'He didn't look like that in his photograph, did he?'

'Use your imagination,' said Bagado, patting the

breast pockets of the shirt, which were empty, while I clenched my jaw and took a closer look at the body.

'He looks the right size, the hair colour's right and that eye's the colour it should be,' I said.

The body's hands were tucked into the waistband of the trousers. Bagado undid the belt and trouser buttons and freed the hands which had no rings, but there was a watch. It was an old Timex. There was a serial number on the back and the usual stuff about water and shock resistance, which hadn't proved to be correct as the watch face was cracked and the inside of the glass was pimpled with droplets of water. He slapped the body on the legs for being so useless at identifying itself and then searched the pockets.

'Ah!' he said, pulling out a wallet.

In it, he found some sodden currency, an unreadable restaurant receipt and nothing else.

'No credit card!' roared Bagado, trying to humiliate the body into identifying itself.

'He was declared bankrupt. He wouldn't have one.'

The body's hands were stiff with rigor mortis. I eased up the fingers.

'He's our man,' I said. 'Paint.'

'Help me roll him over on to his front,' said Bagado.

We rolled him and spun him round so his head was over the pool. Bagado searched the back pockets and came up with a credit card which he handed to me. It was Kershaw's expired AA membership.

'Tell me if anything comes out,' said Bagado, who started to pump against Kershaw's swollen back with the flat of both hands.

'Nothing,' I said.

'Plastic bag,' said Bagado. 'Then thrown in the pool. Let's call the police.'

'There's a call I have to make before that,' I said, and explained.

'You must,' he said, 'or you're a dead man.'

# Chapter 14

It was very hot in the middle of the lawn where Kershaw's body lay on a stretcher. A couple of policemen stood in the shade of a flame tree by the aviary with their hands over their mouths talking to each other. Kershaw's putrefying body filled the air with a sweet sulphurous stench that had instantly attracted a pair of vultures who stood on the wall looking at each other, and then looking down at the corpse. Moses stood with a handkerchief wrapped around his face and a long pole in his hands.

When they'd first arrived, the vultures had landed on the lawn and had bounced around Moses like shadow boxers looking for a line in on their lunch. Moses had been deft with the stick and enjoyed himself hugely. The parrot, from his ringside seat, had urged Moses on with clicks and whistles and the odd squawk when the stick thudded into the solid breast of one or other of the vultures.

I leaned against the french window inside the house trying to erase Kershaw's bloated, rotting, distorted features from my mind. The stench from the garden, the deprived vultures and the sheet-covered mound on the lawn ensured that the image was pin-sharp in my brain.

Bagado had crawled around the pool and patio with his face and fingers at grass level, grooming for clues.

He had produced a little forensic kit and fingerprinted the corpse and found that rigor mortis had come out of the body since we pulled it from the pool. In passing, he had said that rigor mortis lasted for up to four days, which meant that the earliest he could have been killed was Monday, the same day as Perec. He had checked the fingerprints against the whip handle and crocodile clip in the bag, the magazines in the chest and on the paint pots in the back room. They all matched. Then, to give himself a deadline, he had told me to make my call. I'd left a short message on the big man's answering machine, informing him about Kershaw's death and telling him to call this number. While Bagado had run around the house roaring in his own language like a touretter, triple-checking things that he'd already double-checked, a call came through telling me to inform the police. It had given me a number which I'd called.

The arrival of the police had been a relief. Bagado had produced a passport that he'd found in another pocket of the bag, and was talking in French and Ewe, waving the passport in the faces of the six policemen who had formed a semicircle in front of him. They encouraged his narrative with a range of clicks, braying noises and high-pitched squeaks which shot their credibility to pieces. Several of them glanced with sly eyes at the plastic bag with Kershaw's wallet, watch and AA card which hung from Bagado's hand.

On the few occasions that our paths had crossed during his final search, Bagado had told me he would do all the talking.

'I know these people,' he said with a flat hand that

blocked any dispute. He had also been vehement about not mentioning the absence of water in Kershaw's lungs. 'That could be a very serious error. We have no idea what game these people are playing. A slip like that and we could be face down in the lagoon breathing sewage.'

At about eleven o'clock a senior policeman arrived who seemed to be wearing the same uniform he'd been issued with as a cadet. He put his arm around Bagado, like a big gorilla grabbing hold of its young, and steered him off into the garden where they talked with only the parrot in hearing distance. The police officer looked as if he didn't like wearing shoes, because he hobbled around the garden treating Bagado more as a walking frame than a fellow officer. In a short time they were back with the police officer, coughing from the smell in the garden. He gave some brutal commands and the junior policemen stampeded out of the house. Bagado and the policeman went upstairs, Bagado's back straining at every step as the policeman hauled himself up. They made it and the policeman held the banister, his face twisted with pain. They went into the master bedroom.

In the garden, the junior policemen were being ordered to lift the stretcher and take it off down the side of the house to load into the ambulance. The vultures were looking at each other not believing this was happening to them. The police officer giving the orders was the same one running the road block after the riot on Thursday who'd taken me off to meet the big man. He saw me through the french windows and moved off with his men.

There was some loud guffawing from upstairs and Bagado came out of the bedroom with Kershaw's bag in one hand and the policeman leaning on his shoulder. They made it to the bottom of the stairs where they shook hands, the policeman roared again at something that must have been said before, because Bagado hadn't said a word. Bagado gave him the bag and Kershaw's effects and the officer gave him his card and asked him to confirm a time for the body to be identified. The policeman turned and his face dropped as if he had lead in his cheeks.

'What was all that about?' I asked.

'The laughter? These people when they get their own way, they laugh at a blade of grass.'

'What did you give him?'

'Our integrity.'

'Nothing serious, then.'

'I just said we would keep our mouths shut.'

'Does he want anything from us?'

'He wants a very bland statement from me, nothing from you and Moses.'

'You let him have your evidence.'

'Only the things I don't want. This will never make court.'

I told Bagado about the police officer from the road block and he told me what had happened with the Françoise Perec investigation in Cotonou. He had been stuck in a meeting and got to the apartment late. By the time he had arrived, the place had been hoovered and wiped down and the contents removed, apart from the furniture and the coffee filters. The body remained on the bed. The only constructive thing he had managed to do was to get the report into the *Benin Soir*, which he had done by pushing the 'sex session gone too far' theory, which the paper had liked. It meant that Françoise Perec's death was public knowledge, the French were furious and so was his superior officer.

'He took my phone away and suspended me without pay. My boss is a man very strong on irony.'

'The French will get to them in the end.'

'Yes, but too late. The investigation will reopen with nothing to go on. They will have no chance . . . but we will.'

'We?'

'You and I, Bruce.'

I explained that I hadn't finished the job that I had been hired for, that I was supposed to run the sheanut business that Kershaw had been running, that I would have to organize identification of the body which, by the state of the corpse, Mrs Kershaw was going to have to do, that I would have to help her get the body released and out of the country. Bagado listened with a fraction of his brain while the rest of it worked with a ferocity that was showing in his face. His eyes twitched as he slotted other pieces of information next to the facts and theories that tore through his head like ribbons down a wind tunnel.

'Who is your client?' he asked.

'A Syrian businessman in Accra called B.B.'

'B.B.? What is B.B.?'

'It's his name. In full it's unpronounceable.'

'How do you know him?'

'Through Jack Obuasi, another client – an English/

152

Ghanaian who lives here and who I do jobs for in Cotonou.'

'Why can't he do his own jobs?'

'Because he runs a lot of trade along this coast and he doesn't have the time to be in several places at once . . . and he's lazy.'

'Did B.B. contact you directly?'

'No. Wednesday morning, I turn up at Jack's with the money from a job. Jack takes a call and volunteers my services.'

'Money from what job?'

'Seven thousand tons of parboiled rice into Cotonou off a ship called the *Naoki Maru*.'

'When?'

'Tuesday.'

'What did you do?'

'I arranged the papers, received and counted the money. There was a problem.'

'What was the problem?'

The woman . . .'

'Which woman?'

'Madame Severnou.'

'Mr Obuasi does business with Madame Severnou?' said Bagado with a voice that pounced.

'Is that a problem?'

'I wouldn't like to do business with Madame Severnou.'

'Nor would I, but I have,' I said. 'What's so grubby about Madame Severnou?'

'It's not entirely clear where Madame Severnou's money comes from.'

'Meaning?'

'Not very nice people have money that they can't put in banks so they send it to Madame Severnou's laundry.'

'How dirty?'

'Not just kick-backs and bribes.'

'Drug money?'

Bagado nodded. It was well known that Lagos was one of the main trans-shipment points for heroin from Asia and cocaine from South America going into Europe. The corruption was sufficient and the money big enough for the drugs to get in and there were enough unfortunate women prepared to fill their guts full of condoms to courier the drugs to London. Sometimes the condoms broke and the women died, sometimes Heathrow Customs decided to keep the women until they just 'had to go' and sometimes they got through.

'Twenty per cent of the women in British jails are Nigerian drug mules,' said Bagado. 'They all work in the kitchens, and you know the pity of it? The pity of it is that the few pounds' jail pay they get every week they send home to their children. It's good money to them.'

'How many's twenty per cent?'

'About three hundred and fifty.'

Three hundred and fifty women in jail for carrying maybe two to three kilos per head – more than a ton of heroin, and that was the stuff that didn't get in. The mule business was diversionary, gave the drug enforcement agencies plenty of work to process while the big shipments came in containers. None of it was small beer, not even the mules, and it was a better explanation of Madame Severnou's gorillas than Jack's.

'What was the problem with Madame Severnou?' asked Bagado.

The money for the rice was fifty million short and it wasn't part of the plan – not the one in Jack's head, anyway. He tried to cover up by telling me it was part commission payment and part a cotton-fibre deal, but I could tell he was pulling out flannel by the mile.'

'Why?'

'I don't know, but I do know he wanted me away from that rice deal. I was all ready to lean on Madame Severnou but Jack said no, and threw me the Kershaw job. Ever since then it's been "Come back to me"; "Let me know how things are going"; "Call me".'

'You're getting the feel of it now,' said Bagado. 'I can see from your face that you're beginning to understand your duty.'

'*My* duty?'

Bagado walked off down the room, across the squash court floorboards with his hands behind his back, one hand opening and closing with each step. He still had his raincoat on. He turned, walked back and stood in front of me looking into my chest. He cocked an eye up which locked on to my own.

'Where did this rice come from?'

'Thailand.'

'Where is it going?'

'Nigeria.'

'Via Cotonou because of the rice ban?'

I nodded.

'How long will it take to get it across the border?'

'Maximum twelve days – could be a lot less.'

'We're going to take a look at this,' he said, dropping his head and moving off around the room again.

'Jack's got too much money and too little nerve to start dealing drugs.'

'There's no such thing as too much money to rich people. That's why they get richer. As for nerve, if you haven't got it, you're often too stupid to admit it to yourself, and anyway, you're thinking about the money too much to worry about your balls.'

'What's it got to do with Kershaw?'

'He worked in Cotonou.'

'So do I.'

'He was unlucky, maybe, like Françoise Perec.'

Out in the garden, the urn lay on its side by the pool, the rope still attached. The parrot clung to the wire mesh at the front of the aviary with its feet and beak. It opened its wings, stretching, and flapped them once. The heat pressed down on the lawn. The stink of rotten flesh remained. I turned to Bagado.

'You were going to tell me about my duty.'

'Technically, your job is finished. You have found Kershaw.'

'Thanks.'

'Kershaw is dead. We know he's been killed. The officer with the bad feet isn't going to do anything for him, just as the Cotonou police aren't going to do anything for Françoise Perec.'

'You're going to tell me about the duty you feel to these people as a policeman?'

'No, as a human. There's not many of us left. I know this is nothing to do with you. I know the English have a fear of "getting involved" but you're already involved

– Yao's boss has seen to that. I know that law and order should prevail so that you shouldn't have to get involved, but to use an English expression: "It's all fucked up." You are the only person who can do anything for these people. I am suspended. I have no money. Today, I don't even have socks.' Bagado lifted up his trouser legs and showed his bare ankles. Bagado saw me looking out into the garden squinting through the rank air.

'Dead bodies,' said Bagado. 'You've never seen a dead body.'

'Not in that condition.'

'A layer of innocence gone,' said Bagado, flicking nothing with his forefinger out of the french windows. 'We lose them all the time.'

'That was a layer I wouldn't have minded hanging on to.'

'And now it's gone. So you deal with it. We can only learn from experience, but she's a ruthless, barbaric bitch of a teacher.'

'She?'

'*Experience* in French is feminine and most of what I know about myself, I've learnt through women.'

'Where are you taking me, Bagado?'

'Put it this way, I think you think you're unusual. An Englishman living in Africa doing this strange work of yours. An odd job man who looks for missing persons. It sounds unusual. Your friends in England poking around their computers in London must think it's unusual. But to me, it's ordinary. Where you live and what you do doesn't make a man extraordinary. It's what's in here,' he said, thumping his heart and tapping his temple. 'You might have something in there, but you're not showing it and until you do you're just another one of them.'

'Is this what they teach you at the police academy?'

'People murdered with extreme violence, money laundering, drugs, government and police corruption. A nasty combination. I can see why you . . .'

'What about you, Bagado?'

'I made my decision a long time ago, and anyway, I'm naturally curious. I have to know. Are you afraid of death?'

'Only my own.'

'Are you scared?'

'Only the stupid aren't.'

Bagado walked up to a wooden carving about five-foot high. It was of an old woman holding a child. The woman's hair flowed up out of her head like a solid flame – it was the natural grain of the wood. The figure had been carved to that unaltered phenomenon. He stood next to it and put his arm around it. The three of them accused me of something which I didn't like being accused of.

'Charlie is an American,' I said, 'who runs a bar down the coast out of town, about a mile after the port off the Benin road. He told me to talk to an old girlfriend of Kershaw's called Nina Sorvino. She told me that Kershaw was into sadism and bondage which was why she ditched him.'

I told Bagado all I knew about Charlie, Nina, Jack, B.B. and Madame Severnou, not leaving out that four days ago Kershaw had been seen by Charlie with a blonde French woman in his bar. I told him about

158

Dama, and again about Yao and the big man behind Yao. Bagado stormed around the room with his hands in his pockets, walking faster and faster until I had finished and then he tore off his orbit and burst through the french windows and into the escape lane of the garden, where he slowed down just before the pool.

'What is Charlie's surname?'

'Reggiani.'

'Italian?'

'Tajikistani.'

'What!'

''Course it's bloody Italian.'

'I never assume anything,' he said.

'Well, you can assume that.'

'Is or has there been a relationship between Nina and Charlie?'

'Beyond friends and fellow Italian/Americans? I don't know.'

'Somebody wants us to think that Kershaw killed Perec, came back here and killed himself.'

'It seems more likely that somebody else killed Perec, framed Kershaw with the evidence and killed him to make it look like suicide.'

'Charlie?'

'Framing for Kershaw supplied by Nina.'

'What's their relationship and their motive?'

We shrugged at each other. Bagado wanted to follow the Charlie/Nina angle as well as Jack's rice.

'What about Yao and his boss?' I asked.

'That makes me very uncomfortable. He's not operating through legal channels, sending Yao around here, having you picked up, and then when we call the police they come and don't investigate. This whole business could start from him.'

'Kershaw and Perec knew something about him?'

'Maybe there's a link between the big man and Charlie and/or Mr Obuasi.'

'That's not something we're going to find out very easily. He seems the careful type.'

Bagado spent a few minutes staring at the front of my shirt and clicking his teeth with his thumbnail. I knew how he felt with all those ideas, facts, possibilities and theories stumbling about his brain. My head was like a full lift where life is on hold, where only those things in front of your face figure until someone gets off and gives you some space. Heike and Kershaw occupied my entire cerebral scope, the other things were part of the unseen pressure. Bagado's relentless mind landed.

'I know you have a problem with a woman,' he said. 'I know the symptoms very well. I also have a problem with a woman. Françoise Perec. A woman who was tortured and murdered in a terrible way, in a way that makes me ashamed of my gender, in a way that makes me so angry and determined that nothing will stop me from bringing that man down. I will get him,' said Bagado, looking from under his brow and stabbing the air in front of him. 'I will get him. If we are going to work together I have to know that you have the same anger, the same determination. You have to find it in yourself. You have to find your stomach for this work. I know you don't want to disturb your quiet life. I understand you have a personal crisis, you have a distaste for rotting flesh, you fear the megalomania of power and money – all of which is right.

'But forget them. You'll find time to straighten those things out. This evening. Tomorrow. The day after. There will be time. We can't move too quickly. Some big men are playing a game and I don't want to be a pawn in it. For now – get angry!'

Bagado moved into the centre of the room and turned, sweeping his hand before him and with the face of a man stuffed full of pompous vanity said: 'We Africans love to speechify.' He laughed and I wiped the sweat from under my eyes.

I called B.B. He picked up the phone during the first ringing tone.

'Yairs?' he said, through his smoker's throat.

'It's Bruce.'

There was a noise on the line like an industrial grinder so I said I would call him back.

'No, no, Bruise. It's me. I eat some groundnut.'

'I've found Kershaw. He's dead.'

There was an explosion of static which blew the phone off my head. B.B. fought for air. There was the sound of coughing and hoiking and then the phone clattered to the floor. I heard a struggle and the noise of spitting, then the phone was being pulled up by its line, knocking against the arm rest and the table.

'B.B.?'

'Yairs.'

'Everything OK?'

'Is OK. One of the red skins from the groundnut caught in my troat. You found Kershaw. Good. Let me spik to him.'

'He's dead.'

'Whaaat?'

'We found him in the pool at the house in Lomé. The police have just taken away the body. He's in the hospital morgue.'

B.B. was silent. The sweat trickled. The palms stood still in the garden. The heat leaned on the house.

'My God. Is a terrible ting,' he said after some time. I heard him light a cigarette.

'Still smoking?'

'I no can stop. After you left, I call de Armenian friend who have de house in Lomé where you are now. He tell me terrible ting ... my God ... dis world.' I heard the smoke rasping down his congested tubes. 'You know I say dere's a problem in Ivory Coast. Dey kill his son.'

'Who are "they"?'

'I don't know. Is a car bomb. Dey tink political killing or someting like dat.'

'I thought he was a businessman.'

'Yairs. He is businessman. But de people want democracy, you know, free elecsharn. So dey kill de white man to put de pressure. You know, France get very angry, dey tell the Presidarn he haff to do someting or dey tek away de investmarn. Is a terrible ting ... a dutty business ... dutty.'

B.B. agreed to call Kershaw's wife who, given the state of the corpse, would have to come over to identify the body. He told me to call Mrs Kershaw in the afternoon to get her flight details and to keep the fee to pay for her expenses in Lomé and to book a room at the Sarakawa. I took down her London number and asked

162

B.B. to speak to his Armenian friend to find out where the maid lived, telling him Bagado would call later for the information. He said we should use the Armenian's house as our base and that we would talk about the sheanut business when Mrs Kershaw had left. He put the phone down without saying goodbye.

Bagado was excited about the Armenian's son. 'There are too many people dying,' he said.

'Bagado,' I said, 'Françoise Perec was found in Cotonou, Kershaw in Lomé, but in the last half hour you've stretched this investigation from Lagos to Abidjan and thrown in some drug trafficking. Where are the connections?'

'There are none. This is not ordinary police work. Even if we did have the backing of the police they have nothing to help us. As it is, they are against us. They are being paid to cover up. The more people you pay the weaker you become. A material that's stretched has more holes in it. The wider our vision, the more chances we have to force a break from cover. This is how we have to operate. We have no authority and if we're seen to be making our own investigations we'll get ourselves killed.'

'That's what the policeman told you?'

'In his own way. Lots of smiling and laughing. It wouldn't take much. Lomé's become a dangerous place. Lunch?'

'I'll watch.'

'You'll eat.'

We drove the short distance into the centre of town and parked up off the Rue du Commerce. We sat out-

163

side a stall and ordered grilled chicken and salad from a very big woman whose breasts were only marginally less astonishing than her bottom, which behaved like a couple of sacks of restless guinea fowl. The sweat poured down her face as she turned the chicken and she kept up a non-stop monologue which anybody could interrupt if they were man enough to have a go.

Even away from the charcoal the day had built up a terrible heat. My clothes clung to me like a bore at a party. Bagado, still with his raincoat on, threw the occasional comment at the massive cook who roared with laughter, which set her breasts off into a playtex tremble which she had to still like kettle drums. Moses sat with his back to the table and was doing his best with a coquettish Ghanaian girl who was doing *her* best to ignore him.

A man with long white robes and white cylindrical hat washed his hands from a bowl held by a young boy. He splashed the water on his face and ran his hand down again and again over his rubbery features, flicking the water off into the road each time. There weren't many people in the street. It was too hot. The women from the booze stalls lay in the shade of their displays and fingered the shawls over their heads, dozing.

We ate. The food sat in my stomach and fizzed. Afterwards, we went back to the house and lay down. When the time came for me to call London, Bagado told me to be vague with Mrs Kershaw about the cause of her husband's death.

Mrs Kershaw was glad to have someone to talk to. Her voice was panting and nervous and her brain was

164

running faster than her mouth. Bagado was listening on a second earpiece. She gave me the flight details and started on an involved story about the body canister which I interrupted by telling her to make sure she had her jabs, birth and marriage certificates and some wedding photographs.

'We weren't close any more,' she said after a pause that should have terminated the call. 'His financial problems changed him.'

'What were the financial problems?'

'He was a Name at Lloyd's. His syndicate lost a lot on the asbestosis claims. They took everything and the bank pulled out of his business. I'm living in a friend's flat in Clapham now. My husband used to work in Africa so he went there to get a job and save some money to start again.'

'What was his business?'

'Import/export. Is there some doubt? I mean, you're asking these questions as if it wasn't suicide.'

'We don't know, Mrs Kershaw. The police have taken away your husband's body. It's possible that you'll have to answer some questions when you come to Lomé. You might as well be prepared.'

'It'd be better face to face.'

I agreed. She ran through her flight details. I gave her the name of the Hotel Sarakawa where she was going to be staying and she hung up.

'If everybody in Africa with no money killed themselves,' said Bagado, 'we'd be left with a continent of corrupt officials. Imagine the horror. Only the vultures left.'

'It's the First World's disease. Without money you lose your status, your dignity . . .'

'Dignity?' asked Bagado. 'Money doesn't buy dignity.'

'Anyway, she thinks he committed suicide.'

'Does she?' he said, nodding. 'She didn't like your questions.'

'She doesn't know me.'

'It will be interesting to see her identify the body and how easily they release it. It should cost you some money.'

It was time to get back to Cotonou. Bagado said he would stay in Lomé with Moses to find the maid and check on Charlie. I gave him some money for expenses and offered him part of my fee for finding Kershaw. He said he would split one day's fee with me and told me to give it to his wife.

'What about transport?' I asked.

'The taxis are on strike,' said Moses coming out of the kitchen.

'You could . . .'

'We'll give you a lift to the border,' said Bagado.

'Thanks.'

'"We",' he said. 'I mean, it's just a figure of speech, you understand.'

# Chapter 15

The trip from the border to Cotonou was in a Peugeot 504 estate with eight people and a driver, all of whom wanted to be next to a window because the car didn't have air conditioning, and even if it had it wouldn't have worked. The heat towered above us and the air it sent through the windows was like a warm, wet flannel. The smell the eight of us, two long baskets of live guinea fowl and a small bag of dried fish managed to generate would have made a hyena boke. In Cotonou, we fell out of the car and stumbled about with our hands up like survivors of a mortar attack.

The heat and the pressure were stacked up high against the back end of the afternoon and everybody was ready for the storm to come and break them up. It did come, but it rolled overhead with dry rumbles of thunder and gusts of wind bringing foul smells but no rain.

It didn't take long to walk to Bagado's house from the centre of town where the taxi had dropped me off. Bagado's wife was a tall, elegant woman who looked as if she never sweated. She invited me in and when I refused was glad not to press the point. She took the money, and by the way the muscles in her forearm stood out as she gripped the envelope, she was glad to accept it. She asked me to tell Bagado to call Michel and gave me a letter for him from his mother. I drifted off like a vagrant, wading through the afternoon stillness, the dust powdering my shoes.

It was dark, hot and airless when I reached home. The lights were on, which meant a warm shower, cold beer and Heike. She sat at the table in a large, white, airy dress with a cold beer in front of her, smoking the cigarette cocked in her hand which she'd levered to her mouth on automatic. A glance said she was relaxed, a look that she was as tense as a tow cable. I acknowledged her with a palm held high and she waved me into the bathroom with her cigarette.

The taxi ride washed off easily but somehow an essence of it crept into a disused olfactory canal, so that in various lulls of the evening I was brought back sharply to my fellow travellers. A quarter of an hour later, I was sitting in a T-shirt and shorts in front of Heike, watching her plug another cigarette into her holder. I sipped a second beer after the first had shot over my larynx like a white water river. She looked as if she had done a lot of thinking, her brow had lines which pointed to the bridge of her nose.

When Heike had nothing left to do – she'd got her cigarette going, dealt with her hair so that it was slightly worse than before, sipped her beer, taken the sweat off her top lip and flounced her dress a couple of times to get some through draught – she came up with a sigh. Then her face stilled and she flicked her ear a couple of times with her finger and shook her head, opening and closing her eyes. Then she opened and closed her mouth a few times and stretched her neck over to her right shoulder and hit herself twice on the left side of her head with the ball of her palm.

'I've gone deaf,' she said.

'Let me take a look.'

'No.'

'Look, I'll just . . .'

'No,' she said, turning away from me and covering her ear.

'I won't do anything; I'll just look.'

'I don't want you going in there.'

'I'll wipe my feet.'

Her shoulders started to shake. She turned to face me, holding on to her ear and laughing. She was laughing so hard that no sound came out. Then she took a huge breath and there were tears in her eyes and she wasn't laughing any more. She dropped her elbows on to the table, stuck her fists into her forehead and cried into her beer. I rubbed the middle of her back between her shoulder blades and thought, now we're getting to it.

'I don't know what I'm doing any more,' she said, and strode to the bathroom. She reappeared swallowing hard and leaned against the door jamb. She looked small in her dress.

'For peace of mind,' she said, 'a person needs a job, a home and a lover. If you're missing one of those, life is tolerable, two and it's a pain, three and you end up like this.' She hit herself in the breast bone. 'I have a temporary home, a temporary job and a temporary lover. It's making a bloody mess of me.' She had two pockets on the front of her dress which she put her

169

hands in and walked in a slow circle around the room.

'You might be able to solve two of those by going back to Berlin.'

'You overestimate yourself, Bruce.'

'I don't think so. It's not easy to find people you like, let alone go to bed with or love.'

'There are a lot more people in Germany.'

'Choice complicates,' I said, and she shot me a look which I didn't understand. 'There's always the problem of unfinished business.'

'We can't finish unless we've started,' she said, looking at the floor.

'It's difficult to get started with three hundred miles between us.'

She stopped and looked at me sideways across her shoulder.

'How did you feel when I said I was leaving?'

'Bad.'

'So did I.'

'And that's not enough?'

'No, because it's negative,' she said and resumed walking. She walked straight past me into the kitchen. 'Let's have a real drink, my blood's running slow.'

She came back with the rest of the whisky from last night, a bowl of ice, two glasses and a bottle of cold water. She poured two whiskies, ignoring the ice and water, and handed me a glass. We banged them down and she kissed me, her lips stinging with whisky.

'We know how to drink,' I said.

'We know how to do a lot of things.'

She poured more whiskies, with ice and water this time.

170

'Two jobs have come up with the company that runs the project,' she said. 'One in Porto Novo, the other in Berlin.'

'Last night it was Berlin. What is it this evening?'

'Tomorrow evening I'm going to Porto Novo for a dinner, to meet the people I could end up working with. Sunday, I've got a conference about the project. If it all goes well they'll offer me first choice on either job. Three-year contract.'

'They like you.'

'If I choose Berlin, it's unlikely I'll get the opportunity to work in Africa again. If I choose Africa I'll find it difficult to get back into working in Europe.'

'And?'

She sat on the table and put her feet on the chair. 'It's easy to love someone for a weekend every two months.'

'It's not so easy for two people our age to make up their minds. All that history.'

'You're getting everything your own way.'

'How's that?'

'Uncomplicated bi-monthly sex.'

'You want to complicate it?'

'I want more.'

'Then you have to come more often.'

'Not sex.'

Heike looked at her drink as if the ice might tell her something. No air came through the open-slatted windows. The cicadas were whistling. There were no lights outside, the darkness felt close, the noise made it closer. Heike's hair was dark with sweat on the back of her neck.

'Why don't you get air conditioning?' she asked.

'It's part of my campaign for real air. Why did you say you were going to Berlin last night?'

'I was testing.'

'Did I pass?'

'Without honours.'

'Do you think you can handle Germany now? You know, you all have to get up at the same time, go to work at the same time, lots of *Guten Morgen Herr* this and *Guten Tag Frau* that. Everything nice and organized, no margin for error, little margin for creativity; don't rock the boat, keep things predictable, keep things clean. You'll get married to some guy with a name like Horst, have two kids, Dieter and Ingrid, get divorced not because your husband's boring, but your life's too boring. Your only excitement will be when the Far Right fire bomb your offices because you're giving good German money to black people. And I'll have to sit here and wring what humour I can out of the fact that you married. A Man Called Horst.'

'I take it you want me to stay?' she said.

'Yes.'

'Then say it.'

'I want you to stay. I want you to take the job in Porto Novo and live here – with me.'

Heike smiled one of those smiles she'd rather not have given away. She looked around her, drained her whisky, poured herself another one and did the same for me. She picked up her cigarette holder, pulled out the butt and fitted a new one and lit it.

'What about these bedsheets of money and men with guns?' she asked.

'You can't have everything. You'll enjoy a bit of excitement when you come back from the office.'

The phone went. We looked at it and Heike stabbed at the noise with her cigarette. I swam over to it, through the thick, humid air.

'Hot?' asked Bagado.

'Enough,' I said.

'How's my wife?'

'Fine. She said: "Call Michel", and I've got a letter for you.'

'How's your woman problem?'

'Still there.'

'All you have to do is listen.'

After Bagado had dropped me at the border, he'd found that Charlie had been to Cotonou and returned to Lomé on the same day that Françoise Perec had been murdered. On the return journey, his car had passed through the border at the same time as ACR 4750, Kershaw's car.

Bagado had spoken to B.B. about the Armenian's son when B.B. had called to give the maid's address. The Armenian had lived in Paris and had made a lot of money from a nut and bolt factory in Abidjan, which he'd spent on art. He had wanted to paint but lacked the talent and had become a patron and dealer instead. We didn't know what this meant, but it was the first sign of a connection between the young Armenian and Kershaw.

He had found the maid's family in mourning. The maid had been one of the twenty-one bodies floating in the lagoon with bullet holes in the back of their heads. They confirmed that she had worked for a white man who painted a lot in a house near the Grande Marché.

He had staked out Charlie's compound and watched Jack and Nina Sorvino turn up on separate occasions in the late afternoon. Both had talked to Charlie in his house. Charlie was now in the Hotel Sarakawa having dinner with a woman that fitted the description of Yvette.

Bagado had also called the police and had arranged the body identification in the hospital morgue for 11.00 on Monday morning.

'There's nothing unusual about Charlie going to Cotonou,' I said. 'It's just a coincidence that it was on the same day . . .'

'It's a pity there aren't degrees of coincidence. The Armenian's son, the maid, Charlie in Cotonou on the day of the murder. Jack and Nina going to see him.'

'They've known each other a long time.'

'Who's the woman he's having dinner with?'

I told Bagado what I knew about Yvette.

'How long has he known her?' he asked.

'I don't know.'

'Find out. Did you notice anything odd about those magazines in Kershaw's drawer?'

'Apart from the obvious.'

'This was obvious. They were American, priced in dollars only. Kershaw was British; why have American magazines?'

'Perhaps they have more recherché tastes.'

'But the British are the world experts. Haven't you heard the French expression *le vice anglais*?'

'What's that?'

'Spanking, beating, the lash.'

'My French teacher didn't cover that. I'll see you tomorrow.'

Heike stood with an eyebrow raised and a sneering smile sneaking across her lips which finished with a grunt.

'That didn't sound like business.'

'It was. A different type.'

'You used to have conversations about sugar and tyres.'

'I've got involved in something else. I found a dead body this morning.'

Heike didn't want to hear about that and she took hold of my shirt front to tell me. 'What are you playing at now, Bruce?' she said, shoving me backwards, some red creeping into her blue eyes. 'What the hell are you doing?'

'I was asked to find somebody. He was dead. That's all,' I said, thinking – it's coming.

'Then the job's finished,' she said, looking dangerous, a crescendo building. I didn't say anything. 'I've just told you I can't live with this kind of shit on my doorstep, you make a joke of it and seconds later I hear you're in the death business. I don't like it. And if the quarter of a brain you've still got was half working, you shouldn't like it either.' She thumped me in the chest with her free hand. There it is, I thought, the first one. 'You want me to live with you? I have to feel safe. I mean, not in immediate danger. Not listening for the gate all the time.'

She let go of me and held her hands apart and looked at the space in between – warming up. 'That's not a big thing to ask, is it, Bruce? I'm not telling you to stop drinking, I'm not even saying you can't slob around watching football all day, I'm not asking you to put up some new shelves and buy a wardrobe, I'm not asking for triple locks, security fences, alarms, dogs. I'm just saying I can't come back after a day's work to sawn-off shotguns, a head in the freezer, millions of CFA in cash on the floor and brown bags full of a white powder that isn't sugar.'

She stopped, looked up and off into the room somewhere. 'Am I nagging? Shit . . . I never thought it would happen. You've made me start nagging,' she said, and thumped me again, the second one.

'Jesus!' I said grabbing her wrist. 'Who said he was headless?'

'You know what I mean.' She hit me with her other hand and I grabbed that one too. She used her elbows and a knee.

'The money was for rice, for Christ's sake. That's how much seven thousand tons of parboiled costs. There were no drugs. The heavies came round to frighten me, not to kill me. It was business, not Harvard school – Lagos school. I was asked to find somebody. It's happened before. It's just this time the somebody was dead. His wife's coming over on Sunday, she identifies the body on Monday and then finish. No heads in the freezer, only carpets on the floor and flowers on the table.'

She fought her wrists out of my grip using a kick on the shins to help and slapped me around the shoulders until I wrapped both arms around her and she roared for a bit and then gave up. I let go and she lay down on some cushions on the floor and stared at the ceiling, breathing hard. I tried to take her hand. She batted me away.

I went to the kitchen and warmed up some food that Helen had left for us. We sat down to eat, Heike calm now but not talking. It was too hot to eat. The food wouldn't go down so we drank two bottles of cold white wine before drifting back on to the whisky.

Later we turned the lights off and sat in the ambient light from the street. Heike was talking now, coming back round to me, but wary.

'It's not the job,' she said.

'I know.'

'But those kind of people don't care about anything. You know that. Except money.'

'It's nearly over. Let's not talk about it now.'

'You understand though?'

'I've got the bruises.'

We stripped and sat naked in front of a fan, drinking more whisky and as much cold water as we could stand, the sweat trickling down our backs, the fight further off now. I stroked her right nipple with the back of my hand. Heike looked across, lust and reluctance in the same face. She clambered over and sat astride me, easing herself down. The fan blew cool air between my legs, and up Heike's back as she rose and fell against me. The sweat poured down us, our skins slipped against each other's. We finished under the shower, Heike locking my neck in the crook of her elbow and crushing her mouth to mine.

By two o'clock in the morning, we were lying on a sheet on the floor not moving at all, our hair damp and skin still slick with sweat. It was too hot to sleep and too loud to talk. We let the fan scan our bodies like a meticulous and accepted voyeur and had complicated thoughts which looked as if they were worth talking about, except there was no vocabulary for them. By four o'clock, we were dozing like dogs dreaming of rabbits and at first light we were nearly dead. I dreamt very clearly, but other people's dreams have always bored me. It finished with an urgent knocking sound that rang in my head.

The phone wrenched me out of my coma. It was light outside. My scalp was drenched in sweat. Heike lay on her back with beads of moisture between her breasts. The phone insisted. She clicked her tongue against the roof of her mouth. I crawled to the angry phone. On the third croak, someone spoke. It was Nina Sorvino. I said hello, which came out as a single syllable beginning with 'B'. Nina spoke very softly for my well-wrung brain and asked me to an Embassy party in Lomé that evening. We arranged to meet at the Hotel Le Benin, not far from Jack's house, at seven o'clock.

The day was hot and grey like motorway service station coffee. It passed with hostage slowness. There should have been a sense of triumph, a post-row euphoria. I'd asked Heike to live with me. The offer had been received but, I noticed, not accepted. I had that feeling of being on the edge of something great but without knowing whether it was good or bad.

We went to the Sheraton and lay face down on a

couple of loungers under some low palm trees. Once an hour, I slid into the pool on my belly while Heike remained on the lounger with her arms over the side, her cheek flat against the mattress as if weighed down by something. Later she came in and I manoeuvred her around the pool while she stared up at the overcast sky. I was doing what Bagado had told me, I was listening; the only problem, Heike wasn't talking.

The heat and humidity didn't let up and this time the storm didn't even bother to pass drily overhead but slunk off round the side without even a breath of wind. On the way home, I said I wanted to go to Kershaw's office. Heike wasn't happy about it. 'It's not bloody finished yet, is it?' she said, and slouched against the door jamb with her arms folded while I looked around. There wasn't a lot in the room. In the desk was a ledger of the sheanut Kershaw had bought, at what prices and from whom. The filing cabinet was empty, and so was the ashtray. The office plant was a dried yellow husk. There was a clean block of paper on the desk with no imprints left by any previous note. There was an empty coat hanger on a picture hook.

'Where would you put a dirty shirt?' I asked Heike.

'In a plastic bag on the door handle,' she said, yawning. I looked. Nothing.

'That's what people do with dirty shirts, Bruce. They take them home and wash them. Try the answering machine, Sherlock,' she said. 'It's flashing.'

The phone was on a separate shelf below the window, the answering machine next to it. I rewound the tape and played it. B.B.'s voice came on.

'Steef? You dere? Pick up de phone. Bloddy hell!

179

Steeef! Gah! You call me. (A slurping noise.) Tell me how many ton you haff now. Send sample. De last sheanut we send to Aarhus from Lomé de FFA more dan four per cent. Dey not payin' me. You hear? Bah!' The phone clattered. B.B.'s message was laid over another, a different voice speaking French. '... *à vingt-trois heures le vingt-trois septembre. D'accord. Au revoir.*' Then a voice I recognized as Kate Kershaw's. 'It's me. This stuff, where do you want it sent? Lomé or Cotonou? The sable brushes cost a fortune. Bye.' Then blank tape.

'What do you make of it?' asked Heike, sarcasm on full, a cigarette going now.

'I've got to go home before you take me to the taxi station.'

Back at the house I found the direct number of the harbour master's office in Cotonou port. Nobody answered for some time, and then with a Saturday afternoon voice that was sitting around in its vest with its bare feet up on the table next to a radio. I asked him which ship gave an ETA of 23.00 hours on the 23rd September. It took him forever to tell me what I already knew. The *Naoki Maru*.

Heike dropped me at the taxi station. She said she was staying in Porto Novo until Monday or Tuesday, depending on how things went with the conference and job interviews. We kissed and she squeezed my shoulder. She couldn't hold my look. I got out of the car, closed the door and she drove off like a cab driver after a new fare.

# Chapter 16

*Saturday 28th September*

The Hotel Le Benin looked refreshed as if it had just flown in from a short holiday in the Côte d'Azur. It had a smart, cool grandeur to it that night, with the lights trained on to its creamy façade. In the darkness of the gardens, I changed my shirt. Headlights cut through the night as cars swung round the circular driveway. Car doors opened and shut and shoes gritted on the loose surface. There was smoke and chat and the rustle of silk and folding money. The open air restaurant and bar was filling up but there was no Nina there, so I went into the air-conditioned lobby, which was freezing after the smothering heat of the evening, and wandered around like a paying guest.

Seven o'clock came and went, as did seven-thirty. A young African girl came up to me and asked me if I liked dancing; I said yes and she left the hotel without a backward glance. The doorman came up to me and apologized.

'These girls,' he said. 'Very . . . *bad* girls.'

I thought about following and doing some bad dancing with her because I was getting chill from the air conditioning. Then I started thinking that something had happened to Nina as a quarter to eight assumed the position on the lobby clock.

Boredom got its arm round my shoulder and pushed me into an African art boutique and I started playing a game of *wari* with the girl behind the counter who tore me to shreds. My mind wasn't on it. At least that was what I told myself.

'You're pissed, right?' said Nina, in a low wary voice behind me.

'I wish I was.'

She was wearing a blue Chinese silk dress with a high collar and cut at the shoulders. Her hair was tied in a long plait which hung over her right shoulder and needed only six more inches to the top of her thigh. She said it took her an hour to do the plait which she thwacked me with on the arm. It was as solid as a dog's tail.

We drove to the party which was being held in the US Cultural Centre opposite the Embassy. I was wondering whether to tell her about Kershaw, and decided that if she was a New Yorker she must be able to take just about anything, when she asked me if I'd found him. I told her and she didn't like it one bit. She had a lit cigarette in her mouth in less time than it took her to run the red light. She rolled down the window to get some air and all that came in was thick, heavy heat which covered her face like a gloved hand. She threw the cigarette out, rolled up the window and turned up the air conditioning.

We arrived at the Cultural Centre in silence. Nina's jaw was shut tight so that the tendon sprang out by her ear. She had a wide look to her blinking eyes as if she was paranoid. She wasn't just upset about Kershaw, she was scared.

'Nina?'

'What?' she said, with a viciousness that came from speaking with her jaw shut. 'I'm upset, that's all. Haven't had an ex-boyfriend die on me before. You?'

'No.'

'Well, it's like this.' She dropped her head on to the steering wheel. 'Jesus. I'm sorry. I keep you waiting for an hour and then tear your throat out. I'm outa line.'

We sat in the darkness, couples walked past on the way to the party. Nina looked out not seeing them and not blinking either.

'Let's get a drink,' she said. I didn't drag my feet.

We went into the party and immediately ran aground on some of Nina's colleagues who wouldn't let us get near a drink. The waiters with their trays of ready-made drinks sensed a couple of desperate people and kept well away from us. It must be something drummed into them early at waiting school. Nina broke free from the mob with the verbal equivalent of an elbow in the eye. We stood by a waiter, Nina holding him by his arm, and drank two drinks apiece from his tray and took a third. A hand came down on my shoulder and Jack took my arm and spoke in my ear: 'You won.'

'How do you know?'

'Everybody knows, but only I knew you found him.'

'And now everybody knows that.'

He was about to introduce me to a small but very attractive Asian woman with long shiny purple nails, but she sent out a complex message in social semaphore that brought Jack up short. He let go of my arm and followed the Asian woman to a far corner where he stood bent at the middle looking at the ground over her shoulder and made a good show of listening.

Nina returned and introduced me to Elizabeth Harvey who, she explained, was English and married to a prominent banker in the US community. Mrs Harvey was tall enough on her high heels to look me straight in the eye, which she did while I remembered Jack's decadent bet. She had a glassy coolness to her and I felt as if she'd picked me up by the scruff and was inspecting me as she would a yobbish kitten. Her blonde hair was piled high on her head, a single string of pearls circled her neck. Her shoulders were bare and she was thin, so that her clavicles stood out, along with a few other bones that I hadn't seen on myself for a long time. I could just see the top of her raw silk dress which had a blue green sheen and showed that cleavage was not something she possessed. I didn't look any lower.

She didn't seem too displeased with what she saw in me and she put me down and gave me a little stroke. She smiled with a small mouth whose lips looked as if they might be hard to kiss – not difficult, just not very yielding. Her eyes were very blue, too blue to be believable. She must have been wearing coloured contacts.

'I hear you found a body,' she said, and showed me a set of perfect but very small teeth that pointed into her mouth so that if she got them into you, you might find it hard to get them out.

'There've been a lot of them about lately,' I replied. 'I wouldn't like to find one.'

'I didn't enjoy it myself.'

'Was it stiff?'

'Yes, and hard, and bloated and it stank.' It was a hard line to take, but then, she had showed an interest and I saw no reason to hold back. She shivered.

A tall man with grey hair which was swept back and curled above his red and white striped collar appeared at her side and took her elbow. He wore a light grey, lightweight suit and a tie that joined him to a club where people talked quietly while the world haemorrhaged money into their bank accounts. Mrs Harvey introduced me to her husband, Clifford Harvey, without taking her eyes off me. He didn't waste his time shaking my hand and behaved like someone who'd chipped neatly out of the rough and come to pick up his golf bag.

'Darling,' said Mrs Harvey in a bright voice that could shatter crystal.

Clifford held out his hand and we shook. He'd been to handshaking school. He threw the spare hand over his hair and it came to rest half on his neck and half on his cheek with the little finger in the corner of his mouth. His brow had the right concentration lines, his eyes had the alert tiredness of the hardworking, capable, corporate man.

'Mr Medway found a body,' said Elizabeth Harvey. 'What was its name?'

'Steven Kershaw.'

'Who is Steven Kershaw?' drawled Clifford, as if he might be a potential client.

'Was. He's dead now,' said his wife, blinking.

'Who *was* he?' said Clifford, stringing out his already

strung-out American accent to show his wife that her irritating little shots were coming right off the meat.

'An Englishman who did some sheanut business out of Cotonou,' I said. 'I found him in the pool of a house a couple of hundred yards from here.'

Clifford had heard all he wanted to hear. He gripped his wife's elbow and gave her a gentle shunt with his shoulder. She didn't budge. She was more interested in death than hanging off her husband at a party. After all, she was a Catholic and her whole life was invested in death.

'You found him in a pool?' she asked.

'With an urn attached to his feet.'

'Was it suicide?'

'It looked like it.'

'Is this your job?' asked Clifford Harvey, amazed that people could earn a living doing this kind of thing.

'Finding people, not necessarily dead ones. This is the first. I do other things too.'

'You're a private eye,' said Clifford, who in his privileged life had probably run into some things other than bankers, but they'd only made a mess on his windscreen.

'Not exactly. There's not much call for that kind of work on this coast. It's not what you'd call California.'

'You gotta line in acute perception there, Mr . . . ?'

'Medway, darling,' said Mrs Harvey, and I watched my name zip through his head once more without troubling his memory.

Elizabeth Harvey had begun to look about her as if she was fresh off the deck of a sinking liner. Something had clicked inside her and she'd moved into another phase of her programme. She asked me if I was alone and I told her I had come with Nina who was off on the far side of the room talking to Charlie. Of course, she remembered that Nina had introduced us, so I asked her if she knew her. She didn't like that and her eyes popped open and she took a look down her nose at me of the sort that shoe-shine boys must get used to. Clifford was breathing pure steam into her ear and Elizabeth Harvey let herself be led away to meet the owner of an aluminium smelting plant.

'What do you think?' asked Jack from behind my shoulder.

'Very cool.'

'Just right for these hot nights we've been having,' he said, giggling.

'Maybe a little brittle.'

'I can be careful.'

'How does Clifford feel about it?'

'These people only sleep together in the back of limousines after boring bankers' dinners.'

'Does she know your reputation?'

'She's too pure for that.'

'Or too stupid.'

'I'm the only one who's daring enough.'

'The secret of your success.'

Jack was rubbing his hands and looking around.

'Nina Sorvino,' he said.

'Forget it, Jack.'

'Not me, you.'

'I know.'

Nina was still talking to Charlie, who was looking stone-faced at nothing in particular, in the middle of the room. He sipped his drink and turned his head slowly towards her. He said something. She turned and walked out of the room with her chin on her chest. A drink came into my hand and my empty was removed from the other. The service element of the party had improved now that I wasn't desperate. Jack lumbered off through the crowd towards Charlie and knocked the official photographer on the back on the way through. Charlie was having his face kissed by Yvette and it was having the same effect on him as a perfect punch on the point of the chin.

Nina came back into the room, strode across to me and flung the plait around my neck, pulled me to her and kissed me on the mouth. A flash went off. Some people laughed. I pulled back. The plait was like a silk rope on the back of my neck. Nina held on to the other end.

'You could strangle someone with that.'

'I'd have to get very close to do it.'

She let go of the plait and it slipped down my shoulder like a snake moving off. I wasn't feeling very comfortable about this manoeuvre of Nina's. Her kiss had sent a bolt of electricity straight down my spine. I had enough problems of my own without adding hers. She sniffed at me as if a little upset.

'I'm only kidding,' she said. 'I've a reputation for being outrageous. I gotta keep it up.'

'It's a big talent,' I said.

'Are you for real, Bruce? Are you one of the few men who doesn't want a piece of Nina Sorvino.' She put one hand on her hip and flung the other around herself. 'He wants my tits, he wants my ass, he wants

188

my pussy, he wants my mind, he wants my feet,' she said with a deep voice, 'but he's a bit weird.'

'But nobody wants the whole Cadillac,' I finished.

She sniffed again and I thought she was going to cry, but her head came up bright-eyed. 'I'm the spares department.'

We whipped some drinks off a passing tray and looked around. Charlie was shaking hands with the massive Nigerian from AAICT who was held in position across his meaty shoulders by Jack, who seemed to be coming first in an international grinning league. Nina said his name was Bof Awolowo and that he'd made huge money in the seventies from the Nigerian oil boom. He'd somehow managed to squeeze out of Nigeria when they had the clampdown in the eighties.

'He was a lot slimmer then,' she said. 'Now he's back and trying to be legit and getting big in politics. You can imagine, it's not ideology that's gettin' him there.'

'You're impressed.'

'He just wants to put himself in a position where he can rip his country off again.'

'What's he like in business?'

'I met an oil man from Port Harcourt who said: ''His name sounds like a fart in a tub and that's all you get when you do a deal with him.'''

Awolowo's shoulders were shaking and the boom-boom of his laughter rebounded off the walls. His head rocked back and the creases multiplied in his neck. A waiter arrived with a tray and he turned to take a drink; the humour drained from his face and his eyes flickered.

'Has Charlie worked with him?'

'I don't know, but he likes a challenge.'

189

'You know Jack?'

'I never been to bed with him,' said Nina, giving me a sideways glance with slitty eyes and a mouth that should have had a cigar in the corner.

'You're a rare breed.'

'Maybe I'm gonna be extinct the way things are happening round here.'

Nina was carried off by some Embassy people. A small, fat woman with sweat beading through the powder on her nose tapped my elbow and stared up at me. She held a heavily ringed hand with an orange juice in it towards me as if to chink glasses. We juggled our names around until the coaster stuck on the bottom of her glass fell off, then we knocked heads bending down. She was an American and lived in the Hotel Golfe in Abidjan. Her husband was head of Global Bank. She pointed him out. I didn't know whether I was supposed to say he looked nice. I asked her why she was living in a hotel and she told me that Abidjan was very dangerous and they hadn't found secure accommodation. I hadn't thought it was that bad, I said, and she put me right. She was worried about having her head cut off by a machete. I asked her where she came from in the States and she said New York; I mentioned that they had a hell of a lot more crazies in New York than they did in Abidjan and that was the end of it.

Nina was half a mile away by now talking to a large sandy-haired fellow who was fingering her plait and murmuring things to her that might have been offers of money. She was leaning away but the plait moored her to him. I had some telepathic understanding with a waiter who could intuit when the ice in my glass had got to rattling point and would coast by with his tray at just the right speed and level to put a dead glass on and take a live one off.

The official photographer was lining up the Harveys and a bunch of executives from the aluminium smelting plant. One of the team had enough drink inside him to think that he could put his hand on Elizabeth Harvey's bare shoulder. It wasn't there for long and when he took it off he checked it as if he'd lost some skin on cold metal.

Yvette was doing something to the back of Charlie's neck and he had the uncertain look of a man who was thinking that maybe everybody around him could hear his heart beating in his ears as loud as he could. She was wearing a Fortuny-pleated silk cardigan in silver and its intimate rustle was devastating Charlie's hold on himself. He was swallowing a lot. It was a thick lustful swallow which sent whatever was coming up right back down to his loins. Awolowo and Jack had moved on so there was no audience to his restraint.

Yvette whispered something in Charlie's ear. Her lips and tongue made contact with his lobe and his legs trembled in his trousers. She broke away from him, the Fortuny-pleated silk flared trousers she was wearing hushed the conversation where she walked. She reached me and folded the cardigan across herself.

'They tell me you found a body this morning, Bruce,' she said, rolling my name on her tongue.

'Why are women so interested in death?'

'Sex and death is what it's all about. Power and money is for boys.'

'A black widow speaks.'

'That was Jasmin who said that. *I*'ve never killed a man . . . in cold blood,' she said, laughing in the back of her throat.

'Remind me not to get involved.'

She took a cigarette out of her purse, put one in her mouth and was about to light it when she remembered that she was in the American Cultural Centre and the marines were on passive smoking duty. She twiddled the unlit cigarette in her smoking fingers and tickled the gap in her teeth with her tongue.

'This body,' she said. 'It belonged to Mr Kershaw. They tell me another body was found in Mr Kershaw's apartment in Cotonou. That body belonged to a woman.'

'Who's they?'

'I don't remember.'

'You're not trying very hard.'

'Was it suicide?'

'I don't know.'

'He drowned,' she said, neither as a fact nor a question.

'I suppose it's not a normal way of killing yourself,' I said.

'Suicide isn't normal and they say drowning is very nice.'

'If you've had such a nice life that you don't mind it flashing before you.'

'I see your point. An overdose of painkillers is perhaps more usual. How would you . . . ?'

'I wouldn't.'

'How do you know?'

'Suicide is for romantics.'

'And "ruined" financiers,' she said. 'You are not a romantic?'

'There's comfort in escape but no solutions.'

'Perhaps you're more profound than you look?'

'Which is how?' I said, wondering if her English stretched that far.

'*Beau*,' she said, stroking me with her violet eyes.

'You *are* a romantic,' I said, taking a good slug of whisky while I thought about bottling whatever it was that was getting me all this attention.

'I am,' she said, making her top lip shine with the tip of her tongue.

'You should be careful.'

'And why is that?'

'You're opening yourself up to disappointment.'

'Hi, Bruce,' said Charlie, appearing between us. 'What's goin' on. You two comparing notes on marriage again?'

'We're talking about death, as usual,' said Yvette, smiling.

'Americans never talk about death,' said Charlie.

'You just spend a lot of money putting it off,' I said.

'Let's go live some life at my place,' said Charlie, biting his bottom lip and taking Yvette's arm and leading her away.

People were leaving. The tray floated past once more. At the door, Charlie detached himself from Yvette and she passed through first. Nina appeared in the doorway and blocked Charlie's path. Charlie warned her with his index finger and walked through her. By the time I got out, Nina was nowhere to be seen.

She came out of a door down a corridor with her

make-up in place. She told me she was tired and was going to go home. She was sniffing and blinking. We walked to the car, she opened the door, turned and held my face in both hands and kissed me hard. She got in, stared straight ahead, started the car, reversed out of the parking spot and drove off into the darkness with my overnight bag in her boot.

A couple from the party told me Nina lived in Kamina Village in the north of Lomé. I walked the couple of hundred yards back to the Armenian's house in the dreadful heat and sweated whisky.

# Chapter 17

The house was in darkness, the garden velvet black. The faint roar of the traffic and the sea widened the night, but the sky was starless, the low cloud hung overhead and sealed us in. I stumbled into the house expecting steps where none existed and frisked the walls for light switches, which must have been designed out of the house because I couldn't find them. The room pitched in my deprived senses and I reared away from things which turned out to be just more darkness with nothing in it.

A hand locked on to my ankle and I crouched and gripped the wrist. Bagado was lying on the floor in his raincoat doing a very good job of blending in. I gave him the letter from his mother. He propped himself up on an elbow. A match rasped and the room opened up in the uncertain light from an inch of yellow candle at Bagado's side. He drew up his leg and sent two long fingers probing down his sock. They came back with a two-inch penknife between them. He opened the blade, slit the envelope and replaced the closed blade down his sock.

'New socks?' I said.

'Kershaw's.'

'Why the sensory deprivation therapy?'

'The power's off.'

'Drink?'

Bagado read his letter, I poured a couple of fingers of Scotch into two glasses, set one down next to Bagado and sat on the floor at a right angle to him. Bagado folded the letter and blew out the candle. A colony of mosquitoes had moved in from the pool and started a feeding frenzy. We slapped ourselves about a bit, sipped whisky and smelt the snuffed candle twisting in the dead air.

Bagado's voice told me about his phone conversation with his friend Michel who worked in the French Embassy in Cotonou. Françoise Perec was not a French textile designer from Paris. She had been monitoring shipping for the International Maritime Bureau. The IMB was concerned at the increase in piracy along the West African coast and had sent a team to gather information. Françoise Perec had been assigned Lomé and Cotonou. She was ambitious, had done some undercover work before but couldn't be described as experienced. What interested Bagado was that her boyfriend worked for the French police's Drug Squad in Toulouse.

'They are becoming more daring, these pirates,' he said. 'They used to just board the ship and steal money and jewellery. Now they kill the crew, repaint and rename the ship, change the flag and papers and steal the cargo, and any other cargo they can find. They keep going until the ship gets too hot, then they sell it for scrap.'

'They couldn't do that working on their own,' I said.

'Somebody would have to trade the goods for them.'

196

'Somebody would have to organize them. That's a lot of forged paperwork for a bunch of ex-muggers, and how do they know which ships?'

'Perec was following a ship.'

'I found a message on Kershaw's answering machine in his office today. The Cotonou harbour master giving an ETA of the *Naoki Maru*.' Bagado sat up. 'That's the ship which brought in Jack's rice. The captain told me he'd also been to Lomé first to pick up some cashew and he'd already discharged in Abidjan and Tema.'

'Michel told me that these IMB people use local traders for their information. Charlie said that Perec and Kershaw knew each other. They could have been working together. Is the *Naoki Maru* carrying anything apart from rice?'

'Hi-fi.'

'Good cargo to steal.'

'Somebody tells Charlie that Perec and Kershaw are watching the ship. He doesn't like it. Follows them to Cotonou. Tortures Perec to find out what she knows and kills her. But he doesn't kill Kershaw there.'

'He killed him here in the master bedroom. I've found clothing in splinters of the door jamb and down the stairs. It looks as if rigor mortis had set in. He slid him down the stairs like a plank.

'He wanted Kershaw to run. It's more convincing. You could believe that Kershaw killed Perec by accident, panicked, got out of Benin, and drowned himself at the guilt of it. It's easier for the police to tie up and any investigations start moving the wrong way.'

I told Bagado about the party, about Nina's reaction to Kershaw's death and how she and Charlie weren't hitting any high notes together. She was asking him for something he wasn't prepared to give, or she was under some kind of pressure that Charlie could lift but wasn't going to.

'She's doing drugs too.'

'Which?'

'Cocaine. She left the room a few times, came back sniffing and firing on about twelve cylinders with her turbo whistling.'

'Heroin?'

'No needle marks on her arms or legs. If she's doing it, she's got to keep it quiet. She can't work in the US Embassy with needle rash all over her.'

'You think Charlie supplies?'

'What's he get out of it? He's not going to deal on his own doorstep.'

'Information. Control. She's going to do what she's told, isn't she?'

'He gets Nina to leak Kershaw's SM kink to me. I tell her Kershaw's dead and she realizes she's implicated in his death and doesn't like it. The water's got too hot and too deep.'

'Sounds like a good party,' said Bagado, lying back down.

'Yvette was with Charlie again and she knew about the Perec connection.'

'How?'

'She'd just come from nibbling Charlie's ear.'

'Is it Charlie's way of telling you he knows what's going on?'

'She's got Charlie by the pecker, which is how she holds most men. She could get anybody to tell her anything. She could be with Charlie, but she's strong enough to be a free agent.'

'Out for what?'

'Who knows,' I said, sucking some more whisky down. 'I've heard from two sources that Charlie's taken some bad hits trading gold . . . and there's one thing you need a lot of to trade gold.'

'Cash,' said Bagado. 'If this rice is what I think it is then what we need is a link between Charlie and Jack.'

We thought about that until Bagado slapped himself and yawned. I heard the whisky jug down his throat. He said he was going to stake out Charlie tomorrow while I put the pressure on Nina when I went to pick up my bag on the way to the airport. His fingers drummed the floorboards. The cicadas whistled in the garden and all but drowned out the sea and traffic.

'Where's Moses?' I asked.

'He met a big girl called Mercy from Ghana. I hope she shows him some. You owe him some money, too.'

'He always says that.'

'For the photographs.'

'Anything juicy?'

'They're mostly of the paintings, but there's two photographs of Kershaw with someone who I think is Kasparian, our Armenian friend from Abidjan. I'm waiting for B.B. to confirm. That's where Mercy fits in. She's taking the photograph to Accra, but it seems there's a price.'

'In that dimension, Moses is a millionaire.'

'She's a very big girl, Bruce, very big.'

Bagado's stomach made the sound of a distant wolf howling. A mosquito whined and banked off. The

199

whisky streamed off me and my brain fixed on nothing.

'Those paintings were painted by a dying man,' said Bagado out of the black. 'He knew he was going to die.'

'It's the only certainty in a post-Heisenberg world, my friend.'

'Some of us are more certain than others.'

'You've been lying in the dark contemplating mortality?'

'Immortality,' Bagado corrected me. 'It's why we have children. It's why we put flowers on graves.'

'Why people paint pictures.'

'It's an odd thing to do, to paint on the walls when there's yards of unused canvas in the back room,' said Bagado, rolling the empty glass on the floor. 'You can throw canvas away or burn it. The walls, even if they paint them over, are permanent or seem permanent.'

'Are you just being maudlin or are you taking me somewhere?'

'I have the feeling Kershaw was going to kill himself anyway. He's painted everything he's lost: youth, innocence, life. That painting on the ceiling in the other bedroom with the light coming through the clouds. What does that say to you?'

'If it's a vision of death, it's better than mine.'

'It *is* a vision of death. It's *my* vision of death. I used to just see black, now the last few years I'm seeing more light.'

'You're getting older, Bagado.'

'So?'

'You can't afford to be so final.'

'Maybe a power cut's not such a good time to talk about this.'

200

'We seem to be talking about sex and death.'

'Anything wrong with that?'

'Yvette told me sex and death is girls' talk. We get power and money.'

'I'm stronger on the first two.'

'Tell me about sex and death then, and make it simple, they're big themes for the time of night.'

'*A* death,' his voice said after a while. 'And you might not be happy about it.'

'Is this something about *a* death you should have told me before?'

'Maybe. It's something I remembered at the time but forgot a little detail until I called a friend of mine in London.'

'A police friend?'

'A retired detective called Brian Horton. He taught me how to play darts when I first went to London.'

'Must have been interesting for you. Let's have it.'

Bagado rolled his empty glass again and it hit me on the foot. I flicked it back at him.

'In the kitchen on the side,' I said. 'Bring the bottle.'

Bagado crawled on all fours to the kitchen and brailled his way to the whisky bottle. He came back, his hand sweeping across the floor searching for the glass. Liquid poured into the glass. It was a generous measure.

'Don't stint yourself, Bagado.'

'It sounded like two fingers.'

'Gloved. Come on.'

'Some time ago, maybe twenty years, I went to a lecture course called the "Psychology of the Psychopath".'

'Bad start, Bagado.'

'One of the case studies was about the torture and killing of a seventeen-year-old girl.'

'Where was this?'

'I was in London. The girl, I don't know. Brian's looking into it. The girl had been tied down, severely beaten, electricity had been used and she had been strangled.'

'How unusual is that for a modern murder?'

'It wasn't that modern. And there's a detail. The girl had money screwed up in balls and stuffed in her mouth which was taped.'

'And Françoise Perec?'

'When I got there the body hadn't been touched. Her mouth was still taped. I got everybody out of the room and stripped the tape off. Her mouth was stuffed with screwed up five thousand CFA notes, which, as you can imagine, had been well chewed.'

'What was the detail Brian remembered?'

'The notes in the girl's mouth in the case study were ten-dollar bills.'

'You don't remember anything else about this girl?'

'It was twenty years ago, one case in a ten-week lecture course. Neither of us could remember. It was just that the money was the significant psychological detail.'

'And the significance?'

'The idea of "paying back".'

'Where does that get us?'

'Françoise Perec was killed by a psychopath.'

'I hate psychopaths, you know – the accountant with seven wives in the chest freezer, the insurance salesman with a briefcase full of male genitalia. They can do a hard day's work and then come back to some midnight head-boiling. Where do they get the stamina?'

'Their intent, driven by whatever it is ticking away in a dark corner of their minds. One thing,' he said, 'all this psychological profiling, it's all rubbish. You don't try and understand a psychopath, you just try and catch him, which isn't so easy. They're very concentrated on what they are doing.'

'Kershaw's killer wasn't so concentrated. No water in the lungs.'

'Whoever killed Perec didn't kill Kershaw.'

'But it was connected.'

'A hired killer who was told what to do but it didn't turn out right, or it was too difficult to get him in the bath, or he didn't want him to have a lump on his head.'

'And the police were supposed to find the body.'

'Or you were,' he said. 'Time for bed.' Bagado lit the candle. He finished off a half inch of whisky, left the candle on the floor and went upstairs.

'The rest of the photographs are in the kitchen,' he said from the gallery and I heard his door click.

I blew out the candle. It was after midnight, a dangerous hour to start thinking with a headful of junk and system popping with alcohol. The projectionist got up in his box and started changing the reels. Heike's face cartwheeled into focus. Kershaw's stiffened body slid vertically over it and was swiped away by Nina Sorvino's whirling plait and the camera closed in on the thick black rope which became the creases in Bof Awolowo's ox neck which bubbled into the irrepressible rolling boil of a fart in a tub.

I wanted to think about Heike but the whisky wanted to surf the channels. After an hour, I felt like an American in front of a TV, the TV dinner uneaten, the ninety channels viewed for a maximum of thirty seconds each, the brain tired and confused, the body disorientated.

One more jolt of booze and Heike got the screen to herself, there was a net over the lens, soft focus again, the noise of slush filtered through. Another slug and the Bell's was ringing in my head and Heike was clear, sharp, black and white and laughing. We could laugh. That was something. Then cut to Heike naked on a bed. I desired that body. She wanted mine. That was something else. Cut to Heike drinking, then fighting and drinking more, and violence and vowing never to see each other again until morning, when all that remained were bad heads and a millilitre of rancour.

We attracted and repelled each other. Had the moments of repulsion added up? Was she testing me but really wanted out? Had she decided that I couldn't give her what she wanted? Did she know what she wanted? I used to make her feel alive. Maybe she doesn't want to be so alive any more. It was tiring. Did she want someone more house-trained, less of a raggedy old wolf, somebody who will always, and I mean always, put her first? Was I that person?

The sound of a Bakelite door handle wobbling against wood penetrated the refereeing of the cicadas. I was still sitting on the floor and my left eye had a clear line of sight to the door by the kitchen. The little light that came in with my visitor was not enough to show anything, but it meant I could make out the corner of the wall at the end of the corridor between the kitchen and the stairs.

I stood at that corner and listened to a hand moving along the wall, silent where the kitchen door was open and then again rubbing the smooth plaster to where I was standing. The hand reached the corner – a smell of perfume and dainty sweat. I swiped my hand down and connected with the wrist and pulled and twisted it so that the woman would have to spin around into me, which she did.

I was expecting the back of whoever it was to thump into my chest where I could hold her. The back came preceded by a sharp elbow which buried itself in my unprepared stomach wall and I went down with the noise of a cheap plastic sofa that's been sat on. I sensed a knee coming facewards and got both hands up and pitched myself forward, bringing the woman down underneath me. Her smell told me it was Yvette. I rolled off her in the least post-orgasmic way possible. She laughed and I sucked the dust off the floorboards.

'Do you always keep your elbow that sharp?'

'If I'm going out. I need room to dance.'

'Do you get many partners?'

'Only the ones I want.'

I lay on my back and massaged my stomach, suppressing a wriggle of nausea. The adrenaline seemed to have mopped up all the whisky and I felt a hangover doing press-ups in my head. Yvette's tilted face flickered yellow in the darkness and disappeared to a glow as she lit a cigarette. Her breath was sharp as the smoke cut her lungs. She was wearing the same jacket with the same lack of clothing underneath it that I had seen her in at Charlie's on Wednesday night.

'Did you come to steal some African art?'

'No,' she said. 'To see you.'

'What happened to knocking?'

'I thought you might be in bed.'

'Well, I'm still up. What do you want?'

'To talk. I'm a night bird.'

'Who starts?'

'You, if you want.'

'How long have you known Charlie?' I asked.

'Not very long.'

'How long?'

'We met on a Tuesday.'

'Tuesday last year, or five days ago?'

'Five days ago.'

'How did you meet him?'

'I was drinking in his bar.'

Her body shifted. The glow of her cigarette moved to my right. She drew on it, her lips hovered and went. Her face was probably only a few feet from mine. She leant back, I heard the candle plate tip. She flicked her cigarette at it and slid it along the floor.

'Love at first sight for Charlie.'

'My turn, Bruce,' she said, distracted as if she was staring up at the stars. 'Do you know what you are doing?'

'In love or work?'

'Both.'

'Sometimes.'

'That's not an answer.'

'It's your style.'

'Are you married?'

'No.'

'You have a girlfriend?'

'Yes.'

'Are you in love with her?'

The plate rattled on the floor as Yvette crushed her cigarette on to it. She moved closer. The tobacco on her breath and the vestiges of the evening's perfume flavoured the air.

'Are you?' she asked again.

'I don't know.'

'Then you know you're not.'

'A romantic speaks.'

'What about the realist?'

'He thinks: No compromise.'

'He thinks: I want my freedom. You're the sort who get depressed when you see families pushing shopping trolleys around supermarkets at the weekends?'

'I've never stopped to think. You're getting a lot of questions in your turn.'

'I'm curious.'

'Are you in love with Charlie?'

'He has his attractions.'

'Why are you with him?'

'He has a big powerful body.'

'Sex? That's good enough.'

'I wouldn't know.'

'Charity then?'

'My turn,' she said, tapping a fingernail on the floorboard. 'Do you know what you're doing in your work?'

'I had to find Steve Kershaw. I did. He was dead.'

'And now?'

'I'm waiting for his wife to identify the body.'

There was a shift of material, like the weight of her jacket falling off her shoulders. A cigarette slid out of a tight pack. A match ignited. Her face, shoulders and breasts wavered in a light that stilled, and remained, and remained and then was gone.

'Then what?' she asked, the smell of the spent match between us.

'I'll go back to Cotonou and buy sheanut.' I said, my eyes as wary as a bird's in a hedge.

'You know Charlie is a little annoyed with you?'

'No.'

'He thinks you're chickenshit . . . Is that the word?'

'He's a sweet-natured guy.'

'And you get on with women. He doesn't like that so much, either.'

'He didn't like that in Kershaw. Has Charlie got a problem with women?'

'Why do you ask?' she said, and the glow of her cigarette brightened, her lips came and went. Her chin rested on a round bare shoulder, the arm straight to the floor.

'You look as if you might know.'

'Have you ever seen him with a woman?'

'No, but I'm not as close up to him as you are.'

Tobacco and paper crackled and Yvette drew her breath in tight.

'He wants to fuck me,' she said exhaling long and hard.

'Is that unreasonable?'

'He doesn't know how to get me to do it.'

'Are you helping?'

'Why should I, he's old enough now.'

'In some ways.'

'He's good at business.'

'Sure he is.'

'He's ruthless too.'

'He has to be.'

'He's very strong.'

'That's why you said you liked him.'

'But he's a little boy.'

The nose of her cigarette found the candle plate. I felt her breath on my cheek, her breast touched my bare arm. She kissed me on the lips, her small tongue flickered over mine. Our lips parted, her mouth stayed close.

'You're the second woman to kiss me tonight without my asking.'

'We need permission?'

'You need a reason and my good looks aren't enough.'

She shrugged her jacket back over her shoulders. Her smell moved away. A droplet of sweat careened down my spine. The cicadas renewed their whistling, unless they'd been there all along.

'How did you know about the woman in Kershaw's apartment in Cotonou?'

'I had dinner with a friend of mine from the French Embassy last night.'

An aching memory bank told me she was eating with Charlie in the Sarakawa last night. She didn't look like the kind of woman who was taking two dinners a night.

Yvette stood up, I joined her with a rush of blood. I

couldn't make out what time it was. I was sobering badly. Somewhere in the room was a half bottle of vaporized whisky. We found our way into and out of the alley between the maid's quarters and the house. In the street, a light had come on but it had no interest in illuminating beyond itself. Outside the front gate, Yvette's taxi with the blue furry dashboard stood with its driver sprawled back in his seat as if he'd had his throat slit. I opened the door for Yvette and the driver hit his seat mechanism which jack-knifed him against his windscreen.

As she got in, I could see in the dim neon light that her face had collapsed with tiredness. She said good night and closed the door. Her head clicked back as if a screw had loosened, her arms supported her on either side. The driver got the engine started seventh go. Yvette didn't move. The taxi rocked over the mud road. Its single working tail light blinked and went out. I stood in the shadow of the wall, my head hung on my chest. After a few moments, a dark car with no lights on pulled out fifty yards further on and settled behind the taxi.

I couldn't find any keys to the gate or the front door so I left them open. I found a mosquito net in the bottom of Kershaw's wardrobe, rigged it up and flopped down underneath it in the nude. It was still and hot and sleep didn't come as easily as I expected. In the tumble dryer of my desiccated brain turned the questions: Who was Yvette? She came here for information, but for who? She talked Charlie down and vamped me out. She looked as tired as an actress after a long West End run.

The reel changed. Heike came back on and looked at me and smoked. It was a shrewd look, one that I didn't much like. The straining street light collapsed and died. The celluloid ran out on Heike. I slept.

The street light was on again when I rolled out from under the mosquito net. I walked to the bathroom and relieved myself lengthily until something hard pressed into my right kidney and stopped my flow. A voice said: 'Whatever you're doing or thinking of doing, drop it.' There was a flash of white and then the edges of my vision turned green, the floor rushed up to meet me and the lavatory became my friend.

I came to with my arms around the base of the toilet and my face cold against the tiled floor. I drew my head up to the bowl and vomited something ghastly into it, then crawled back to bed and lay down, shivering.

# Chapter 18

I didn't feel so amusing in the morning. I woke up with a mouthful of bad-egg saliva and a lump on my head like a horse's knee. Strange messages made their way down some bad wiring in my spine and my leg fizzed as if it was shorting out. My stomach made a noise like a dog yawning and I thought it might force me into another gruesome duet with my old pal.

On the way to the bathroom, I looked in on Bagado, who had gone. I showered and put on one of Kershaw's shirts and would have looked quite fetching with a foot of bare torso showing if it had been ridged and rock hard. It wasn't and the shirt came off with the sound of an ill-treated sack. I put on last night's shirt and smelled like a night club barman's table wipe at four o'clock in the morning.

Overnight, the stairs had become impossible to negotiate and the banister proved invaluable as my feet seemed to be doing both parts in the world's most complicated fandango. The fridge opened on to a grapefruit and a soggy pawpaw. The pawpaw didn't hold out both hands and I took the grapefruit, which had more pith on it than an Oscar Wilde aphorism. The first segment made me coy and put my parotid glands on red alert.

My head stepped in with some lefts and rights to the lower cortex and I put the grapefruit down and gave myself a minute's silence.

The car keys to my Peugeot were on the side next to the instant coffee, which backed away from me. The photographs were in their packet leaning up against a jar of gherkins. I picked them up and left the house, shouting for Moses and wearing somebody's sunglasses that held my head like a pair of ice tongs. The phone went and I returned and picked it up. It was B.B. confirming that the man in the photo was Armen Kasparian, the son of his Armenian friend who had been killed by the car bomb. B.B. was as keen to chat as I was to throw up so I just cut him off mid-sentence.

I made another attempt to leave the house and this time got as far as the alley when the phone went off again. I thought it might be B.B. looking for a rematch and was going to ignore it, but then I realized it might be Bagado or Moses. Clifford Harvey surprised me by remembering my name and inviting me to his house that night for a drink.

'Seven o'clock sharp, don't be late and don't be early.'

'Are you going to tell me why?'

'Not on the phone. It'll only take five minutes.'

'Short drink.'

'It's not social. G'bye.'

The third time I made it to the car, which was half under the shade of a bougainvillaea. It was the wrong half. The sun had carved itself a good space in the cloud and was hammering down. Moses hadn't showed and the driver's seat was hotter than a griddle. I threw the

213

photographs in the glove compartment and, alternating buttocks, drove north out of town to Kamina Village, a smart community for expats and rich Togolese with neat houses and gardens full of gardeners.

I passed the English school and the tennis club whose baked red courts were empty, but whose swimming pool fought it out with a hundred dive-bombing children with cream puffs on their arms. I asked a European woman, who was directing her gardener from a deck chair on her verandah, where Nina Sorvino lived. She took in my car, my unbrushed hair and unshaven face, and said she didn't know.

I cruised around feeling unwelcome amongst the hissing water sprinklers until I saw a guy in his late fifties who looked worse than I did, washing his car. Nobody washed their car who lived in this neighbourhood, so he stood out like a skull cap in Mecca. His limbs, sticking out of a tennis shirt and a pair of shorts that lost the Empire, were shaking more than an agoraphobic greyhound. He cared as much for Nina's security as he did for washing his car. He told me the way, and with a sly eye seemed to be on the brink of asking me in for a drink, when his wife came to the porch and shouted something that would have made a dog salute.

I left and watched in the rearview as the wife came down the drive and gave him a slap on the back of the legs and pulled him into the house by his ear. This rare scene left me feeling cold and depressed, even with the sun rippling through the high trees and children's voices not giving a damn for Sunday morning sleepers.

I took his directions past houses walled up against

the surrounding poverty beyond the Village and found Nina's house in a quiet corner on the outer perimeter. Her car was parked in an open garage. I walked up the short driveway, and the next-door neighbour's dog, which had been noisily lapping its genitals, stopped, looked up, flicked an ear and went back to his laborious task.

I knocked on the front door, then saw the bell, which must have been set at a pitch that only the dog could hear because he let out a belching growl. I went back to knocking then walked along the verandah and, after a scuffle with an aggressive banana palm that slapped me about and let me go, reached an air-conditioning unit that sighed even hotter air into the steamy late morning. There was a sleeping form beyond the light curtains in the room. It was after 11.30 which seemed respectable enough, even for the old soak washing his car, so I thumped on her window frame. I pounded, rattled and tapped. I whistled, hollered and roared. The dog came up on to the fence with his front paws, ears up and a look of total consternation across his intelligent face. He barked but it didn't help. I was getting uneasy.

At the end of the garage was a door. It opened into the kitchen and there was a door to the left into the living room. On the other side of the living room was a curtain and behind that two doors, one of which opened into Nina's frozen room.

She lay on the bed, twisted in a white sheet like a body committed to the deep. She had a black sleeping mask on that I had thought was strictly Hollywood. Her face was white, her lips pale. I expected to see a mist of snow sweeping across the Arctic floor. On the bedside table was a plastic container of pills with nothing in it.

I touched her arm which was cold, but not as cold as Kershaw had been. I tore off the mask, took hold of both shoulders, shook her and yelled her name. Her head lolled around and the sound of a very drunk person trying to say the word 'ululation' came out of her. I laid her back on the pillow and slapped her face gently from side to side until she showed me the whites of her eyes and begged me to stop. I made a cup of coffee that would have woken the entire audience of a Rotarian's after-dinner speech. She got it down and began to say my name in just two syllables. I got her on her feet and let her pin-ball her way to the bathroom for a half-hour shower. She came out with a towel round her head and a long T-shirt on. Her eyes looked like fresh picked mushrooms.

'Who cut me out of the freeway bridge?' she said.

'Who poured you in there? How many of these did you take?'

'I don't know. I couldn't sleep. Is there any more coffee?'

I poured her another cup. She stepped backwards as if she was on the gym beam and sat on a chair with her last night's clothes under her. Big fat tears started to roll down her cheeks and her shoulders began to shake. Her mouth came open with strings of saliva between her teeth and she let out a terrible wail. I took the coffee from her and she seemed to fall in on herself, shuddering from the wide black sobs that the pit of her stomach sent up through her body. After a minute, she stopped and held out her hand for the coffee as if she had been through nothing more than a mild choking fit.

'I get these crying jags,' she said, as if it might have slipped past me.

'You've just taken enough sleeping tabs to put the whole of Brooklyn under . . .'

'Yeah, tell me about it, Bruce. What you doin' here anyway?'

'You drove off with my bag.'

'I did? That's why you smell like the bottom of last night's glass.'

'Can I use your shower?'

'Maybe I'll hose you down in the garden. You might ruin the bacteria balance in my septic tank.'

She gave me the keys and I took the bag out of the boot. I showered and shaved, which did my head no good, and I looked in her medicine cabinet for an aspirin. I took three and put the bottle back and found a razor blade, a hand mirror and a little baggie of white powder at the back of the bottom shelf. I dipped a wet finger in and rubbed my gums. It was cocaine. She was snorting herself up with the coke and bringing herself back down with the sleepers.

She was still sitting on her clothes when I came out. She stared at the S-bend of the sheets on her bed and held the coffee cup in the palm of her hand.

'Do your crying jags have anything to do with Kershaw?' I said to the back of her head.

'He's dead.'

'You were upset last night.'

'I was?'

217

'More upset than you should be for someone you ditched as a pervert.'

Her towelled head straightened and after a few moments she turned and looked at me out of the corner of her eye. Too much was going on in the puffy eye that she fixed on me for me to understand a fraction of what was happening in there. She turned back as if she was performing her morning stretch exercises.

'I'm pregnant,' she said.

'By Kershaw?'

Her neck shook as if it was suddenly too fragile to support her piled head. She held out the coffee cup and said: 'Gimme a drink and I'll tell you about it.'

I filled the cup in the kitchen and came back to find Nina on the sofa in the living room with a bottle of brandy in her lap and a cigarette in her mouth. She put the cigarette down on the edge of the table and took the coffee, sipped it and poured a slug of brandy in, then sipped it again and poured some more brandy in.

'Do you want ice and soda with that?' I asked, and she answered by plugging the cigarette back into her mouth.

'Six months ago I started a relationship with Charlie. Shit, relationship – I call it that but it was more like seeing a married man who's getting the blahs from sex with his wife. I go round to his place, we fuck, he comes round to my place, we fuck. Hell, a girl gets tired of being a semen deposit.

'I pushed him for more; you know, something really demanding like dinner out together once in a while. He gave me the: "Yeah, sure honey", and two weeks later I'm still the exercise bike. The problem is, I like him. He's a big strong guy and . . . hell, there ain't nobody else, that's for sure. But I reckon I got some class so I tell him' – she sipped her coffee and dragged on the cigarette – 'I tell him I'm gonna have to look for someone else who gives me a bit more of their time. He laughed at me.

'I meet Steve. Not really my type. He made me feel kinda big. But a hell of a lot better than the Lebanese. We date. I stop seeing Charlie. Charlie's pissed as hell. Gets all proprietorial and shit. I mean, the guy's shown me as much attention as a rubber doll and then when somebody else gets on, he flips.

'He says he can't stand Steve. Says he's gonna kill him. All that kinda baby stuff. The guy's shit hot in business, he pulls off deals that nobody else can, he talks to anyone from the President down to the *gardien* but with women he's like a kid with a toy.

'So, Steve starts to get weird. I make a mistake. I tell Charlie. I mean, I need to talk to somebody and Charlie's the guy I want to notice me so I tell him. Charlie sends someone round to "talk" to Steve. I mean, you gotta understand the hate going on here. The sexual jealousy was incredible.'

'When did all this happen?'

'A couple of weeks ago. I told you I saw him in the restaurant a couple of weekends ago. Charlie had already "spoken" to him by then.'

'What did he say?'

'He told me he asked Steve to leave me alone or he'd have him killed.'

'What sort of talk was that?'

219

'Unnecessary. Steve didn't give a shit about me any more.'

'But did Charlie mean it?'

'It was just talk, Bruce,' she said leaning forward giving me a deep dumbo voice. She lit another cigarette from the one she was about to put out and sipped the brandy. She put her feet up on the sofa, crossed at the ankles, and lay her head back in the cushioned corner and smoked at the ceiling.

'You saw Charlie again after this?'

'Whaddaya mean "saw". You going biblical on me?'

'Did you sleep with Charlie again?'

'Hell, Bruce, this is private. Jesus. What's with this cop stuff?'

'A woman was found dead in Kershaw's apartment in Cotonou. Kershaw was found dead in his house in Lomé. It looks as if they caught it on the same day.'

'What's that gotta do with me going to bed with Charlie?'

'I'm trying to work out what was happening last night.'

'I'm not following you.'

'Between you and Charlie at the party.'

'Oh, that. Nothing special.'

'You were asking him for something he didn't want to give you.'

'No, I wasn't and no, he wasn't.'

'Do you know whose baby it is? Was that what it was?'

I was standing in the middle of the floor looking down at her. She got up and stood in front of me, her face a few inches from my chest and tilted her head up to look at me.

'I told you last night I liked you. Now I'm going to

show you how much I like you.' She saw my eyes flicker. 'That means I'm gonna trust you, not fuck you. There's not many people round here who can say that.' She puffed aggressively on her cigarette and squinted at me through the smoke. 'How much more have you gotta do on Steve's case?'

'Meet his wife this afternoon and identify the body tomorrow.'

'Just do that and then drop it.'

'Drop it?'

'That's what I said – it's American for quit.'

'That's what somebody else said to me at four o'clock this morning.'

'Who?'

'I don't know, but they seemed to think I needed a close look at the bathroom floor.'

'Then take the advice,' she said, and went back to the sofa and crushed her cigarette out, stabbing at the ashtray.

'Tell me about Yvette.'

'She's a lady who's got her hooks into Charlie.'

'What else?'

'I don't know. She hasn't been around long enough.' She lit up again.

'You've spoken to her?'

'We've met,' she said, with nothing in her face except three strands of smoke.

'What about the drugs?'

'Bruce!' she said through gritted teeth. 'You're not doing what you've been told.'

'You're snorting coke, popping downers and drinking brandy in your nightshirt.'

'Back off!'

'Are you scared?'

'Not as much as you could be.'

'Charlie supplies the drugs. What do you give him? Sex and soul?'

'Get outa here,' she said taking a rip drag from her cigarette and pointing the two fingers that held it at me. 'I said I'd trust you and you're kicking me in the teeth.'

'You haven't trusted me with anything.'

'I've trusted you with the advice that's gonna keep you alive.'

'Tell me something.'

'This is a dangerous situation and a difficult person. If I tell you anything you'll stick your nose in and get your head taken off.'

'I don't buy this crap about Kershaw and bondage. It's too pat. A dead girl's body is found in a bad way in Kershaw's apartment and a couple of days later you push me this line about Kershaw hurting you. Did Charlie put you up to that?'

Nina shook from her head to her heels in one zigzag shudder and she reached for the brandy bottle. The neck didn't rattle against the coffee cup rim as she poured, but it wanted to.

'Who's this girl you keep talking about?' she asked, looking into the cup.

'Ask Charlie, he'll fill you in. Tell him not to spare the details. It might change your mind about going to bed with him again.'

'I've got lunch at the golf club. You better go.'

'Lucky I came along. You wouldn't have come out of that until Monday morning.'

'If I need a nanny, I'll give you a call.'

'Maybe Kershaw gave you the drugs, just like Kershaw got a kick out of hurting you. Dead men are good to have round. You can dump all the shitty stuff on them and they never squeal.'

I went into her room and picked up my bag; she stood in the same spot, cup and cigarette attached.

'If you *are* pregnant, I should ease up on the drugs, booze and fags or you'll give birth to a stand-up comedian.'

'Fags?' she frowned.

'Thanks for the shower.'

'Any time, Mom.'

We arrived at the front door together. She leaned against the jamb. We faced each other.

'You're angry, which is not cool,' she said, weighing every word. 'Just calm down and take the advice.'

'I thought advice was the stuff that businessmen give you a lot of before you succeed and after you fail.'

'Sometimes it's the stuff that friends give each other so they can ignore it.'

'You tell me why I should and I'll take it.'

'But you won't and you'll get yourself killed.'

'I still won't and I'll still get myself killed.'

I turned and she said to the back of my head, 'Can you keep my out of hours habits to yourself. I've gotta job I need to keep.'

I walked to the car thinking Charlie must have that on her as well. The next-door's dog kept pace with me to the gate and got his paws up on it. I threw the bag in the car and got in after it. Nina stood in the doorway with her arms folded and smoke curling off her shoulder. I started the car and the dog's ears flickered and he looked across at Nina, concerned. Maybe he came from a broken home. I drove out of the Village and headed east to the airport.

# Chapter 19

Along the road in the red dust was a different suburb of Lomé. Pock-marked mud walls supported sheets of rusted corrugated iron. Spastic wooden frames were held together by thatched palm leaf. Woodsmoke rolled its shoulders out of fires which heated large black cauldrons in which three-foot wooden spoons stirred a white gelatinous cake.

A couple of girls with better shoulder muscle definition than a pro boxer took it in turns to pound cassava. Three girls sat in a line. The eldest plaited the middle girl's hair into perfect pentagonal shapes tying a little tail in each. The middle girl plaited the youngest one's hair into tight rat's tail braids, the unfinished side of her head looking like an exploded mattress.

I stopped at a stall where a despondent teenager sat in front of a pile of green oranges. She opened up a couple of them for me, I paid and she rolled the money up in her wrap. A group of boys played with their homemade toys. The biggest had a truck made out of coat hanger wire, the youngest a chariot made out of a tomato purée tin and two beer bottle tops for wheels.

A *tam-tam* started and all the bodies, sitting or standing, responded. A pink baby was getting a wash from a gigantic woman who tossed it around like a pineapple she was about to buy. The baby was showing her what a pair of small untrained lungs could do and two young boys stood on one leg apiece with sticks in their mouths and watched.

When I got back to my car, two girls in second-hand dresses which were split down their backs to their pants were preening themselves in the wing mirror. They saw me and ran off and started playing a pat-a-cake game which involved sudden pronking and mid-air footwork which would have left my feet tied in a bowline.

The oranges injected me with something lacking in my system and I approached feeling reasonable with understandable care. Ten minutes later, I arrived at the airport which looked like an American country club with palm trees, green lawns and flowers. I parked up and a group of kids sprinted over and volunteered to guard the car. I asked them against what and a cocky-looking fellow with one eye said: 'Us, we slash your tyres you no pay us.'

I span a coin in the air and a cartoon brawl started with a lot of dust, feet and fists until one boy shot out pursued by the pack and they ran out of the parking area.

A woman at the information desk with half-shut eyelids managed to tell me that the KLM flight was delayed with no ETA. Moments later, her head lay on her fleshy arm on the desk.

In Arrivals, a large, well-trussed woman in bright green and red cloth fanned herself with a postcard while her ascetic husband, a hat on the back of his head, appraised the way his fingertips met each other between his knees. I reached the glass partition between

Arrivals and Departures and supported myself on the aluminium frame. I was about to let my brain slide into 'motor reflexes only' mode when I saw Jack and Charlie arrive in the Departures hall, followed by Bagado who, mirrored in the polished floor, strode with the purpose of a fare-paying passenger who was a little late. Jack and Charlie checked in at the Nigeria Airways desk for the 13.10 Lomé/Lagos flight that was leaving in thirty minutes. They got their boarding passes and went through passport control, leaving Bagado spinning like an ice-skater on an empty rink.

I went round to the Departures hall and Bagado skimmed across and fell on me as if I'd just taken the china he'd wanted at the Harrods sale. I handed him a fold of notes and he pushed away from me arriving at the check-in desk with a toe-stubbing abruptness. The Nigeria Airways girl told him that the flight was fully booked but that two passengers so far hadn't showed and if one of those failed to check in he could buy that seat. Bagado turned in a monstrous performance about how people should be checked in at least an hour and a half before take-off, but this cut no ice with the girl at the desk who pointed out that he hadn't been either, and he didn't even have a ticket.

He asked the girl how long he had to wait before she would sell him the ticket. She looked at a slim, expensive gold watch on her wrist and, enjoying every syllable of her power, told him five minutes. Bagado then stood in front of the desk with the malevolent body language of a defensive linebacker.

An American turned up wearing a pair of trainers which looked as if they had a tank of goldfish in the soles and Bagado gave him the ocular equivalent of a straight-arm tackle. The American veered away and straightening his Red Sox baseball cap came in from another angle. Bagado stood at the desk with his back to the American. The girl looked over his shoulder and asked for his ticket which the American passed over Bagado's head. She checked the American in. Bagado whipped back on to her and told her the five minutes were up. She flicked her wrist up and said: 'Four minutes and fifteen seconds.'

Bagado put an elbow up on the desk and turned to give me a look of nodding smugness that in an instant changed to slit-eyed intent. His poisonous look fell on a small bearded man with swivelling eyes, drinker's purple on his cheeks and nose, and a blue funk vapour trailing off him. Bagado came to my side and hissed, 'Keep him away from here.'

I was on the bearded guy in a matter of seconds and caught him by the arm which had a maroon Qantas bag over the shoulder and hopped him to the restaurant steps.

'What's going on?' he said in an Australian accent.

'I'm sorry, sir. My name is Zeger Van Harten; I work for KLM.'

'I'm not flying with KLM.'

'But we want you to. It's part of our new publicity programme. We establish that all the check-ins are closed and then we choose at random somebody to be our guest for lunch.'

'All the check-ins are closed?'

'Yes, sir,' I said. He looked around and I swayed in front of him.

'Well, you know, I don't mind if I do,' he said, holding out his hand. 'Mike Pocklington.'

'Pleased to meet you, Mike. You're Australian, aren't you?'

'That's a pretty good English accent you've got there, Zeger.'

'Thank you,' I said, hoping I didn't have to demonstrate my Dutch.

Once I got him in there and we were sitting in front of a perfect *steak, frites, salade* with a bottle of cold Beaujolais, he relaxed a little more than I expected him to and we had an interesting conversation about Australian Aboriginal and African animist religions. There was a sweaty moment during the second bottle of Beaujolais and a slice of brie when a badged KLM rep walked past and Mike, the red veins cracking on his nose, took the opportunity to thank the staff. I smiled and managed to convey with my eyebrows only, that my companion was on the fourth day of a seven-day bender.

I paid the bill and asked Mike what he was going to do in Lagos.

'Lagos?' he said. 'I'm going to Ouagadougou, mate.'

I've never liked eating alone and I've got a butter mountain of generosity in my soul but I found myself hard-pressed to smile when I found the Ougadougou flight didn't take off until 16.15.

'What were you doing here at quarter to one, Mike? Three and a half hours before your flight, and where's your luggage?'

He patted his Qantas bag and blinked at me through the haze of red wine that shimmered off his nose. 'I get nervous, I don't like getting bumped off, I have to find out what plane it is, I have to get a seat near the emergency exit, I have to go to the toilet, everything has to be right . . .'

I patted his shoulder and walked away from him before I stiffed him into a baggage trolley.

# Chapter 20

The Nigerian Airways girl confirmed that Bagado had got the flight and the last passenger had never showed. There was a return flight that evening and another tomorrow morning, early. Back in Arrivals, the KLM flight had an ETA of four o'clock. I sat down next to the woman fanning herself with the postcard and dozed on my Beaujolais pillow for an hour.

At four o'clock, I went to the car. The covert surveillance team had been as good as their word and not slashed the tyres, although since they'd scarpered the car had let itself go and taken on the over-relaxed air of a couch potato. I took a couple of old fan belts out of the front seat well, cleaned the tray beneath the glove compartment of old bulbs and petrol filters and thumped the upholstery. I found a piece of paper on the back seat, shook the red dust off it and with the intestine of an old biro wrote 'KERSHAW' on it.

I took the photographs out of the glove compartment and flicked through them until I got to the one remaining photo of Kershaw with Armen Kasparian. Kershaw had his arm around Armen's neck in a mock lock and Armen was supporting himself on Kershaw's stomach. They were standing in front of the right-hand half of the painting of the girl with the bowl of fruit and both were laughing. I folded them away and threw them back in the glove.

The Customs officials were enjoying themselves going through wealthy people's bags and occasionally held up items which the passengers would rather not have had on public display. At half past four, a woman with shoulder-length brown hair, already lank from the heat, approached me and held out her hand.

Catherine, or Kate, as she preferred, was unhealthily slim. Her arms were all tendons and sinew with dog-bone elbows and wrists. Her small, sharp breasts jutted through the faded material of her shrunken T-shirt like two teepees and her baggy jeans with their nail-tearing grip on her hip bones looked as if they were about to disgrace her. This was a woman who had lost a lot of weight in a short time.

Her skin colour was muddy, an old tan overlaid with London grey and pricked with half an hour of tropical heat. Her skull was evident around her eye sockets, her cheekbones sending scimitar blades off to her ears and her hatchet-sharp nose had nostrils that winced under the strain. Her mouth had full lips, incongruous amongst all the edges, but she had a pleasant smile if you ignored the nicotine-stained teeth and a tongue still with its travel coat on.

I took her bag and walked her to the car. We left the airport with my head aching, but feeling comfortable with the self-possession of the woman sitting next to me who smoked with her elbow on the window ledge and her hand held out into the oncoming breeze.

'This is my first time in Africa,' she said, her lips kissing the filter of her cigarette.

'It's a bit different over this side.'

'I was going to ask you. Where are the animals? Where are the thorn trees? Where are those tall red natives standing on one leg with big holes in their ears drinking cow's blood and milk cocktails?'

'I saw an elephant in Nigeria once and some Yahoo baboons, there are thorn trees in the sub-Sahara, but I've never seen a Masai anywhere near here.'

'It's not as dirty as I expected.'

'It tries a bit harder when it rains.'

'So does London.'

'How is it?'

'Well, you know, property is falling, businesses are folding, school standards are dropping, hospitals are closing, crime is rising, homelessness is getting worse and the "green shoots of recovery" are supposed to be protruding, but they don't like it.'

'Any good news?'

'The banks are suffering, and I bought you some Marmite – already open, I'm afraid. It's all I could think of in the time. Is that OK?'

'Inspired.' My last visitor had bought me custard powder. I hated it, he loved it. He was the kind of kid who bought his mother a football for her birthday.

I took her the most scenic route possible across the lagoon and through town to the coast road. The town was quiet, still a little bruised after the rioting, and with a Sunday suicide feel to it. We hit the sea and Kate's polluted spirits rose as she saw the spangled water, kids playing football and palms applauding shabbily in the breeze. She asked if she could go and see the house and her husband's work. 'Those kids play-ing football reminded me. Steve described a painting to me, one with two boys on the beach playing with a lemon.'

She didn't want to take a shower and change first, so a few minutes later we pulled up outside the house. Before we went in, I gave her the photograph of Armen and her husband. She looked at it and something strange happened to her face. She started to smile and then stiffened as if she'd had a backhander across the cheek instead of a caress. She asked to keep it. I shrugged, got out of the car and opened the gate for her. Kate fingered the ducks and tortoise knocker. I opened the side door to the house but Kate carried on into the garden.

She looked at the pool. The parrot whistled her up and she crossed the lawn to the aviary. He put his beak through the chicken wire and with one eye dared Kate to scratch it, which she did. The parrot said something along the lines of 'Sniggedy', which neither of us under-stood, but it prompted Kate to talk.

'I told you we weren't close, which was true. In the last three or four months before he went away, I didn't see much of him, but we spoke on the phone. We've been married for twenty years,' she said, pulling her finger away from the nut-cracking beak just in time. 'I miss him.'

We walked back to the house, the parrot giving us the bird. 'He couldn't get over losing it all. Everything he'd worked for gone. I told him it didn't matter. I'm not a great one for the luxuries of life. But he thought he'd failed me. He didn't believe me that it didn't matter. He left me and came down here. He'd done some business in Africa. I suppose coming here, he didn't feel like such a failure. You know, success is rammed down your throat everyday in England. You read the Sunday newspapers and you think everybody's made it except you.

'Then he asked me to send the art materials down. He sounded positive. He'd picked up the job, which meant he could move out of the hotel. And he got inspired to paint again. He used to paint when we first got married, portraits, mostly of me. Not good enough to sell, but I liked them. Then he got involved in work and that was the end of it. Until Africa . . .'

She went upstairs and looked at the paintings on her own while I fed and watered the parrot. Afterwards, I sat down next to the woman and child wood carving and thought about cold beer. She came down half an hour later and sat on the sofa opposite me. The sun was on its way down but it was hot, and fresh from England, Kate was wilting like a snapped-off house plant. She looked like someone who needed a cold beer and I went into the kitchen and split a big Eku into two glasses. She took two large gulps from her frosted glass which started tears in her eyes and I went back and picked up the kitchen paper roll and put it next to her. She put her glass down and tore off three feet and buried her face in it.

'What do we do?' she asked.

'Do you want to go through this now?' I said, unprepared for what I had to do. I shuffled around for easy ways into what was going to be a difficult discussion. Kate just nodded, picked up the beer and sipped it.

'We're going to identify the body tomorrow morning at the hospital morgue. I've no idea what the police are going to say to you. I don't even know what verdict they will record. I'm fairly sure they haven't done any investigation and knowing Africa they'll just want a little bribe and get everything out of the way with as little trouble as possible. But I don't know. I think it's best you get all the facts so whatever they say you're not going to get any surprises, because if they think they can roll you, we could be here for months.'

She put her glass between her knees and pulled a pack of cigarettes from a carton of twenty which she stashed back in her large handbag. She lit up and held the glass between the fingertips of both hands. The smoke curled up over the rim of the glass and Kate stared down at the white frothy head of her beer.

I started with what B.B. had said about Kershaw. When I mentioned B.B.'s opinion about Kershaw's fondness for talking to women, Kate flinched, but no more than I'd expected. I moved on to Charlie, told her about the bar and how Kershaw was seen frequenting it with a number of different women. Kate tensed, the skin seemed tighter across her cheekbones and the wrinkles around her eyes smoothed out. The tendons in the back of her hands stood out and each metacarpal with them. I moved on to Nina Sorvino and felt the sweat trickling over each vertebra on its way down my back as I came closer to the point.

'And?' asked Kate.

'She ditched him, she says, because he was into bondage and sado-masochism.'

Kate's spine stretched about a foot with indignation

and she sat bolt upright, her eyes slashing through the smoke that hung in the purple light between us. Her top lip tightened against her teeth and began to go white.

'Is this woman reliable?'

'I don't think so, but I'm not sure.'

'Is she a tart?'

'No.'

'Who the hell is she that she can say these things about my husband to you?'

'I'm telling you what's happened and what's been said. Let me finish. It'll make other things clear.'

She sat back in the sofa with her pointed chin on her evident sternum and looked at me from under her forehead, her eyes barely visible.

'A woman called Françoise Perec was found dead in your husband's flat in Cotonou. She was tortured and murdered, we think on Monday morning. Your husband died here, we think in the evening. The bag containing the instruments used to kill Françoise Perec was found upstairs. The police have it now.'

Kate Kershaw didn't say anything to that. There wasn't a lot to be said, apart from something like 'Jesus Christ'. Her smoking rate went up to forty drags a minute and I broke another Eku out of the fridge. I took her upstairs and opened up the chest of drawers. She peered in gingerly and reared away from the hideous pornography.

'Your husband's prints are on these magazines. They were also on the whip handle which the police took away.'

'Mr Medway,' she said, having called me Bruce up

237

until now. 'Do you think the person who painted these pictures could hurt anybody?'

'No, I don't. Although there are plenty of people who would tell you that sex isn't logical and that Africa can have a strange effect on people.'

This earned me a steady look from her that demanded an explanation.

'I'm saying your husband's been framed.'

'How do you know?'

'I know he was murdered.'

'Do you have any proof?'

'When I pulled him out of the pool there was no water in his lungs.'

She sat down on the bed. The light in the room was deep purple and then suddenly it was night. I switched the light on. Kate took a golf ball of tissue out of her pocket, unravelled it and blew her nose.

'This is Africa, Kate,' I said. 'Things happen differently here. The police are being controlled. There was no investigation here and there was a cover-up of the Françoise Perec killing in Cotonou. It's possible when we go to the morgue you'll find that you'll be required to sign release papers that indicate your husband died from drowning and that he committed suicide. This is not true but if you kick up a fuss about the autopsy and try going to the British Embassy for help you'll find a lot of obstacles, not least of which is some damning evidence. It'll take a long time and you'll need money. I am trying to find out what happened to Françoise Perec and your husband, but people are not being very helpful.'

'I have no time and no money.'

'I know. I'm only telling you all this because you look like someone who'd want to know what happened.'

'Do you suspect anybody?'

'A local businessman.'

'What about the trollop?'

'Nina? She knows something but she's too scared.'

'Why?'

'I don't know.'

'What do you think?'

'I'm still not sure.'

'What would you do?'

'In your situation I would sign the papers, take your husband's body home, bury him and forget all about it.'

'In fact, I have no choice.'

We went back downstairs and finished the beers in silence. Kate smoked slowly but with such intensity that the cigarettes burned like a bush fire just to get it over with. We left the house and drove to the Hotel Sarakawa.

A band littered the lobby with musical instruments and splayed legs. I booked Kate in and asked her if she would like to have dinner later on. She said she'd prefer to be on her own, and looking at the frown lines on her forehead and the yellowing bruise of the nicotine stains on her fingers, I was glad. I was about to give her some money for expenses when she had second thoughts.

'Come and have a drink,' she said. 'I can't face dinner. I can't really face the bar with all these people. I'd like it though. We've had a lot to go through for a couple of strangers . . . unless you're just being polite?'

'It'll have to be now,' I said, looking at my watch.
'Fine. I'll take a shower. You get the drinks.'
We followed the young bellhop to her room.

Kate took her bag into the bathroom and I took up one of my favourite pastimes – wrecking the mini bar. Kate shouted for gin and tonic and I poured myself a double Red Label. I slid open the balcony door and walked out into the sea breeze and the purling light from the underwater-lit swimming pool below. It was quiet out there, with only the palm trees rattling and distant voices insulated by darkness.

A barman in a short white jacket wiped down the pool bar counter and drew the shutter. He came out of a door at the side and reached in to turn off the light, his hand in his pocket after the key. A voice called him from a table set back from the pool half in the dark. He walked over. There were two women sitting there. *'C'est fermé maintenant,'* he said.

One of the women gave him a note and said something, leaning across the table, her face in the light from the pool. It was Jasmin. The barman went back to his bar and came back out with two drinks on a silver tray which he set on the table. *'Merci. Bonne soirée,'* he said and backed off. He locked up and walked off around the pool and into the hotel.

Yvette, the other woman, was standing by the pool now with her back to the water talking to Jasmin and using her sandalled foot to scratch the bare tendon of her left leg. Jasmin leaned forward in her usual T-shirt and jeans and slurped the top off her over-full drink. Yvette went back to her chair and on the way ran her hand around Jasmin's shoulder, stroking her neck and hair and then held her head to her stomach while Jasmin leaned in like a cat, enjoying it. There was something in that gesture which was more than just girlish affection. These were two people who were used to touching each other, who were lovers and had been for some time.

'Bruce?' said a voice behind me which sent a bolt of white hot iron up my back.

Kate Kershaw stood at the balcony door in a fresh T-shirt and cotton trousers with a towel around her shoulders, rubbing her hair.

'Your gin and tonic's on the bedside table,' I said, feeling furtive and trying to keep it down, out of my eyes. She didn't move for it, but rubbed her hair and looked through me.

'Are you married?'

'No,' I said. 'I don't seem to be the type.'

'What type are you?'

'The type who does the wrong kind of work with the wrong kind of people. The type that doesn't give enough of the right sort of attention. The type ... Christ, the wrong type, that's all.'

'Are you the faithful type?' she asked the night air over my left shoulder before focusing on me and regretting the question. 'You don't have to answer.'

She turned into the room and picked up her drink and took a three-fingered slug of it. The coldness and the fizz springing tears which she wiped with the towel. I ducked into the room.

'I've tried being unfaithful,' I said. 'Didn't like it.'

'Not even the screwing?'

'The lying was the problem.'

She finished her drink, handed me the empty glass and I made her another.

'He's dead,' she said, taking the full glass from me, 'and all I can think of is the bloody women.'

'When my father died from a lung disease my mother spent a month asking me why the bloody fool had to keep smoking – the only time I heard her swear.'

'The women didn't kill Steve though, did they?'

'You have to get angry with him for something. You've been left behind.'

She sat up straight at that, and lit another cigarette, the smoke not mingling well with the smell of soap and shampoo and wet towelling in the room.

'That must be it,' she said, smoking with her mind off the job, her hand going up automatically, the smoke leaking out of her from everywhere.

I put my empty glass down.

'You want another ... Help yourself,' she said, crushing her cigarette out.

'I can drop by later if you want.'

'I'll be fine,' she said. 'You go. I'll see you tomorrow.'

I opened the door looking back. She lay on the bed now, her feet crossed at the ankles. She waved and then stared at the ceiling, folding her hands across her stomach.

Down in the lobby where the band was still waiting, I spoke to a friend who worked in reception who said he would look out for Kate in case she needed anything. I was about to leave when Yvette and Jasmin drifted over. They asked for a single room key. Despite the time of night, Yvette was wearing sunglasses. She saw me and pushed them down her nose and looked over the top of them in the only way possible.

'I had a visit from someone after you left last night,' I said.

'Someone I know?'

'Perhaps mutual.'

'What happened?'

'He hit me on the head.'

'Hard?'

'No, with a rolled up comic . . . What do you think?'

'Did he say why?'

'He told me to drop what I was doing.'

'And what *were* you doing?'

'At the time I was having a pee.'

'Bad advice.'

'Your taxi was followed last night after you left.'

She took her sunglasses off and swung them by the arm between her thumb and forefinger. Jasmin looked over Yvette's shoulder, the room key swinging from her hand.

'What are you doing here, Yvette?'

'I'm buying African art.'

'Are you?'

'I am,' she said, locking antlers. 'I buy in Zaire, Cameroon, Gabon, Nigeria, Benin, Togo, Ghana and Ivory Coast. We're thinking of expanding north to Burkina and Mali later this year.' She tapped Jasmin on the arm, who took a card from her purse, and gave it to me. Yvette Dussolier – L'Art des Africains and an address in Paris which meant nothing to me.

I clicked the card on my thumbnail. 'I might have something for you,' I said.

'Call me,' she said, raising her eyebrows.

'You must know a lot.'

'Enough so they don't roll me,' she said, walking to the lift.

I asked my friend if I could use the phone to call Gérard, a French retired hydrologist who collected African art, books and empty whisky bottles. While his phone rang, I got annoyed with Yvette and her fabricated sexiness, her cocky, air-plucked intelligence, her practised coolness. She was a fine act with a tough veneer but no heart to pull it off. The manipulation was showing like suspenders and stocking tops below a hemline. Gérard answered and I arranged to meet him at his house for a drink at ten o'clock. I turned away from the counter and ran into one of the musicians, a colossal African, who was as annoyed as I was, who'd done 'waiting in the lobby' for too long, whose face looked as if a bee had just flown up one of his cavernous nostrils.

# Chapter 21

The Harveys' house wasn't far from the Sarakawa but I was still going to fail on the first of Clifford Harvey's requests. It was close to half past seven when I arrived at his solid wooden gate. I pressed the bell and was surprised by the man himself answering on the intercom.

'You're late. Stay where you are,' he said.

I leaned back against the car and twenty seconds later Clifford appeared at the gate, well-dressed for an unobtrusive night-time chat in a lemon polo shirt, sky blue slacks and white shoes.

'I been calling you not to bother come,' he said. 'You can't turn up on time, I got no use for you.'

'Shall we call it good night then?' I said, getting into my car.

'You wait a minute!' he said in a voice that drew blood.

'I'm not the obedient type,' I said, closing the car door and fitting the keys in the ignition.

'This is delicate, Mr Medway,' he said, changing his tack but not his tone.

'How'd you get my number?' I asked, trying to get a better hold on the client relationship.

'Nina Sorvino gave it to me last night. Now look . . .'

'You look,' I said. 'Your money doesn't buy my

knuckles to rap. It buys me to work for you. Now what is it that we have to hang around outside your house exchanging pleasantries in the dark?'

He stared in at me through the open car window. The chief executive in him wanted to strip the pips off me but the man needed something so he took the bite out of his voice, just leaving the bark.

'My wife is having an affair. I want you to find out who with and get me photographic evidence that's good enough to use in a divorce court. You get it and you're two million CFA richer.'

'And how much richer are you, Mr Harvey?'

'That's none of your goddamn business.'

'I don't do domestics,' I said, starting the car. He didn't understand. 'I don't follow people's wives or husbands, loved or unloved ones. It's tacky and I have enough trouble looking at myself in the mirror every morning as it is.' I put the car in gear. 'What you've told me is totally confidential . . . even though I'm not working for you. Good night.' I drove off with Clifford Harvey featuring in my rearview for three hundred metres before I turned right and up on to the coast road to go back into central Lomé. I was glad I didn't have the time nor need the money so badly that I might've had to reconsider one of my two business ethics. As it was, if Bagado was right about Jack's rice that was my first business ethic shot to hell. If I'd had to take to snapping Jack with Elizabeth Harvey I could have found myself on the same ethical footing as a paparazzo.

I was looking forward to a lie-down with some aspirin in my veins and something cool on the back of my head. I pulled up outside the wooden gates to the house and didn't see them at first under the trees overhanging the wall on the other side of the street. I got out of the car. The officer who'd been in charge of the road block and who had also taken Kershaw's body away was sitting on the bonnet of his Peugeot. He beckoned me over.

'*Je suis fatigué*,' I said. '*Je vais me coucher.*'

Three of the car doors opened at once and four soldiers got out.

'*Je viens de repenser . . .*' I said, putting my hands up.

'*C'est bon ça*,' said the officer.

I was thrown into the same footwell as before. I recognized some of the same smells. The feet were planted on my back, the rifle butts next to them. There was little air down there and the sweat sprang out in fat gobs and ran into my hair. The car moved off. The deep breathing began and I noticed that the flash of anger I'd felt seeing Yvette gliding through the lobby with her lover had moved from the back of my head. It was now settled in my stomach. I could feel it like a hot crystal as I lay contorted over the hump of the drive shaft.

In twenty minutes, I was in the same leather and book room with the lazy overhead fan. There was the smell of pear drops, a solvent, as if someone had recently rain-proofed some sensitive buckskin shoes.

'Thank you for your call the other day,' said the deep voice in French. 'I'm sorry to drag you out at this time of night.'

'It's not the time of night, it's the dragging I'm not so keen on.'

'How very . . .'

'Don't talk to me about my amazing sang-froid, and don't call me M. Medway. The name's Bruce. What do you want this time?'

'More cooperation,' he said, with a little steeliness to his voice.

'The guy's dead. There's not much more I can do for you on that front.'

'I know he's dead,' said the big man in a way that told me the ice was getting thinner. 'Do you know how he died?'

I didn't answer that one and heard the man shift in his seat.

'The message you left said he'd been found in the pool.'

'That's right.'

'Drowned?'

'I presume.'

'You're wrong. I had an autopsy done. I'm told he was smothered by a pillow or cushion. What does this *tell* you?'

'He was murdered?'

'So that it would look like suicide.'

'And you're going to tell me why.'

'M. Kershaw had some money of mine,' he said, letting out a pained sigh. 'I gave it to him to trade with. He said he would give me a return of nine per cent.'

'What sort of trade?'

'Sheanut, cashew nut, cashew nut shell liquid, cotton seed and oil, cocoa . . . that kind of thing.'

'How much did you give him?'

248

'A million.'

'You're sending me to the ninth circle of hell and back for a million CFA ... For four and half thousand dollars?'

'Who said CFA?'

'If it's francs that's more the ticket.'

'Dollars,' he whispered.

I could hear him sweating now, and shaking out a large piece of cloth to mop it up with. I've found that with being in the presence of men who've taken bad financial hits in their lives the best policy was respectful silence. The thought of losing a million dollars could bring on sudden spasms of violence. Things could be bad – your wife could have left you, you could have a terminal disease but if you wanted to discuss those things with someone it's best not to choose a million-dollar loser because they'd just think you're whingeing.

When the big man finally spoke he'd got himself under control and I didn't think he'd start any casual baseball practice around my head.

'Whoever killed M. Kershaw has got my money. I want you to find him and I want you to get my money back.'

'What's wrong with the police?'

'This is not a police matter.'

'I'm not talking about official police. What about the people who took away the body, the officer with Kershaw's bag, the goons who bring me here. Why not them?'

'They are very loyal. They are my people. But I cannot have my people involved in my private affairs. You understand, I think.'

What I understood was that the big man had given Kershaw a million dollars of kick-back money to trade with and either somebody knew about it or Kershaw was careless and had got himself killed and the money stolen. The only person I knew who needed that kind of money and could get ugly enough to kill for it was Charlie Reggiani.

'I'll get back to you,' I said.

'I hope with good news this time,' said the big man from behind my head.

'You took your time coming back to me considering the money involved.'

'You've been away. I've had affairs of state. I have appearances . . .' He trailed off.

'When did you give Kershaw this money?'

'Last Sunday evening.'

'Why didn't you just take the money to Switzerland, for Christ's sake, like everybody else does?'

'You have to pay to keep it in Switzerland . . .'

'Not as much as it's cost you to give it to Kershaw.'

'. . . and these days, they're more careful about whose money they take.' He searched around in his head for another good reason. 'And M. Kershaw was a very capable man.'

'Is that it?'

'It's time for you to leave,' he said, irritated again, moving to the door.

'One thing,' I said. 'I need a favour from you. Mrs Kershaw is here to identify her husband's body and take it back to England. You don't need that body any more. I don't want any obstacles and I don't want to have to pay anything.'

'I guarantee it,' he said.

He knocked on the door. The boys came in.

'Do I have to travel underneath their boots?'

'If you're not seen you have a better chance of staying alive.'

I had another dark, uncomfortable drive back home during which I didn't protest, but calculated from the coolness of my sweat that the level of threat in the big man's final words might merit some measure of respect.

It was nearly ten o'clock by the time they dropped me off. I found a new bottle of Ballantines in the cabinet in the sitting room and went to meet Gérard. I thought about walking it but there was barely enough oxygen in the stagnant heat outside to light a match.

I parked outside Gérard's large crumbling house and pulled the metal hand that hung on a chain underneath the bougainvillaea that rolled over the walls. A boy came to the gate in a luminous white shirt.

He showed me to the living room. The walls were covered with shelves of books, and most of the floor space was occupied by piles of books, some of which had collapsed. In one corner, a drift of books reached four feet up the walls. Gérard lay on an ancient divan that spewed thick bolts of stuffing from several holes. His head was propped up on a faded rose bolster. He was reading by the light of two hurricane lamps, holding the book so close to his half-moon specs they must have been making contact.

He wore a faded blue shirt, open, with the tails hanging out and a pair of brown shorts. His gut rose and fell with the lack of rhythm of a man who fights hard for his air. I touched his bare calloused foot and he dropped the book on to his chest. I put the whisky on the table and Gérard muttered something. His boy must have had the hearing of a bat-eared fox because he came in with a pair of glasses and some ice.

We drank and Gérard stroked his short grey hair that was combed forward so that he had an inch of fringe at the top of his forehead. He disentangled himself from his wiry specs and rubbed the two divots on either side of his nose. His red face was lined with unmatching creases so that he looked as if he had two different sun-blasted faces put together. He began to brush the underside of his hairless chin with the back of his hand and his jowls quivered, connected as they were to his neck by two webs of slack, silky skin.

Gérard was prepared to read in English but he didn't like speaking it, and as he now knew I wanted something from him we spoke in French, me not understanding much of his Cevennes accent and he shuddering at my butchery. I asked him if he could give me something that would test the skill of an African art buyer. He smiled showing me a set of teeth that would have made an American faint. He had a couple of black ones, three yellow, and one a disturbing green. He put a finger up in the air, which gave me something else to look at apart from his ailing maw.

He had three goes at getting off the divan, slapping away my hands, and eventually opted for the western roll off the side on to all fours. He raised himself up and rested his hand on his belly and thought in silence for several minutes like a man with two storeys of chaos and no filing system. He picked up a lamp and limped off in one direction, sprawling a pile of books into another with his knee. He snapped the waistband of his shorts, and then, given his dire physical state, executed a competent sidestep and left the room.

His leathery soles scuffed the dry marble floor in the hall. A banister creaked and he climbed the stairs with hollow, boxy thumps. He gathered breath on the landing and resumed. I threw the whisky down and poured another and flung my arm over the two-seater sofa I was sitting in. It hit something hard and hairy. I glanced over the back, and a hog's head with some vicious tusks stared me out. There was a shout from upstairs and the boy flitted through in his ectoplasmic shirt and stuttered up the stairs making sure he used each step.

Their return journey was a laborious affair which saw off another glass of whisky and they emerged into the room with the boy carrying a sackcloth bundle and the lamp and Gérard holding the lad's head for support. Gérard sat down and hurled his drink into his mouth. The boy poured another, holding the bottle in two hands as if it was an elixir. Gérard brushed him away and the boy skipped off. He opened the sackcloth which held four bronze bell heads; two were identical figures cast sharp with all their edges and clappers intact. The other two were more primitive and pock-marked, without clappers.

Gérard asked me which were the fakes. I pointed at the two perfectly cast ones and then handled the other two which looked more genuine but revealed nothing to me. Gérard told me it depended on the meaning of genuine. The perfectly cast bell heads were genuine fakes cast by a British foundry and sold openly in Nigeria at affordable prices for the local Yoruba people's religious ceremonies from the beginning of the century. The more primitive ones were made by local Nigerian foundries a couple of years ago, imitating the old 'lost wax' technique to produce 'genuine' bronzes that they could sell at high prices to gullible white people.

He told me someone buying African art should be able to tell as much as he could from the bell heads and, although they were worth less than the whisky left in the bottle, he wanted them back. I left the whisky with him and said I'd bring the bronzes back the next day.

On the way back to the house, I found a second wind and decided to go and visit Charlie and see if there was a different smell to a man with a million-dollar solution to his problems. I also thought I might be able to get him to corroborate parts of Nina's story just to make sure she wasn't 'putting me on' again.

Half an hour later it was just after eleven o'clock and I was approaching Charlie, who was dressed in a white dinner jacket and a black bow tie and was standing at the empty bar with a tumbler of whisky in front of him and a black look that could have started a monsoon. I wanted to get out as soon as I got in. The neat-haired pianist was clawing the air with her voice singing Patsy Cline's 'Crazy' and a frightened boy was clearing glasses off the tables. The boy looked up at me when I came in, like a cat who didn't care for strangers.

A girl stood up behind the bar. I ordered a Scotch.

'We're closed,' said Charlie.

The girl ducked down behind the bar with the speed of someone who's just seen six-guns coming out of holsters.

'I just want to talk, Charlie,' I said, feeling suicidal with the music.

'I got nothing to say.'

'You didn't tell me you and Nina had been an item.'

'The boy's deaf,' said Charlie to himself.

'You didn't tell me you had a "talk" with Kershaw about his "problem" with Nina.'

'I don't have to *tell* you anything,' he said, turning his face to me and burying his tumbler in his hairy fist. He finished his drink without taking his eyes off me and put the glass down on the bar. His face was still. '*Arrêtez la musique!*' he roared in an American accent and the pianist stopped as if she'd been garrotted and slammed the cover over the keys.

'Did I get a visit from you last night?' I asked.

'Blow away, Brucey,' he replied in the sort of quiet voice a man might use before he opened your face down to the bone with a cut-throat. I didn't hang around to find out if that was his intention.

Something had happened since I'd seen Charlie last night. If he'd solved his cash flow problem he wasn't showing it. What he was showing was a healthy dislike for my person which he was stoking with some outside help. Nina must have told him about my visit and the ugliness of my questions. Charlie looked as if he was planning something personal to persuade me that my present occupation was not a great career move.

\* \* \*

Back at the house, I locked the metal gate that gave out on to the street and locked the side door in the alley. The power was off again indoors. Bagado wasn't back. He must have gone for the morning flight. I grovelled around the floor looking for the candle and some matches. In its tired light my huge shadow wavered across the painted walls in the gallery above. I went into the kitchen and hovered over the last drop of Bell's and found myself too weary to go through with it. I took a couple of aspirin, filled a plastic bag with ice, went to bed, stuck the cool bag on the back of my head and slept.

It doesn't take a medium for anybody to know that they're not alone in a room. The brain throws a switch and the body powers out of deep sleep into instant consciousness. A hand gripped the back of my neck, a knee came down hard in the middle of my spine, another hand tore a fistful of hair and rammed my face into the pillow. My brain crashed down a luge tube of panic into a tight black curve that replaced all body muscle with toasted marshmallow. Then my head was torn back, my throat stretched to ripping point, my mouth taut and wide open with as much scream in it as Munch's painting. An urgent, hoarse whisper scoured my ear.

'Listen! When you're told to drop it, you drop it. I don't want to have to come back and hold you down for the last time.'

The hands thumped my face back into the pillow. Red lights burned in my sockets, swimming to green, then black and white lines rushed towards me, going to black. Panic burst into every limb and they lashed out, my body bucking and twisting, my heart and lungs yowling at the white hot needle that eased in from spine to sternum until something broke and then there was nothing.

# *Chapter 22*

I came to in what I first assumed was the afterlife. A faint light was easing across a morning sky and I watched it grow from behind a gauze sheet, so that I began to think all those films were based on fact and that there was soft focus after death. I scooped the mosquito netting away and sat on the edge of the bed, the soft nylon on my shoulders. The plastic bag lay empty like a patch of saliva on the damp pillow case. I fingered my head, the bump was down to the size and texture of a strawberry left in the sun. The brain inside felt cramped and stifled. My neck had two steel struts riveted between the scapulae and lower cortex which made nodding a no-no. I pulled on a pair of trousers and went downstairs and made a cup of coffee, squeezing the remains of the Bell's into it.

There was a knock on the door which was still locked. Bagado stood there yawning down to his knees with a paper bag in his hands. It was half past seven, he'd come straight off the morning flight. He could smell the whisky in my coffee and, showing his usual restraint, asked me if I had a problem. I told him how difficult I was finding it to get a full night's uninterrupted sleep in this house. We searched inside and out to find the point of entry but none of the locks had been picked, all the windows were intact and there were no marks on the floors or walls. Bagado knew the outside gate was still locked because he'd had to climb over it and there were no prints at the foot of the walls and no sign of disturbance on the top of them either.

'He must have had the keys,' said Bagado, hunching his shoulders to shrug but not following through.

'Whose?'

'Kershaw's?'

'There was a set of keys in the door when I first got here and ran into Yao.'

'Probably the maid's, but it's something to think about.'

We were standing on the small patio with the three urns in front of the pool. Where the patio met the grass was a shallow trench a few inches wide, overgrown with grass. Bagado was standing at the corner where the missing urn, which was still in the middle of the lawn, should have been. He knelt down and ran his hand along the trench and he came up with something that looked like a credit card. He read it and handed it over. It was an expired Bloomingdale's store card in the name of C. Reggiani.

'That was dropped between Thursday night and today,' said Bagado.

'What happened to precision?'

'What can *you* tell me about it?'

'Nothing.'

'There's no rain marks on it, no mud. It was dropped

after it rained on Thursday night and probably once it had dried on Friday.'

'Did you check this trench after we'd found the body on Friday?'

'I'm sure I did.'

'So it could have been dropped on this visit or the one I had on Saturday night?'

'Yes, but I don't like it,' he said, taking the card off me and putting it in his pocket. I knew he'd heard me when I'd mentioned Saturday night but he didn't have the energy to take me up on it. Bagado hadn't slept well and he looked as if he'd got to the age when he needed to.

'I've bought some food,' he said, shrinking into his rumpled mac. I followed his stiff walk to the kitchen.

Bagado produced the croissants from his paper bag and we leaned against the sideboard eating them and drinking coffee. In a tired and hoarse voice he told me he'd followed Charlie and Jack to the offices of AAICT in Ikeja, a Lagos suburb, where they had a meeting with Bof Awolowo and Madame Severnou. He knew this when the four of them came out of the offices and went for a late lunch in the Hotel Sheraton nearby.

Bagado watched them order their food and then went back to the AAICT offices. The break-in hadn't required anything more than a penknife. He'd found a vacant lot behind the offices and an open door to a defunct central air-conditioning unit. He slipped the lock on the next door which let him up some stairs and into the main body of the office building. The offices were on three floors and Bof Awolowo's was on the top at the front. His office was open. It hadn't been so easy to find the relevant papers. Bagado hadn't been sure what he was looking for.

'I found a contract between Carlo Reggiani and AAICT. He's bought five hundred tons of cotton fibre c.i.f. delivered Oporto Portugal. What's c.i.f.?'

'Carriage, insurance and freight included. But Charlie wouldn't buy c.i.f. He's the kind of guy does his own shipping. He finds these Polish two thousand-tonners to do it for bunkers only.'

'What's the price of cotton fibre per ton?,' asked Bagado.

'About one thousand five hundred dollars f.o.b.'

That's without freight?'

'Right, free on board, the freight would be around sixty dollars per ton.'

'The c.i.f. price in the contract was one thousand four hundred and twenty-five dollars per ton.'

'Cheap.'

'But not so cheap that you'd be suspicious.'

'Unless you knew.'

'Why do the deal on a Sunday?'

'Not that unusual,' I said, 'except that they all met last night at the party, apart from Madame Severnou.'

'It could mean that they're nearly ready.'

'Why not just do the deal here?'

'Madame Severnou wanted to be there?'

'Was there a ship's name on the contract?'

'*Osanyin*.'

Bagado had left the building with an hour and a half to go to the return flight to Lomé. He dropped in at the Sheraton in time to see Jack and Charlie getting in the back of Awolowo's dark-windowed Mercedes. He followed them to the airport where they boarded the plane, then took another taxi to the Apapa docks to look for the *Osanyin*.

'Why bother?'

'It's an unusual name for a ship.'

'What does it mean?'

'Osanyin is the Yoruba god of medicine. I thought it might be a sick joke to move drugs on a ship called that.'

'You found the ship?'

'Yes, she'd just docked. Good-looking ship,' he nodded. 'New paintwork, Liberian flag . . .'

'Did you get on board?'

'I tried. They wouldn't let me on. They said my police badge was no good. They were aggressive.'

Without my asking, a clip of the rusty *Naoki Maru* slid into my head and I got a frisson of excitement at the possibility.

'Was the ship's generator working?'

'There was an engine running. It didn't sound very healthy.'

'Did you notice the lifting gear over the cargo holds?'

'Why?'

'There's a single hold at the back of the ship behind the bridge and living quarters. Did you notice whether the lifting gear over it was broken?'

'I wasn't looking at the lifting gear.'

'If it was, then it was the *Naoki Maru*.'

Bagado pinched his nose at that and asked if we could check the position of the *Naoki Maru* and the ownership and registration of the *Osanyin* without drawing attention. I went into the living room and wrote the following fax message to a friend of mine in the shipping company I used to work for.

Attn. Elwin Taylor
Frm. Bruce Medway                    Date 30/9

Pls confirm with owners position of Vsl *Naoki Maru* 14,000 dwt. Korean flag.
Last known position 24/9 Cotonou to disch 7000 tons rice ex Thailand.
Previous positions – Discharge containers Abidjan and Tema.
                              Load Cashew Lomé
Future positions – Lagos to discharge hi-fi.
Pls confirm ownership and reg. of Vsl *Osanyin* Liberian Flag no further info.
Keep Strictly P+C. Pls fax ASAP.
                    Rgds BM.

Today may be our last chance to see what's happening with the rice,' said Bagado as we watched the fax going through. 'If the *Osanyin* is the *Naoki Maru* then they wouldn't let her dock unless they were ready to load.'

'Wrong. They're going to buy bunkers. The master would have run the bunkers down to zero to buy cheap fuel in Lagos. We've still got time. It'll take her two days to refuel if they pay the right people.'

'We still have to go today. The *Osanyin* might not load but the cargo could be ready. We can't lose the rice. We have to know where it goes.'

'There's one thing not clicking with me in all this. If there's drugs in the rice then Jack and Madame Severnou are partners. Why would Madame Severnou rip Jack off for fifty million?'

'What kind of business ethics do you expect in a drugs deal?'

'That's my point – I'd have thought they'd have to be straight, or people start getting killed.'

'You said Jack didn't have the nerve to deal drugs. Maybe he doesn't, maybe Madame Severnou is stronger than him in the hierarchy of the deal. Maybe Jack's a temporary member of the team.'

Bagado finished his coffee and brushed the flakes of croissant from his raincoat.

'What I keep thinking about,' he said, 'is the Armenian's son and the maid. Why were they killed? The maid must have seen something. Fine. But Kasparian was five hundred miles away.'

'Does there have to be a connection, apart from the fact that Kershaw could paint and Kasparian was interested in art?'

'Just give me some ideas,' said Bagado. 'You can start with the art.'

'I haven't got any ideas,' I said, irritated. 'I've got a dent in my head about half the depth of a gun barrel and my brain didn't get as much oxygen as it wanted to last night.'

I told him about Saturday night's two visitors – Yvette and the mystery man who'd used the same terminology as last night's uninvited guest. I also told him about Nina Sorvino's Sunday morning performance.

'If somebody's nervous enough to hit you, and Nina's frightened enough to warn you off and arrange for you to get another visit, then we must be getting warm.'

'Nina's on the edge. She's strung out on drugs and booze. She's playing tough but she can't hold out much longer. I'm going to check her out this morning, see if she pays any visits before work. And you might like to know that the big man forced another appointment on me. He's anxious about the one million dollars he gave Kershaw to trade with, thinks it might have something to do with him ending up in the pool.'

'A million dollars,' said Bagado twitching his head. 'That explains the cover-up.'

'It might explain the seven hundred thousand dollars that Charlie's supposed to have gone down for trading gold,' I said. 'I went over to his place last night, see how he was under all that strain. He doesn't like me any more.'

'You've been busy.'

'The one person I don't understand in all of this is Yvette. She hangs around in the Sarakawa with her lady lover and some strange information about a dead person in a Cotonou apartment, she's teasing Charlie and she's tapping me for everything I've got and giving nothing back.'

'Maybe she has a nose for money.'

'She knows about Kershaw, she knows about Françoise Perec. Today, I'm going to find out if she knows anything about African art; my bet is she doesn't.'

'You're sounding angry.'

'I'm getting hacked off with people who take one

look at me and think: "Here's someone we can bury in shit and tell him it's going to make him grow."'

'I like the sound of you, Bruce. You're talking from your stomach.'

# Chapter 23

At ten past eight, I was sitting in my car two hundred yards down the road from Nina Sorvino's house with a view through some low palms of her red Citroën which was parked in her garage. At half past eight she got into the Citroën and left Kamina Village for downtown Lomé. If she was going to the Embassy she was taking the long way round.

I tailed her to the Pharmacie pour Tous on the Route de Kpalimé which was as far from the Embassy as you could get and had a lab that did analysis. She walked in and came straight out with an envelope which she opened in her car. I followed her to the German Restaurant in the centre of town, where she went in and made a telephone call. She came out after five minutes and I went straight in and asked to use the phone while the owner asked me since when did he become the PTT. I hit the 'Redial' button and waited. The phone rang four times before it was picked up by Elizabeth Harvey, who gave her name.

She had been very low down on my list of people that Nina Sorvino would call and I just managed to throw an American accent together and pass myself off as Sal Goblowski. I asked for her husband, who she told me was in his office and had been for the last hour. I went back to the house and passed the Embassy on the way. Nina Sorvino's car was there.

Bagado was asleep upstairs on his bed with a three-month-old *Times* crossword on his chest. I showered and shaved and changed into my last set of clothes. I sat on the bed and stared at a beetle that had recently landed in an undiscovered world and was finding it hard going through the wisps of fuzz on the floor.

One of the best teachers in my short academic life taught me English. She wanted me to write poetry, which goes to show that people can be good at some things and still have terrible judgement. She managed to persuade me that there were other ways of thinking than with your brain and from between your legs.

*Always go for the idea you don't know you have.*

Ah, right, I thought, assuming a standing start and coming up with a big blank.

*The idea that bobs into your consciousness and then slips away. That's the right idea for you.*

I was the poet from hell but I learnt how to think. Something had been nagging at me for the last twenty-four hours which was nothing to do with Nina Sorvino's pregnancy test. It had something to do with the photographs.

I went to the car and took them out of the glove, went back upstairs and laid them all out on the bed. There were several photos of each piece of work, a wide shot then some close-ups. I compared them to the originals on the walls. I looked for any differences but they were shots of the finished paintings and there were no differences.

Had it been something in the shot that I'd let Kate

take away? I checked the negative but couldn't tell anything from it. I gathered the photographs and went back to the car and drove to a shop in the Rue du Commerce where I gave them the strip of negative for the two-shot of Kasparian and Kershaw and they said they could do it for me while I waited. They gave me prints of all five shots on the negative strip. I looked closely at the two-shot and the background which was the right-hand half of the girl with the fruit bowl. It didn't say anything to me. I put the main packet of photographs in the glove compartment. The five prints that had just been done, I kept in the map shelf under the steering wheel so that I could get at them if I felt the need. By this time it was half past ten and I had to get to the Sarakawa to pick up Kate Kershaw for the body identification.

At reception they called Kate's room and while I waited I spoke to the guy I'd asked to look out for her. He told me that she'd left the hotel just after seven-thirty last night and hadn't come back until eleven o'clock. The taxi she had used stood in line in the car park and I found the driver sleeping at the wheel with his hand down his trousers. She had asked him to take her to a restaurant in town and he'd dropped her at the German place in the centre. She wasn't in there when he'd cruised past the open air restaurant on his way back to the Sarakawa.

Kate appeared in reception and we drove to the hospital in silence. She wasn't looking chatty and I wasn't looking forward to smelling hospital again. The sterilized instruments, syringed medication, rattling trolleys, distraught relatives, the noise of nurses' starched uniforms knifing through the air and the occasional groan from the patient with the untreated gunshot wound who's been left in the corridor brought on an anticipation of nausea.

The nausea nearly culminated in another bowl-hugging melodrama when I saw the pickled sweetmeats in large Le Parfait jars on shelves around the medical examiner's office.

The policeman with the bad feet was already there when we arrived, holding a plastic bag with Kershaw's effects in it which he gave to Kate as I introduced them. She looked in the bag and nodded. The policeman and the medical examiner spoke to each other in the Ewe language and looked at us. We shuffled out of the office in file through swing doors into the morgue. The smell of formaldehyde was one I knew well from post-school lunch dissection classes with unlucky newts and frogs. Renewing its acquaintance was not the nostalgic trip I'd been looking for.

In this part of the morgue there were just four tables, three with white sheets laid over lumps and the fourth empty. The medical examiner stopped at the first table, raised the corner of the sheet and his eyebrows as he revealed a long black foot with a card attached to the big toe. The second table, the foot was smaller with painted toenails but still black, and the third had no foot at all, just a rounded black stump.

The policeman hobbled forward and let out a yell and the swing doors at the other end of the morgue exploded open and blasted out two hospital porters, the one taller than the other by about a foot and a half. They stood in front of us, hands clasped in front of them, heads bowed and eyes searching the floor like cabaret spotlights. The medical examiner gave them seven blasts of a verbal shotgun and they ran back through the swing doors which fanned each other on their maligned hinges to a standstill.

After several minutes of silence, during which the policeman stared at the swing doors so hard they looked as if they might open on their own just to please him, we heard the far-off manoeuvrings of a trolley. We all turned as the doors behind us banged open and, preceded by his two big feet, came another hospital porter riding on the front end of a trolley with a sheet-covered lump on it, pushed with toe-digging effort by his sweaty colleague. They sailed through us, the front porter unable to throw himself off without being run over, and disappeared through the other swing doors.

The policeman and the medical examiner didn't appear too uncomfortable with this farce and, satisfied with the very frightened African voices on the other side of the doors, turned to us and smiled. The trolley came back in at a funereal pace. The two porters lifted the body on to the table with undertakers' solemnity and the medical examiner lifted the sheet corner over a white foot. He checked the card and nodded at us.

Kate, whose only noises this morning had been a mumbled thank you to the policeman, moved forward on stiff legs. She looked as if she'd had a bad night, but it was difficult to tell given her normal haggard look. It was a feeling she gave off – a feeling of 'don't get too close', 'definitely don't touch or stroke', 'just keep your distance and you won't have claw marks down your face'. I stood next to her at the head of the body.

The examiner's cherubic black face looked up and he peeled back the sheet. Kershaw looked no better, in fact, he looked worse – as if he'd been left out in the sun with the old folk. More skin had decomposed so that more of the skull was visible. His teeth snarled through where his cheek used to be. Kate took her bottom lip between her teeth and bit it white. She touched the brown hair, her face twitching. Then she took the sheet and whipped it off down to the cadaver's legs. The chest and torso weren't decomposed. There were the roughly stitched, brutal autopsy scars but all eyes skated over these to Kershaw's genitals. The policeman's eyeballs sprung out at me. Kershaw's penis lay between his thighs, long, thick, fat and misshapen like a homemade chorico. Kate threw the sheet back over the head and said: 'That's him,' and left the morgue.

The policeman's shoulders were shaking and he showed me a set of brilliant white teeth and a twelve-ounce raw burger tongue and said: 'There're some things a woman never forgets.'

'Like the mole on the top of the left thigh,' I said. The policeman peeked under the sheet and roared and grabbed at my shoulder for support.

In the examiner's office, all the paperwork for the release of the body was ready. The cause of death was given as drowning and the verdict, misadventure. Kate signed them and the policeman witnessed. We talked about the airline and the time of the flight, which was just after midnight that night. Hands were shaken, no money was in them. It was the cleanest piece of African red tape I've ever seen.

\*     \*     \*

We arrived at KLM's offices just before they closed at 12.00 and a very efficient woman with the inauspicious name of Fafa said she would handle all the arrangements and Kate gave her the release papers.

Twenty minutes later, we sat at the traffic lights and a boy knocked on Kate's window and she opened it. He raised a filthy bandage over his eye and showed Kate the empty socket, who yelped and grabbed a handful of my shirt. I gave the boy some coins and he left with the whimper of a dying lettuce.

'You were out last night?' I asked.

'I was,' she said.

'Anything wrong with the hotel?'

'I don't like luxury. It makes me feel dead. Steve was crazy for it. Room service, mini bars, buffets, drinks by the pool, all that kind of thing – he'd have killed for it.' She shrugged her expression off with her eyebrows.

'Where did you go?'

'I wanted to go to a restaurant. The taxi driver dropped me off at a German place which wasn't what I wanted. I found a place with a more African menu and ate there. It's called Keur Rama, do you know it?'

'My favourite place. Are you hungry?'

'No thanks.'

I took Kate back to the Sarakawa. She said she didn't need me to take her to the airport so we said goodbye. I watched her go up to her room. I asked reception if room 405 had made any calls last night and they said she hadn't but that she had received one. They didn't know whether it was local or long distance.

On the hotel steps, I met Yvette with a spinnaker of blue silk billowing out behind her.

'Did she identify the body?' she asked, her eyes searching me under her bluebottle sunglasses.

'She did,' I said. 'I didn't know art buyers were so nosey.'

'It must have been very difficult for her,' she said, raising her sunglasses. 'The body was in the water a long time – in very warm water with lots of things in it.' She hooked and unhooked her finger at me like a small aquatic beast picking at its food.

'Her husband had a big dick,' I said, and her sunglasses slipped down and slammed her eyes shut like a visor.

'That helps,' she said, with a pout of her lips.

'I have something for you,' I said, walking to the car. I opened the glove to take out the sackcloth which wrapped the bell heads and noticed that the photographs in there had gone. I leaned further in and saw that the prints I'd had done earlier were still in the map tray. I stood and opened up the sackcloth on the car roof.

'What do you think?' I said, standing the bell heads up.

She put her sunglasses on the roof and examined the bronzes. She could see that the sharper bronzes were fakes but she thought the primitive imitation bronzes were genuine and offered 4000 French francs a piece. I rewrapped the bell heads and put them back in the glove and turned to Yvette.

'Yvette Dussolier,' I said, 'if that's your name, you

know as much about African art as an Eskimo, and that's being tough on Eskimos.'

Yvette didn't like me looking at her and she didn't like being without the protection of her sunglasses, which she reached for on the roof. I got to them first.

'It's time we talked, don't you think?'

She led me back into the Sarakawa and up to her room. She knocked three times on the door and waited. The door opened an inch. Yvette paused a second and went in. I followed. Jasmin startled me by appearing from the bathroom, but she had nothing in her hand and just filed in behind me. I sat down on the bed opposite Yvette. Jasmin stood behind her.

'You were saying,' said Yvette.

'I was saying you don't know anything about African art, which you don't. You know less than I do, which for someone who's said they know enough "not to get rolled" means you must have a big hole in your bank account. You *do* know a lot about Françoise Perec and Steve Kershaw. And I get the feeling you'd like to know more. So would I. You've been using the one big advantage you've got in life to try and do that, by getting close to Charlie Reggiani and, on one occasion, me, except . . . I know you don't like men, not in that way anyway.' Yvette didn't flinch. Jasmin tucked her T-shirt into her jeans. 'What I don't know is why you're going to all this trouble, unless it's the sad old reason why anybody does anything. The money.'

'The money?' asked Yvette.

'Your turn.'

Yvette stood up, went to her purse and took out an ID card.

'Françoise Perec was my colleague. I work for the IMB out of Abidjan.' She handed me her ID card. 'I am not here in an official capacity. I am here because I don't like what happened to my friend. I am trying to find out who killed her and, as it turns out, Steven Kershaw. Michel, the same Michel as your friend knows in the French Embassy in Cotonou, has been helping me with information. I am interested in Kershaw because he was the last person that we knew of who saw her alive, and I am interested in Charlie because according to her report, that was the last place she'd been before her death. I could have joined you and your friend Bagado, but that is not how I work. I always work alone. The less people know about me the better.' She paused and lit one of her thick white cigarettes. 'What money?' she asked.

I told her as much as I could remember at the time and we came to an agreement. Bagado and I would continue with what we were doing and she would keep her hooks into Charlie. She said that she couldn't spend all her time with Charlie, that he was cooking her dinner the following night but that it wasn't very classy to sit around on his white leather sofas painting her nails all day like a gangster's moll. I told her that Moses, if I could find him, would do his usual excellent job of hanging around doing nothing in Charlie's compound. When I stood up to leave, I held out my hand to Yvette.

'Still angry with me?' she asked.

'Not any more,' I said. 'Since we're on the same side.' She took my hand and kissed me on both cheeks as if she were about to present me with the *Légion d'Honneur*. 'You're making me feel as if I'm on my way to certain death.'

She laughed and said, 'And we never got married.'

I left the Sarakawa at one o'clock and drove to the Keur Rama and spoke to the owner, who told me that no foreigners had eaten in his restaurant last night.

Outside the German Restaurant there were four or five fruit and vegetable stalls run by young women selling the same, but more expensive, versions of what you could get in the market. A 1000 CFA bought me the information that Kate Kershaw had taken another taxi from the restaurant. A further 1000 CFA to one of the women who knew the driver a lot better than others bought me the taxi's number and she told me through all the giggling that its usual hangout was in the rank outside the Sarakawa.

The cab driver was fourth in line and asleep but wasn't too annoyed at being woken up by a 1000 CFA fluttering under his nose. He remembered Kate Kershaw and said he'd dropped her off at eight o'clock outside the Hotel de La Paix which was further along the coast road than the Sarakawa and would have been much easier to get to with one taxi than two.

I drove to the Hotel de La Paix and found a waiter who had served Kate Kershaw with a gin and tonic. She'd sipped it for fifteen minutes and then left, her glass still half full. I asked the hotel doorman if he'd seen Kate Kershaw or ordered a taxi for her and tried to jog his memory with my last 1000 CFA note, which he accepted before telling me he wasn't on duty last night. I stripped the note out of his hand before it found its way into his pocket and after I'd spoken to everybody I could find who'd been there last night, I gave up and headed back to the house.

# Chapter 24

Bagado had moved down from his bed and was lying on the floor, still with the crossword on his chest, staring at the ceiling. Moses was sleeping on the sofa.

'Hello, driver,' I said and Moses's sleepy head came off the pillow of his elbow.

He stood up and refused to look at me.

'Yes please, sir,' he volunteered.

'Where the hell have you been?'

Moses looked at Bagado, who had sat up. He wasn't sure what line he was going to take and he hoped Bagado's face would give him some ideas. Bagado put his head over to one side like a dog that doesn't understand.

'Lying in the arms of Mercy?' I asked.

'Or was it Patience?' offered Bagado.

'Or Faith, Hope and bleeding Charity,' I said, and Moses picked his cuticles.

'Grace,' he said.

'You use the condoms I give you?'

'Yes please, sir.'

'How many.'

'Oh, all of them please, sir.'

'I gave you twenty.'

'Yes please, sir. All gone.'

'You going to marry this girl?'

'Oh no please, sir. She is very bad girl.'

'What happened to Mercy?'

'The big girl,' Bagado reminded him.

'Oh, no, no, no, please sir,' said Moses in a deepening voice as if we were going to make him do something again that had taken a terrible physical toll first time around. 'She too much, Mister Bruce. Too many. She brekkin' me no small. I . . . no, no please sir, Mister Bruce.'

'Bagado and I are going to Cotonou. You are staying here. We drop you at Charlie's bar and you keep watch. See what happen. You be inconspicuous.'

'Whassat please, Mister Bruce?'

'Invisible . . . which doesn't mean "not there".'

'No please, sir.'

'You leave Grace alone small.'

'Yes please, Mister Bruce.'

'Let big fellow sleep small.'

'Yes please, Mister Bruce.'

'Or Mercy she comin' back brekkin' you no small.'

Moses's face widened in horror and then, if it was possible, broadened further into a wide smile. 'But she likin' me no small, Mister Bruce, you unnerstan'.'

'I think I do, Moses.'

We dropped Moses off at Charlie's just after two o'clock and he took off across the wasteland like a car thief. The sun was high in the sky and the pressure and humidity as normal as West Africa allowed. We drove with the windows open, Bagado hunched in his raincoat. I told him about Yvette, who didn't concern him, and Kate Kershaw, whose theft of the photos and night-time sortie did. He had the five photos I'd had printed this morning in his hands and was going through them over and over again, waiting for the epiphany.

'Why does the wife lie?' he asked.

'She went to see somebody.'

'Who did she see that's worth lying about?'

'Somebody who knew her husband.'

'Somebody who killed her husband?'

'She doesn't look the type, and how would she fit in with the Perec killing?'

'This killing might not be about Françoise Perec, it might just be about other women, *and* a million dollars,' he said. 'And what *does* Mrs Kershaw look like?'

'In need of food.'

'Thin people can still get upset by their husband's infidelity and have a taste for luxury.'

'She is upset by her husband's infidelity but she says she doesn't like luxury,' I said.

'The Perec killing could be connected to Kershaw's death,' said Bagado, tapping his lips as another wild theory curved into his brain. 'Mrs Kershaw tells her "friend" that she wants to get rid of her husband. Her "friend" needs to get rid of Perec. The "friend" provides the connection. He gets rid of his problem and uses Kershaw to do it *and* maybe gets paid for it.'

'You'd have to be very trusting with the money.'

'I was just thinking she might not know about the million dollars. That might have been something between Kershaw and the big man. She's found out about another woman, and she's had enough of her husband's infidelity and is angry enough to have him killed.'

'How would she know the "friend" who's going to do this for her, how's she going to find the money when she's broke?'

'Somebody who knows the Kershaws, somebody who's in contact with both of them, somebody who knows Jack, somebody . . .'

'B.B.,' I said, without thinking. 'He wouldn't be doing it for the money.'

'What about love?'

'That's nearly unimaginable.'

'Charlie?'

'His bar's not too far from the Hotel de La Paix.'

'It's an interesting possibility,' said Bagado, looking out of the window at some diseased coconut palms. 'I had a call from Brian Horton in London. He found out about the girl in the psychopath lecture. Her name was Cassie Mills, born 15th March 1937. Murdered 23rd September 1954 in Rockford, Illinois. Case unsolved. No suspects.'

'Perec was killed on the 23rd September,' I reminded him.

'Coincidence.'

'It's a pity there aren't degrees of coincidence.'

'When I first beat Brian Horton at darts he said to me: "Bagado, nobody likes a smart-arse."'

'I've noticed that myself,' I said.

We crossed the lagoon at Aneho and watched a lonely figure far out on the tip of the sandbar staring out to sea.

'I'm beginning to feel like a pawn,' said Bagado.

'I hope it's a strategic one?'

'No, as usual, an expendable one.'

'Only a bad player throws away his pawns.'

'A small hope for us to cling to.'

We crossed the border and got through a congested Cotonou using Bagado's lung power and a police motorcyclist who I dashed some money for petrol. We rolled into Porto Novo at half past four. Bagado had been interrogating and I had been spilling it about Heike.

'She wants children. They all want children,' he said.

'She's never talked about children.'

'Women don't. They think about it and the need just creeps up on them. They wake up one day and want to be pregnant. How old is she?'

'Thirty.'

'That's the age. They think it's their last chance. They have to act quickly.'

'She just talks about her work. She's down here for a conference and to sort out her career move. She hasn't, as far as I know, been found standing with her head to one side and her mouth open outside primary school playgrounds. What she's been thinking about is whether she stays in Africa or goes back to Berlin.'

'And what's the first thing she does?'

'I don't know what . . .'

'You do.'

'What?'

'She comes to see you.'

'I live down here.'

'You've never been married.'

'No.'

'You've never been close to marrying.'

'No.'

'You've had girlfriends, but nobody important.'

'But I'm not a virgin.'

'You're how old?'

'Thirty-eight. I'm a late developer.'

'Do you love her?' asked Bagado, slipping in the crucial question amongst the easy ones in that natural policeman-like way.

There was a bit of a pause while I wrestled that question to the ground and pinned it down, only for it to wriggle away and get me around the neck with its knee in my back.

'She's different,' I said.

'Isn't that what people say about modern art when they don't like it?'

'I didn't say I was *fond* of her.'

'That would have been worse, but *different* is a failure. A woman doesn't give you everything if she's just *different* to you. She wants you to look her in the eye and say you love her.'

'She asked me how I felt about her leaving. I said – "Bad". She told me that wasn't good enough because it was negative.'

'Ah, Heike, I like her,' he said, grunting at his inadvertent rhyme. 'She came here to test you. She's confused. She's got the ache for children. Work is still important but everything has changed. Her life still seems to be the same but it isn't. She's begun to look around her and she sees you – the right man in the wrong circumstances.'

'What are these "wrong circumstances"?'

'The nest, security, someone who will look after her, someone reliable with money coming in . . .'

'Someone who doesn't get visits from hitmen in the night. Someone who doesn't go looking for trouble with his new pal Bagado, who, incidentally, isn't paid and spends days away from his home and loving wife and children.'

'We all have to make our choices,' he said. 'It may be small consolation to you, but I know of women who have got over this need for children . . . The right man wasn't there at the time and the feeling faded.'

Bagado stretched his arms forward and put his hands on the dashboard. 'Bah!' he said lifting them off. 'You people in Europe are too selfish anyway.'

We stopped at a traffic light and looked at the people crossing the road. A group parted as it straggled across and Heike, the only white person in the crowd, appeared in the road almost in front of us.

'Christ, that's her!' I said, getting out of the car, confused at seeing her, not thinking what I was doing. Bagado held my arm. I shrugged him off, thinking he was just worried about the traffic, but I looked back and he jerked his head in Heike's direction. She was walking away from us, her skirt swinging on her hips. I had only seen her at first, but now, with a sharp shock, I saw that her hand was held by another, bigger hand. She was walking alongside a European man a little taller than her. They were talking and Heike's head was toppling back, she was showing him her throat and laughing about it. The man kissed her there on the neck and horns went off behind me.

The car stalled, I restarted it and pulled away from

the slogans on my stunted manhood. Bagado folded in on himself and looked out from behind the collar of his raincoat. 'Choice complicates,' I said to myself, and understood the look Heike had given me. It was a look I'd seen on a few other faces recently.

It wasn't an elbow-out-the-window-shirt-flapping-in-the-breeze kind of drive to the Benin/Nigeria border. A lot of concentration poured through the windscreen but it wasn't directed at the road. I hunched over the wheel and found that it wanted to remain attached to the steering column. Bagado applied a lot of brake in his foot well. We arrived and I uncoiled myself while Bagado went to the warehouse alone.

The car was parked away from the border amongst fifty overladen trucks with skewed chassis waiting to cross into Nigeria. Bagado checked out the warehouse while I waited and ran the gauntlet of every emotion going. I finished by getting on the highest horse there was and stared down its snorting nostrils at Heike's deceit, only to come to the lurching conclusion that this rearing, tooth-baring, nostril-flaring stallion wasn't righteous indignation, it was far worse, and again, something that I'd seen in a few other people recently.

Bagado appeared running up the road from the border, his raincoat flapping like crows' wings. In West Africa, only athletes and children under twelve run, so I started the car and turned it around ready to go south across the coastal border. Bagado got in and the car squirmed on the grit, the engine howling before the tyres caught and we kicked off the blocks.

By five o'clock, Bagado had got us through the Benin

part of the frontier and was working on the Nigerians. They weren't so understanding and he called me over.

'They want to see the white man.'

I took out my fold of money and peeled off two 5000 CFA notes and put one in each breast pocket of my shirt. I rolled the rest up and shoved it in my sock.

As I walked to Immigration, there was a shout from the Customs shed and a crowd of people scattered, slowed and then turned. In the clearing were two men, one with a bottle. The one without the bottle shouted: 'I kill you,' which struck me as unlikely since he had as much muscle on him as a praying mantis. The man with the bottle was winding it round in his big fist. He had a divoted, shaved head with a two-inch white scar above the ear where they must have taken the brain out. His neck was built with industrial grade steel rods and his arms hammered out of some bronze alloy. He was smaller than a scrap metal truck, which was the only human observation I could make. The crowd urged them to get on with it.

A policeman barged through the people, snicking them out of the way with his truncheon. He burst into the clearing and with no introduction cracked the bottle man across the bridge of the nose with a straight-armed sweep across his body. The man dropped to his knees with his hands on his face, the red blood filling them and seeping through the cracks in his fingers. The policeman rose on his toes and came down with his truncheon on the back of the ridged, shaved pate and there was a noise like a distant cricket match. His opponent threw his hands up in the air, victorious. He strutted to the crowd who wide-eyed him in silence.

The policeman stepped forward like a batsman on to his front foot and drove the man's head into the boundary of the crowd. He hit the deck with the face of a moron.

A sign at the end of the Customs shed said: 'Welcome to Nigeria.' I went into Immigration, leaving the policeman surveying the crowd and washing his truncheon under a tap with the meanest look I've seen on a human outside prison.

We went into a dark and dirty office which had a slit window big enough for a rifle, but too little for a view. A weak light bulb developed four Immigration officers in light brown uniforms like an ancient sepia print. Bagado was told to wait outside. A policeman shut the door. The Immigration officers positioned their sneers.

Each had his elbows and forearms horizontal on the table with hands on top of each other. They had the slim, fine features of northerners. Two of them asked a different question at the same time. The one with the most ribbons stared down the table and then said: 'Your ticket, please.'

'No ticket.'

'You need a ticket for onward travel out of Nigeria.'

'I'm in a car.'

'But you have to prove that you will leave Nigeria on a certain date.'

'I promise.'

The officer with the ribbons stood up and kicked the chair back. He put his hands behind his back and paced round his colleagues in a perfect imitation of a British official, circa 1950. There was a little game to be played now and I had to show that I had all the time in the world to play it.

'You have broken the law of our country, Mr Medway,' said an officer.

'You haven't let me in to break it.'

'And you, one of our previous colonial masters,' said another.

'I should have known better.'

'You are on Nigerian soil now,' said the man with the ribbons, staring at the floor with a look so grave I thought he was going to make me plough it.

A policeman opened the door and threw a bundle in which landed on the floor behind me. He closed the door again. The bundle was alive. He was a pitiful wretch. He looked up from the floor with the undefiant look of something hog-tied for market. The officers peered over the desk. They spoke to each other in Hausa saying: 'Let's get some money off the white man and let him go.'

I had enough Hausa to offer a contribution to the Immigration Officers' Holiday Fund and they all roared with laughter and one said: 'I see you have imbibed some of our culture.'

'A man can't move without imbibing the culture.'

They all laughed again and clapped their hands. I gave them one 5000 CFA note between them and that was enough. As I left, the policeman outside the door was practising cuts with a three-foot piece of cane, which gave me some painful reminders of black days at a school where discipline was enjoyed.

# Chapter 25

Bagado looked like the relieved accomplice who hadn't been snitched on. I thought he might ask me how many I'd got, but he just climbed in the car and pointed east. We wanted to get to the Nigerian side of the border to where the porters were bringing the rice across, so we went east to Badagri, turned north to Ado, and finally west back to Idiroko which was on the Nigerian side of the border from Porto Novo. Bagado was surging forward in his seat like a jockey and twitching me on with a whiplash voice when he wanted me to overtake. He had seen that the warehouse on the Benin side was nearly empty. Madame Severnou had moved the rice in half the time I'd expected.

We took the road out of Idiroko to the border and on the outskirts of town saw a truck loaded with rice turning off the main road. We followed it for about a mile to a warehouse with other trucks of rice waiting to unload outside. Whitened stick men in soiled loincloths walked up and down wooden planks, storing the rice in the warehouse.

Opposite the warehouse, which had its own chain-link compound, were three crumbling buildings and to one side some mud-walled houses with corrugated iron roofs. There were some trees with good shade and some homemade wooden seating with no ground clearance.

Beyond was another street and some more mud-walled houses. We parked up behind the crumbling buildings in a street where a black stinking liquid ran in the gutters. A dog stood looking at us, a nothing dog, neither big nor small and with a rough coat the same colour as the red dust. It shook with fever and tics. Blood gathered at the teddy bear point of his lips. Flies settled there, took off and relanded.

We found a dark corner by one of the mud-walled houses which was shaded by a tree with thick heavy leaves coloured red by the dust. We sat on some wood with our backs to the mud wall and waited. For a moment, the sun turned the whole sky a deep orange pink, a rare West African sunset against which some skeletal trees blackened, faded and merged when it was finally dark. It was just after six o'clock. Lights came on around the compound and in the warehouse.

It didn't take someone with an MBA to realize that they shouldn't have been unloading here at all. The rice was destined for Lagos and Ibadan and it didn't make sense to load and unload twice.

As the sacks were taken off, two tall, well-built young Africans in grey slacks and white shirts, looking as if they were off an American college football team, ran detectors over each sack as it came into the warehouse. In the hour after dark, one sack was put aside to join four others in a corner by the warehouse office and something was recorded on a clipboard attached to a string on the wall.

Women with bundles of washing on their heads walked past without seeing us. Children played by the road in the light from the compound. A boy beat a hoop with a stick. The hoop outpaced him and crossed the road, missed by a truck and a car, it lodged itself in a ditch. Another truck arrived, the sacks queued off. Not a lot was happening, apart from phase three of an international drugs operation.

Bagado's distant voice was telling me how clever this operation was. The idea of smuggling something more valuable inside something else being smuggled was, to his mind, brilliant.

'Why make something look clean when it's already dirty?' he said. 'Anything clean here stinks like hell.'

He was right. It was a regular piece of Nigerian business and what was more, it wasn't happening in a port, nor in a city warehouse, nor in an airport with a lot of curious people around who talk to other people who cost money. It was happening in a dusty, shitty little border town sixty miles from Lagos with people who were glad to get some work.

Other thoughts turned over with the weight and monotony of ploughed earth. The film clip of Heike with her lover played and replayed itself in my head. Bagado and Heike were right. I'd never made a decision about her. I hadn't realized how much my own stability relied on her. I hadn't understood what a difference she made, or maybe I had and chose to ignore it because things like that can get difficult.

The truth was I didn't want to lose her, and not just because I could see her being taken away but because I realized in my near-forty dotage that I needed her – positively needed her. Things I knew already but kept back behind the fences crept to the front of my mind. I admired her for the work she did, I respected her for the way she did it – the toughness, the resilience, and I loved her for the hair at the back of her neck, the large hands holding the cigarette in its holder, the way she sat in that big dress and drank with me, glass for glass. And I knew I believed it because the feeling I had didn't come from my mushy, inconsistent head nor that over-flattered fragile organ, the heart, but high up in the stomach, around the diaphragm, where a sharp tap can take all the wind out of you.

Bagado hit me on the arm and told me it was all over. The last truck had arrived half loaded. Another sack had been put aside and one of the college boys was doing a final count. He let the clipboard fall and spoke to his friend who gave him his detector, walked out of the compound and crossed the road into one of the crumbling buildings. The other guy was winding his arm around as if he was cranking an engine and the workers broke into a run. They took the ramps off the two trucks they had been unloading whose diesel engines farted thick smoke and reversed out of the compound. The half-loaded truck crawled in. The ramps were attached. The other college boy crossed the road back to the compound. The workers unloaded the last truck at a sprint.

In a quarter of an hour, the last truck left. The workers queued up to be paid. They crossed the road with their clothes over their arms, counting their money. The fierce halogen light in the compound imploded.

The metal sheeting of the warehouse doors walloped against the frames as they ran the doors closed. A padlock clicked into place. In the weak light cast from one of the crumbling buildings we could see the college

293

boys' white shirts. One appeared to be jogging on the spot, just lifting his heels, hands behind his back. The other stood still. The only car that passed in the next three quarters of an hour had one headlight and a knocking sound from one of the front wheels.

We heard the sound of expensive wide tyres kissing the metalled road. Madame Severnou's graphite grey Mercedes slowed, feinted left and swung right into the compound. The boys opened the doors and the car reversed in.

We ran for the Peugeot. The light shed as we opened the doors showed the dog lying on its side like an abandoned toy whose trolley had been ripped off to make a skateboard. Flies busied themselves over the already swollen body. We waited in the car under the tree where we had been sitting. The Mercedes, low at the back, rolled out; one of the boys shut the warehouse doors. The Mercedes continued out of the compound and the boy followed with a length of chain hanging from his hand and locked the gate. He got in the car which accelerated up on to the tarmac. We followed with sidelights only until we joined the main road into Idiroko.

We made quick time to the Abeokuta turn-off on the road to Lagos, but as we came into Ikeja, just after Lagos's Murtala Mohammed airport, the traffic solidified. We crawled past the Sheraton, the fumes thick in the still night air. The Mercedes was seven or eight cars ahead in the fast lane of a three-lane highway which had now become six lanes of cars. Taxi drivers swore with monumental gestures. A large woman with a gold watch that cut into her fat wrist stared out of her red air-conditioned BMW at the stock car race she'd found herself in.

Madame Severnou's Mercedes pulled away. We remained. Bagado rolled down his window and sat on the ledge. Twenty yards ahead, two taxi drivers were throwing abuse at each other like old china until one of them produced a wrench and the other didn't like the size of it and moved off, his fan belt screeching like a pig that's seen the knife. We moved again, seething into any available pocket. Bagado thumped the roof with his hand and slid back in. We'd lost them.

We drifted into some orange street lighting, which poisoned an already polluted scene, and I saw the Mercedes coming towards us on the other side of the highway. Bagado watched it turn right into an estate about a quarter of a mile behind us. Its taillights dodged from tree to tree and disappeared.

The Peugeot took a few knocks to the body as we crossed four lanes of cars to the next exit and Bagado shredded his larynx on some razor-wire invective. Ten minutes later, we were cruising the lanes of the estate where the Mercedes had gone. The estate was set out in a grid system on three parallel roads. The first two roads were private houses for middle-class Nigerians. The third road had private houses on one side and office buildings and storage on the other. Beyond this was a tree-lined wall. We found the Mercedes parked in a cul-de-sac on two strips of concrete which ran down into weeds and long grass. The boot was open and one back door.

We turned left and parked out of sight, to the side of a private house. I told Bagado I wasn't going to sit around waiting any more, replaying my least favourite film clip, and he said he'd give me fifteen minutes.

'Before what?'

'Before I go in there myself.'

'And get us both caught.'

'All right, I'll leave you to die.'

'OK. Come in with your thimble blazing.'

One side of the cul-de-sac was a two-storey office building and behind it a low Nissen hut with a walled yard. A shaved head bobbed along the wall and came out through a narrow gate attached to a body, which was naked apart from a pair of shorts. The body was wide, the shoulders, pectorals and abdominals cast like an armoured breast plate, the fingers of the ribs dovetailing with the muscle. The quadraceps wobbled and set as the man walked.

He bent over the boot and as he uprighted a pair of sacks, the ridges and plateaux of muscle in his back shifted along the deep rift of his spine. He wiped his hands on his shorts, they were as big as a statue's. He scratched the back of his calf with an unshod foot – it would have needed a shipyard to build it a shoe. He picked each fifty-kilo sack up by the ear with his thumb and forefinger and walked sideways through the gate as if he had nothing more than the weekend's groceries.

I walked across the front of the office building and went down an alleyway on the other side of it. The wall at the end was about eight foot high, and with a short run I hooked my leg up on to it, knelt and stood up. The courtyard behind the Nissen hut was full of broken pallets and a fork lift with an empty pallet sheathing the forks. The corrugated asbestos roofing of

296

the hut overhung the front walls and made a narrow verandah. A pair of dusty shoes crossed a shaft of light from the hut which showed the planking of the verandah and the ground of the courtyard covered in weeds, empty cardboard cartons and skeins of plastic sheeting.

The shoes I'd seen darted out of the light and a large rat pelted into the courtyard, followed by the grotesque feet of the rice porter. There was a squeal, a high laugh and a crunch and the rat, flattened, came from the dark of the courtyard and landed on the verandah. The dusty shoes came back out and kicked it off. There was no way down into the courtyard from the wall; I let myself down and walked back to the Mercedes whose doors and boot were now closed.

I walked through the gate without thinking about it, and to my right saw that there was a three-foot gap between the hut and the office building. It stank of stale urine. A light from the hut was cast on to a window sill of the office building from a ventilation grate.

The grate was a foot above my head; I pulled myself up on the window sill and looked over my left shoulder into the hut. There was a partition wall over which I could see a store room stacked to the ceiling with lavatories, bidets, wash basins and cisterns. Over my right shoulder were pallets of floor and wall tiles positioned at random around the room and, in a clearing in the middle of the hut, Madame Severnou was watching the rat-crushing porter unstitch a sack. There was a plastic sheet with a bathful of rice on it. The two college boys were refilling empty sacks with rice from the bath using aluminium jugs.

The porter emptied the sack into the bath and the

boys picked out the four brown paper packages that fell out. These were stacked on a table next to Madame Severnou with twenty other packages. I let myself down and let my shoulders burn through my shirt.

Grit twisted under shoe leather. Somebody appeared at the end of the gap and grunted. A zipper rippled the air. There was an ill-tempered rustle and then the sound of piss hitting concrete and a man breathing through his nose. He must have had a bladder the size of a zeppelin because his jet of urine drilled at the concrete for several minutes and streams trickled around my feet.

He left and I pulled myself up again. The bath was empty and a pair of hands stitched a rice sack. By the table was a cotton bale. Madame Severnou looked at the stack of packages and said something in Yoruba. I only understood the words 'Awolowo' and 'cotton bale' and from the way the college boy jotted it down in his notebook, they needed another one. The rat crusher began stuffing the packages into the cotton bale and I dropped to the floor, lathered in sweat.

After a few minutes, I paddled through the urine to the end of the gap. The voices were muffled inside the hut. I took five steps to the gate and arrived at the same time as the rat flattener coming the other way.

'Excuse me,' I said and he stepped to one side. I passed through. A hand came down on my shoulder and took a big handful of me in a grip with some kind of built-in steel clip. It spun me round and sent me back through the gate and I hit the Nissen hut face first.

A steel baseball bat was the minimum requirement for handling this specimen and I had a set of house keys.

A part of my brain with a sense of humour reminded me to put everything I'd got into the first assault and not to go for the head. I looked at the head that I wasn't supposed to hit and it looked back with eyes that told me it had a cranium filled with solid bone. I put enough beef into a right hook to his heart to have put a pit pony out of the game for life and I got a coat hanger grin back from my opponent. He balled his fist and weighed it on the end of his arm like a sack of bolts. My jawline suddenly felt like the finest crystal. I held my good hand up in a gesture of surrender and he picked me up, tucked me under his arm and carried me head first into the hut, where he threw me in the bath.

Madame Severnou stood with her jewelled hands clasped in front of her. The bright blue and yellow cloth of her dress was new and her headpiece in the same material looked like an exotic bird landing. Her face, however, was still. Her unblinking stare permafrosted the sweat-filled air. Her mouth was open a crack and her tongue rested between her teeth.

'Kill him,' she said, without moving her lips, and her tongue disappeared.

# Chapter 26

I was relieved to find that there wasn't an immediate reaction to this command. From my position of towering strength, lying in the bath with rice up my sweaty forearms, I could see the two college boys in their white shirts, grey slacks and Gucci loafers had the kind of body language I liked – very reluctant. The bone-headed, rat-flattening rice porter, with the body recently panel beaten out of half-inch bronze sheeting, didn't have any body language. He was just a natural, absent-minded, killing sort of a guy.

There was a long pause which was about to expand into a silence when one of the college boys said: 'Who?' which just seemed to be a way of filling time and space because there were no options.

'Dayo,' said Madame Severnou, cocking her head at the obvious candidate.

'How?' said the other college boy.

'I go break his neck,' said Dayo, holding up a pair of unartistic hands that would have found the task trifling.

'What about the body?'

'Throw it in the lagoon,' said Madame Severnou.

Messrs Harvard and Yale didn't like it. Their intelligent faces looked for a way out. Dayo spat on his hands. This was his kind of work. That was what those hands had been made for.

'It's not so easy,' the boys said together.

'It's very difficult to throw big things away,' I said. 'You get seen.'

'Shut up,' said Madame Severnou, her voice hitting a very flat high C and she flung her heavy hand out in my direction and half a pound of gold slashed across my face. It was like getting hit with a brick. My teeth tore into the inside of my cheek and blood spilled on to my chin.

'He has to be killed. He's seen everything,' she said. 'But not now.'

'We kill him now and we have to get rid of him. He'll stink within hours.'

'We get rid of him and we get seen, or his body's found.'

'A white man's body in the lagoon is big trouble.'

'And the shipment goes tomorrow. Why not keep it quiet until then?'

It was a virtuoso performance by the college debating team and Madame Severnou was vicious, mean and tough but not stupid. She thought for a few minutes while I decided how long it would be before Bagado showed this crowd his nine-millimetre, semi-automatic finger.

'OK,' said Madame Severnou, drawing out the 'K'. 'Keep him here tonight. Dayo and you stay –' She pointed to one of the boys. 'You and I will bring two more cotton bales tomorrow. One for these packages and the other for him. We load him on the ship and put him over the side at sea. No problem.'

And it wouldn't be, the college boys loved it, no dirty work. Dayo was disappointed and slouched off to the door, leant against it and looked out into the courtyard like a spoilt kid. Madame Severnou thought of something else.

'How did you get here?'

'Taxi.'

The jewelled hand flashed in the corner of my eye, my head kicked back. The inside of my mouth was all ploughed up. Dayo grabbed the front of my shirt and held me up to his face and I bubbled blood at him. Madame Severnou tapped him on the shoulder and said something in Yoruba, he dropped me and left the hut, clipping the door frame with his shoulder and rocking the whole structure.

Behind my head, in the alleyway, I heard Bagado pulling back the trigger of his thumb. The trick wasn't so effective front on, even to someone of Dayo's academic standing. There was the sound of someone being squeezed very hard and Dayo reappeared in the doorway with Bagado under his arm, limp as a roll of cheap carpeting. He dropped him by the bath and Bagado clawed his way up to my level.

'Who is he?' said Madame Severnou.

'My driver.'

'Where's Moses?'

'Sick.'

Madame Severnou's face stilled again, her lids seemed to puff out and her eyes slitted. After a minute's silence in which nobody moved, not even the rats, Madame Severnou spoke.

'I told Jack Obuasi you big mistake.'

'Jack's never been a great listener.'

'If my men in Cotonou kill you from start, we no have problem we have now.'

302

'Is that why you sent them?'

'Only to frighten small and . . .' she stopped herself.

'. . . and take some more money?'

'Why not?'

'Jack was upset.'

'Jack,' she said, as if it was something cockroaches fed on. 'He come tellin' me you lookin' for Kershaw man now. Keepin' you away from this thing we doin' here. Now look' – she pointed at me and looked up at the college boys – 'this what happen when Mister Jack done thinkin'.'

'Sounds like you've got a lot of respect for him.'

Her eyes swivelled and fastened on Bagado who had taken on the miserable look of the boss's driver who was about to die.

'Three cotton bales,' she said, and Harvard took his notebook out again.

'How much heroin did you bring in?' I asked.

'Beat them,' she said and moved to the door.

Dayo warmed to this like a pyromaniac with a box of matches and a licence to torch the joint. He hauled me out of the bath and lifted Bagado to his feet. He put the bath on top of a pallet of floor tiles, took an empty pallet and broke off three lengths of wood. He threw two at the college boys. There was a swift crack, our knees buckled and we hit the plastic sheet. We put our hands over our heads and the blows rained down. We rolled on to our sides and the pine planks continued to cut through the air, thudding into us sometimes with a sharper snapping sound if the wood hit a bone close to the surface. The first minute was bad. The pain was new, unexpected and specific. Later, my body reached a plateau of agony above which the nerves and brain were not prepared to go.

Madame Severnou said something in Yoruba from the doorway. They rolled us on to our fronts. Bagado's raincoat was stripped off, our ankles and knees tied and then our wrists behind our backs. Dayo picked up Bagado by the waistband of his trousers and took him to the store room where the lavatories, bidets and wash basins were stacked to the ceiling and threw him in. Bagado let out a half shout, half scream and then was silent. Dayo came back for me and hurled me into the same room, my forehead connecting with the rim of a toilet bowl. The room tilted and things seemed far off and infused with green. White lights arced in the dark planetarium of my skull and nothing seemed familiar, not even my huge tongue in the vast, unmapped cavern of my mouth.

The concept of time passing came back as slowly as it took for the picture in my eyes to click sharp without drifting or fish-eyeing. Sweat poured off me into a dark patch where my head made contact with the grit on the concrete floor. Nausea crept up my throat and I breathed it back down. My head was huge and somebody else's, all the joints in my body ground into each other. A weak light came from under the door and over the top of the partition wall. There was the sound of crying in the room. I rolled over and pain shunted down the nerve tracks. Bagado lay with his back to me, his shoulders shaking.

'Are you all right?' I asked.

The sobbing became more intense.

'Are you crying?'

'I'm laughing.'

'I didn't hear the punchline.'

'There's no joke. It's just very bleak . . . the outlook.
I get hysterical. I think my collar bone is broken.'

A chair scraped, footsteps approached through the
pallets next door. A body brushed against some plastic
wrapping around the cartons of tiles outside. I rolled
back. The door opened, a torch light bounced around
the room. The door closed, the footsteps retreated, two
voices exchanged something.

The smooth, rounded, glazed contours of the sani-
taryware offered little in the way of comfort and nothing to cut through rope. I squirmed around on the floor
looking between the stacked columns for something
with an edge. Bagado asked me what I was doing and
then told me about the penknife in his sock. I worked
my way round to Bagado's feet and with my crushed
and split fingers eased the penknife out. We opened it
between us and fixed it in Bagado's hand.

The rope was a very tough kind of hemp and the
one and a half inch blade didn't rip into it with chainsaw
enthusiasm. Bagado's collar bone, a couple of visits
from Dayo, and the awkwardness of the angle meant
that after three quarters of an hour we were still not
through the rope.

I reminded Bagado that the inside of a cotton bale
is a very warm place to be with a limited supply of
oxygen and the only water to look forward to, salty. I
strained at my wrists against the rope and felt the
strands of hemp snapping. A chair toppled. Bagado
stopped sawing. I urged him on. A table leg shifted.

Bagado forced the blade down. Footsteps neared and then receded and came back again quicker. The hemp snapped. I came up on to my knees. The door handle turned. I stood and leaned against the columns of toilets. The door opened. I picked up a lavatory and in one movement swung it across my body, lifted and slammed the thick rim of the bowl into Dayo's face.

For a moment, I thought he wouldn't fall but would just give me a last look at his clean white teeth before he put his hand through my chest and tore my spine out through the front. He did fall, straight as a plank, and the back of his head hit the concrete floor and didn't bounce. Something metallic skittered away amongst the pallets.

I tore the knife out of Bagado's hands and sawed the rope between my knees. The boy who'd stayed with Dayo was muttering Yoruba in a hoarse whisper. I started on the ankle rope and looked round the door jamb and saw the college boy's head outside the hut. He was crouched below the window line. The only light was on the verandah. It shone across the plastic wrapping on the tops of the pallets of floor and wall tiles at the front of the hut. Here in the back it was dark. The boy crawled through the door. I heard his gun's action sliding and the safety snicking off.

The ropes around my ankles loosened. There was a slap of a hand on plastic. Bagado panted with adrenaline. Sweat dripped off my face and spotted my shirt. A foot made contact with a wooden pallet. A shirt brushed against cardboard cartons. I picked up a handful of six inch by six inch wall tiles. They were thin with sharp corners.

I crawled out of the store room and frisbeed a wall tile into the far corner of the hut. A silenced gun spat a bullet into the same corner. The boy was to my right, about fifteen feet away, and nervous that whatever was in here had chewed Dayo off and spat him out. His head ducked behind a palletful of tiles about three feet high. Dayo lay at my feet, his gorilla hands empty, the torch by his head, broken. The lavatory with a large chunk missing from the rim lay on its side beyond him. A dark stain edged out in the concrete by his left shoulder.

The college boy moved again. Stealth was not his best quality. I stayed still, with my back against the wall next to the store room door, and hidden by two pallets of tiles stacked on top of each other about seven feet high. The boy was on the other side, breathing in too much air. I held two wall tiles, one in either hand in the shape of a diamond. His back shifted along the plastic covering of the pallet of tiles. I stood up, my knees didn't crack. His head appeared two feet off the ground, then his shoulders and a leg. He turned his back square to me and brought the gun up in front of him in both hands and rested it on some cartons. I took one step and jammed the two sharp corners of the wall tiles into his face.

His scream was terrible, starting off as a bellow like a cow in labour and reaching the shriek of a frightened monkey. He twisted round and two shots thumped out of his gun into the roof before it toppled from the back of his hand and he fell backwards into me, tearing at his face. The back of my head cracked into the door jamb, a glancing blow. The college boy bounced off the partition wall, twisting and writhing, his hands at his face and just a high-pitched whine coming from his wide open mouth. I picked up the lavatory bowl next to Dayo and cuffed him across the face with it. He collapsed across a pallet of tiles.

I dropped the toilet and in the light from the verandah saw that he had pulled one tile out of his right eye, which was punctured, and a clear, gelatinous liquid oozed on to his cheek. The other tile remained stuck just below the left eye. I dropped to my knees and vomited a gob of bitter mucus on to the floor, where my hand found his gun.

There was a Stanley knife on one of the pallets of tiles for slashing plastic and I used it to cut Bagado free. On the back of a chair on the verandah was a jacket with a clip of bullets in the pocket for the gun. My keys lay on the table, the car was in the courtyard. A warm wetness oozed from the old wound on the back of my head. Bagado had found his raincoat but couldn't put it on. He had split four packages from the table and was sprinkling heroin around the warehouse like rat poison.

# Chapter 27

It took some time for me to open the gates with a set of fat fingers which felt as if a microsurgeon had attached them to the wrong knuckles. So that by the time I'd scraped not just one, but both car doors getting out of the tight corner of the cul-de-sac, it was first light. Bagado sat with his arm crossed over to his opposite shoulder. We came out of the estate on to an empty highway and rather than go into Lagos continued back to Idiroko. I turned south off the Idiroko road to Ado where we stopped and cleaned ourselves up. There was blood down my shirt and I couldn't cross the border like that. Under my shirt I was almost the same colour as Bagado.

'Now you know what it's like to be black,' he said.

'I do?'

'It hurts,' he said, holding off a laugh. We reached Badagri at eight o'clock and I bought a second-hand shirt from a stall in the market. It was the only one in my size – a bat-winged affair in turquoise and pink. I looked like a jobbing flamenco guitarist from a package resort hotel who'd thrown himself under a truck. I tucked the gun and the spare clip in the springs under the driver's seat. Bagado lay in the back under his raincoat and looked malarial without trying.

There were a lot of checkpoints leading up to the

border, but most of the officials were having breakfast and waving people through. We weren't sure whether Madame Severnou would have found Dayo and the college boy and if she had, whether she had the influence to have us detained at the border before she came and rag-dolled us for good. We drove into the border post compound pumped up with adrenaline with Bagado intoning the word 'calm' as if he was on a language tape.

An Immigration official with half-closed muddy eyes stamped my passport and flipped Bagado's identity card back at me without looking at it. I walked to Customs where a large pot-bellied officer with the bottom four buttons of his tunic open finished eating. He washed his hands and face from a bowl held for him by a small boy and raised his large frame off the small stool he'd been sitting on. He eyed me with an apparent lack of interest while he cleaned his teeth with his tongue and wrestled his tunic over his tight brown gut. He hitched his trousers up.

'I like your shirt,' he said and walked past me, taking my passport as he went.

He walked with a solid step, the heel hitting the ground as if he was preparing it for a place kick. He rolled his head on his neck and fluttered his hand over his hair, hovering at a bald patch that had just started in the centre of his crown.

The sun was already hot at half past eight. The officer stuck his fingers into his waistband, flapped his arms, revealing two plate-sized damp patches, and wafted his pungent sweat smell in my direction. He stopped at the boot of the car and pointed a finger which he wiggled as if he was bouncing a miniature ball on its end. I opened the boot. He didn't look in, but looked around him, surveying the people in the compound and nodding as if counting them off. Then, with the same finger, he bounced the ball down again. I shut the boot thinking this was all we needed – a performance from one of the great Nigerian hams.

The officer had composed himself about five yards from the rear door and clasped his hands in front of his groin. He nodded at the door, which I opened. Again, he looked away at the crowd and brought his hands up to his hips. One hand slid up to his breast pocket and brought out a toothpick which he put in his mouth. He looked in the car and his eyes popped out and his mouth dropped open, leaving the toothpick jammed in between two teeth.

'What is this?'

'He's my driver. He's sick.'

He folded his face back down again.

'Driver!' he roared.

'Yessir,' said Bagado.

'Your driver is alive,' he said showing me his teeth, tongue and quivering uvula as if he was considering eating him.

I shut the door. He opened the driver's door himself, went down on his haunches, and his knees cracked like plastic bottles in the sun. He put his hands under the seat. I went down next to him and stared at his neck. I could see Bagado's eyes through the gap behind the seat and they weren't 'calm' any more. The Customs buffoon took his hands out and put them on the sill. For a moment, nothing happened. Our eyes connected.

311

What I saw in them was not what I had expected –
pain and embarrassment. I blinked the white fear in
my own away and the policeman whispered: 'Help me.'

His knees had locked. I stood behind him and shoved
both my hands into the moist underworld of his armpits. A white hot needle shot through my ribs. With
both of us grunting, we still couldn't get his knees
beyond ninety degrees. I walked him back to the Customs shed and fitted him on to a stool where he wrote
out my gate pass.

At the barrier, I gave the old man the pass and 100
CFA and the white metal pole shot up. There was a
shout. Bagado yelled something from the back. The
barrier dropped. Bagado groaned.

'Now we are dead people,' he said.

A young man in a floor-length white robe strode
with the maximum stride that the robe permitted and
arrived at my window. He bowed and put his hand into
a slit pocket and took out my passport.

'Good journey,' he said, and Bagado laughed like a
hyena.

In forty minutes we were in the Cocotiers district of
Cotonou where they have the airport, the Sheraton, all
the Embassy residents and a private clinic. I made a
deposit of 75,000 CFA for Bagado's treatment and they
told me to come back in an hour.

I drove back to the house using the accelerator and
the horn with occasional reference to the brake. I was
crazed with lack of sleep and wild with hope that Heike
would be there and that, for the first time in my history
of human relations, I could come up with something

tender, loving and careful. I wasn't dressed for the mission and my brains were leaking out of my head, which wasn't encouraging, but a reckless voice somewhere in the muddle was yelling: 'What the hell, go to it' and other high-spirited exhortations. It hadn't escaped my attention that tightening around my empty stomach was a thin garrotte of fear, that I'd look and sound pathetic, that she wouldn't believe me, that she'd be gone already.

I left the car outside the gates to the house and saw Heike's 2CV in the garage. I ran up the steps of the house, stripping off the flamenco shirt which hung on me like a three-toed sloth. The front door was open and part of the door jamb split. The banister saved me from an involuntary Acapulco dive back to the car. I got the gun out and, in a time that wasn't going to win me any prizes, found that there was a bullet in the chamber and the safety was already off.

I pushed the door open. The furniture was pleased to see me, piled as it was with cushions and carpets to the ceiling in a corner of the room. There was an envelope on the stripped floor addressed to me in Heike's writing.

*6.30 Tues 1st Oct.*
*You were told to leave this alone. I told you to leave this alone. Now these people are taking me somewhere and they're telling you that if you involve the police or continue whatever it is you think you are doing, they will kill me.*
*H.*

The sun was hot on my legs. I moved out of the doorway and stood in the room with my thoughts in Brownian motion. I felt sick, with nothing in my stomach but concentrated hydrochloric acid. The wild hope had addled, the fear of not knowing what to say had curdled into a terrible anguish and my mouth was suddenly full of ghastly-tasting spit. This was the worst possible thing that could have happened. This was worse than any tragedy. This was going to be unforgivable. I went to the kitchen and picked up a bottle of water off the flooded floor. It had been thrown out of the now empty and defrosted fridge. I rinsed out my mouth and looked at a broken bottle of separating mayonnaise.

In the wreck of the bedroom, I stripped and through some psychosympathy stubbed my toe on the way to taking a long shower, during which my thought processes steeplechased over an impossible course, the blood thundering in my ears.

Big blue contusions marbled with a sickly yellow covered all available skin area. Several of my fingers were swollen fat like sausages in the sun and the skin around the nails split like overripe tomatoes and my head was soft and lumpy like slapdash mash. I was becoming a canteen meal. I was sick of getting whacked around the place. This didn't use to happen. I did my job, got paid little bits of money, drank some beer, some whisky, read a few books and yet somehow did something which shot my horoscope into another galaxy where nothing was panning out and everything was screwing up.

I swam briskly through that sea of self-pity and

settled on the jagged problem that even if it was resolved was going to shatter another person's life and my own in the process. I didn't tread lightly on the broken glass but ground it in and stoked up some top grade, undiluted, sulphuric wrath. Somebody was going to suffer and it was probably going to be me again, but before that happened Jack Obuasi was going to feel my hard, blunt knee in his flaccid undercarriage.

Dressed, with a long-sleeved shirt on, I looked like the lucky one in a fifteen-car pile-up. I improved my speed with the gun, the mirror telling me I needed a badly chewed cigar. A clip of film ran in my head. Dayo lying on his back with the stain growing around his head, and the college boy with a gob of gelatine on his cheek. Something like a cold hand landed on my back, slid over my shoulder and caught me by the throat. My heart surged and pushed a huge quantity of blood into my brain and I leaned against the wall with my vision throbbing red. It was over in a moment, leaving me with a mark, black and deep somewhere in me I didn't know I had, but which reminded me with unfading permanence that I had killed a man.

I took the last money I had out of a window box on the verandah and, as I got into the car, had a sudden insight about the photographs. It was something about the two-shot of Kasparian and Kershaw. I took the photo out and drove back to the clinic.

Bagado was in reception with his arm in a plaster cast above his head looking despondent. There was no change from the deposit I'd given the clinic and we left and sat in the car. I showed Bagado the photograph and what I'd thought was suddenly important now looked less so, and I realized that I hadn't solved the whole puzzle but I had an interesting part of it in place.

'I assumed it was a self-timer,' I said.

'And now?'

'I know it's not.'

'How?'

'There isn't the posiness that self-timers have. The person who's pressed the button always has an inanity to their face. It comes from not trusting the camera to take the picture on its own. This photograph was taken by somebody.'

'The killer?'

I shrugged. 'The "friend" of Mrs Kershaw, perhaps.'

Bagado handed back the print, he was tired and in pain.

'You may be right, but it doesn't get us very far.'

I took Bagado back to my house with his arm out the window and told him about Heike. We came up with a plan, which began with a visit to Jack and ended with a confrontation with Charlie. With a gun in my hand and most of the puzzle in place I should be able to get Heike released. Bagado was going to contact his friends in Interpol about the heroin in Madame Severnou's warehouse and I would call him from the house in Lomé about the fax on the *Osanyin*.

It was going to take some time for the investigative system to kick in, Madame Severnou could have cleared the warehouse, we didn't know where the cotton bales were, and it was conceivable that the *Osanyin* was already loaded and steaming for Europe. Our only advantage was that Madame Severnou didn't know that we had any idea about the *Osanyin*.

Bagado was going to get some sleep then wait by the phone in my house from eight o'clock that evening. I was going to take a room in a hotel in Lomé, sleep, pick up the fax and then get to work on Jack Obuasi.

I left Bagado outside my house waving at me with the fingers of his permanently raised hand. I made quick time to the border and ate my first food for twenty-four hours. At two o'clock, I booked myself into the Hotel Ahodikpe Eboma, whose name sounded dyspeptic but whose rooms were large and had fans. I lay on the bed with the gun under the pillow and went to sleep fully clothed with the fan churning the heavy afternoon air.

I woke up with something in my throat that wanted to be a loud scream. It was dark. The heat was packed hard into the room and the fan barely turned. I lay on my back with a weight on my chest which proved to be my hand. The pillow was sodden. Passing cars lit the room through the slatted blinds in rushes. My watch told me it was eight-thirty. There was the sound of people drinking outside in the street. I showered and dressed in a loose T-shirt, jeans and black trainers. I put the gun in the bag, went down and paid for the room and drove to the Lomé house where I hoped the fax and nobody else would be waiting.

I parked some way from the house, near the Grande Marché, and, armed with the gun, walked across the wasteland which brought me to the garden wall. I climbed the wall, which left me feeling trampled to death on the other side. I set off towards the french windows and the parrot treated me like a piece of skirt it had just seen from its scaffolding; I stopped dead, waiting for the searchlights to come on. Nothing happened. I reached the french windows which were locked. I should have done something nifty with a credit card but I didn't carry one. I kicked the door open, which juddered to its hinges, and I just saved the glass from smashing against the wood carving.

I found the fax from my friend Elwin Taylor curled up under the table. It told me that the owners of the *Naoki Maru* had received reports of engine trouble between Cotonou and Lagos and then lost contact with the vessel Thursday 26th September, 20.00 hrs. The *Osanyin* hadn't been so easy to track down. Elwin hadn't been able to get any information on the ship from any UK source connected with the Baltic Exchange or Lloyd's. He had found it very difficult to get through to Monrovia, the Liberian capital, and when he had, the official he had been speaking to cut the line after he had given the vessel type (an SK-14, same as the *Naoki Maru*) and owner's name, A & S Shipping Ltd, Lagos. There was no such company traceable in Lagos. Elwin, being of the rare, intelligent type of broker, had then contacted some agents he knew in Lagos who had told him that A & S Shipping Ltd did not exist but the *Osanyin* was at dock in Apapa. The agents knew this because they had arranged a part to repair some lifting gear over No. 5 hold so that a consignment of hi-fi could be discharged. Payment for everything was being made in cash, in dollars. The fax finished with the words: 'Does this help?'

I phoned Bagado and left the house by the same

route as I'd arrived. I drove to Jack's house, trying to kill a mosquito that I could hear whining in my ear with the insistence of an untrapped idea.

# Chapter 28

As I passed the wall to the side of Jack's house I could see a low light in his bedroom and the rest of the house in darkness. I parked behind the house several streets down, where local people sat outside a bar drinking beer and jiving in their seats to music. I took the gun out, unscrewed the silencer which I put in my pocket and jammed the gun in the waistband of my jeans, folding the T-shirt over it. I walked around Jack's house and listened. Everybody had been given the night off. I hopped over the wall, which didn't do the ribs any good, and nearly emasculated myself on the gun. I let myself in at the back of the house through the double doors of the dining room. What noise I made was drowned by the air-conditioner breathing out of Jack's room into a night thick with wet heat, cicada noise and bamboo growing audibly in the garden.

I ran up the carpeted stairs, screwing the silencer on the gun, and padded down the marble-tiled corridor, the air-conditioner's breathing getting louder and louder. Above the noise came a sound of methodical, concentrated grunting and a bedstead bucking against the wall. I waited until the condenser in the air-conditioner cut in with a metallic whingeing and opened the door.

Jack was naked with his back to the door, kneeling on the bed, his buttocks pumping and squeezing as he thrust at the raised white bottom of a woman in front of him. His dark hand was stark against the creamy white skin where he gripped her hip. Her blonde head lay on the pillow, her arms thrown out on either side, her hands clenching wads of sheet, her back sloping up, her sex abandoned to the vehemence of Jack's powerful and quickening shunts. Their moist skins slapped together. Jack's breathing grew harder and a low growl came from the woman's throat. I placed the barrel of the silencer on the nape of Jack's neck. He shuddered to a halt, his back quivering with the lost rhythm.

'Come on!' said the woman, thrusting her bottom back. 'Come on, for God's sake!'

'You won't be doing that for a long time, Jack,' I said.

'I hope that's a gun, Bruce. I'm not the sharing type.'

'I'm not finding things so funny these days.'

'Don't go losing your sense of humour on me . . .'

'Shut up, Jack,' I said quietly, and he did.

As soon as the woman heard an alien voice in the room, she'd thrown herself forward from Jack and turned, scrabbling for the sheet to cover herself. It was Elizabeth Harvey. Her hair no longer piled high on her head but torn apart like a hayrick in a gale.

'Success at last,' I said, prodding Jack with the gun. 'Nearly.'

'Into the bathroom please, Mrs Harvey,' I said. She skipped in there, sporting Jack's paw marks on her hips. I told Jack to get dressed.

'It's time to see what you and Charlie have got to say to each other.'

As I shut the bathroom door, Elizabeth Harvey opened her lips to show me those sloping back teeth of hers. There was no fear in her, but her eyes were black with humiliation and anger. I closed the heavy mahogany bathroom door and locked it. That was one guest list I was never going to get on.

Jack limped around the room picking up his clothes, his semi-erect penis making him look foolish. Mrs Harvey's clothes lay neatly folded on a chair weighed down by a densely packed purse. There'd been no passionate ravishment in *her* corner.

Jack was dressed. I stood in front of him and held the gun in his gut. I raised my knee so hard into his groin that he came off the floor and slid backwards off my leg on to the polished tiles where he held his aching genitals and bit the air.

'That's for involving Heike in this business.'

I followed up by drilling a penalty kick into his partially protected testicles and he slid across the floor, cracking his head on the wardrobe.

'And that's for involving me in this business.'

I picked him up by the scruff of his shirt and hauled him out of the room, pushing him down the corridor and stairs, kicking him out on to the portico and dragging him to his car. I let him squirm on the floor for a few minutes until his breath stopped coming out in lumps, and then I kicked him in the legs until he stood up. I pushed him into the passenger seat and shoved him over the gear shift into the driver's seat.

Jack drove down the coast road with a gun under his ribs and his eyes wincing from his aching, undischarged testicles. To the left, the town was very quiet and to the right, the sea barely turned in a wave. There was nobody out and no cars on the road. A tyre burned where the road forked at the Mobil garage. As we passed the Sarakawa, I looked back and saw, far behind us, a single set of headlights.

'I'm sorry,' said Jack, gnawing at his lower lip trying to think how to get started.

'I believe you.'

'OK, you're right,' he said, thinking again, looking for a way in. 'I'm not sorry.'

'Go on, Jack, bare your bleeding heart and try not to make me puke.'

'Why the fuck d'you have to poke your nose in so far?'

'Why did you stick my nose in it in the first place?'

'Because you were there,' he said, and that was enough to set me off.

'Jack,' I said, staring out of the windscreen, 'you've got an honesty span of about three words. Maybe you started out in life thinking straight, I don't know, but somebody made the big mistake of teaching you how to speak and you picked up a vocabulary of concentrated shit to draw on. And since then, when you haven't been balls-out lying, you've been persuading yourself, and all the poor bastards who've bothered to listen, that you're OK, that you're as big on the inside as you are on your feet. But there's nothing there, is there, Jack? Maybe that's why you never sleep with the same woman twice. It's not because you get bored easily. It's because they find out they've been had. Been had by one of the hollow men, a shit-filled rubber doll, a stupid prick on the end of a bladder.'

'Buzz me when you're finished,' he said, bored.

'Don't tell me you're sorry, or you're not sorry. I don't want to know. Like all the other stuff that comes out of you, it doesn't mean anything. You shoved me in it with Madame Severnou because you didn't want to get dirt down your own shirt front. You threw me into the Kershaw business to get me away from the rice and to keep whatever information there was around coming your way. But you don't tell the gofer anything, you just use him to keep all the nasty stuff away. You're chicken, Jack, corn-fed, yellow-belly with skimmed milk for blood in your veins. All that crap about "sometimes I think you're my brother, other times my son" – it's just video pap, soap bubbles – you'd tip your brother and your son into a meat grinder if it was going to save your ass.'

Jack pulled up on the roundabout by the port for a road block – not a police or a military road block but a multi-party democracy road block. A young man stuck his head in the window and took a good look in the car.

'What do you want?' I asked.

'You give us something. Show you support democracy.'

'Open the barrier.'

'You give us something first.'

'I give you nothing.'

'Maybe we think you love the President,' he said, taking out a knife.

'That's an undemocratic-looking knife you've got there,' I said.

'You pay, yovo*!' he said through tight lips.

---

* Yovo – white man in Mina language.

'This is my undemocratic-looking gun,' I said, putting the muzzle of the gun into the eyeball of the young man. 'Open the barrier!'

He shouted something and two boys pulled away the rocks and tyres in the road.

*'Vive le Mouvement Togolais pour la Démocratie,'* I said and waved.

The headlights behind us had disappeared.

Jack buzzed the window up and we returned to our air-conditioned bubble. A few minutes later, we pulled over to cross the wasteland to Charlie's bar. I looked back at the road and a car drove past towards Cotonou, and then slowed and took the right turn to Al Fresco's, keeping parallel with us across the wasteland.

'Two hundred thousand dollars,' said Jack, with a green tinge across his features from the luminous dashboard.

'You're going to buy me like you buy your women?'

'It's all about money, isn't it?'

'You seem to think it is. What's two hundred thousand dollars?'

'Half the money from the heroin deal.'

'Sounds like you're getting ripped off.'

'I'll throw in the profit from the rice on top. Thirty-five thousand.'

'What do I have to do?'

'Let me drive back home. Forget all about it.'

'What about Heike?'

'I'll sort that out.'

'Just like you sorted Madame Severnou out,' I said. 'Let's face it together, Jack – sorting out is not one of your talents. We're driving along and you think it's still

325

all nicey-nicey, don't you, Jack? You think your part of the deal's done and you're going to get paid just like you do in any ordinary piece of business.

'But even ordinary business screws up. Product gets lost. People don't pay. Cheques bounce. But you've always got the law to fall back on. The only thing is, now you're outside the law and we both know that you're not a hard enough man to provide your own law. That's why you employ me to do your dirty work for you in Cotonou. You haven't got the stomach for it. You want to be liked too much. Smiling Jack of the Gold Coast.

'But people don't laugh very much when they're dealing drugs. The money's too big. They get a sudden feeling they don't like you, don't like your smiling face, don't like the way they have to pay you for doing not very much, don't like the way you've become an expensive, big-mouthed overhead that cuts into their percentage and then they just think: "Let's shut him down, wet him, clip him, whack him, waste him, top him, max him, rub him out." You ever wonder why these people have so many different ways of saying the same thing? It's because they do it everyday and they get bored of saying the word "kill".

'So before you start offering me part of your share, you better make sure you've got the balls to make him give it to you. You didn't have the balls to make Madame Severnou give you back your fifty million, did you? But maybe you've got a better chance with Charlie than you have with her. She's got about as much respect for Iron Jack as a whore for a sad-arsed punter.'

Jack blinked and passed a dry tongue over his lips,

our bodies rocked together as the car dipped and rolled over the mud road, his cheeks shook.

'You don't know shit,' he said.

The car that had been making its way to Al Fresco's had stopped, its lights cut; I couldn't see if anybody got out.

Jack and I cruised through the barrier of Charlie's compound at 10.30. The *gardien* had lifted the red and white pole as soon as he had seen Jack's car. The restaurant and bar were shut. We walked down towards the sea and crossed in front of the bar to the door at the side of Charlie's house. Jack tried the door, which opened.

The light coned down on to the jug which was still in the hall, the flower with the excited comb not looking as interested in life as it had before. I glanced down as I stepped in and sensed a movement. Jack wasn't in my line of sight any more. I angled the gun towards him and felt something hard nudge up behind my ear. That was when I knew the difference between a finger with a thimble on the end of it and a large-gauged handgun with a sight on the barrel.

'Know what this is?' asked Charlie.

'A gun?' I hazarded.

'That's right, Brucey, but what type?'

'A Smith and Wesson Schlong?'

'Wise ass. It's a Colt Python.'

'That's marketing for you,' I said. 'Nobody's going to buy a Colt Asp.'

'Still feeling clever, huh? If I shoot this it'll take your head off. If I hit you with it you might wake up for Christmas.'

'All right, you persuaded me. I'm dumb.'

'Moses is here. Says you'll explain everything. He's been sweating it out in the genny house the last twenty-four hours. Let's have the gun.'

I handed him the gun and walked down the corridor, smelling a familiar perfume. He jabbed me into the living room and pushed me down on to a sofa. Jack relaxed in the middle of the sofa opposite. Charlie fixed a couple of drinks. One wasn't for me.

'Yvette here?' I asked.

'What's it to you?' snarled Charlie.

He put my gun down on the glass tabletop and sat down along the sofa from me, his leg crooked up and his tongue licking the whisky off his dark lips.

'Let's go, Bru – shoot.'

'Where do you want me to start?'

'Let's start with why you got Moses snooping around and why you come here with a gun up Jack's ass.'

'Moses loves the beach.'

'Don't fuck with me, Bruce,' he said in that cold, quiet voice that came off the peg whenever I was in the room.

'Moses was staking you out. I came here with "a gun up Jack's ass" because I wanted to hear the two of you discussing your cotton shipment out of Lagos tonight.'

Jack slapped his leg and leant back on the sofa giggling.

'You getting something out of this whisky I'm not?' asked Charlie, moving his eyes over Jack without turning his head.

Jack sat back, threw his arm along the back of the sofa and closed his mouth.

'What the fuck business is it of yours what I do with cotton out of Lagos?'

'It's not my business,' said. 'It's yours, and that's bad news for you.'

'What's this asshole talking about?' Charlie asked Jack, and Jack played dumb with all the natural talent he possessed. 'Bru, we don't know what you're talking about. Start at the beginning. It's easier for us.' Charlie looked at me with mock-enthusiasm and waved the big black hole of the gun barrel at me along the back of the sofa.

'The Python's making me nervous.'

'Percy?' said Charlie, looking at the gun. 'Yeah, that's what he's supposed to do.'

'Are we going to talk like real people?' I said, suddenly needled by Charlie and his big boy's gun. 'Or do we just get our dicks out on the table and measure up?'

'You just tell me what you fucking know,' said Charlie, putting the gun in my cheek. 'And don't try and run this show. It's not yours to run. Now sick it up like a good boy.'

'Where's Heike?'

'Goddammit, start at the fucking beginning.'

'Why're you making me tell you what you already know?'

'I like hearing stories about myself.'

Jack sat with his arms straight, hands on either side of him on the sofa, back stiff, the tendons of his neck standing out, legs splayed, his testicles probably still pulsating. He was comfortable but not as comfortable as he would have been with a gun in his hand. His eyes didn't know which of us to look at. Charlie flicked the gun back with his wrist, the nickel-plated sight flashed and before it ripped across my nostrils I came up with a version of the story so far delivered at pace.

'On the 23rd September, Françoise Perec, an operative for the International Maritime Bureau, was tortured and killed in Steve Kershaw's apartment in Cotonou. Kershaw found her, panicked and ran for it back to his house in Lomé. Somebody caught up with him, suffocated him, framed him with the Perec killing tools, stole a million dollars cash from him and dumped him in the pool, making it look a bit like suicide, which it wasn't. The maid was found floating face down in the lagoon and an Armenian businessman's wealth was redistributed by a car bomb in Abidjan.

'You, Charlie, told me three things. The first that Kershaw had been with a blonde Frenchwoman in your bar; the second, that Kershaw had had an affair with Nina Sorvino which ended on a sick note; and the third, that you didn't much care for Steve. There were a few things you didn't tell me. You didn't tell me that you had had a relationship with Nina, that you hated Kershaw because he walked off with your woman, that you knew exactly what had happened between Nina and Kershaw and gave Kershaw a "talking to" about it.

'On 23rd September you were in Cotonou. The same day Perec caught it. An expired Bloomingdale's store card in your name was found in the garden of the house where Kershaw died. I got two visits from people telling me to back off; the first hit me on the head with something hard, heavy and Pythonesque. The second showed me what happened to Kershaw before he was dumped in the pool. Both used the same terminology which was: Drop it!

'When I told Nina about Kershaw's "drowning" she got scared. I watched her at the Embassy party trying to give you a hard time. You'd implicated her in Kershaw's death because you persuaded her to tell me about Kershaw's bondage tastes, and she didn't like it. You reckoned you'd paid off the police in Cotonou and the big man's illegally acquired million dollars was enough to keep the heat off in Lomé and she'd got nothing to worry about.

'The next day I trod on Nina. She told me about your very romantic liaison. She told me she's pregnant and she wants to get back with you, which was maybe another reason she was leaning on you at the party. She told me that you bent Kershaw's arm about how he got his kicks. And I found she's got a drug problem. Where was she getting the drugs from, Charlie?

'Jack's rice was shipped in from Thailand on a vessel called the *Naoki Maru*. That was the ship that Perec was getting too warm on and why you had to find out what she knew. There's a rice ban in Nigeria so Madame Severnou is brought in to smuggle it across the border at Idiroko. But she's been in on it all the time because it wasn't just rice in those sacks.

'Some of the sacks unloaded at a warehouse in Idiroko were taken to another warehouse in Ikeja where they were emptied out and small kilo-size brown packages were found inside. These brown packages contained a white powder which wasn't rat poison but just as good. They were stuffed into cotton bales which were purchased at one thousand four hundred and twenty-five dollars per ton c.i.f. delivered Oporto from AAICT by the buyer, one Carlo Reggiani at the AAICT offices in Ikeja, Lagos in the presence of Jack Obuasi, Madame Severnou and Bof Awolowo on Sunday 29th September. The cotton bales are being shipped ex Lagos probably tonight, 1st October, on the vessel *Osanyin* aka *Naoki Maru*. Have I left anything out? Oh yes, the dirt around town is that Charlie Reggiani took some bad hits playing with gold . . . they say the man needs some money. They say it was seven hundred thousand dollars.'

Charlie had walked over to a sideboard with a set of shelves above it and pulled down an ebony bowl which was full of credit cards. He flicked through them all and put the bowl back up on the shelf.

'What was that about a million dollars?' asked Jack.

'Shut the fuck up,' said Charlie, cuffing Jack across the back of his head with the tips of his fingers. He sat back down on the sofa, looking hard at Jack who did his best to stay still and failed. He put his left ankle on his right knee and held it there with both hands and tried to stare Charlie out. Charlie turned to me and asked the one question I hadn't expected.

'What's with you and Yvette?'

'What do you mean?'

'You came in here sniffing the air, asking after her. You got something going together?'

'Like what exactly?'

'You wanna be English about this, I'll be American. Are you fucking her?'

'Charlie, I'm the punchbag in this. I nose around in

dirty laundry, get caught and get the shit beaten out of me. I don't have time . . .'

'You've fucked her,' he said. 'You have. First time you saw her . . . all that marriage and *concubinage* shit . . . You fucked her.' His lips had gone white at the edges and the teak dome of his head had taken on a purplish colour.

'I haven't done anything to anyone, apart from kick Jack in the balls and he's had that coming a long time,' I said, finding myself looking down what seemed to be a one-inch hole which was the Colt Python's barrel.

'Just tell me the truth. Nothing will happen if you tell me,' said Charlie. 'Just don't lie to me.'

I didn't want to tell him the truth because he would think I'd lied to him and I didn't want to lie to him because the size of the bullet that would come out of that hole was going to make me an instant airhead. I came up with: 'She's your woman,' which didn't end in a big bang.

'I know that,' he said sweetly, 'but it didn't stop her from going round to your place after the party Saturday night and it didn't stop you two dickering over something outside the Sarakawa yesterday, and didn't stop you going into the Sarakawa with her and staying in there for Christ knows however long it took you to give her a good schtupping.'

The barrel of the gun was shaking. He was gripping the butt so hard his forearm stood out swollen with pumped muscle, his flexed triceps were set solid, his neck was bright red where it came out of his chest hair, his mouth was closed, and his clenched jaw muscles worked hard. Jack was sitting forward on his sofa. I was pressed back hard into the corner of mine.

The door opened. Charlie's head twitched and he lowered the gun behind a cushion on the sofa. Yvette came in, followed by a vapour trail of perfume. She was in a blue short-sleeved dress and no shoes with a purse held tight against her hip.

'Honey, this is business,' said Charlie. 'Can you give us a few minutes?'

Yvette stood between the two sofas at the end of the glass-top table. Her face was still and white, her mouth closed in a bloodless line. Her body was taut, a line of muscle ran the length of her calf from knee to ankle. Her flat stomach pumped in and out as she panted air through her nose. She slipped past me and stood in front of Charlie between the sofa and the table. She clicked open her purse. Charlie spoke to her in a quiet, intimate way, as if we weren't supposed to hear.

'Honey. Look, this is serious. Fix a drink if you want, but it's better you wait outside.'

She was pulling out a pack of cigarettes and Charlie leaned forward to pick up the table lighter for her and his face ran into a small shiny black gun that Yvette held in her hand. He sank back into the sofa with his face in his lap. Jack's mouth opened slowly with the weight of his jaw. I managed the least moronic look in the room just by holding my teeth together.

'Put the gun down on the table,' she said, her small tongue wetting her lips. Charlie hesitated, still in shock. 'Put it on the table, you fucking bastard!'

Charlie was looking at me as if I was responsible for

this. He slid the gun out from under the cushion until it was flat on the sofa and angled towards me.

'You did, didn't you?' he said to me, the gun now up off the sofa, going towards the table.

There was the sound of a shot. A pane of glass from one of the windows cracked and collapsed; large shards fell on to the floor and shattered as Jack's head kicked back with the snapping sound of a dry twig and most of the back of his head sprayed itself over the sofa, sideboard and living room wall.

Yvette fired her gun on a reflex and Charlie his. The noise filled the room like a jet engine in a public toilet. Charlie's body twitched and arched up off the sofa, while Yvette's feet left the ground, her body twisted, and she came down on her face across the glass tabletop, which shattered. Then the lights went out and the faint hiss of the air conditioning cut.

Through the high-pitched whine in my ears, I could hear Charlie grunting in the dark as if he was lifting a big weight off his chest. There was the sound of dripping and the sea had come closer. Warm, wet air rolled in from outside and the cicadas blew the whistle on the show.

'She shot me,' said Charlie, as if he was speaking through a rag someone was stuffing down his throat. 'The bitch shot me.'

Yvette was silent. Her perfume still hung in the air, as did some acrid sweat and cordite. And there was another smell, sweet and metallic, that grew in the room with the heat.

'She fucking shot *me*,' said Charlie from the back corner of his mouth.

I slid off the sofa and knelt. I found Yvette's leg amongst the glass and moved my hand up over her thigh and hip. My fingers moved up her back, up her shoulders to her neck. There was still a pulse. She moaned and I moved my hand away to the point of her shoulder which was wet and ragged.

'You hit her, Charlie.'

'I'm hit myself, for Chrissakes.'

I found the table lighter whose yellow flame illuminated the scene. The predominant colour was black. The floor was black, the back of Jack's sofa, the sideboard and the wall were black. I turned to Charlie and pulled his hand away and wrestled his shirt up over his gut. There was a small black hole in his flank but not as much blood as I expected. I felt behind him. There was an exit hole.

'Straight through, Charlie. Blubber only,' I said, and he grunted.

I called for an ambulance from Charlie's study. Charlie told me where the torch was. I picked up my gun from where it was tucked in under Yvette's body and ricocheted out of the house towards the beach to the generator house.

Bagado had been right, Charlie was in the clear. That Bloomingdale's card had been one piece of evidence too much for Bagado's liking. Jack must have lifted the card and somebody planted it at the house. Charlie didn't know what was going on; as soon as I told him about his cotton shipment he let me play him in so that he could nail Jack. Just as I was beginning to doubt Bagado and believe my own bullshit, Charlie leant in with what he really wanted to know from me. What was *I* doing with Yvette? Christ, what a thing to ask *me* – the man with a love life like a train wreck.

The generator house door was open. I called out to Moses whose confidence had taken a huge knock since Grace had built it up. I found the starter key to the 13.5 Kva Lister and it roared and then settled. A dim light came on. Moses was standing behind four drums of diesel.

'Did you see him?'

'No please, sir.'

Outside, there was a clear line of sight to the house. In the red dust were some footmarks, a trainer of some kind without a brand name in the sole. I shone the torch down the fence and found more marks. He must have opened up the generator house, shot Jack, cut the generator and run back down the beach to Al Fresco's. Whoever it was had been sent to kill Jack at his own house and followed us to Charlie's.

In the living room, Yvette, her face cut up, had rolled over on the broken glass and was sobbing and trying to reach her torn shoulder with her hand. Charlie was half conscious and blabbering on a red mess on the leather sofa which wasn't soaking in, but dripped on to the carpet. I wrapped some towels around Yvette's shoulder and moved her into the bedroom, where she fainted. I found some more linen for Charlie's middle and bandaged him up. He was silent now and breathing heavily. I hoped they'd stay that way until the ambulance arrived. I didn't think they were two people who were going to socialize much in the future, given that their first penetrative exchanges had been bullets.

Jack was lying with one leg off the sofa, half his back

on the seat, the other half up the back of the sofa, his head in the apex. A huge quantity of blood and white and grey bits in it and black skin and curly hair spattered the sofa and wall and sideboard. His eyes didn't see the hole where his nose had been. He still showed his teeth, but not even a madman could call it a smile.

Outside, I called for Moses, who had lost his nerve and ran off into the night risking the beach muggers. The *gardien* had fled as well. I'd already decided on my third visit of the evening as the adrenaline rushing my brain decoded the confusion of what had just happened. I opened the barrier, fixed it and drove Jack's Mercedes out into the wasteland, out there, in the bleak and suffocating darkness, the missing detail from the photographs came to me and although I still didn't know who was behind the camera taking the shot on that sunny afternoon when Kasparian and Kershaw posed for him, I did know where he was.

# Chapter 29

By the time I hit the roundabout by Lomé port, the democratic road block had been moved away and I put my gun down on the passenger seat and enjoyed the clear run through down the coast road back to Jack's house. I was glad it was clear because I found that Jack's Mercedes was capable of 154 m.p.h.

I parked by my own car to pick up the photographs and checked them: even in the dim courtesy light of the Peugeot the missing detail stood out. All it had needed was a change of thinking, instead of looking for what was in the picture I looked for what wasn't. Then I drove to Kamina Village in Jack's Mercedes, but didn't go in because it was barriered off at night. I parked outside on the road by the hedge around Nina Sorvino's garden, put the photographs in my breast pocket and pushed the gun down the front of my trousers with the T-shirt over it.

I skipped over the shallow ditch and ran straight through the half-hearted hedge, which brought me out at the back of Nina's house. I walked around to the front and up on to the terrace outside her bedroom window. The light was on in the empty bedroom and there was an open packing case on the bed.

Through the living room window, I saw Nina in her stockinged feet standing in front of a full-length mirror on the far wall, her hair tied in a temporary ponytail. She was wearing a red raw silk suit and was looking over her shoulder to see what her bottom looked like with all that material stretched over it. She turned and positioned her feet so that she looked slimmer, less curvaceous and placed both hands on the tops of her thighs and leant back slightly. She pouted and then she laughed as if she was the luckiest bitch in the world.

I went into the garage and tried the door at the end of it, which, like the last time, was unlocked. I waited and listened to Nina shuffling in front of the mirror and then I heard her go into the bedroom. I went into a living room redolent of expensive perfume and sat on the sofa which backed on to her bedroom wall and stared at the empty TV screen and full bottles on the sideboard in front of me. There were three other suitcases parked by the front door.

She came back in again, at a swift pace now, with some high heels chocking the tiled floor and her hair loose, holding a red hat in her hands which she set on her head in front of the mirror. I got up and stood about five metres behind her. She was so in love with her situation that she didn't see me for a while and when she did she walked towards the mirror as if there was a problem with it. It was only when she turned that reality closed in on her and she squeaked.

'Going somewhere?'

'As a matter of fact, I am.'

'Far?'

'Up north, Kara for a few days.'

'Four suitcases for a few days?'

340

She moved towards the table and I lifted the T-shirt and showed her the gun.

'No cheap lines, Nina.'

'I wanna cigarette.'

'You're going to need more than that to get you through.'

She lit a cigarette. I asked her to get some whisky. She poured two stiff ones into some glasses on the sideboard with the TV.

'Four suitcases?'

'I travel heavy,' she said, taking a good suck on the whisky.

'When are you going?'

Tomorrow morning.'

'Who with?'

'On my own.'

'You always like to look good and smell nice for yourself, on your own? You always like to dance around in front of the mirror with your new clothes on and your fancy new hat before you hit the hot spots of the Hotel Kara on your own? You always pout and laugh at yourself in the mirror the night *before* you go somewhere . . . on your own?'

Nina sucked hard on her cigarette in the hope that the nicotine could do more for her than calm her down. She wanted something with a little more punch to it that was going to make all this nastiness go away. I handed her the photograph of Kasparian and Kershaw. She took it and stiffened.

'There are three people involved in that photograph. Kasparian, he's the one on the left, Kershaw, you know, and the third guy's behind the camera. Two of them are dead. Now, this is by way of a test, Nina. I want to make sure you don't start off our discussion by lying to me, which is what you seem to like doing. So I ask a question and you tell the truth and if you don't . . .' I took out the gun, pointed it at her and clicked off the safety. 'Which two are dead?'

'Kasparian . . . and . . . Kersh . . .'

She didn't finish and I'd just found out how difficult it was to shoot straight with a handgun with a silencer attached. I'd aimed a yard to her right but the bullet, I could tell from the mark on the wall behind her, must have passed close enough to go through that thick black mane of hers. She screamed, dropped her glass, cigarette and the photograph and wet herself. A dark patch spread out in the raw red silk of her skirt.

'Oh Christ!' she said, holding her cheeks. 'Oh, my God!'

'Two people you haven't had much contact with recently,' I said. 'Now, pick up the photograph.' She knelt in the tight skirt, cutting a knee on the broken glass. The cigarette had been doused by the whisky. She slipped the photograph off the wet floor.

'Cigarette?' she said.

I picked one out of the packet on the table, lit it and gave it to her.

'Try again.'

'Kasparian,' she said and dragged on the cigarette, 'and Gildas Sologne.'

'Thanks. I didn't know who he was, but I knew he was dead. He's the painter who was in the pool, right?'

She nodded, finding her mouth with the cigarette.

'Do you want to know how I know?'

She nodded again.

'Look in the bottom right-hand corner of the painting.' She looked. 'There's nothing there.'

'So?'

'There should be a signature that says "Kershaw", but it doesn't because Gildas Sologne is still alive and Steve hasn't painted on his signature yet.'

'Next question. Ready, Nina? Where's Kershaw?'

'I don't . . .' She didn't finish again, and this time I shot straight and over her other shoulder, and with a splat a hole appeared in the mirror glass which held for a moment and shifted and then fell to the floor in pieces.

'There doesn't seem to be any point in asking you these questions. You're just a junkie. A compulsive, lying junkie.'

'The Harveys,' she said in a half scream, looking back at the mirror which no longer reflected her tight, red, stained backside.

'Good. That's right. That's why when I followed you from the Pharmacie pour Tous on Route de Kpalimé and you went to the German Restaurant in town, you called the Harveys. I went in there after you and hit the 'Redial' button but I didn't know why someone like you would want to talk to someone like Elizabeth Harvey about you being pregnant.'

Nina was shaking now and it was with some difficulty that she took the cigarette out of her mouth.

'Last question before we leave. Where's Heike?'

She held out both her hands, waving them at me, the hot long cone of the over-smoked cigarette fell off and hissed in the liquid at her feet. The red of her lipstick had broken its boundary and huge fat tears were rolling down her cheeks, bringing black mascara that left tracks to the corners of her mouth. She coughed her first sob. I picked her handbag up and checked it, then took some Kleenex out of a box on the sideboard and handed them to her.

'Clean up; we're going.'

'Why?' she asked, with some distant logic for her present position.

'You're my currency of exchange. I hope you're worth something.'

While Nina patched up the damage to her face, I picked up the phone and left a very quiet message on an answering machine which I hoped would get listened to.

Nina wasn't capable of driving. I pushed her through to the passenger seat and drove myself with her curled in the corner of the seat looking into the ball of tissue in her hand. The Harveys' house was back on the east side of town between the Sarakawa and the Hotel de La Paix. We were there in a quarter of an hour and Nina had got herself back together. I told her to leave her high heels behind. She took two minutes to put some make-up back on so that she looked just right for the man in her life.

# Chapter 30

A twelve-foot wall stood between us and the front door of the Harvey mansion which was in darkness. Two wrought iron gates showed a driveway up to the garage at the side of the house, but these gates had harpoon-barbed spikes on the top so that it would take a surgeon with a ladder to get you off them. A small Peugeot was parked in the road which was probably Elizabeth Harvey's runabout and I thought for a couple of seconds that we could climb up on the roof and scale the wall from there, but my body staged a wild-cat strike that brought the management to its knees.

Next to the Peugeot was another gate which was fitted into the wall and was the one where Clifford and I had exchanged views what seemed like a few months ago. There was no way round it, over it or under it unless you were an airmail envelope. There was a *chien méchant* sign on the gate. I clicked back the latch and pushed the gate. It opened on to a narrow path which took us between two massive palms and twenty feet of lawn to the front door.

Bad 'bad dogs' tell you where they are from some way off. They growl, tap dance with their toenails on the concrete, slaver large quantities of goo and bark. Good 'bad dogs' are preceded in the last moments only by a rush of air before a white-toothed, hot-breathed necklace clamps on to your carotid. I held Nina by the collar of her suit and pirouetted up that path like a pansy up a drag queen catwalk and we reached the front door without Dobermans hanging off our necks.

The door was a large piece of mahogany with a shining brass dolphin leaping out of it. It wasn't the kind of door you took a run at and dropped your shoulder into unless you were so hardboiled you couldn't be eaten for breakfast. It opened on Teflon hinges with a push from one of my *merguez* fingers. The only thing that was missing was a gold-embossed invitation.

There was no sign or sound of air conditioning. There was a fan in the hall but it wasn't doing anything interesting. I crossed the hall with the gun in my hand and pushed Nina through some double doors into a living room with a half mile of sofa in it. There was a lamp in one corner with a Chinaman's hat shade about three foot across and it showed that nobody was round for drinks and that the carpet was being held down by a perspex table with magazines under its veneer, which showed you how life should be lived and by whom.

We hiked across the room and went through some sliding glass doors to the swimming pool and garden. The garden was walled with high, dreadlocked palms guarding it. A frangipani spread itself in one corner like a curtsying ballerina. The underwater-lit, kidney-shaped pool lapped and gurgled and simmered at my feet. I left Nina at the door and walked around the pool through the warm chlorinated air and looked up at the back of the house. A dim light shone in one room in the middle.

By the time we got to the top of the stairs my T-shirt

was like a tiresome girl at a disco. The stairs split in two at the second landing. I went left, pulling Nina, and found a bedroom with a sunken bath in the corner, full and steaming with nobody in it. The other stairway led us to a corridor with double doors off it on either side.

Faint light shone from the crack under the doors to the back of the house. I opened one door into a huge room with little in it apart from an acre of carpet and a desk. A cone of light shone from a downlighter on to the desk. A fan above sliced shadows on to a man in a white shirt. Clifford Harvey sat in profile in a large scoop of black leather chair. There was an upright chair on the side of the desk nearest me.

It was a jog to the desk but Nina and I walked it for effect. Clifford Harvey swivelled in his chair and put his elbows on a blotter in front of him that hadn't blotted anything since the ballpoint came in. He steepled his fingers. His shirt was advertisement-white with blade creases from the shoulders to the cuffs. The collar was detachable and starch-sharp and cut him across the carotid. His tie looked like open heart surgery.

'You look like someone who's going to say: "I've been expecting you,"' I said.

'You took your time,' he drawled. 'Put the gun down and take a seat.'

'I'll stick with the gun.'

'It's better you put it down.'

I backed away from the desk feeling for the chair. I didn't find the chair but I did find a rifle barrel in my spine. The voice that came with it was male and bored.

'Put the gun on the table, Bruce.'

'Not before I've put a hole through Nina, Steve,' I said in my best tough guy's voice.

'You do that,' he said, and Nina shuddered.

'Give me Heike and I won't have to.'

Kershaw laughed. I adjusted my grip. Some silence eased past.

'No bollocks,' he said. 'That's your problem. Go on, stick it to her,' he said, prodding me in the back with the rifle.

There was some sweat coming off me now and Clifford had reached forward and put his glasses on so that he could get a better view of the show. Nina's head was wobbling on her shaky neck.

'Come on, you bag of shit,' said Kershaw. 'Stick it to her . . . or put the fucking gun on the table.'

Nina's whole body was trembling now which was unnecessary because I knew I couldn't shoot her. I put the gun on the table.

'Rule number one,' said Kershaw. 'Don't threaten unless you can follow through. Your problem is you think too much. Don't think, just shoot. Bang. Next.'

Kershaw was standing in front of me. He was more of a spidery-looking guy than I'd expected from his photograph. He held the rifle in one hand. He was dressed in black – black trainers, black ankle-length cycling slicks, black long-sleeved sweatshirt. His hands and clean-shaven face were blacked up and he had a black hat on. He was perspiring big gobs of sweat through his boot black. He pulled the hat off and revealed a brown fuzz of crew cut hair beneath. He prodded my stomach with the rifle and I sat down. Nina threw her arms around him and buried her face in his neck, just as she'd been taught from the best years of her life watching B movies.

'We're very touched,' I said and Clifford grunted and took his glasses off and put them in his shirt pocket. Nina peeled herself away from Kershaw and turned to me. She was feeling a little cockier now that she didn't have bullets ripping past her ears. I could tell she was still smarting from the humiliation and her damp skirt reminded her of it. She swung her arm back and pre-pared to give me a taste of her open palm. Kershaw caught her by the wrist and shook his head at her with some meaning in his eyes. He took her by the hand to a door covered by a curtain at the side of the room and opened it. They whispered a few things and he came back to me and searched my pockets and found Jack's keys. He went back to the door. There was some more discussion and she disappeared.

Clifford pushed some cold cream and Kleenex over to Kershaw and moved a bin around with his feet. Kershaw watched me as he wiped his face off, throwing heavy handfuls of tissue into the bin. His eyes were hollow, the cheekbones pronounced, the jawline sharp and with muscular corners, but he had full lips that looked as if they'd done some kissing in their time but belonged to a bigger face. He finished cleaning himself and put his head down into the light and looked at me with wide eyes and a question mark on his forehead.

'Like it?' he asked.

'Impressive,' I said.

'You don't recognize me?'

'You lost a lot of weight.'

'Two 'n' 'alf stone,' he said, with some of his native

south London accent creeping over the Home Counties stuff he'd recently learned.

'Been enjoying yourself in the afterlife, Steve?'

'No.' He snapped it off like a piece of rock. 'I 'aven't. Apart from being very hungry, you've been giving me a lot of trouble.'

'Trouble's one thing dead men don't usually get.'

'My wife's been giving me hell.'

'Maybe you wronged her in a previous existence.'

'I'm not laughing,' he said looking at me straight, his head cocked to one side. 'And nor is she.'

'What was it, Steve?' I said, crossing a leg. 'The infidelity, the perversion, the lust, the greed, or the brutality.'

'Christ, you've got some fucking gob on you.'

'Right now it's all I've got.'

'Steve,' said Clifford, and Kershaw turned to see him gently batting the air over the blotter with his hands.

'My wife might not look very much but she's got a temper on her.'

'What's she done to you? Tied you down and slapped you about a bit. Or is that private?'

'She was pro-castration at one point.'

'That's the least she could do for humanity,' I said. 'Is she still here then?'

'Flight delayed,' said Steve. 'Now listen to me, Brucey boy, because this is going to keep you alive. If she comes in here before we get you out, I want you to keep your big gob shut.'

'About what?'

'Women.'

'Like Nina?'

350

'You're not listening to me, are you, Bruce?'

'Like Françoise Perec?'

He picked up the rifle. 'You ever caught one of these in your teeth?'

'Steve,' said Clifford, cautioning him again.

Kershaw's lips had disappeared into thin dark lines. They were stretched tight across his teeth, which looked sharp. His eyes hadn't narrowed but something behind them had. His pupils were smaller than a snake's nostril.

'Sorry, pal,' I said.

'I'm not convinced.'

'I'll pull a hair from my nose.'

'You won't have to when you see what Clifford's going to do to your Kraut bird.'

Clifford's hands were clasped across the blotter and he looked out into the room as if he was invigilating an exam. The downlighter hooded his eyes and did nothing for his image as a patrician banker.

'Clifford's got a taste for it after the Perec girl. He's got some new ideas. He's better prepared. So this is what'll happen. You'll go for a drive with Clifford to one of the bank's guest houses on Lake Togo; very quiet, very isolated, nobody for miles, you'll like it. Clifford'll show you his new techniques. He likes an audience. I haven't got the stomach for it. When he's finished with the girl, you know, after a couple of hours or so, he'll take your gun, stick it in that big mouth of yours and give you a new skylight. So keep it shut and it might not happen.'

Kershaw sat on the corner of the desk, which Clifford wasn't happy about, and clasped his hands around one knee. He looked at me as if he expected me to believe him. Me, who'd just seen the rough trepan work he'd done on his late partner's head and whose last words to me were: 'You don't know shit.' Shit was something I was beginning to know a lot about. I'd been submerged in it for a week now, and that's the best way to learn a language.

In the silence that followed Kershaw's offer, Clifford got to his feet with some plastic cuffs in his hand. He was going to put them on me when Kate Kershaw entered the cone of light. Clifford went back to his seat and opened and closed a drawer. I did my best to relax now that I knew I had more time, and Steve tensed. Kate was dressed in her usual no-frills way – a black T-shirt, a short black skirt and black pumps. Her legs were strips of muscle secured to the knuckles of her knees and ankles. Her hair was wet and she smelled of soap. She had her head back and sniffed the air which wasn't that nice to sniff.

'Still here?' I said, and she turned to me.

'What's left of me, Mr Medway. They say I'm leaving at four or five in the morning.'

'How's Elizabeth?' asked Clifford.

'Sleeping.'

'She must be tired,' I said, 'after breaking down that bathroom door.' Kate frowned at me, Kershaw let his knee go and brushed non-existent lint off his slicks. Clifford, the iceman in his alabaster shirt, seemed to stop breathing.

Kate Kershaw was definitely not 'in'. I didn't know if she was as far 'out' as Jack had been, but she definitely wasn't 'in' with this particular 'in' crowd. It didn't mean that she was *with* me, but it probably meant she wasn't against me. Looking at the other two possibilities in the room, she was the only chance of an ally I had.

'I don't understand, Mr Medway,' she said.

'It's nothing, Mrs Kershaw. I'm just tired and talking rubbish.' Steve and Clifford relaxed and I brought myself up to the marks for the final push.

'Why did you have to kill Gildas Sologne?' I asked.

'You know why?' Kershaw said to his wife.

'My husband needed an ID change,' said Kate. 'Been a naughty boy as usual –'

'Gildas Sologne,' Kershaw interrupted with the sort of French accent that orders fish and chips on the Cannes Croisette and never gets served, 'couldn't paint his way into a corner. Bloody load of crap. All that lost youth and innocence. Bollocks to it. "Faggy stuff" Clifford called it. He was as queer as a short-necked giraffe.'

'You killed him because he was gay?' I asked. 'Or because you didn't like his painting?'

Kershaw had blundered around that first question with the talent of a mountain bear in a dentist's waiting room. Kate was making him tense. He got himself under control and threw out a dead-end remark.

'He was HIV positive.'

'Put him out of his misery.'

'Why not?'

'Come on, Steve, why did you kill him?'

'Why did I kill him?' he said to himself, trying to work out where this was going to lead him and whether he minded being led there.

'You haven't forgotten?' asked Kate, the interest bristling off her. Kershaw twitched his head at her.

'He was the right size, right hair colour, right eye colour.'

'Yes.'

'And the only two people who knew he was there was me and Armen and he never left the house.'

'Why was Gildas here?' I asked.

'Like I said, he was HIV positive. He hadn't known for long and he got this romantic idea into his head that he would leave Paris, come to Africa and paint. Then, when he was ill, he'd kill himself or get Armen to help him. Armen and him lived together in Paris.'

'Who killed Armen Kasparian?' I asked, trying to keep him working.

'Professional,' said Clifford. 'A Chicago friend of mine knew some buck-hungry Liberians with some Semtex. They hopped over the border and snipped him off for fifteen grand. Gildas had already told Steve everything he needed to know. Even gave him Kasparian's card. A very trusting kind of guy.'

'You don't have to feel too sorry for Kasparian,' said Steve. 'He was HIV positive too.'

'The "me" generation gets into mercy killing.'

Steve snorted back a laugh.

'When did you know you were going to kill Gildas?'

'Weeks ago. He told me everything about himself within the first four days. He didn't have anybody to talk to, you see, so he tells me his whole life story and leaves me thinking this is a gift. So a few weeks ago, I start showing B.B. the sketches and get Kate to talk to him about art materials and stuff.'

'Nice touch with the baboon.'

'He told you that, did he? It didn't fool him. It was

his way of showing he liked me. I think he knew I was up to something, but that was the kind of bloke he liked.'

'Crooks and killers.'

'Crooks. He loved watching people trying to rip him off. He thought I might be a candidate. I must have disappointed him by not clearing the bank account out. I just didn't think of it.' Kershaw was more relaxed now, answering questions that didn't get too close to the bone. I was planning on a little lull before we got to the hard stuff.

During the grilling, I checked out Kate Kershaw to see if anything else was a surprise to her. From the start she believed that she was down here to get her husband a new ID, and now it was up to me to show her, without too much desperation, that there was a greater scheme which didn't include her future.

She surprised me. I didn't have her down as the brutal type. She wasn't unnerved by her husband and his convenience killing. Then again, she wasn't a pretty woman and Steve liked pretty women. When I'd first mentioned Nina Sorvino and Steve's sadistic tastes to her, that indignation wasn't fake. She hadn't liked the idea of her husband's infidelity but Steve had somehow persuaded her it was part of the plan. She must have met him that night when she went missing from the Sarakawa saying she was in the Keur Rama restaurant. He must have smoothed her over and even persuaded her to steal the photographs whose missing detail she'd noticed when I first showed her the two-shot in the car.

Her problem was that she loved Kershaw and she

was totally loyal to him. She looked as if she might have a job to hang on to him with just her natural beauty. So she'd got plenty on him. I should think she had enough to put him away for the rest of this millennium and most of the next, but plain Kate went along with whatever Steve said as long as he stuck with her. Steve hadn't liked to swerve out of line too much in case she'd got talkative, so he kept his part of the bargain and did his best to love her back.

Nina's packed cases had made it clear that Steve was planning on a greater disappearing act than Kate had envisaged when she agreed to go along with his new ID scam. I had that feeling from the way Kate had sniffed the changing wind when she first came in that she was beginning to realize this. It was bad luck on Steve that her flight had been delayed and she'd got involved in this ugly postmortem. It probably meant that he was going to have to kill her. Something that wouldn't be as easy for him as: Bang. Next.

'Why did you kill him, when you killed him?' asked Kate, showing him he wasn't home free just yet.

'I told you.'

'The Perec girl recognized you.'

'That's it.'

'Take us through it.'

Kate folded her arms, leant back and put out an aggressive toe in Kershaw's direction. His eyebrows flickered as if he just realized something, but he shrugged and straightened himself up, putting his hands under his armpits. I liked the way she'd used the word 'us'.

'Authority's a funny thing.'

'Tell me about it,' said Clifford, who rocked back in his chair and showed me that he did have a pair of eyes and not just burnt-out sockets.

'I will. Twenty years ago my car gets towed away in London.'

'And you've never forgiven them,' said Kate.

'Shut up and listen,' he said, spearing his lips. 'I send a mate down to pick it up so I don't have to pay all my parking tickets. He gets there and the copper in the Met car pound recognizes him for non-payment of alimony and does him. This Perec bird is supposed to be a textile designer but she's working for the IMB and she's got a boyfriend in the Drug Squad. She recognizes me as Stan Davidge, a known drug trafficker. I'm three stone lighter, tanned and working in Africa buying sheanut and she nails me.'

'Are you on the run?' I asked.

'No.'

'You just didn't want her sticking her nose into your latest piece of business.'

'Top marks, Bruce.'

'Why the new ID then?'

'The heat back in the UK. Nothing chargeable, but uncomfortable.'

'And not just for him,' said Kate.

'No, I should imagine you've been through a great deal,' I said.

'How do you know she recognized you?' asked Kate.

'You know me, Kate, I'm paranoid,' he said, drilling her with a hard look. 'I know trouble when I see it. If I'd seen Bruce I wouldn't have let him anywhere near this. Jolly Jack Tar thought he was being bloody clever when –'

'But how *exactly* did it happen?' asked Kate, her voice hacking away at him like a machete.

'I told you,' he said, kicking back at the desk which put a crease in Clifford's shirt.

'I want the detail,' she said, her back straightening, her neck fanning out.

'It was a look.'

'When did this *look* happen?' She gripped the back of my chair which cracked.

'Sunday before last.'

'Where?'

'In Cotonou.'

'In the flat?'

'That's right.'

'In the kitchen making tea?' she sneered.

'Leave off, Kate.'

'In the living room over G and T?'

'Christ.'

'Or looking at each other's sunburn in the bedroom.'

'Don't tell me – "I'd fuck a frog if it stopped hopping",' sneered Kershaw.

'I will, you would, and you have. Now let's have it,' said Kate.

'We left Lomé Sunday and got to Cotonou before dark. I needed something from the office so we go straight there. We get in the office and I got a clean shirt so I changed. Then I leave her on her own while I go for a piss. I come back and I see her going through the desk. I watch her for a bit, make a noise, you know, and let her get away with it.

'We go back to the flat. I get her into bed.' Kershaw lifted himself up off the desk with his arms straight and the desk groaned. Kate, who was still holding the back of my chair, tensed. The chair didn't like it and nor did Clifford who was getting fed up with the Kershaws' slap-happy attitude towards his furniture.

'Keep going,' said Kate.

'I can tell she's not into it so I know she's found something in the desk. I slap her about a bit and try and get her to talk. She starts fighting back so I have to hit her hard and put her out. I tie her down and call Clifford in Lomé. He flies in the next morning and does a number on her and she says she knows who I am, that she's been tracking the *Naoki Maru* and she knows that I'm interested in it as well.

'She only found two things while I was having a piss. A passport photo of me when I was a bit heavier with a moustache and a piece of paper in my dirty shirt with the ETA of the *Naoki Maru* written on it. She was good, was Françoise.

'It was afterwards when I was asking Cliff what we do with the body that he hits on the idea of framing Gildas as me for the Perec girl's killing.' Clifford twitched at this point, as if there was something not quite straight about Kershaw's story, but let it ride. Steve's mouth motored on. 'He calls the Cotonou police and tells his mate there that a friend of his has had a problem with a girl and can he do a clean-up job on it while he gets his friend out of the country.'

'How much did that cost you, Clifford?' I asked.

'Ten thousand bucks,' said Clifford, still as a lizard.

'So we pack up the gear in my bag. Clifford flies on

to Lagos for a meeting and I drive back to Lomé. We get together in the evening and Clifford gives me the bondage mags to plant in my chest of drawers.'

'No wonder you're CEO of a bank, Clifford,' I said, and Clifford stared down at his fascinating blotter.

'You don't look like a killer, Clifford,' I said.

Clifford's eyes might have looked at me but I couldn't tell.

'She had information that could have blown a deal. We had to find out what it was and we had to ensure our own safety,' he said as if he was reading a corporate manual.

'What part did you like, Clifford, the killing or the hurting.'

He went back to whatever his blotter was telling him and rubbed a finger over one of his lapis-lazuli cufflinks.

Steve was glad to have the heat off him for a while but I didn't want him sitting back just yet.

'What about Gildas's dick, so that Kate could identify him.'

'Oh, he *had* him as well,' snorted Kate.

'He painted in the nude. Spent most of the day naked. Only dressed for meal times so he wouldn't frighten the maid.'

'You killed her as well.'

'I haven't finished with Gildas yet.'

'It's time to go,' said Clifford from so far back down his throat I thought he was talking in his sleep.

'We want to hear the happy ending,' said Kate.

'So I get the mags off Cliff.'

'Clifford, Steve, Cliff-ford.'

'Yeah. I get the mags, go back to the house and he's

lying on his bed, naked as usual. I smother him with his pillow.'

'One of your specialities, Steve?' I said, looking at Clifford who'd let a frown crease his brow for a second.

'As a matter of fact, it is. You were getting a bit nosey so I thought a little scare job was in order.'

'You had the keys.'

'I did.'

'You dropped Charlie's card.'

'That too,' he said, raising his eyebrows for more questions.

'Jack lifted that for you?'

'About the only thing he did do for us that didn't get us up to our hairlines in shit,' said Clifford. 'The guy had no fucking sense of responsibility.'

'Are you finished?' asked Kershaw. 'So, Gildas is on the bed. The maid arrives. I tell her he's got malaria and he's not eating. She makes something for me and I start thinking what I've got to do. It's a rush job now. I mean, I knew I was going to dump Gildas in the pool. It hadn't been cleaned for years and there was no chlorine in it. It was full of bugs, and in this heat there wouldn't be much left of him after a few days. Plus, if he was underwater it would keep the pong down. But what about the maid? I didn't want the maid dead on the premises, did I?'

'Hell of a problem, Steve,' I said.

'Right. The maid cleans up and goes off to read her Bible and I start to get Gildas ready before the rigor mortis sets in. I get him into my clothes and stick my wallet and watch on him.'

'I liked the AA membership card.'

'That was there, was it? Lovely job.'

'You an alcy?' croaked Clifford.

'Automobile Association.'

'Jesus,' said Clifford, sinking back into his chair and swivelling it to face the other way.

'I wiped off the mags and put his prints on them and did the same with the whip handle and crocodile clip. I pushed his hands in his trousers so that if the rigor mortis came out early his arms wouldn't float up. I tied the rope around his ankles and left some spare for the urn. I got all his stuff together and shoved it in his suitcase.

'I called Clifford to see if he could come up with any ideas for the maid. He told me he had to go out to dinner and I should put her under and bring her to the house. I had some smack with me so I give her a shot and she's out. Then I put on a pair of surgical gloves that Clifford gave me and clean the house from top to bottom. Biggest shag of my life, that was. Then I paint my name on to Gildas's paintings.'

'Why didn't you drown him in the bath?' I asked, coming back to it, looking at Clifford. 'He'd have had water in his lungs then.'

Clifford reacted again, looking across at Kershaw this time, interested.

'It would never've looked good enough,' he said, and continued without missing a beat. 'About midnight I took the maid to Clifford's. We kept her drugged the next day but we still don't know what we're going to do with her. Then on the Wednesday night, Clifford's out to dinner and a minister tells him that some dead bodies had been found in the lagoon, shot in the back

362

of the head. Clifford calls me from the dinner. So I shoot the maid, put her in the back seat of the car and drive to a quiet part of one of the lagoons and slip her in. There was nobody about. They must have heard of the death squads and stayed in to watch telly. I found out the next day that the bodies were all over the place so the maid fitted in nicely.'

'At least you didn't kill the other twenty people in the lagoon just to make it look good.'

'You'll like this,' said Kershaw. 'I dumped Gildas's clothes in a part of town which looked as if they could use them.'

'Somebody got something out of this,' said Kate.

'I've always given to charity,' he snapped.

'Narc. Anon?'

'Save the Children.'

'You're going to tell me you can paint next.'

'I can. That's how we met,' he said, looking at Kate.

'You called it painting. I called it lying on the floor out of your brains on hash in Morocco,' said Kate.

Steve pulled out a phial on a necklace from inside his sweatshirt. He unscrewed the top, which had a little spoon attached, crossed his black, slick legs and snorted a dab of coke from off the end of it.

'Where are you from, Clifford?' I asked, just to give Steve some time to feel cocky with the coke.

'What's it to you?'

'I'm doing a thesis on American regional accents.'

'It'd give me a thrill to read that.'

'It's not New York?'

'Illinois,' he said, shaking his head.

'Chicago?'

'Rockford,' he said. 'Look, guys, I hate to break this up but we've got a lot to do tonight and I suggest we get it on the road.'

Steve smiled to himself and took another dab of coke on the end of his spoon and snorted it up the other nostril. I decided the time was right for Kershaw to get back to work.

'You must have supplied that stuff to Nina Sorvino,' I said.

Nothing happened except a little time dragged past. There was no significant movement. Kate's already white knuckles whitened to the bone on the back of the chair. Kershaw's crossed legs tightened. Clifford's white shirt creaked. Apart from that, the ceiling seemed to get lower and the walls closer. The pressure of people not saying anything thickened the air and the fan had a job cutting through it.

# Chapter 31

The cicadas sensed that they had a part to play in this and brought in a whole new chorus so that there wasn't a moment's silence. Four tired people looked at each other, no longer careful to disguise their irritability. Clifford sat forward, the shadows of the fan blades slapping over his grey head. Something sharp, hard and cold was coming in my direction from Kershaw who was getting the same from his wife. Kate was close to tearing the back of the chair off. Clifford had some anxious body language but it was difficult to tell about what. Maybe it was his furniture, maybe he just wanted to get to work.

'Nina's snorting enough of that stuff to get the snow ploughs out,' I said. 'And topping it off with enough downers to leave a big gap in her weekend. Any reason for this, Steve? She shouldn't be doing that kind of thing, especially if she's preg –'

The chair cracked and I came off it fist-balled and fast. Steve was faster. He flipped himself off the desk and buried his knuckles in my bruised belly. Air hissed out of every orifice and I hit the floor like a truckload of logs.

I was making a big fuss down there on the carpet, cycling my legs, hoping to remind myself how to breathe. Nobody took any notice. Their words flashed above my head while I contributed some constipated heaving noises until a crack of air slid into a lung and gave me something to hold on to.

Breathing crawled back like a wounded soldier from no-man's-land. I flopped around and got myself on to all fours and hung my head. Kershaw was a few feet from me and I decided it was time the cocky Londoner found out what it was like to have a meaty shoulder in his diaphragm.

'Don't even think about it,' said Clifford.

My left eye swivelled to see Clifford leaning over the desk with the rifle in one hand, the barrel a foot from my cheek. Jack's brains exiting from the back of his head was still a clean print in my current stock of ugly clips. I stood up. I didn't bother to listen to the Kershaws, who sounded like any married couple having a fight in the kitchen at a cocktail party. I sat in the chair which had a wobble in its back legs like mine. The Kershaws finished their exchange of diplomatic gifts and split. I was nearly halfway there.

Clifford laid the rifle across the desk, the barrel pointing at me. Kate lit a cigarette which Clifford thought about requesting her not to, until he saw her sharp, irritated breasts daring him. From my angle I could see how pointed her elbow was and I liked the idea of it finding its way into her husband's gut.

'I'm not a pro, as you'd put it, Steve,' I said. 'I'm a greenhorn when it comes to nailing crims. Never done it. Don't have the psycho's brain. Dead in the head for clues and motives. I thought the whole business was Charlie's. I thought Charlie told Nina.'

'Shut it!' roared Kershaw. It was good to know Nina was such a sensitive spot.

'I thought Charlie told Nina to feed me about your taste in bondage. But now I can see that's what you were into all the time. You had to be, didn't you, Steve, or did you?'

Kershaw picked up my gun and took two steps towards me.

'I'm going to do it now, you big fuck,' he said, and Clifford stood up, concerned at the future mess on his carpet. Kate came between us, and, biting her bottom lip with her front teeth, floored Kershaw with a swift dig in the solar plexus. That elbow must have been honed on a whetstone of pure spite because it didn't stop until it got to his spine. Kershaw's eyes came out on stalks, his tongue wagged like a gargoyle's and he kissed the carpet like the best Muslim in the mosque.

'Carry on,' said Kate, picking up the gun by the barrel and holding it by her side.

'When I realized Charlie was in the clear, I started thinking about Nina. When I saw Steve's name was missing off the paintings in the photographs, I knew that he set the whole thing up with Nina's help. The first time I spoke to her she told me he was a pervert, but at that stage nobody knew how Perec had been killed. Nina was prepping me for when I found out. That means that either Steve was a pervert or Nina was in on it from the beginning. Which?'

'Both,' said Kate.

'Why was Nina in on it from the beginning, Steve? Don't get up, I'll answer for you. Nina's pregnant, she told me on Sunday. I thought it was yours but you were dead. Then I thought it might be Charlie's and he didn't want it, or Nina was trying to persuade Charlie that he was responsible. Then I followed Nina and got lucky when she went to get her test. I didn't understand why the first person she called was Elizabeth Harvey but things have got a little clearer in the last hour.

'Nina's packed, four suitcases ready to go. I dropped by. She was trying on her new clothes. They look great. She was wearing her most expensive perfume. Had a nice hat on. New shoes. She'll be a credit to you. That's what all this is about, isn't it, Steve?' Kate's face fractured, the bitterness in her gut finding its way to her mouth, her tongue pushing through her stained teeth as if forcing a mouthful of grounds out. The lines on her anorexic face which had never met with any grace before, now looked horrific, as a freak's. '*You* want to get away from *her*!' I said, and Kate's face which had started to break up, stilled.

'But there's one thing that nobody knows about in here except you and me, isn't there, Steve?' Kershaw's mouth was wide open and most of his tongue was out on the carpet. I could hear Clifford listening now. 'Old Clifford's sitting there smugging for America. He knows all about Nina. He's known it all the time. He doesn't give a damn. He's colder than a North Sea cod on ice. He *does* care about money though, Steve, and that's where you haven't been so straight with Cliff, isn't it? We all know you're a greedy bastard, we all know there's only one number one, but only I know how greedy. It wasn't Clifford who came up with the idea of framing Gildas for the Perec killing, it was you. You wanted to get rid of Gildas as soon as possible. And it wasn't Clifford's idea that you didn't drown him in the bath, it was yours. You wanted it to look like suspicious suicide because you were trying to persuade somebody that you'd been done and the killer had run away with' – Clifford was leaning forward, his slack neck hanging over the collar of his shirt – 'with the million dollars.'

'Who's the somebody and what million dollars?' asked Clifford.

'I've had a couple of blindfolded interviews with a big man in the Togolese government who gave Steve a million bucks of his kick-back money to trade with, except Steve died and the million bucks got lost and the big man's very upset.'

Clifford was on his feet leaning over the desk to see if there was any chance of a word from between Kershaw's clenched teeth. I began to think that the big man had given up waiting by his answering machine. Kate looked as if she had indigestion. Some more time crawled past while three brains chewed their way through the lean meat I'd just thrown. Kershaw was still jawing with the carpet. Kate was rubbing her heartburn. Clifford's pink body stood encased in its white shirt like *saumon froid en papillote*. He looked out of the cone of light. Honour, that miraculous thing which is supposed to exist amongst thieves, was nowhere to be seen.

'Who's the big man?' he asked anybody who was prepared to answer.

'I don't know,' I said. 'Steve?'

Steve wasn't feeling so tiptop. It was good to see him on the floor mopping up his cockiness. He didn't look like somebody who'd been at boot height for some time. We watched him as he pulled himself up on an invisible rung, stepped back and held on to the desk facing Clifford. Clifford showed the anxiety of a man who is about to get puked on by an overdrunk friend, but Steve rolled on his hip and sat on the corner of the desk.

'Who is he?' asked Clifford again, and still Kershaw didn't speak. I glanced over my shoulder. Kate had left the room.

'I've got a couple of clues,' I said. 'He likes to wear expensive buckskin shoes and his assistant is . . .'

I didn't need to say who the assistant was because Clifford stiffened as if someone had eased an ice cold shiv in between ribs three and four of his back.

'You stupid fuck,' he said to Steve, the clubby banker suddenly out to lunch, the language dropping a hundred floors of the World Trade Center to the street. 'You custard-brained, Limey fuck. Jeez, I thought Jack was a headless fuck, but you, I fucking told you when I introduced you to that guy not . . . to . . . fucking . . . touch! We gotta get outa here,' he said, quickly opening the drawer and taking out the plastic cuffs, a handkerchief, some gaffer tape and a gun. He got to me in three strides, lifted me off the chair, spun me round and cuffed me. Kershaw, still rubbing his gut, picked up the rifle, leant it against the chair and took the handkerchief off Clifford.

'You had your chance,' he said.

'As much as Jack did,' I said.

'You fucked up like him 'n' all.'

'Even if he hadn't, he still wouldn't be here.'

'He only had eyes for the money. That was Jack's problem . . . and keeping trouble outside his garden wall. That's no way to be in this business.'

'Especially with you two for partners.'

'He thought he was running the show – getting you to look for me, cuddling up to Awolowo, fucking Cliff's wife . . .'

'Maybe you should have told him you were going to disappear.'

'Too big a mouth,' he said, taking hold of my jaw. 'Like you.'

'You knew I'd talk about the women, didn't you? You wanted me to talk about the women. You wanted it to hurt, you sadistic little shit. You just didn't know I knew about the money.'

Kershaw grinned, letting a bit of insanity into his eyes. 'I've been looking forward to this,' he said, and grabbing my jaw he stuffed the handkerchief well down my throat until I gagged. Clifford stuck the tape across my mouth and wrapped it around my head. Kershaw clapped me on the shoulder like a good old boy and sat back on the desk.

'I'm going to kill my wife now,' he said.

'Not in the house,' said Clifford. 'No killing in the house. You've fucked up enough as it is.' He pushed me to the door and before we went down the corridor he took a last look at Kershaw. 'When you're finished, go to Nina's and get outa Togo and don't fucking come back.'

The corridor was dark and hot. The bedroom where there'd been the steaming bath was in darkness. There was no sound of Kate Kershaw and there was no sound of the big man's goons coming to the rescue. Clifford took me down to his Mercedes in the garage. He opened the boot and folded a duvet up into the back underneath the rear shelf. I got in and he jammed me in with another duvet so that I was hot and immobile. He loaded crates of wine in front of me.

The lid came down. The garage door opened. The wrought iron gates squealed. The car huffed as Clifford got in and the motor seemed to come on without any ignition. We rolled out. The gates shut like two guinea fowl calling.

# Chapter 32

There was a police post at the main turn-off to the lake, but we didn't reach it. We turned off left down a bumpy track which joined a smoother one and we began to circle the lake. Clifford wasn't in a hurry. I was thinking of ways to keep him occupied for three or four hours but none of them were as interesting as what he had in mind.

It was hot work. Four pounds of fear soaked into the duvets, just leaving the salt in all the cuts and grazes on my body to remind me how uncomfortable being alive could be. By the time we arrived at a gate, which Clifford opened, I was rebreathing the boot air for the seventh time and it had lost a lot of its flavour.

The boot opened and the hot air that flooded into my black hole felt like a fresh breeze whipping off the lake. Clifford unloaded a few crates, pulled me out, stripped off the tape and pulled the handkerchief out. The pressure was high. Over the tops of the tall dark trees around the lake, the black sky flickered like newsreel of the Blitz. We crossed a mud courtyard with high walls around with shards of broken bottles set in cement on top. The house was a single storey fronting on to the lake. We walked in between two semicircles of lawn to the front door.

'Why did you want me to follow your wife, Clifford?' I asked, because nothing else came to mind.

'Forget it,' he said. 'You're dead. I got nothin' to say to you.'

'You didn't like Steve's private million-dollar deal, did you, Clifford? Thought it might jeopardize the big one. It has. I called the big man before I left Nina's, left a message for him to come and look you up.' If Clifford's life had just fallen to pieces with that bland statement, you wouldn't have known it.

'It'll cost me a million and a half, but I can handle that,' he said, calmer now. He motioned me forward with the gun and told me to kick in the door so that it looked like breaking and entering. I took two steps back.

'What's the name of the Yoruba god of medicine, Clifford?'

'The fuck are you talking about now?' he asked, suddenly dog-tired.

'Osanyin,' I said, and kicked the door just below the lock and a pane of glass shattered as the handle hit the wall and the top hinge popped out. A four-foot splinter of wood flik-flakked across the hall and down a few steps to the living room whose shuttered windows would have given us a view of the lake. Clifford hadn't moved. He held the gun on me and blinked only twice in a minute.

'It's over, Clifford,' I said. 'You don't want to go adding double murder to your problems.'

He didn't answer for some time. If I could have seen inside his head, I might have been damned scared, as it was from my side, he looked old and tired. When he did finally speak I almost missed it he said it so quietly and with an odd squeak in his voice that distorted the sound. It let me know, if I still had any doubts, that under the handmade shirt, the Italian tie, the pleated slacks, the buffed black Oxfords on his feet, Clifford Harvey was as mad as a split-gowned maximum-security headcase.

'Cut,' was the word he used.

With a new and disturbing energy he steered me to the left and opened the door in front of me. He flicked the light on with a surgically gloved hand and leaned something up against the wall behind me.

To my right, Heike was lying on her front on the bed, her wrists and ankles tied to each corner with a sheet over her. Her head moved as if she'd been sleeping and then stilled. The calico curtains were drawn and dusty. There was an air-conditioner in the corner of the window frame and the curtain had been cut round it. It hadn't been turned on and there was no fan. The only smell was of the mustiness of the infrequently used bed linen. Clifford threw the bag over to the bed, took the cuffs off and told me to strip. He stood in front of me, holding the gun waist-high, his elbow tight against his body.

When I was down to my underpants he unzipped the bag, took out a pair of lycra shorts and told me to strip and put them on. Heike's head moved again; I looked, Clifford didn't. He positioned a chair three feet from the bottom right-hand corner of the bed. He wanted it just right and was nudging the front legs with his foot when I lunged at him. He didn't bother to shoot but side-swiped my head with the barrel which hit me across the cheekbone and temple and the room spun on the wrong axis.

He pulled me up by the hair and fitted the barrel

under my ear. I sat in the chair and he cuffed my wrists under the seat so that my chin was on my knees and tied my feet together at the ankles with some nylon rope.

He drew out a floor-length brown plastic apron from the bag, put it over his head and tied it around himself. He took his glasses out of his shirt pocket and put them on. There was a long, low table for a suitcase by the window and he positioned that in front of me. He picked up what he had leaned against the wall, which was a long plastic case like a gun cover. Out of it, he pulled a three-foot long rhino hide sjambok. From the case, he took a length of smooth metal tubing with two wires attached, a switch and a two-point plug, two crocodile clips attached to wires, again with a switch and a two-point plug, a gang socket with an extension, a length of hard plastic with two holes in it and a loop of rope through the holes, a packet of cigarettes, a lighter and some lighter fuel, a ball of rags, a scalpel, a box of chilli powder, a rusty coat hanger, some gaffer tape, a pair of long-nosed pliers, a plastic bag and from the side pocket, a clean slab of fresh money.

'What's the game, Clifford?'

'There's no game.'

'You take the tray away and I have to remember what's on it?'

'I said, it's not a game.'

'Bankers don't do this kind of thing, Clifford.'

'We have other instruments.'

He put each of the instruments in my hands and I printed them up for him. He moved the table over to the bed and looked down at Heike, swallowing hard.

He rubbed his thumb and forefinger together. His neck was shaking. He took a corner of the sheet and walked off with it behind me, leaving Heike naked on the bed. I kicked my fear back down the basement stairs when I saw Heike's white vulnerable nudity next to Clifford's terrible implements.

The air-conditioner came on, roared and smoothed out to a steely hum. The cool air chilled the sweat on my back and Clifford's voice raised the atavistic hairs up my neck. The sprawling, relaxed business drawl had gone and a constricted throat said: 'You've wet the bed.'

He strode past me. I roared at him. He took Heike's shoulders and shook them, her head lolled. He dropped her and stood back, his neck and cheeks red. Heike opened her mouth which was dry and clogged with a thick, sticky saliva. Her eyes opened and I watched the memory and the terror worm in. I called her name and she looked at me with black, shiny eyes. She put everything she could into her scream, her whole body dipped into the bed but nothing came out.

Clifford picked up the slab of money, pulled a few notes out and screwed them into balls.

'Why the money, Clifford?'

'Everybody's gotta get paid.'

'Why her?'

'You get paid for everything.'

'What do you mean?'

'Life's all about moving money around.'

'You only get paid for doing something.'

'She's going to. She's going to suffer.'

'What for?'

'Because she gets paid. They all get paid.'

'What did you pay Cassie Mills for?'

Clifford stopped screwing up the money, his head clicked up and his eyes bolted on to mine.

'Cassie Mills, Rockford, Illinois, 23rd September 1954,' I said, and time crawled forward on its elbows while Clifford's face lost all expression.

'I paid her back,' he said, only moving his lips, the slab of money cocked stiff in his hand.

'You paid her back for making you suffer.'

'Yes, I did.'

'What did she do?'

Clifford's mouth clamped shut. His eyes stared through me.

'What didn't she do?' I asked.

'She didn't mean anything.'

'To you?'

'She didn't *mean* anything.'

'She lied to you.'

'They all lied to me.'

White deposits had gathered at the corner of Clifford's mouth. His tongue tried to lick them away but they were tacky like glue and they stuck his mouth together. He was swallowing a lot but nothing was going down.

'They all lied to you?'

'Cassie, Bob, Whitey, Doug, Lena . . .'

'Your friends?'

'My friends,' he said, with matte black eyes. His body was still, his breathing shallow. There was a long pause filled by the cool air rushing from the air-conditioner. Clifford seemed to have dropped below some horizon. He was out in an open boat again, surviving a childhood trauma that had never fitted into the way he was told things should be.

'She paid them,' he said from a long way off.

'Cassie?'

'Mom.'

'Mom paid Cassie?'

'Thirty bucks a week.'

'She told you?'

'She told me. She got a five-buck bonus for kissing. She told me.'

'When did she tell you?'

'We were doing it. She got double for doing it. She told me.'

'What about Bob?'

'Ten bucks. Whitey ten. Doug twelve, he was on the softball team. They showed me the money. They all showed it me. They all showed me they got paid to be my friends.'

'What did your mom say?'

'I found the cheque book. Hundred bucks every Friday. Pay day. They always had money at the weekend.'

'You paid Cassie back?'

'I paid her back.'

'It's quits.'

'Uh huh. They all have to pay.'

'Where's Mom?'

'They all have to pay.'

He looked at the money in his hand and peeled notes off and screwed them up and dropped them to the floor. He went down on his knees and pulled Heike's head back and pushed the balls of money into her mouth.

He filled her cheeks and then taped her mouth over. He picked up the sjambok.

'It didn't happen, Clifford. Your mom didn't pay them. She took a hundred bucks out on Fridays for weekend shopping. They were just kids having a sick joke like kids do. Listen to me. You killed Cassie Mills. Did they come looking for you? They would have linked you to her. They would have found out about the money if your mom had paid them. They didn't. You never went down for her killing. You weren't even a suspect. Clifford!' I roared. 'CLIFFORD!'

He stood both feet apart and brought the sjambok above his head. I threw myself forward and hit him in the leg with my head. Clifford went down hard, the sjambok toppled out of his hand and sprang off one end into the corner of the room. Clifford clawed away from me in a panic before he realized I had turned turtle. I could see he had a cut on his head and his glasses hung over his mouth. He pushed himself up on his good leg, straightened his glasses and hobbled over to the sjambok.

He brought the sjambok down across my face and chest, across my shoulder, then the stomach, the legs, the arms and ribs. Blood ran, pain opened in lines across my body with junctions of agony. Warm blood pooled in my eye and ran over my forehead. The sjambok slashed the cool air and white hot welts swelled. New pain stopped. The chair lifted and fell on its side, my wrist trapped underneath. Heike thrashed about on the bed, her head whipping from side to side. The sjambok thumped across my ear and I felt an eyebrow split. I swung round, using my wrist as a pivot, and caught

Clifford below the knee with my bound feet and he went down again. I heard the glasses fall off his face.

'Fuck . . . ,' he said. 'You fuck . . .'

Across the floor, the door opened.

'Clifford!' a voice said.

'Mom?' he said, in a voice so strange my scalp tightened over my cranium.

Two thin legs in flat black shoes appeared. I turned to Clifford, who stood over me, his hands empty. His glasses crunched underfoot. Kate Kershaw put three bullets into his chest and a fourth into the wall. Clifford fell back with three black holes in the bib of his apron. His body crashed through the table of instruments and his head bounced off the bedside table, dislodging the lamp which shattered on the floor. The white deposits at the corners of his mouth frothed in small bubbles like boiled milk, blood appeared in the foam which turned pink and darkened to a thick red. He ended on his back, his head crooked up against the blood-smeared wall, a surgically gloved hand across himself and the other arm twisted behind him.

# Chapter 33

Kate left the room and came back with a chopping knife in her hand. She cut the leather strips at Heike's wrists and ankles. Heike tore off the gaffer tape and spewed out the saliva-coated balls of money. She pulled the sheet around her. Kate picked up Clifford's gun and stuck it in a bag over her shoulder. She cut the plastic wrist cuffs and the rope around my ankles.

I showered a lot of blood off me and got dressed. Only the split eyebrow continued to bleed. Kate found a first aid kit and sealed the cut. Heike's clothes were in a plastic bag in the bathroom. She dressed on automatic. Kate cleaned the floor and asked me to wipe off all the instruments. Heike started to shake as if she was malarial.

'What's going on?' I asked.

'Clean up and go,' said Kate. 'KLM have confirmed my take-off for 5 a.m. There's a walk to the car.'

She kicked the air-conditioner off. Dry thunder growled somewhere over Benin. Heike got to her feet and leaned on me. We left the house with Kate knocking the light switches off with her elbow. She picked up a torch she'd left by the front door. After the chill of the room, the heat hugged us like a duck-down duvet. We crossed the baked mud of the courtyard, closed the gates and walked down the tree-lined path next to the lake. There were no lights around the lake. The storm was closer. The lightning flickered longer and the thunder rumbled nearer.

Kate gave Heike the cigarettes and told her to light one up for her and anyone else who needed the calm. She kept her distance, the gun still in her right hand, her finger on the trigger guard, the torch in her left armpit, shining on the path. The lightning shattered the dark long enough to show her face, her eyes fixed open, the brain engaged elsewhere, her mouth open a crack where the cigarette burned. She was going to tell us something and I couldn't be bothered to tell her we didn't want to know.

'I'm not a very impressive person,' she said slowly, the line coming out of the dark like a stage prompt. 'I have my weaknesses.'

'Don't we all?' said Heike.

'But they don't screw up your life like they have mine.'

'They haven't yet.'

'If I told you . . .' She stopped herself. 'Not if . . . I'm going to tell you something you won't understand, that pretty people don't understand. Why I . . .' She drew on the cigarette, trying to get it all in the right order. 'Pretty people don't know what it's like to be missed, I mean, overlooked, not noticed. I've watched them, the pretty people, sitting in cafés, standing around in bars, hotel lobbies, at parties, weddings, the races, even funerals, for God's sake . . . They're always getting something. They're always getting seen, they're always getting touched, things are said to them . . . They get given to. They get attention. I never had that. I'd been hungry for it all my life until I met Stan, Steve, whatever you call him. He said things to me, nice things, he looked at me, he touched me, he made me feel . . . He let me know what it was like to be a beautiful woman. You don't understand that, do you? Sometimes I don't. Sometimes when I stopped to think how much I was paying for it, I really didn't understand it either. And Christ, did I pay for it. Everyday I paid for it. I've had to turn my back on some terrible things. I've waited for some very long nights to be over. I've spent a lifetime and a half scared to death. And this . . . now . . . this was supposed to be the end. The death of the old Stan Davidge. The end of fear. And it happened. Everything was going to plan. His plan. With me out of it.' She straightened the torch, drew on the cigarette again. The trees on the other side of the lake rushed with the wind and settled.

'He lied to me. He thinks after twenty years he can still lie to me and I don't know it. I let him do it. I let him get away with it. He's lied to me about his business, he's lied to me about the women, he used to lie to me about whether he'd been to the fucking bank or not. He lied to me about killing Françoise Perec and Gildas Sologne. He lied to me about Nina Sorvino. And I let myself believe him, and I let myself believe him again and again, because I wanted to be with him . . . But,' she said, through a long, exhausted, predictable sigh, 'I found the suitcase with the money. I found the two airline tickets, one with his new name – Michael Caswell, the other with Nina Sorvino's name on it. It was there waiting in his room, waiting for me to leave, waiting for me to be out of the picture. Then I realized it wasn't me, wasn't just me . . . that he's planning his new life with Nina bloody Sorvino and – this is when you know you're doing the world a favour – he's fucking Françoise Perec while he's doing it. And after that he can sit there and watch her being killed . . .'

She'd already smoked her cigarette down to the filter. She threw it down the path, the tip splintering into sparks. She asked Heike for another. The thunder and lightning of a different storm crackled in the distance somewhere out to sea.

'I've done a lot for my husband. I've put up with a lot. I used to get sick from all the police pressure. I hated the types he had to deal with. Strong and nasty with tinted glasses and too much jewellery and a fondness for small children.' The lightning etched her face out of the night for a moment and it broke whatever thready line of thought was going through her. 'I shot him,' she said. 'I shot him where it didn't hurt. I shot him how he said to shoot people. Don't think about it. Bang. Next. He's in the bath. When you left he came looking for me. Calling me in his soft voice, using his pet name for me. Chicken. When I heard that, I knew. I waited for him in the dark room, his voice getting closer. The smell of his new woman's perfume still up my nose. I turned the light on and I didn't give him time to smile.'

The thunder crashed almost overhead, and the trees roared in the wind blowing across the lake. She threw away her newly lit cigarette in disgust.

'I heard Clifford putting you in his car, I followed in Elizabeth's. Clifford's insane,' she said, in case we hadn't realized it. 'He's been on the brink for some time. If he hadn't been married to Elizabeth, he'd have been put away a long time ago.'

'What was he doing here?'

'He was a New York banker who laundered drug money until they cracked down on it. The bank let him go and nobody would touch him. He had a reputation. He liked hurting women. When he was powerful in the bank because of the drug money they put up with him. They knew what he was doing, but all these guys are into something. When the drug money went, he was out. He picked up the Lomé job through Awolowo, who pushed money through him in the old days.'

'What's the connection between Steve and Clifford?'

'Stan knew Clifford since he came down a couple of years ago to put a Nigerian connection into his European operation. They just teamed up again.'

Kate's mind wandered off and we finished the walk to the car in silence, the storm shunting around in the background, hanging off for the moment but building. Kate got in and rolled down the window, asking Heike for the cigarettes. 'I can't trust you not to call the police. Maybe I deserve it but I'm not spending any more time in this place than I have to. You're walking from here.'

'Where's the money?'

'Goodbye.'

'You're taking it with you?'

She nodded once as she closed the window and then drove back to the guest house to turn around. A few minutes later, she floated past us, staring straight ahead. The red taillights disappeared into the trees. The lightning whited Heike out, the clouds boiled overhead before returning to a deeper black. The thunder woke up in long, lazy, discontented growls, stretching itself out, its bones and tendons cracking further and further away to some distant point over the sea where the last joint in the furthest reaching knuckle clicked.

I had a lot to say to Heike. She had more to say to me but not what I wanted to hear. I took hold of her hand and she didn't bat me away. My eyes, just used to the dark, could see her, with her hair blowing across her face, her eyebrows questioning, her slim white shoulders, tired. I pulled her to me and didn't get a dead leg from it. We held each other, not with the usual urgency and desire but something better. She pressed her face into my neck and whispered: 'I've been waiting for hours.'

'It took some time.'

She leaned back from me and held my beaten head in her hands, but softly so I only winced from what she might have done.

'When she was talking about the pretty people, she didn't mean you,' she said. I laughed. She smiled and then wiped it off her face. 'Don't think, for a moment, I've forgiven you.'

'It hadn't crossed my mind.'

'That's good,' she said, letting me go.

'I've got a lot of work to do, I take it?'

'A life's work . . .' she said. 'Maybe more.'

The lightning flashed overhead. Wild and angry, it hovered so that the whole lake burned itself on my retina. After a fraction of a second, something thumped the air hard in the gut and the thunder cracked like a rock split down its back. Another stronger wind rushed across the lake, the water chopped up and Heike's dress snapped like a flapped flag. A single drop of water hit me on the back and then warm rain poured down in sheets.

It was a long walk back to the road for two people who'd arrived in car boots. Paths had disappeared in the storm and become white water streams. Thigh-high puddles thirty metres across confused the outline of the lake. We headed for higher ground which was swallowed before we got there. After an hour, we found a high grassy bank. The rain had eased off from a vertical drilling into a slanting lash. At the top of the bank was the old road. By the time we hit the tarmac of the new road, the rain was down to a nervous spray. It was just after five o'clock. There was no traffic.

There was still no traffic when we walked into Baguida at 7.30. We found a bar that served coffee, baguette and margarine, and cakes. We ate without speaking for ten minutes while a Togolese woman with the behind of a hippo talked to a young girl no bigger than her leg, who was serving behind the bar.

'Was his name Horst?' I asked.

'Who?'

'The guy in Porto Novo.'

Heike asked the woman to bring her some cigarettes and matches. The woman shouted into the bar from her position on a three-foot bench, where her vast buttocks spread like a flat truck tyre. The young girl's flip flops skidded behind me and the cigarettes materialized from under her hand. Heike lit up and sucked the smoke in down to her kneecaps and held it there.

'Wolfgang,' she said, breathing out the smoke.

'What does Wolfy do?'

'He runs the aid project.'

'You known him long?'

'Two years.'

'Same as me.'

'Not in the same way though.'

'How long have you known him biblically?'

'Two months,' she said. 'I didn't think you were the jealous type.'

'I am.'

A smile sneaked across her face which it shouldn't have, but she couldn't suppress her enjoyment of that second small victory and I couldn't blame her.

'Do you want children?' I asked and Heike's eyebrows took off into her hairline and wouldn't come out.

'Who've you been talking to?'

'Nobody you know.'

She drew a ferocious drag from her cigarette, straining at the neck like a dog backing away from its leash. The smoke cut into her throat and a small croak crept out of her mouth.

'It's just a feeling I've got,' she said.

'Who do you want to have them with?'

She crossed her forearms and bounced the two fingers holding the cigarette on the metal tabletop. Smoke jetted out of her nostrils.

'The best father.'

'My point score must have dropped back in the last few days.'

She nodded and pursed her lips at me. 'You have a negative point score.'

'How's that?'

'I've only been counting the last few days.'

'I suppose bloody Wolfgang's off the end of the scoreboard.'

'Different league.'

'I can never be *that* good.'

She smiled, not such a big smile that I thought she would forget Clifford's punctured body and horrible instruments, but enough of one to let me know that Wolfgang wasn't coasting to the finishing line with time to wave at the crowd.

'Have you got any money?' she asked, and I shook my head.

She pulled out the slab of fresh money bent down the middle by Clifford's thumb and peeled off a 5000 CFA note and put it on the table.

# Chapter 34

*Friday 4th October*

I asked Moses to drive me into Accra along the coast road. We stopped at the point where the road first hit the sea. On the right, was a deep green malarial marshland and on the left, rows of very high diseased coconut palms. In front of them was a rocky strip on to which the tight tubular waves burst, creating a fine mist. Accra, which normally looked like the innards of a TV set, looked its best through the chiffon haze.

A woman begged me to come to her fish stall, taking my forearm in her two strong hands which, flaked with fish scales, gave me a jolt of anxiety that she was passing on a touch of wet leprosy. I let her take me to her table where she threw back a piece of sacking and I met the reproachful, gelatinous eye of a large silver fish.

I asked her to cut me a good hunk and she tried to persuade me to buy the whole thing. Moses stepped into the discussion, speaking to the woman in Gaa, and I looked down the coast and watched a group of boys playing soccer on the beach a mile away. The action was around the far goalmouth which was just visible through the zest coming off the sea. The goalkeeper nearest me was practising diving saves of greater and greater swank, leaping further and further from his goal. The action moved. The goalkeeper was embedded in the sand. The ball sailed through the unprotected goalmouth and his team mates fell on the stranded goalie with less mercy than a jackal pack.

When Heike and I had got back into Lomé on Wednesday morning, we took a room in the Hotel Golfe in the centre of town. Heike went to sleep and I called the big man and left a message on the answering machine. This time he called me back.

'What happened to you?' I asked.

'What?'

'I left a message last night on your answering machine.'

'You did?' he said. It was a reply that made me feel very tired.

I told him that his million dollars had left the country in a suitcase owned by Mrs Kate Kershaw who took off on a KLM flight early that morning. I told him that if he'd listened to his messages last night he could have had the opportunity of a face-to-face discussion with Steve Kershaw himself. As it was, the man was taking a long bath in the Harveys' mansion with a hole where his heart should have been. The big man didn't understand this and it wasn't a matter of five minutes to explain it all to him.

What he did do was arrange a reception committee for Kate Kershaw at Schipol airport, but she didn't show. It was only later when he checked the KLM manifest that he found that Kate Kershaw didn't leave on that flight after all. She had taken a storm-delayed flight to Rio de Janeiro on which Michael Caswell and

Nina Sorvino were supposed to be but didn't make it.

Nina Sorvino probably waited until half an hour before that flight until she took some kind of action to find out where Kershaw was. She may have called the Harvey mansion and received no reply. She may have gone to the house and found Kershaw dressed in black taking a blood red bath.

There wasn't that much speculation because there wasn't a lot that Nina Sorvino could tell anybody. She had mixed herself a large speedball, a mixture of cocaine and heroin, and injected it into her left arm on the inside of the elbow joint with a syringe taken from her emergency anti-HIV kit. She was found dead. The left side of her body on which she was lying was grape dark where the blood had settled, her lips were the colour of sloes and her swollen tongue, bigger than a black plum, protruded between her teeth. Needle marks were found on the soles of her feet.

Bagado had contacted his friends in Interpol who linked up with the Nigerian police and boarded the *Osanyin* before it left the Apapa docks. There was an exchange of fire which only two of the pirate gang survived. They then woke up Bof Awolowo, who, half an hour later, barefoot and dozy, wearing a pair of pyjamas made with enough silk to kit out a parachute regiment, found himself being fingerprinted in a police station in central Lagos. Madame Severnou, whose ear had been closer to the ground than Awolowo's on his pillow, had disappeared.

The Togolese police spent a long time in Charlie's living room getting sick from the smell of blood. Charlie had been taken to the clinic and had his wound cleaned, as had Yvette, who had ended up in the same ambulance. They didn't speak.

Elizabeth Harvey woke up at four o'clock in the afternoon on Thursday 3rd October after a long drug-induced sleep during which her whole life changed. She didn't find Bobo, her houseboy, waiting by the side of her bed with a cup of china tea, but an Interpol detective who was looking for an explanation of her movements on the night of 1st October and the morning of 2nd October.

She was astonished to hear that Steven Kershaw was found dead in her sunken bath and remembered to collapse into instant grief at the news of her husband's traumatic and fatal chest wounds. She was very helpful in explaining the intricacies of the drug-trafficking operation that her husband and Steve Kershaw had been running for the last few years.

Jack was the same as when I had left him except a little colder in his eight-foot sliding cabinet in the hospital morgue.

Heike had gone back to Germany. The day after her kidnap she seemed to be over-calm. She brought the Teutonic side of her character in to deal with the trauma. At night, however, she woke me with a scream loud enough so that, once I'd unhooked my claws from the ceiling, I found that most of the hotel's clientele were in the corridor outside our room. They wouldn't leave until they saw her alive and they weren't easily convinced by my appearance, nor by the Heike-shaped lump hiding under the sheet.

Yesterday I took her to the airport. Clifford's money paid for the ticket. This whole mess had cleaned me out. We had a discussion about my 'job' on the way. It wasn't healthy for me – nothing broken, but well flayed. I tried to explain that while she was a high noble creature intent on helping others, I was a lower animal who loved to scrabble about in other people's dirt. She didn't buy it, but in several moments of the time we'd spent with each other since the early hours of Wednesday morning, I'd told her that I loved her and this had persuaded her to come back, just to see if I was worth the trouble. I still had the feeling of her trembling bird-like body against mine from when we kissed goodbye at the airport.

'She go give you this mush, Mister Bruce, two thousand cedis,' said Moses.

I nodded and the woman slid her knife into the silver skin. She wrapped it in newspaper. We drove to B.B.'s house. As we turned right to go on the ring road via the Trade Center, there was a stall with a sprawl of watermelons falling away from it. I bought one for B.B. Twenty minutes later, we arrived at his house.

He opened the door himself, looking dressed this time. He wore a well-pressed short-sleeved shirt which just made it around the bole of his stomach. Several buttons' teeth gritted under the strain, which gave his string vest a view of the world. The shirt overhung some grey slacks which fell in folds like elephants' skin, and he wore a pair of shoes which looked as if they'd just played football on the gravel drive.

'What happen to you?' he asked.

'I fell over.'

'Cushion, Bruise. You haff to look where you going.'

I gave him the fish and the watermelon. He put the fish on the table and roared for Mary. He walked to his chair with the watermelon tucked under his arm.

He crashed back into the chair, whose legs screeched across the marble floor. He put the watermelon in his lap and alternately tapped it with his knuckles and slapped it with his palm.

'Ka-ka-ka-ka-ka-Mary!' he roared again.

'Sah!' she yelled back from the kitchen, and came in tucking her wrap into her waistband. She slowed and walked swinging her arm wide like an army recruit taking the piss. B.B. held up the watermelon on his fingertips and Mary snatched it away.

'Da-de-de-Mary,' he said, more subdued.

'Sah!' she replied before he'd finished.

'De fish, on de table, you fry it. And mek de hot peppy sauce. You want beer, Bruise?'

I nodded and Mary threw the watermelon up in the air over her head and turned to catch it, which involved a desperate lunge and a near miss for her head and shoulders in the dinner service cupboard.

'Yairs,' said B.B. after several minutes to the usual non-existent question. 'My God, is a terrible ting.'

He tapped the arm of the chair and knocked his feet together. Mary put the sliced watermelon in front of him and B.B. hefted his feet off the table and nearly threw his shoulder out reaching for the quarter circles of green-rinded pink flesh.

'Wait, B.B.,' I said.

B.B. looked at me as if he'd never received a command in his life and never obeyed one either. I picked up ten napkins and laid them across his belly.

'Very good, Bruise. You are tinking correck.'

He dropped his head into the watermelon and like a good carnivore kept one wary eye up. He spat the pips into the fist of his spare hand.

'You see what I tell you, Bruise?'

'Tell me again.'

'I tell you what I told you.'

I nodded him on.

'Now you see what happen,' he breathed through his nose, which wasn't occupied by the melon. 'Jack, he greedy. He say to me he doing a lot of business, he making lot of monny. But, I tell you, Bruise, is not so easy now. He see he haff to wok for de monny, and when de monny given to you in firs place you no like it. I see in his face he want more monny. But he no show me de eyes of a wokker. He show me de eyes of a lazy man, a foolish man.' He whimpered, suddenly petulant, and then shouted so that everything stood still. 'Why he need more monny! He haff a good life. He no need more monny. But' – he said softly, holding up a finger – 'he tink he does.'

I inspected the cotton weave of my trousers until I heard a noise of somebody fighting for air. B.B. was leaning forward, his eyes popping, his face reddening. His spare hand opened and the small change of melon pips fell out. He coughed with his shoulders and a melon pip tore past me and ricocheted off the slatted windows and landed on the table, spinning.

'Is difficult when you haff everting. Is no purpose. Why you want to have more dan everting? Thassway he never happy. Always different woman. Always tinking there someting better he no haff. I tell you, Bruise.

I tell you and you no listen. You tink B.B. an old man, a stupid man, but I tell you correck.' He paused, stopped eating and frowned with neanderthal intensity. 'You haff my monny?' he asked.

'Sorry,' I said, which he took to mean I'd misheard him.

'My monny. You tek your fee, and expenses for de wife. You have some left?'

'I owe you one hundred thousand CFA.'

'You owe me? You no haff it? Where dit go?'

'I'm broke.'

'This no very good business you in.'

'You don't need to tell me.'

The sun shone on the back of B.B.'s head. He was thinking, and held a piece of melon up so that it glowed red in the light. The garden boy's machete whipped the grass outside. A banana palm flexed and flapped. B.B. sucked the flesh off the rind and bunched up the napkins in his fist, wiped his mouth and said: 'I haff small problem in Korhogo.'

I sat back in the hot afternoon. I had no wish to listen to B.B.'s problems. Big or small, they were always about money and the talk of money now brought on a metallic taste in my mouth, not unlike blood, and I found myself thinking of Kate Kershaw, alone under the Brazilian sky with a straw hat and sunglasses, measuring her life in cigarette stubs, waiting for a hopeful glance, watching the pretty people, feeling hungry.

# Blood is Dirt

## Robert Wilson

Bruce Medway, fixer and debt collector in Benin, West Africa, has heard a few stories in his time. The one that Napier Briggs tells him is patchy but it doesn't exclude the vital fact that two million dollars have gone missing. Bruce is used to imperfect information from clients embarrassed at their own stupidity. But this time it leads to a gruesome death.

It would all have ended there but for Napier's daughter, the sexy, sassy and sussed Selina Aguia, a commodities broker. She launches Bruce into the savage world that her apparently innocuous father had chosen to inhabit – a world of oil and toxic waste scams, of mafia money laundering, of death and violence fuelled by drink, drugs and sex. Worse for Bruce, Selina wants revenge, and with the scam she invents it looks as though she'll get it. But this is a world where blood is dirt – nobody really cares. Not even if they love you.

'A vivid and steamy stumble on the wild side'

VAL McDERMID

ISBN: 0 00 713041 4

# The Company of Strangers

## Robert Wilson

Lisbon 1944. In the torrid summer heat, as the streets of the capital seethe with spies and informers, the endgame of the Intelligence war is being silently fought.

Andrea Aspinall, mathematician and spy, enters this sophisticated world through a wealthy household in Estoril. Karl Voss, military attaché to the German Legation, has arrived embittered by his implication in the murder of a Reichsminister and traumatized by Stalingrad, on a mission to rescue Germany from annihilation. In the lethal tranquillity of this corrupted paradise they meet and attempt to find love in a world where no-one can be believed.

After a night of extreme violence, Andrea is left with a life-long addiction to the clandestine world that leads her from the brutal Portuguese fascist régime to the paranoia of Cold War Germany, where she is forced to make the final and the hardest choice.

'Displaying once again Wilson's gifts for atmospheric depiction of place, this ambitious experiment is streets ahead of most other thrillers'

JOHN DUGDALE, *Sunday Times*

'A big, meaty novel of love and deceit . . . with this novel Wilson vaults to the front-rank of thriller writers'

PETER GUTTRIDGE, *Observer*

ISBN: 0 00 651203 8

# A Small Death in Lisbon

## Robert Wilson

A Portuguese bank is founded on the back of Nazi wartime deals. Over half a century later a young girl is murdered in Lisbon.

1941. Klaus Felsen, SS officer, arrives in Lisbon and the strangest party in history, where Nazis and Allies, refugees and entrepreneurs, dance to the strains of opportunism and despair. Felsen's war takes him to the mountains of the north where a brutal battle is being fought for an element vital to Hitler's blitzkrieg. There he meets the man who makes the first turn of the wheel of greed and revenge which rolls through to the century's end.

Late 1990s, Lisbon. Inspector Zé Coelho is investigating the murder of a young girl. As he digs deeper, Zé over-turns the dark soil of history and unearths old bones. The 1974 revolution has left injustices of the old fascist regime unresolved. But there's an older, greater injustice, for which this small death in Lisbon is horrific compensation, and in his final push for the truth, Zé must face the most chilling opposition.

'Compulsively readable, with the cop's quest burning its way through a narrative rich in history and intrigue, love and death'                           *Literary Review*

ISBN: 0 00 651202 X

# The Big Killing

## Robert Wilson

Bruce Medway, go-between and fixer for traders in West Africa, smells trouble when a porn merchant asks him to deliver a video at a secret location. Things look up, though, when he's hired to act as minder to Ron Collins, a spoilt playboy looking for diamonds. Medway thinks this could be the answer to his cashflow crisis, but when the video delivery leads to a shootout and the discovery of a mutilated body, the prospect of retreating to his bolthole in Benin becomes increasingly attractive – especially as the manner of the victim's death is too similar to a current notorious political murder for comfort.

His obligations, though, keep him fixed in the Ivory Coast and he is soon caught up in a terrifying cycle of violence. But does it stem from the political upheavals in nearby Liberia, or from the cutthroat business of diamonds? Unless Medway can get to the bottom of the mystery, he knows that for the savage killer out there in the African night, he is the next target . . .

'A narrative distilled from pure protein: potent, fiercely imagined and not a little frightening'    *Literary Review*

ISBN 0 00 647986 3

# A Darkening Stain

## Robert Wilson

Bruce Medway, fixer for the great unfixed, does not see the disappearance of schoolgirls off the streets of Cotonou, Benin, as any of his business. That is the domain of his ex-partner, police detective Bagado, and his corrupt boss. Bruce has the more pressing matter of a visit from two sweet-natured mafiosi who want him to find Jean-Luc Marnier, a French businessman in for something nastier than a wrist-slapping.

Then an important schoolgirl goes missing and Bruce gets involved, descending into a deeper darkness of police corruption, mafia revenge, sexual depravity and illegally mined gold. To save himself he conceives a scam, one that will excite the natural greed that prevails along this coast and, when executed out on the black waters of the huge lagoon system, inevitably result in death. But then innocence has always been the burden of dark experience.

'Unmissable . . . Unflinchingly imagined and executed. No hint of competition'                    *Literary Review*

ISBN: 0 00 713042 2